Angel Maker

A Karen Memory Adventure: Book 3

Elizabeth Bear

Acknowledgements

Please give it up for the amazing team who went into making this publication a reality: Cynthia Sheppard (cover art); Lauren Hougen (copyeditor); Clarissa CS Ryan (cover design); and Casey Blair (interior design and typesetting).

I'd like to thank my agent, Jennifer Jackson, and her assistant Michael Curry, for their hard work on audiobook and other sub rights. The friends and colleagues who listened to my whining about the inevitable struggle of getting the original rough manuscript written and then hammered into its polished form were invaluable—Jodi Meadows, Amal El-Mohtar, Amanda Downum, Alex Haist, Arkady Martine, Arula Ratnakar, Benjamin C. Kinney, C. L. Polk, Celia Marsh, Devin Singer, Fade Manley, Liz Bourke, Max Gladstone, Fran Wilde, Jodi Meadows, John Chu, John Wiswell, Sarah Monette, R.S.A. Garcia, Ryan Van Loan, Jamie Rosen, and Clarissa CS Ryan.

I'd also like to thank the Patreon patrons who've opted in to being acknowledged here. Thank you so much to Sarah Smith, Karl

Gustav Dandenell, Heather K Veitch, Gerald Sofaman, Kevin J. "Womzilla" Maroney, Tegan M, Dennis P Smith, CAZ, M&M Reppy, Toni, Fran Wilde, Alexis Elder, John Whitley, Kristen N. Keegan, Laura Bailey, Avani Gadani, Dawn Mueller, Mike Breen, S.C. Kaplan, Chris Dwan, Deirdre Culhane, Sara Hiat, Siobhan Kelly-Martens, David Lars Chamberlain, E.E.Yore, Jon Singer, Jo Miles, Patrick Nielsen Hayden, Phil Margolies, H. C. Morris, Karen S. Ireland-Phillips, Merridew, Ella Barnum, BC Brugger, Grey Walker, Edmund Schweppe, Brooks Moses, Kelly Brennan, Emily Gladstone Cole, Brad Roberts, Graeme Wiliams, Jack Gulick, and Max Kaehn for helping keep my pets fed and housed, not to mention me.

And last but not least, my family: my mother, Karen Westerholm; her partner Beth Coughlin; my father Steve Wishnevsky; and especially my beloved husband, Scott Lynch, who puts up with all the slings and arrows of self-doubt that plague any novelist.

To Alex and Devin

Chapter One

You'd reckon by now I would've gotten out of the adventuring business.

If I had any sense, which I patently haven't, because there I was clinging to the stagecoach harness of a mare at a canter, trying to crawl up her back so as to get to the reins, with my skirts flapping all around me...

Come to think of it, maybe I'd better go back in history and start this story a couple of days previous. Step with me into the time machine, mesdames and messieurs!

My friend Beatrice would say it just like that. Though her accent is prettier.

It was a bright chilly day in April when my wife, Priya, took me to Chinatown. She was looking for some special things for cooking with.

Now that Madame is the mayor in Rapid City, the cribhouses has got to be licensed and inspected and the girls paid a wage—a poor wage, but something—and allowed out on days off and allowed to send letters home to their families and such. Which, it ain't perfect, and a lot of them is too ashamed to tell their families what they've been doing to earn their livings or knows their parents would disown 'em if they found out, so they lie and send money home claiming it's domestic wages.

And they get paid a little better now, so they can send that money home and buy enough to eat. Bit by bit, things get better.

If you make 'em.

Anyway, there's shops in Chinatown as sell the kinds of flours and spices and such the Indian girls like, as well as the kinds the Chinese girls do, and the prices are better there. Even in a gold rush town. So Priya took me into town looking for ground-up lentils and beans, what she calls dal flour and gram flour, and cardamom pods and mustard seed and I don't even know what, but the bags smelled amazing. And rice. So much rice.

I was trying not to think about the money we was spending. Not that we was destitute; we could afford it, for now. But we was still working on getting established as businesswomen. Our infamy was good for something: the demimondaine trusted me and Priya on most things. But I needed to figure out some way to convince such of the good people of Rapid City as had means and need to keep livestock that I knew my way around a stable as well as a whorehouse.

The thing was, we needed money. Not immediate like: there was enough left of the reward to hold us for a bit longer. And we weren't gonna lose the ranch, because that was paid for. But stock has got to be fed, and women too, and feeding don't get no cheaper year by year.

And my wife was going to need buying into an apprenticeship, if she was going to chase her Mad Science, and then there was parts and tools to think of. I could do some earning, but people won't pay a woman horse tamer what they'll pay a man, though they'll hold her to a higher standard and rate her lower when she's better at the job.

I had thought about looking for work as a rodeo clown, thinking the novelty of a girl in skirts flirting the bulls might make a selling point. But you got to travel the circuit for that work, and Priya told me outright that she'd break my ankle if I tried it—"Just the one, so you may still manage the chores on crutches"—and that pretty much put paid to that notion.

Nevertheless, I'll stand by my reputation for being able to stay aboard just about any old thing you like until it quits bucking. And I thought there had to be a living in that, even if I couldn't cowpoke in a dress.

We was outside Mama Cheyong's, juggling our paper sacks into our shopping baskets and figuring out how best to balance them on my mare Molly's flanks, when we heard a commotion up the top of Nome Street and more or less froze in place. Molly's head came up, ears pricked, like she was thinking of yanking her reins, but I put a hand on her neck and she didn't... soften, exactly, but she at least got down off her tiptoes and let her breath out. She weren't used to all this town bustle yet, having just come on a train her own self a month before from Hay Camp. My old neighbor Lutz had sent her back to me. He'd tried not to take any pay, but I'd given him fair price for her and her tack, wired by Western Union, so he could afford to buy a mare of his own.

I'm a big enough girl, but when Molly went up tall like that I couldn't see over her withers. She's not quite seventeen hands, a strawberry roan with a shoulder blanket. She's a real Nez Perce warhorse my Da bought as a foal.

Her face is fine-boned for a Palouse, flecked gray and red down the long soft line of her nose, and I was looking at the pink underside of her jaw while she cased the situation. Luckily for me, though it was all pretty unfamiliar to her she's not a flibbertigibbet, and I got her attention right back when I rummaged in the saddle pocket where I keep the carrot ends and whatnot. I gave her a hard candy and a tired carrot—last year's stock—once I was pretty sure she'd forgotten that she'd been thinking about being spooky.

Half of horse taming, or horse whispering as some mountebanks call it, is thinking *like* a horse and then being just a tad bit smarter. You got to think around the corners. Fortunately, horses ain't got much attention span. And this one liked her groceries, which didn't hurt at all when it came to maintaining her focus.

Once she was busy snuffling my apron pockets in case I had something more tucked away in there, I peered over her neck to see what was going on. My darling Priya, who can be a bit spooky her own self, had put her back to Molly's shoulder and was craning her neck uphill.

I said it was a commotion, but that's a mite nonspecific. What we heard was the usual bustle of people, plus all kind of animal noises, and additionally a harsh rattle and a metallic clank that repeated at what you call imprecise intervals. This all added up to more fuss than usual even for a train unloading.

It seemed too soon for the circus to be coming back to town—there'd been one through just the last autumn—but at first that's what I thought I was looking at. Off a little ways down the siding, two wranglers held a half-dozen horses, what must have just been unloaded from the train. A flat car had been towed up next, with what looked like an honest-to-Betsy Wells Fargo stagecoach and a couple of smaller kits balanced on top. The teamsters were making short work of getting those down.

The clanking, though. That sounded like Mad Science, and it was what Priya and me was both craning our heads for. Finally, I saw the source of it: a rail-thin sort of a person in a duster what had once been black and was now living up to its name. Their right hand gleamed hard metal when they raised it to puff on a big cheroot so the rare spring sunlight could catch it below the coat cuff. Said personage was also wearing a worn-in Boss of the Plains in much worse shape than my own treasured secondhand hat. Straw-yellow hair stuck out from under it in a greased-up duck's tail, and a pair of Frye boots with much-scuffed toes and plenty of stirrup wear in the arches. No spurs, though.

Trail boss, unless I missed my guess. With a metal arm, like our own Miss Lizzie. Except maybe fancier, as there seemed to be curls of steam rising from it in the cold morning air.

"That ain't no circus," I said.

Priya knew me well enough that she didn't ask why in hell I was thinking about circuses. She just nodded and said, "I think it is a Wild West show," in her lilting accent and precise manner on which I was such a terrible influence, with my careless plain speech.

"Who the Hell brings a Wild West show to the wild, wild west?" I asked her.

In response, she handed me a two-bite chunk of the sweet sticky rice ball she'd been munching on, which in retrospect was a pretty good answer. I chewed on it and leaned on Molly while we watched the Wild West show unload. It was a pretty good sight, and we weren't the only ones interested. All of Chinatown—or at least all of Nome Street—seemed to have stopped what they were doing and come out on the front steps to watch the fun. The way was lined with shopkeepers, customers, layabouts, and as you like it, and I was taller than most—them being mainly Celestials and Indians—so I had a pretty good view especially once I stepped around Molly.

I had looked down at my feet, as makes sense in Rapid City as otherwise you are like to step in something awful, and when I looked back up again what I saw struck me totally still. Not because there was four matched bays being harnessed up to that stage—though they was worth looking at, if you like looking at horseflesh—but because of the conglomeration doing the harnessing.

Gentle readers, it were a machine. And the primary source of that clanking I'd wrongfully assigned to the trail boss.

A mechanical cowboy, to be exact, from his sheet-tin boot tops to his sheet-tin ten-gallon hat. He shone in the sun like a regular porch-roof mobile, and he chimed like one, too. I could see his pistons rising and falling. The small gears in his clockworks whirred under milky-veined transparent covers over his chest and back. I wondered if they was carved out of rock crystal—it didn't seem like any glass could be tough enough. Anyway, I could see 'em plain because while he wore riveted denim trousers he was stripped to the waist like any roustabout.

His parts replicated human contours in a most disturbing manner.

As I watched, I realized that there was a man behind another contraption—this one mounted on a tripod with rollers—following him. The tripod had a big head on it with a whirring wheel, like a sewing machine, and a long barrel. The man was bent down, peering through some kind of a range finder or eyepiece.

A motion picture Kinematoscope. They was making a motion picture right there in front of Priya and me. Just like we could go see in the nickel theatre down on Mulberry Street. They were making a *motion picture* right there in front of me.

Maybe I was a little starstruck, now that you mention.

I checked on Priya. She was staring, too—gaze fixed on the mechanical, eyes as big as saucers, and her fingers curving sharply though her hands hung at her sides.

"Hey," I said gently. "Ask permission before you go rooting around in that gentleman's clockworks."

She glanced over at me, eyes laughing while her mouth stayed firm.

That was when all hell broke loose, and then some.

Chapter Two

It started with a flat, hard bang like a shotgun going off, followed by the sound of wood splintering. I couldn't tell exactly what was happening on the top of the hill, but all of a sudden people who had been loitering in the middle of the street went dashing for the plank sidewalks like watching the Red Sea part.

Priya either had a better line of sight than I did, faster reflexes, or more native caution—probably all three. She grabbed Molly's reins above my hand and hauled Molly *and* me up onto the sidewalk. It was only a four-inch curb, but the extra height let me get a clearer view of what was going on.

There was a cart—a caravan, really, like a little house on wheels—with a panicked horse attached, rolling backward down the steepness of the hill.

It was supposed to be a two-in-hand, and you could see that plain because one of the shafts wasn't hooked up to a harness and was dragging. Somebody must have forgot to set the brake, or the brake had slipped, and before the second horse could be put in the traces the whole equipage had started bumping backward over the cobblestones. It was speeding up and gaining impetus and pulling the terrified dun that *was* in the traces backward on the slippery stones with no chance to brace herself.

"Hold Molly," I said to Priya, and let go of the reins.

"Karen Grace Memery!" she yelled. And something afterward that I didn't catch, because I was darting out the opposite way from everybody else, toward that dragging caravan and its sideways mare.

The caravan was bulky, but it didn't look too heavy for one horse to brace if she could get her weight into it proper. The problem was that she was only traced on the right hand side, so she was crooked and staggering sideways, struggling to keep her feet under her. And the cart was a doubletree type, so the left-hand shaft had swung out and was dragging.

The disaster weren't moving fast, understand, but it was building up some steam, and you wouldn't want to be caught under it. Or between it and a wall.

Or harnessed to it with no way to get loose.

The whole mess made a terrible rumble as it skittered down the hill, the steel-shod wheels and the steel-shod hooves striking sparks off the cobbles. That mare grimly fought for balance, snorting and struggling and thrashing her hooves around, too terrified—or working too hard—even to neigh in fear.

I sprinted uphill, pushing against the folds of my skirts and cursing my corsetry. I had a decent turn of speed on me, though I weren't no whippet like Priya, and I got up ahead of that cart without getting crushed by it, though I dodged back and forth a little before darting past. Something horrible squished under my boot and I thought I felt bones in it. I didn't look down.

The traces dragged off the left-hand shaft, and I almost tripped on 'em and got tangled. That would have been an ignominious fate—dragged to death by a caravan—and no mistaking it, but I somehow tottered and kept upright.

Me and the dun mare, partners in not dying. If you've got that in common, you don't need much else to establish a friendly relationship on the pronto.

She had traces dragging under her feet, too, which wasn't helping her keep her footing. I couldn't do much about that, but I did grab the ones that were attached to the left-hand shaft. Which rapidly became the right hand-shaft, because as I lifted it up and started pulling on it, the momentum of the cart swung me around to face the assemblage and almost tossed me under the hooves.

This close, the lather rubbed off the mare's hide under the harness flicked my face and dress as she surged against the traces. She almost had it. I'd thought she was panicking, but she must have been a seasoned cart-horse, because even with her ears flat with effort and the whites showing at the edges of her horrified eyes, even with only half her traces connected, she was trying to manage that caravan like a professional on a tough job they somehow got stuck with.

That dun mare saved both our bacon. Because all *I* did was skitter in close to her, staying away from her thrashing head and those hooves still scrabbling on the cobbles like so many unaimed hammers, then grab her breast band in my left hand while I was holding on to the traces wrapped around my fist and wrist with the right.

I held on tight and *pulled*.

I had always been a strong girl, and I'd only gotten stronger running our little ranch with just Priya and me. She was the

Mad Scientist (*future apprentice* Mad Scientist, to be sure) and I weren't. But every Mad Scientist needs a burly assistant to lean on wrenches and hold great piles of metal in place for fitting. And every farm needs somebody to throw around bales of hay.

Not to mention all the mucking out and hauling water and chopping wood I'd been doing of late. While Priya was the deft one of the two of us, and the brains of the operation—and while she was taller'n me these days—she was also a willow maid.

Now me? I was the brawn.

My hands were hard, my biceps were bulging, and I'd had to let out all my shirtwaists and all my dresses across the shoulders twice.

I heard the one I was wearing right now tear in just that spot, and cursed under my breath in a most unladylike fashion as I pulled harder. It was my best town dress and there wouldn't be no replacing that until we had more money coming in.

The strain dragged across my chest and shoulders as I bent my elbows. It hit every fiber in the muscles and I didn't like the sensation none. My arms felt like to be pulled out of their sockets, my feet skidded on the cobblestones, and the mare's tossing head thumped on my left shoulder so hard I thought she was going to break my collarbone. Or my shoulder. Or—based on the pain—that maybe she had already done.

My fingers held on to the breast strap though, so I guessed I was just bruised up. I tried to lean my head away so she wouldn't flatten my nose while she was in there. Her hoof caught my shin. I felt the thick hot blood and didn't dare look down because me tossing up all that Chinatown food wouldn't do much to strengthen my arm.

Thing was, the more I pulled, the more I helped the mare's balance, because I was pulling her straight in the shafts. And if she weren't sideways, she had a chance of throwing her weight on the evener and dragging the cart to a halt. So I pulled, and skipped along so *I* didn't get dragged, and helped her stay upright and pointed uphill... and inch by inch, one horsepower and one woman-power, we got the caravan and the whole mess slowed.

It was a sapheaded move, to be utterly certain. It wasn't made any less sapheaded by the fact that it was working. Might even have kept working, too, if I hadn't been not having the best of luck with keeping my *own* balance.

The mare was better at staying upright than I was, though in my defense she had an extra set of legs. I was using her and the cart to stay on my feet now, arms flexed and pulling as hard as I could, and my feet were all but slipping out from under me. I was wearing little girl boots with a heel and about ten dozen mother-of-pearl buttons, and the buttons one by one were giving way—threads popping—my boots going loose around my ankles.

Now I pride myself on my command of colorful imprecations, but reader, I had my hands full at just that particular.

"Aw, jeez," I said as I started to fall.

But as I pitched forward, the caravan stopped dead with a lurch.

I held on to the harness and the traces, which were a good thing, because I would have left teeth in the road if I'd hit the wagon tree face-first, which was how I was oriented. Instead, I hung there like a fly in a big spider's web, keeping myself in place by main strength and the grace of that bay dun mare. My feet touched the ground, sure. But they weren't holding me up. The mare was, and the traces.

The mare staggered and panic flared through me, but she weren't falling. She was just getting her feet under herself, and then she braced there solid and let me pull my own self upright and stable against her harness. Good mare. Better than these fool teamsters deserved.

I unwound my right hand and dropped the shaft with a clatter. The mare jumped and I shushed her. That had been stupid of me. I risked a glance at my hand; it was leather-burned and whatnot, my kid gloves cut to ribbons, but they'd saved me from doing more than welting my skin. I might have cut it to the bone with that trick, calluses or no calluses, if I hadn't been dressed for town.

It were utterly quiet on all sides. Chinatown, of all the places on the green earth, had went silent as water in a glass. So silent I could hear that ringing in my ear what's been there since the explosion last autumn.

The mare nosed my hair. I patted her shoulder and she lipped the edge of my town hat, which had on it a small garden of straw flowers, as if she was thinking about a snack. I bumped her off with a fist and somehow managed to unwind my cramped fingers from her breast band, though it took me both hands to do it. I had some half-considered idea to go around the side of the caravan and make sure the brake was set. So I stepped over the dropped shaft, steadying myself against the caravan's corner, wobbling in my undone boots.

And met Priya coming the other way, fear in her and a scowl on her face.

"Karen! Karen, are you—"

She saw me, and took in my shredded gloves at a glance. And the blood soaking my left boot and the hem of my dress.

"Set the brake," I said.

She snorted at me. "How do you think I stopped the cart?"

My heart kicked and I caught a breath, thinking of her darting in behind the sliding caravan to grab hold of the brake lever and pull it hard to lock the wheel. I opened my mouth—

I looked at her and she looked at me, and I laughed. "All right," I said, at last. "Well, I been saying for six months that you're the brains of the operation. I don't want to hear no guff about me taking silly chances, though, when I was uphill of the catastrophe."

She thought about it, sure. Then she sighed and shook her head. "Damn your eyes, Karen Memery Jones. I'm afraid you have caught me out this time."

If she were indulging in her little game of adding bits and bobs and filigrees and folderols to my name, I weren't in too much trouble. And she couldn't be in trouble with me, unless I were a worse kind of hypocrite than I have yet managed.

I would have kissed her then, but we was in front of God and everybody, and while it is my own considered and contemplated opinions that God would not much have cared, it's likely that some of the good folk of Rapid City might have.

I looked around for Molly, instead, and saw her craning her neck jealously from where a newsboy was holding her, still up safe on the boardwalk though we'd slid well past where she and Priya had been.

"I hope somebody fires the teamster who didn't set that brake." I said it loud, looking away from Priya. She wanted to bend down and fuss with my bloody ankle, but I grabbed her elbow and held her upright for the nonce. We could deal with the gash and whatever else when we was safe home; the wound weren't going to get no cleaner for fooling around with it on the mucky street, and the blood might clean it out a little. As long as I didn't look down and get a glimpse. Inadvertent like.

"Somebody might," said a voice behind me. Male voice, medium timbre. "Are you ladies all right?"

Priya jumped, because she does that when she's startled. I put a hand on her arm for a second, then turned around.

I was looking at a man dressed like he thought you had to audition to be a cowboy. Worn gingham check shirt in blue and white; suede waistcoat that matched his scuffed, buff boots; Levi blue jeans soft at the knees. He was a little drawn under the cheekbones, the kind of big man who gets rangy when he's down flesh rather than wiry or slender.

"I'm Miss Memery," I said, holding out my hand in its tattered glove. By the time I noticed, it was too late to pull it back. At least he was gentle when he bowed over it. "This is my business partner, Miss Swati. We own the Bent D Ranch outside town."

"I'm Black." He took Priya's hand, too, and didn't seem to have to pause to think about it, which made me like him right off the bat. You'd be surprised how often that ain't the case. "You're horsebreakers?"

"I'm more of a horse tamer," I said. "Miss Swati is working on her sciencing license."

He handed me a card. When I took it, he noticed the blood on my gloves from where the harness leather had broken my skin. I turned my hand over real quick so I couldn't see the red. I smiled at him gamely while trying to keep my weight on my right leg.

He whistled. "You just saved me a whole lot of explaining and a whole passel of lawsuits from the locals for broken shop windows and from feet and puppy dogs getting run over. And the loss of a cart and a good horse. So if you want jobs, ladies, look me up."

I looked at the card. It didn't have no local contact information on it, just an address in San Diego, all the way down the other end of the coast in California. I'd heard it was dry and sunny there.

He seemed to comprehend my quandary. "You come on out to the Kindness ranch, if you've heard of it. The Lazy B."

The Kindnesses was our neighbors higher up the mountain.

"I might want a job. Wrangling?" I gestured to the mare and the cart Priya and me'd saved. "Because it seems to me you got some piss-poor wranglers, for a Wild West show."

"We're not a Wild West show," he said, smirking. "You'd be working on a motion picture."

I must have looked like a thumped fish, because he grinned at me. I'd been right about the Kinematoscope.

"All right," he allowed. "It's a motion picture about a Wild West show. But you should come on out. The pay is all right. And who doesn't want to be in pictures?"

"I ain't never considered it," I said, 'cause I hadn't.

"Can you ride sidesaddle, Miss Memery?"

I sighed. One reason I'd rather live in Rapid City than most places is pure and simple, nobody here looks askance at a woman who don't want to risk her neck clinging to a sidesaddle to get from place to place.

Whatever's expected as a woman, men set it up so it's twice as hard, and then look down on us for doing it merely twice as well.

Anyway, plenty of women in the territories are widowed or grass-widowed and fork a horse to ride for their own stock and ain't nobody going to give her fuss about it except maybe some society folk who ain't got nothing better to do. And nobody takes those types without a bit of sugar to help 'em down, so it's fine.

But. He said they paid well.

"If I got to," I allowed.

"We have a job for a stunt double for a lady," he said. "She's a mite smaller than you, but I reckon you'd be more convincing than a lad in a dress."

I was just about to say yes. And then Priya cleared her throat, and I looked at her frown, and I said, "Let me think about it."

Chapter Three

Priya wanted to stop by the fairgrounds on the way out of town and watch the big mechs fighting. It weren't a real duel day—not one where some Mad Scientist said something about another one's mother's way with a crescent wrench, anyway, and then Honor Must Be Satisfied. But there was three practice bouts going on in roped-off arenas and those are always worth a watch.

A lot more fun for me than the real thing, honestly. Because the odds of either a scientist or a bystander getting maimed or squished are so much lower that the racehorse accountants don't even bother to run a book on it.

This was more like puppies wrestling. Big, ten-ton metal puppies. But the object was to play and test their machines instead of to hurt one another, except when it wasn't. Or when something went wrong.

We left Molly at the picket line with a few dozen other horses after making sure our groceries were secure. Odds were pretty good nobody would try to lift them; everybody in Rapid City already knows who that ridiculous-looking spotted animal belongs to.

We wandered past the first mechanical wrestling match, which Priya deemed "insufficiently interesting," and settled on the second. I limped along behind my wife until Priya leaned on the ropes, right up close, making me jumpy as a pocket gopher chewing tobacco.

I would rather have been a quarter mile back from the Mega-Armatures, which are maybe four times the size of our little wearable Singer sewing machine. That's more than enough exoskeleton for my taste.

"That's Professor Emil in the blue Megarm," Priya said. "and Doctor von Hammerstein in the fawn-colored one."

Oh, so that's why we were here. Doctor Stella von Hammerstein was Priya's idol. The Mad Scientist she dreamed of studying under.

The big mechanicals circled each other, mimicking the movements of the tiny people inside them. Their hands darted out and pulled back as they looked for a grappling advantage, neither quite committing.

Priya sighed.

I said, "I can still go work clown rodeos."

"I'm not burying you," she told me.

I waved at the Megarms as the fawn one abruptly lunged, picked the blue one up, and flipped it, like one of those Celestial martial arts they do instead of boxing. The flipped one landed hard on its back—I heard the scientist inside yelp and grunt even from behind the ropes—and waved feebly, like an inverted turtle.

"Bad design," Priya muttered. "You should have a gimbal in the knee joints so it can lever itself back up. Though how you'd make it strong enough…"

"You've got some nerve telling me what I do is too dangerous." I knew I sounded put out and I expected her to flare back, but she settled into herself instead.

That's how I knew she was really feeling low.

"There's not money for it anyway," Priya said with a sigh. "I need to come up with some other calling on which to focus my life, and we both know it. Maybe I can go back to apprenticing under Miss Lizzie."

Miss Lizzie was marvelous. She'd saved Priya's life, and mine, and her mechanical skills had kept the Singer and the octodoc and all the other equipment at the Hôtel Ma Cherie on Amity Street running smooth as butter. But she wasn't Doctor von Hammerstein, and we both knew it.

Just like we both knew we couldn't afford Doctor von Hammerstein's apprenticeship fees.

As I said, we wasn't flat busted. Hell, we weren't even down to the second lucky silver dollar I got from Marshal Bass Reeves.

But we was getting there. And nothing on earth shy of Priya's life or death was going to make me spend that dollar.

I sighed, thinking. You got to be who you got to be, and you got to not be who you ain't, and somehow you got to bend that around the person your lover needs you to be and be that person, too—at least acceptably well—and you got to make room for your lover to be who they is while still not giving up your own self, and it ain't half a wonder we don't all live in caves and meet once a year to trade hides and salt and onions. It's all a big pickle, ain't it?

Priya's chosen work was dangerous. And my da died taming horses, so I can't claim I don't know that ain't nohow safe, neither. But we both had to be who we were.

"We can go work for that motion picture," said me. "They've got mechanicals; they must need engineers. And that Black fellow said the pay was good."

I fished his visiting card from my pocket. *Mr. Walker Black, Head Wrangler.*

"They almost got you killed already." Priya pointed to my feet, which were bare and cold in the dusty grass. My pocket was full of mother-of-pearl buttons I was going to be sewing back on my dress-up boots when we got home. I thought we'd found most of them, with help from some bystanding Celestials, but I might have to add a few mismatched ones from the button jar.

She made a wistful mouth at the mechs. The blue one was still struggling to rise as Dr. von Hammerstein turned directly toward us, and took a bow at Priya.

Well, I guessed the admiration there was mutual.

"Go over there and talk to her," I said, ignoring the pain in my leg and privately wishing Priya would remember it and say, "No, let's go home and get you taken care of."

She was on her own set of tenterhooks, though, and I watched her wobble back and forth on the balls of her feet for a good minute before she squared up her shoulders in her blue-checked shirt, took in a big breath, and blew it out through her lips like a horse. She eeled under the rope like someone marching cold-eyed to an execution.

I gave her a head start, then ducked the rope myself and walked more slowly after her, picking across the furrowed earth.

Doctor von Hammerstein was a true yellow blonde with that see-through hair and skin you don't get much of in Rapid City. Her eyes were ghosty, and she weaseled herself out of the carapace of the fawn-colored Megarm like a ferret sliding out of a birdcage, nimble and long-legged.

She might have been about fifty and she still had all her own teeth and limbs, which was a mite unusual for a Mad Scientist.

"Priya!" she said, drawing herself up with the perfect posture that always made me wonder if she was a real finishing-school baroness. "I hope you have good news for me!"

I didn't hear Priya's reply because I was still well back, and Priya was facing away. But her gesture indicated she weren't so sure of her answer.

I dodged a splintered bit of metal and came within earshot as the doctor lowered her voice. "I understand. You must realize that the apprentice fees aren't punitive."

"I know," Priya said. "It is about investment."

Von Hammerstein smiled. She had an accent, but it weren't strong. "It is also about simply paying for materials. As I am sure you know from your own tinkering."

Priya flinched at the word "tinkering," but nodded. I wanted to snipe at von Hammerstein for dismissing her but I knew Priya wouldn't thank me, so I twisted my fingers together behind my back and concentrated on the throbbing in my shin.

The rest of the conversation weren't nothing but pleasantries, as the doctor howdied me and I howdied her and then she went off in the other direction, her armature following her like a large ungainly kind of pet.

Priya watched her go with another heavy sigh.

I put a hand on her shoulder and she leaned into it. Then she looked down. "You're bleeding."

"That horse split my shin, remember?"

I could see from her face that she had plumb forgot me getting hurt, she was so wrapped up in her own feelings. She shook them off and said, "Damnation. Let us go home and get your leg cleaned up."

By then I was chilled enough that I was barely limping.

"I see why you want to learn from her," I said as we picked our way past the other Mad Scientist and his efforts to right his Mega-Armature with two apprentices, a journeyman, and a great big jack. The mechanical sort, not the donkey kind.

"I don't just want to learn from her," Priya said, glancing over her shoulder. "I want to learn enough from her to beat her someday."

I felt my mouth twist funny and hastened to smooth it. Priya's got a fightin' streak that I don't share: she always wants to be the best at anything. It makes me a mite uncomfortable, sometimes, but it don't make me love her any less and it's who she is, so I try not to comment.

"It's a lot of money," I said. "But it's also who you are. And I don't think you should have to give up who you are because of money."

"Would the motion picture money cover a year of fees?"

"I don't know," I said. "But it would cover more than we got now, to begin with."

"I don't know," she said, with a totally different meaning than when I had said it. Which was better than no thank you.

I didn't tell Priya that motion picture stunts was probably more dangerous than running from bulls in polka-dot bloomers. Me wearing the bloomers, that is, not the bulls, though I reckon a bull in bloomers would be a caution for as long as it lasted.

Some of them Eastern ladies as put skirts on pianos would likely think it only proper, bulls having bull parts and all.

The best part was, a runaway pony, a sciencing duel, and the offer of a job weren't the only things of interest to take place on that particular morning. Because as me and Priya was riding back home, double on Molly, wedged in between her baskets and panniers and saddlebags full of marketing all anyway, we passed a tent setting up at the back edge of the fairgrounds where we'd seen that circus just the year previous. We slowed down to give it a look over.

It weren't no circus tent. It was a rectangular tent with bamboo poles, and it was all plain yellow canvas. There was a low stage at one end—just a few dozen square feet of boards on top of trestles—and it looked like the whole thing had been pulled out the back of the wagon parked opposite. There was three men setting it up. Two of 'em was stripped to the waist despite the chill. The third one was in shirtsleeves.

My hands was smarting and my leg was throbbing. I was hungry and wanted to go home, but Priya craned her neck, seeming fascinated. Motion caught my eye. A small dark-haired boy in short pants was running toward us as fast as his knobby knees could pump.

Molly was only moving at an amble, so it weren't no trick for the boy to catch us up. I thought he'd want to pet the horse, or gawk at Priya—which she hates, though she's getting more used to it and the people of Rapid City are getting more used to Indian girls in trousers—but all he did was jump up and shove a paper into my hand.

It was a handbill. Still wet enough to smear on my ruined glove, paper a little warm from the press. It smelled of printer's ink. I glanced over at the smaller tent that was already up, over by the wagon. The boy had come from in there.

The handbill read:

FOUR DAYS Only
Father POSTLETHWAIT Prayer Revival Meeting
GOOD FOR WHAT AILS YOU
Pleurisy, Consumption, Black Lung, Angina,
Sciatica, Dropsy, Diabetes, Tumors malignant and benign.
Rickets, Beriberi, Goiter, Scurvy, Scrofula, Sprockets.
ALL CURED BY THE POWER of the LORD
ACTING THROUGH THE PIOUS FATHER POSTLETHWAIT
PSYCHIC SURGERY
THE LAME SHALL WALK
YOUR PRAYERS ANSWERED.

There was a little note underneath saying *Rapid City Fairgrounds, Thursday-Friday-Saturday-Sunday, April 10-13, 1879.* Which was of course that very week and weekend. Through Good Friday and Easter, so I thought he might draw a pretty good crowd.

"This one's a rebel," I remarked offhand to Priya, giving her the handbill.

She perused it closely. If I was to turn my head sideways, I would have seen her dark brown eyebrows drawing together over her dark brown eyes. "He is a fakir?"

"Faith healer," I said. "Medicine show. Question is whether it's laying on of hands or patent medicine that's probably got poison in it. I'm guessing laying on of hands, since he ain't going by 'Doctor' and it says 'psychic surgery' down here."

We'd had an adventure with a fine matched pair of mountebank Spiritualists only that winter and it were still fresh in my mind. That, and possibly all that botheration the year before with goddamned Peter Bantle and his goddamned mind-control whatsis, had left me singularly uncharitable where flimflam artists was concerned.

"Hmm." She handed me back the bill, let her fingers brush mine. It went through me like a shock. "So how is he a 'rebel,' my Karen?"

"These fellows usually refer to themselves as 'Brother' rather than 'Father.'

She laughed so hard the men setting up the tent paused in their mallet blows and turned to watch us go.

Priya got me and Molly home, and the vegetables and flour and spices and like unloaded, and Molly untacked and turned out to roll and graze while I hobbled into the house and pumped water and blew the fire up and put the kettle on for it to boil. When she came in with the last load of groceries, I was sitting in one of our two ladder-backed pine chairs with my leg propped on the other and a clean towel draped over my dress and my stocking so I wouldn't have to look at the blood.

"As if you weren't a strapping great girl," Priya said, thumping a bag of gram flour down on the big old farmhouse table that had come with the ranch house, the previous owner's heirs having deemed it too inconvenient to move and rolled it into their asking price. "I have no idea how on earth you handle your monthlies."

"I try not to look too close until I get the rags into soapy water," I said. "There's enough to clean up without adding a load of sick on top."

She had some odd ideas about being in her flowers, for sure, including not touching food other people was going to eat when she was on it. But that was her culture, and we'd worked out some compromises, such that though she did most of the cooking, I did it at that time of the month.

I took it as a sign of how far she'd relaxed that she was willing to joke about it now. She'd been such a starved rabbit when we took up together, anyway, I don't think she'd had a cycle in a year. So I was glad she was back on the regular even if it inconvenienced me.

"Close your eyes, Karen." She undid my bloodied skirts and slid them out from under me as I lifted myself up in the chair with my good leg. I distracted myself with the boots; I was going to be an aeon sewing those damned buttons back on. That would teach me to wear riding boots for everything.

I giggled giddily at a little mental cartoon of myself in a swagged silk evening dress with opera gloves and tooled leather boots. Meanwhile, Priya got my stocking stripped off and managed not to hiss too loudly when she looked at my leg.

"How bad is it?" I couldn't keep my eyes closed, but I kept my gaze on the ceiling.

"I can't see the bone," she said cheerily. "I'm going to have to put a couple of stitches in this, Karen."

One thing about Priya. She's never a one to lie to you to comfort your heart.

Just then the kettle boiled, and she grabbed up the fire poker and swung the hook out.

I closed my top lights again, as directed, before she could catch me peeking. Through such subtle counterfeits were domestic harmony ensured. It was for my own good, anyway.

So I didn't look again, despite the splashing and the wringing sounds and the stinging going on for a good while longer than I felt a simple kick on the shin probably warranted. I held my peace, though, until she dropped a scalding cloth over my raw, open wound. Then I yelped out loud and levitated off the hard wooden chair like a fakir's rope, speaking of fakirs, even though she'd wrung it out and given it time to cool a little.

After the sting of heat the burning started. She'd put some rum in her wash water, and now it was searing the flesh of the kicked leg. My exposed thighs were all over gooseflesh because the rekindled fire hadn't driven the chill out of that cold kitchen yet. That rag was *hot*.

"Don't be such a baby," Priya said sympathetically. "Do you wish to die of gangrene?"

She was a stoic at heart, but she didn't hold others to her own standards. Her hands were gentle even when her words tried to be stern.

Priya said, "I know this is not the first time you have been kicked by a horse."

"It's like falling in love." I clutched the edges of my chair. "Every time hurts worse than the one before."

"And you would know this how, Karen Joy? Have you been falling in love willy-nilly while my back is turned?" She bathed my leg with short strokes, moving away from the wound.

"Over and over again." That hurt less, and slowly I was relaxing. Funny how you never noticed that a chair was uncomfortable until you tried to relax against it.

"Here come the stitches," she said. "Would you like a piece of leather to bite on?"

"Yes," I said, and she handed me the strop we used to sharpen our knives for butchering. It tasted of machine oil and tanning oak, and I concentrated on not biting so hard I bit through it. Or broke a tooth, for that matter.

The puncture and tug at the edge of raw flesh hurt, but I had been anticipating it hurting so much more that I actually kind of relaxed into it.

"That wasn't so bad," I said when she was done.

I felt the tautness of cloth and the tug that told me she was binding the wound at last, and I dared to open my eyes. "I keep falling in love with this black-haired girl who doesn't know I'm alive."

Priya blew dark fringe off her forehead. "Perhaps you should consider a redhead next time. Although I hear they are even more fickle."

"Darling, you are the least fickle creature I have ever known." I sniffed. The dressing she'd put on me had a strong scent. Like somebody had dragged a Christmas cookie through a eucalyptus grove. "What on earth did you dress that with?"

It felt better already, but I wasn't about to admit that until I found out what weird tropical plants she'd packed my wound with.

"It is clove oil," she said. "And neem, and powdered yarrow."

"Yarrow. My mother swore by it." I dropped the leg off the other chair and tested it. "Clove oil?"

"It is a—" She waved her hand in that frustrated gesture she made when she didn't know the word for something. "It stops pain. Like willow bark but you put it on the wound. And neem will keep you from getting the pus and the red lines and fever—"

"Oh." I was thinking about the horrid abscesses of my ma's teeth that had killed her. And *that* made me think about money, and having enough of it not to worry, because everything made me think about money when I didn't know where the next infusion of capital, as they say, was coming from. "Pree... I think I ought to take that wrangling job."

She looked at me skeptical like. Head to one side and lips all cattywampus.

"We ain't got a solid income." I looked around for my skirts.

Priya already had 'em soaking in a bucket of cold water to get the blood out, which didn't do my cold legs any benefit. She must have noticed me casting about like a hound that's off the scent, though, because she picked up a slightly scorched-smelling wool blanket that was warm from the fire and dropped it over me.

It was so hot it was almost uncomfortable, and I savored that.

"There's the work I do with Miss Lizzie," she protested.

"Sure," I said. "It's good money when you get the work. How many folk in Rapid City going to want—or be able to afford—a *lift* in their house? This town's got some gold money, sure. But it's only two streets or so of rich folk. What do we do next, when all such as want one got it?"

She looked stricken, so I said, "There might be another fad, you know. And right now you're supporting us. I just don't want to rely on fads to do it."

"Something will turn up," she said confidently. "We're both hard workers. If it comes to the worst, I will telegraph Missus Horner, the lady magician, and take her up on her kind offer of employment. She pays so well I am certain it would be easy to send money home."

You ever feel your eyelid just kind of start in twitching? A most discombobulating sensation, as if some part of you that ain't your heartbeat or bowels has suddenly decided it's a grown-up adult person that can make decisions on its own.

Well, mine was twitching then. The last thing in the world I wanted was Priya taking off to have adventures far away from me.

And suddenly I understood a little better why she weren't having none of me as a rodeo clown.

"So this Black wants you to be a wrangler on that motion picture. And me to... he doesn't even know, he has not figured out yet, what I am good for. But he saw you being Karen, and me being Karen's rescuer, and so he wants to give us work? That ain't no recipe for turtle soup, my love."

Oh, my Priyadarshini. If there is any other thing in the world that can pierce my heart the way it does when she talks like her own sweet self one moment and then talks like some gold miner washed up in a dockside tavern the next, I haven't found it yet. I suppose it's just as well. Nobody should have too many weaknesses on that level.

"If we do this, we might have enough money not to worry."

Priya put her hand on my cheek. "Dear Karen," she said. "How much money, for you, is enough so as not to worry?"

Well, fair shooting and she had a point. But also easy for her to say.

"I gotta do something useful." The blanket was so warm I like to drifted off, but I pulled myself back. I wished I had some coffee, but Priya can't be trusted to make it. She's good at tea, and tea is fine and tasty, but when you're plain tired it just can't bring you back to life the way an old pot of proper black joe can. "I'm not some fluffy Chinese lapdog, Pree. I'm one of those shepherd breeds with the ticked red coats. I need to be *doing*."

"And you need to feel safe." She was looking at me with that perception that made me feel naked. Which, in fairness, I was. Half-naked, anyway. "And saving money, having a nest egg, is a way for you to feel safer."

I nodded.

"Even if you riding stunts for people who will not appreciate you, and who might get you bucked off or trampled, is from a logical standard *less* safe. Also, you feel like you are not doing enough to pull your weight. Despite—"

I tried to break in, but she kept talking.

"Despite all the cooking and cleaning and hostlering and brush clearing and bramble planting—"

"I'm a horsetamer," I interrupted.

She seemed about to roll over me, but she reined in her tongue and leaned back with her elbows on the table. "Just pretend I made a joke about heartbreakers here," she said.

I scowled at her, but I couldn't really muster up meaning it. "It's not just the money," I said.

She drew up so sharp that if she was a pony you would have seen her set her haunches. She didn't say nothing, just waited for me to go on.

"I don't have a reputation here." I'd written the speech all careful like in my head, but what happened in the real world was that the actual confrontation arose, and all my pretty words vanished in a puff of me hemming and straying.

She snorted dismissively.

"I mean, I do. But I don't have a reputation around horses. And horses are what I'm good at, Pree. Horses are what I do *well*."

"And you think if you go work for this Black fellow, it will cement your reputation as a horse tamer. Because you will have—what do you call it?"

"Credibility," I said.

She nodded. Her eyes were fixed on mine. She didn't say a word.

"It's the same thing you would get apprenticing to Doctor von Hammerstein," I said, aggravated that she could not see that parallel. "She teaches you, and in a few years everybody assumes you know your stuff, because you came up as Doctor Stella's apprentice. Well, Pree, if I go and sign up on this motion picture, darling, I can spend the next ten years putting *Motion picture wrangler* and *Motion picture stunt rider* on my visiting card. Don't pretend to me that you don't see how that could benefit us."

Not meeting my eyes, she sighed. "So it's not just about *this* money."

"It's about all the money forever after," I said. "It's about financial stability."

"It's a terrible idea," she said.

I grinned. "Remember Black said there was a job for you, too."

She sighed again. "All right, let's talk to him and see if it's going to be *enough* money. Because if we're doing this, we are not doing it for pennies."

Chapter Four

We went down to the Kindness ranch first thing the following morning, riding double on Molly. We weren't such large persons—I mean, I was plump and tall, but not heavy-built, and Priya was tall but she was sewn out of scraps and stretched on a rack, a rag doll if ever a creature was one—and Molly carried us like it weren't nothing, clopping down the road that hadn't had time to get dusty yet because it was still raining two or three times almost every day. Spring in Rapid City is a regular Amazon.

My leg weren't happy with me, but I had it bandaged up, and the cuts on my hands was scabbed up nice and down to a dull roar under a layer of salve and riding gloves.

Priya was still a mite restless and uncertain about the whole shebang. So was I, but we'd agreed to give it a chance and see what happened and where it got us. Which, if you're honest with yourself, is all anybody's ever doing. We act like our plans got some kind of permanence to them. But the world just shrugs and does what it were gonna do with you or without you, and if you're in the way when the roof comes down, well, I reckon what you were planning on having for lunch on Tuesday doesn't much matter anymore. Man plans and God laughs, as the saying goes.

Course, not having a plan is as deadly, too.

The ranch was abustle when we got there. So many people, it was like the market down by the pier of a Friday morning. Except instead of stalls of vegetables and fish and flowers, it was just people.

People and machinery.

We rode Molly up to the gate, which was standing open. The Kindness ranch were a neat little place, pretty as a picture and kept up better than the place Priya and me had bought that winter. Otis and Mourning Kindness is colored folk, and colored folk always keep their property nice if they got it.

Which wasn't to say our place wasn't *going* to be a stunner when we'd gotten around to window boxes and such geegaws, but somebody cared enough about this little ranch to whitewash anything that would stand still for it. If I spotted a cat, I wouldn't be surprised to find out that it had been given a good coat of limewash, too.

It struck me odd that there was half a hundred people about, and not one single head of cattle. I wondered what the Kindnesses had done with their stock. I didn't know the couple except to nod to them on the road, but Rapid wasn't so big that I hadn't heard their names. I knowed they was folk with no children, which is a toll on a farm family, and I knowed their stock was beef cattle, mostly, which they grazed out on some good land that ran along the flank of a minor mountain on one side and a bluff down into the Sound on the other. I didn't see any evidence of cattle around the ranch house, anyway. Maybe it was out to pasturage.

You wouldn't have wanted cattle around with all the swarming going on, in any measure. There were a dozen or so caravans set up off to the left—one of them the one Priya and me had stopped from rolling down the hill—and off to the right, a few dozen horses were in the corrals close to the barn. I was looking at the horses, of course—absolutely because I figured we should report to Mr. Black, and Mr. Black being a wrangler would be close to the stock (and if you believe that I got a souvenir tract of swampland to sell you)—and just realizing that the shaggy licorice-brown hills in the corral at the back of the row weren't extra-large haystacks but were, in fact, three plains buffalo large as life—in fact, even larger. They were enormous. And I thought these were all cows. What was a bull like, in that case?

I'd seen a few off the train when I was coming to Rapid City, but dots in the distance ain't nothing like animals a couple hundred yards away and standing next to a horse for scale.

I laid eyes on my friend the bay dun mare, my shin giving a throb of recognition, in with a half-dozen other mares and geldings who was standing around bored in a corral swatting nonexistent flies off one another. They all looked mostly healthy, at least. Not a half-starved beast among 'em, and nobody favoring a foot, which was next to a miracle after train travel.

"Aren't motion picture people supposed to be superstitious?" Priya said in my ear.

I jumped guiltily and pulled my attention back. "I don't rightly know."

"There's thirteen caravans." She pointed with her chin, moving against my back. Molly sidestepped to stay under Priya so Priya didn't even notice she'd nearly overbalanced and fell.

Priya's good at so many things that I'm a little reassured by what a terrible rider she is, truth be told. She forgets her body exists, never mind that she's got to know where all its bits are if she's on the back of a horse—yes, and all the horse's bits, too.

I twisted over my shoulder to gawk at her, then looked back and counted again. She was right, of course. Priya ain't never wrong about figures and figuring and such.

Somebody was coming up the ranch road—a cowpath, it weren't more than two parallel tracks in the grass with some mud in a dip here or there—toward us. I forced my hands to stay loose on the reins as I realized it was the mechanical with the carved crystal chest muscles. Blessedly, wearing a size 40ish flannel check shirt now. I couldn't imagine mechanicals felt an April chill, so it must have been for camouflage and protecting the sensibilities of the ladies.

It stopped in the middle of the road and bowed to us. I was tightening up a little. I made myself think about my seat, and getting deep and loose, because I knew if I weren't, Molly'd feel it and complain. Or maybe get nervous herself.

I don't know what it was about that mechanical that got to me. I'd read about 'em, of course, but they was a fancy East Coast toy like them clockwork bicycles, and I ain't never see'd one before. And that thing—pardon me for saying so—sent a shiver right up my back and into the part of my brain that worrits on about things like earthquakes and house fires and whether a sea monster is gonna rise up out of the Sound and just plumb eat us all. It was just... too close to human, but it didn't move like a human being at all.

Priya, of course, was enchanted. She sat up tall on the blanket behind me—we was riding bareback and I promise it weren't to show off to Mr. Black, it was just more comfortable than trying to fit two in the saddle—trying to peer over my shoulder. That didn't get her a close enough look to suit her, so she wriggled her leg over and slid down Molly's flank on her belly, hitting the ground with a little *oof* like a dramatic cat. Molly's a tall mare, I think I mentioned.

Priya took two quick steps up to the mechanical. I wanted to jump down and grab her, which was totally off the tracks because as I said I've been reading the papers and I knowed mechanicals was built so they couldn't hurt nobody, whether they wanted to or not, and there was a bunch of argument about if they wanted things at all. And Priya was close enough to the thing to touch.

"Pardon me," she said to the top of its cowboy hat. "Are you trying to get our attention?"

It straightened up. "Good morning, misses. I'm very sorry, but this is a closed set."

"Oh." Priya looked at me. "We're invited. Mister Black asked us to come by about a job."

"We're the people who stopped the cart yesterday." I tried to sound decisive and businesslike. I asked myself, *What would Miss Francina do?*

I believe firmly that you can get through just about any sticky situation in life by asking yourself that question.

"Oh, yes, we were told to expect you." Its voice was not what I would have expected, if'n I'd had the wherewithal to expect anything at all. It was melodious, and each word was fluently spoken but sometimes the quiets *between* the words was just slightly at the wrong angle, if you understand what I mean. I was put in mind of a player piano.

I wondered if the mechanical had a roll inside it that had every word it might want to say, but that seemed cumbrous, so I resolved to ask Priya how she thought it might work when the mechanical weren't listening. Which is ridiculous fastidious on the face of it, because why would a mechanical care about that any more than I'd care if it asked how my heart pumped blood and through what mechanism that blood happened to circulate—

—I take that back. I might just find that line of questioning a tad bit menacing, after all.

"I am Priyadarshini Swati," Priya said, thrusting out her hand like the ranch owner she was. I never got tired of watching her put on that little showmanship bluster. "This is my business partner, Miss Karen Memery. I am a mechanic and she is a horse tamer."

The mechanical froze in place like it was a feature in one of those photographs where they prop up dead babies and try to make them look lifelike for a keepsake. I froze, too, and Molly picked up my mood and sidled and stamped. Her head came up, ears twitching.

"Steady," I said. "Steady."

She didn't think much of me yelling at her with my seat about how there was a snake or a mountain lion around somewhere, when she couldn't make out any such monster. She knew it couldn't be the mechanical that had me upset, because it didn't seem to bother her in the slightest. It weren't too smelly and though it clanked a bit it made a hell of a lot less noise and steam than the industrial Singer sewing machine we had back at the ranch, that Priya had kitted out for heavy labor.

The Singer made skidding in logs easier for Priya, for me, and for Molly, too, and she'd gotten pretty used to one of us wandering around the dooryard in the great clanking thing, driving fence posts or what have you.

Better than a man about the place any day.

So Molly wasn't bothered by the mechanical. Just I was.

I quieted my seat and my hands. Molly settled, and when I scratched under her mane she gave a little sigh and relaxed. I took my own chance and slid off her before I could upset her any more, passing the reins under her neck to lead her with.

The mechanical moved again. Gingerly, it reached out and accepted Priya's grip. It gave her two formal, slow pumps of the hand. "I am called Cowboy."

Of course it was, with the tin boots and the tin hat. Now that it was at eye level, I could see it had a tin face, too, with jointed eyelids and eyebrows and a hinged jaw that could only be designed to give the thing mobile expressions. It was a cartoonish sort of sculptured face, long and long-jawed and long-nosed, not unhandsome for a bit of tin. His "eyes" were glass eyes, hazel-green, just like people who got half-blinded wear. Just looking at those human peepers staring out of that dull-coated metal face gave me the heehaws and the vapors.

I wasn't going to be outdone, though. I looked at Priya, who still seemed to have all her fingers—and how long was *that* likely to last, in her line of work?—and gritted my teeth and stuck out my own hand.

Cowboy took it gingerly and gave me the same two measured pumps before gently releasing. All my fingers seemed to have made it through the process also. "A pleasure to meet you, Miss Memery. Shall I show you into the barn?"

"Sure thing," I said, grateful when it turned away and I was no longer subject to that wet-looking, human-looking gaze. Surely the mechanical couldn't *see* out of those glass eyes, could it? How did it see, if not? Were there Kinematoscope lenses somewhere?

It walked at a smooth place, though its balance was slightly jerky and bizarre. Priya followed closely, bending unsubtly from side to side to examine Cowboy's mechanisms from a variety of angles. She looked like a wind-lashed sapling. I stayed back a yard or two with Molly, and the overwhelming impression I got was of a washing machine that's gotten its load unbalanced and is tipping from side to side erratically, walking itself forward under momentum. Like that, but with two legs that bent at the hip and knee. I wondered if there was a big weight on a wheel inside the chassis that served as a counterbalance, moving the thing from side to side. Then I realized I would have to ask the mechanical to take its shirt off again to be sure, and that quelled that line of curiosity pretty darn quick.

It led us up to the barn, frustrating me greatly because it took us to the big doors and not past the corrals. There's no such thing in this world as a horsewoman who can resist a chance to gawk at the livestock, and some of this was livestock worth gawking at. Also I wanted to check on my bay dun friend and see if she was recovering all right, or if she had some tendon soreness or other injury. She seemed okay—she was nose-down in a pile of hay beside her paddockmates—but I still was just plain itching to get my hands on her and see what I could feel.

Cowboy walked us up the center aisle of the barn. There was four big loose boxes in addition to the storage areas in here, but only one of those loose boxes had a horse in it—a tired looking chestnut I figured for the Kindness's horse. He was a gelding and looked like he'd had food through the winter, but not quite enough and too much hard work. That confirmed some things the Kindnesses' carefully mended, whitewashed, but threadbare operation had suggested to me. They didn't have much money, I reckoned. They were house-proud, though, and probably worked their own fingers to the bone. This one fifteen-ish-year-old gelding was one of their more valuable assets, and they took what care of him they could.

But that care didn't extend to grain, even when he was being ridden pretty hard, because grain was prohibitive. To coin a phrase.

I thought I might conspire to sneak him some as the opportunity arose. After all, I would be feeding Molly during the day and it wasn't fair to grain one horse and not the other.

Black was working at the far end of the barn. He was just as tall and spare as the day before, but the hat had come off him and he was wiping his face with a bandanna that sweat and sun had faded to the color of tomato bisque. It looked soft, though, and I wanted to reach for my own just to feel the flannelly texture of much-washed cotton in my hand.

The mechanical pointed him out—just in case we didn't remember what he looked like, I supposed—and excused itself before we got close to him, saying it had stock to finish seeing to. I watched it beat tin feet back the way we'd come, noticing it avoided the closer entrance.

Black, having spotted us, slipped his bandanna into a pocket and walked down the aisle. I wondered how long it has been since there was three other horses. Or maybe oxen. Oxen was better on a farm, often, then horses. True, you can't ride oxen, and they ain't so fast pulling a cart, and they're not going to impress the neighbors with their elegance. But they're strong, and easy keepers, and honestly you'd rather have a team of oxen pulling a plow than most horses, excepting the heavy dray breeds. Those animals are huge, and don't get me wrong, they're powerful. But they ain't cheap to feed.

Black looked me over, and Priya, and Molly behind us. Molly was turning her head a little to look at that chestnut, because she wanted to go over to him. Horses need horses. It's just sort of who they are.

"That's a flashy mare," he said.

"She's been mine since I was a girl." I hoped that would shut down any ideas he might have had about buying her. Molly was staying with me, and that was that.

"You can put her in that loose box," he said. "Get her some water from the pump and a fork of hay. She'll be fine in here. The hands will leave her alone."

"What do the Kindnesses have to say about that?"

He shrugged. "We're paying for the whole property. The deal is that they keep their stock sorted out from ours and vice versa. Horses inside the barn are not the production's, and all the hands are going to know that." He clapped his hands. "Well, don't be a laggard. There's plenty of work to be done. You ride tricks?"

"A few," I admitted.

"And bareback."

"Or with a saddle." I glanced back over my shoulder at the retreating mechanical. "Doesn't that thing scare the animals?"

"Cowboy," Black said. "No, he's a good guy, for a machine. And the horses nearly don't care about him, except with one or two exceptions. They're all pretty used to machines. Besides, most of what he does here ain't labor."

"What's it do then?"

"He goes by he," Black corrected gently. "He's a shootist. Part of the Wild West show."

"I thought you said this was a motion picture."

"It is." Black grinned wickedly and reminded me, "It's a motion picture *about* a Wild West show."

While I was soaking that up, he waved me and Priya—who hadn't said a peep—toward one of those loose boxes. "Go, on, get your mare set up. I'll meet you outside. You can get acquainted with the stock, and meet Annie."

I felt profoundly dumb, and out of my depth also. "Who's Annie?"

Black grinned. "Phoebe Mosey, goes by Annie. She's our other shootist. Not a mechanical, though. Tiniest girl gunslinger you ever did see. You'll be working closely with her."

"Will I?" I said. Priya still wasn't giving me a word of help. She was throwing hay to Molly.

"Sure," Black said. "After all, you're hiring on as her stunt double."

"About that," I said. "We're leaving our ranch chores to be here. So we need to talk about the rates."

"We can pay you each a hundred a week, two weeks guaranteed. Plus fifty a day if you ride stunts that day. Assuming you earn it." He shrugged. "I reckon we'll know by the end of today if you're gonna work out."

It was, as promised, *extremely* good money. It would take care of the ranch all through next winter, and it would cover Priya's upfronts to sign on as apprentice to Doctor von Hammerstein.

Priya and I caught gazes over Black's shoulder. She nodded. I said, "You just hired yourself a mechanic and a wrangler."

———————————

You don't often see a white man and a colored man hunched over with their heads bent together close, thick as thieves and whispering like the wind. So when Black and Priya and me come out of the barn and that was exactly what we saw, it like to have caught my attention.

They was standing on the back porch of the Kindness house, and I recognized the black one so I knowed he was Otis Kindness. He was little and weary and didn't look like the years and labor had been as his name to him. I hadn't an inkling who the other one might be. Excepting the suit he was wearing probably could have paid for the entire Kindness ranch, and his shoes might have covered the livestock on it.

Those two men had a big piece of paper with crease folds in it, like a blueprint or a map, and they had it spread out against the topmost porch rail so it were facing away from me. Curiosity pinched me. I looked over at Priya, though, and she seemed pretty thoughtful. That line between her eyes meant she was unhappy about something.

Black and Priya and me approached the two men, and I might even have believed it when the white man raised his voice to be overheard and said, "Yes, it looks like the eastern exposure along the Sound will give us the best early light. I'll talk to Max about shooting there on Tuesday morning," if I hadn't seen how guilty they both started when Black and Priya and me hove into view.

Not that I cared. It weren't none of my business. And if I hadn't been able to tell from the white man's suit that he was somebody important, I would have been able to tell from the way Black approached him, a little sidelong, like a dog that wants to be noticed but has a little pride, or maybe just doesn't want to risk being yelled at for being in the way, so it won't go right up to nudge its master's hand. I tagged along a little to the left and a step behind, and Priya was my silent shadow. We was both trying to project a cloud of invisibility around ourselves like squid ink. *Step along smart. Nothing to see here.*

"That's Mike Evans," Black said out of the corner of his mouth. "He's the producer."

I didn't know what a producer was when they was at home or why it was important, but Black sure seemed impressed by it. So I was brooding on a suspicion that whatever they called Mr. Evans, what he *was*… was where the money come from.

Black stopped a good way off from the railing and waited. He didn't clear his throat or nothing, just settled back on his heels and waited for that Evans to notice him. After a minute or two, Evans gave the map back to Mr. Kindness, who folded it up right careful like so all the creases matched. The white man came down the porch steps and listened with half an ear, checking his pocket watch as Black introduced him to Priya and to me. He didn't look me in the eye, but he stuck his hand out and bowed over mine just like I was a lady, and over Priya's, too.

A door shut behind us. When I glanced back at the house, the porch was empty. Otis Kindness must have gone inside.

Evans seemed to be going in the same direction we was.

Black explained that the "set," which was where they was filming that morning, was a quarter hour's walk away and he'd be sending me over there once he'd shown me around the stock and helped me get kitted up. Evans was off to the "shooting location," and since it was past the barns and corrals, he walked with us that far, all side by side together.

Chapter Five

Once Evans headed away, Black sent Priya off to find Cowboy again and get him to introduce her to what he called riggers and gaffers and grips. I had no idea what riggers and gaffers and grips might be, in this context, but I'm pretty sure it had less to do with a sailing ship than you might expect.

As for me, Black took charge of me himself, and took me out to meet the stock.

"The buffalo are my problem," he said as I leaned over the rail gawking at them. "You stay out of that corral unless you've absolutely got no better options."

"They're big." I hopped down off the railing.

"Yeah. And they're a hell of a lot stronger than you are, and unlike horses, they got no illusions about who might win in a fight. So don't take any risks around 'em."

"Right." I dusted my hands on my dungarees. "Just as happy to stick to the horses, honestly. I know my way around horses."

He grinned at me sideways, but he didn't say a word. I guess he believed me.

The stock was stock, pretty much—little groups of mares and geldings standing around munching hay, where there was hay to munch, and swatting flies off one another with companionable tails. But there was one horse off by himself who wasn't a mare *or* a gelding, and who was more worth looking at than most.

"Who's that?" I asked Black with a casual tip of my head. I had my hair in one long braid, no ribbons and no fuss, and it slid over my flannel shirt and thumped me on the shoulder. If I was a horse, I would have startled.

He followed the line of my gaze and considered for a moment, though I didn't think he needed to.

"That's Angel Maker," he told me eventually.

"He's gorgeous," I said. "Does he come by that monicker honestly?"

"Or dishonestly, if you prefer." Black tipped his head at the stud, lips pursed in what I took for regret.

"Is he mean?"

"He's something."

I walked over beside Black and we both leaned up against the fence rails. They was four foot high and whitewashed like everything else around here. The horse on the other side was calmly eating his hay, as if we didn't exist, but I could tell from the swishing tail and the side-eye that he was aware of us. And wary, too.

Every cowboy story has got to have the horse nobody can ride. Nobody except the hero, that is, who befriends him through shared adversity and then they're inseparable. He's big horse, always a stud, more wild than tame and the fastest and toughest animal around. He's always snow white or coal black, or maybe once in a while a bright palomino.

Well, I guess this here is a cowboy story. Because that was the day that I met Angel Maker.

Now you know when you meet a horse with a name like that, it's one of two things. I have known my share of ponies called things like Piledriver and Widowmaker and Peaceful and Sarcophagus and Hellbitch—although the meanest colt I ever met was a hammerheaded son of a snake who gloried in the monicker of "Bob"—and it goes one of two ways. Either that horse is an unmanageable, murderous half-ton monster... or they've got a little jackass back there and a terrible sense of humor and they're *smart.*

Well, this horse was a stud, all right, and he was over seventeen hands and built broad, too. But he weren't no parade-horse color. He was a big old sooty buckskin with those black socks like he'd been cleaning out the hearth and that dark stripe down his spine. His body was dark oat-straw gold, but his head was all caramel shades that hid how finely modeled the bones in the big, broad skull were. He finished his hay and pivoted that head up to watch me and Black as we idled there against the fence beside the lane through the corrals, and I couldn't help but notice the muscle in his neck and shoulder, the deep crease on his haunch. He stood stock-still, except the jet-black tail jerking up and down in a warning of what a curly wolf he thought he was.

I hadn't had much intention coming out there except walking around and eyeing the stock, getting an idea of what was what. I'd been mostly thinking about the money—and it were good money, don't get me wrong—versus what I'd heard studios did to the horses to get those spectacular stunt falls. I was trying to figure out how to raise the subject with Black when that buckskin stud locked eyes on me and I stopped just as still as him.

Now, I couldn't tell you what the horse was feeling, but for me it was love at first sight. I tried to play it cool, just turned to Black and said, "Is that a Spanish horse?"

"Up from Mexico," he said. "Pretty to look at, but unrideable. One of their bullfighting breeds."

"I thought those were supposed to be real easy handlers."

"Sure. All sorts of things are supposed to be other things." Black shrugged. "Things are what they are. Expecting 'em to be different don't change anything."

Truer words, and so forth. I guess Black was what you call a philosopher.

"I don't meant to argue my first day on the job..."

"Spit it out." He suited action to words, leaving a spill of tobacco juice in the dirt by the rail. "I got no use for mealymouthed wranglers."

All right then. "I've met very few unrideable horses in my life."

He eyed me. "All fifteen years of it."

"Seventeen, actually." I grinned to show I could take a joke.

"You wanna fork him?"

"Right this instant?" I answered. "It seems like I should probably make his acquaintance first."

It was so easy to fall back into the banter. To sparkle at him. I didn't mean nothing by it, you realize. It was just a professional skill. And him bantering right back made me feel right at home, especially when he didn't seem to mean nothing by it, either.

Professional respect. You don't get that often from a man. It's a real rare pleasure when it happens.

"So what's he here for, if he's unrideable?"

Black spat tobacco again, and tilted his hat down to shade his eyes a little more. "Well, depending on how the scenario works out, I suppose you might wind up riding him after all."

"What does that mean?" I walked to one side a little. Sound construction on that animal. If he looked as good moving as he did standing still, and if his temperament weren't actually fire-breathing dragon when he was handled right... there was a stud I wouldn't mind breeding to. "Is he saddle broke at all?"

Angel Maker snorted and struck the damp earth of his corral with a foreleg, just to let us know he could have taken us both out—*if* he could be bothered to walk over.

Black said, "He's the bronc for the Wild West show."

The walk to the set took ten minutes, each of us leading two horses. One of mine was my bay dun friend—it turned out her name was Copper—and the other was a sorrel Justin Morgan gelding called Danegelt. My mom being Danish, I even knew what that meant, and I thought it was pretty funny.

There were even more caravans here, and tents galore. We picked our way among them until we found a makeshift corral and put the horses in it. Apparently these were the ones who would be needed for shooting today. A caravan with one side dropped down to make an open shed with a ramp held tack, and that make-believe Wells Fargo coach was lined up beside a selection of other equipage.

We got there just in time to almost get knocked over by a burly brown-haired man with a set jaw and a long-ago broken nose, who shouldered me in particular aside as he was passing. "Hey, careful there!" I muttered after him.

"That's Brent Bolan," Black said. "The man who was wrangling Copper and Danegelt here yesterday. I imagine Mister Evans just told him to get off the set."

"Oh," said I. "Then I imagine he ain't too happy with me."

"He ought to be unhappy with himself," said Black. "It weren't you that walked away from that cart with the brake not set."

I'm afraid I kept pestering poor Black with questions as he walked me over to the caravans. "What's a scenario?" (Answer: it's akin to a playscript, but since it's for a motion picture it ain't got no dialogue in it, just the action sequences and tableaux that make up the story. It's written out by a scenarist, working with the director. The actors make up the dialogue that goes on the title cards later.) "What's the difference between a scenarist and a director?" (Answer: the scenarist works for the director, not the other way around.) "How come you're up here in the rain instead of down in sunny California?" (Answer: I didn't get one, because there was a ruckus.)

It didn't look to *start* as a ruckus. But ruckuses come when you least expect 'em, I suppose.

There was a lot of bustle, sure, plenty of toing and froing and inning and outing. Those tents they had set up—pavilions, I guess you'd call 'em—a good most of those had a whole side or two roped up to facilitate folk moving between the interior and the exterior en masse, since it weren't just then raining. I recognized a machine shop—no sign of Priya, though I craned to look—and a mess tent, and what would have been instantaneously recognizable to any girl who'd worked a parlor house as a beauty salon, hair and makeup in progress on a half-dozen heads both male and female. That looked interesting, and I was glad to see that Black seemed to be leading me in that direction.

I had to draw myself up sharp to keep from getting walked into by a bountifully voluptuous woman with a sea of red hair who clutched a fluttering fistful of papers and moved like she were on a mission. Admittedly, everybody here was moving like they was on a mission, so it didn't signify. But she nodded sideways and gave a little smile when Black lifted his hat and said, "Morning, Miss Celia."

A moment after she sailed through, a honey-blond showstopper no bigger than pocket-sized came out of the very tent we was aimed at. It was Miss Helene Roman, who I recognized from the silver screen in the Rapid City Odeon, and who had obviously just had her hair and makeup done. She stepped down from the platform casually, standing out from the rest in part because she was, as I intimated, a showstopper. In part, because she made a show.

Of not being in a hurry, for one thing, which made her by my reckoning the only individual in the observable portions of the Washington Territory who was not.

"That's Helene Roman," Black said, unnecessarily, pronouncing her name in the French manner.

My heart had already skipped a little beat. I guessed I had been saying her name wrong. If Priya had been anywhere in sight I would have grabbed her hand and squealed so loud they would have heard me all the way to the Odeon.

Miss Roman also made a show of rummaging up her compact from her reticule. Right there in front of the girls who had just done her hair and paint to an immaculate standard! Though the paint was overdramatic for day, I reckoned the exaggeration was to benefit the Kinematoscope.

We was headed right for her, so I didn't have to crane my neck or be in any way obvious as I inspected her. And anyway she was so all caught up in her own reflection I don't think she would have noticed if I was bare-breasted and waving a French flag. She weren't much older than me, and she was a wee slip of a thing. But she had that air of taking up space some small women cultivate, and it weren't *all* down to her bustle being three times as big around as I was.

She pursed her perfect painted Cupid's bow as we came up on her. Then she pulled out a lipstick and made the result bigger, redder, and faintly ridiculous.

I thought about offering a word of advice, but she has that haughtiness hung on her, and women in kid boots, pearl earrings, and shot silk by the hectare don't generally flock to hear fashion tips from women with scuffed toes and manure on their blue jeans cuffs. So I let it slide, and we just walked on by. Black tipped his hat to this lady, too, but he didn't speak to her.

She batted her eyelashes at him, smiled prettily, then looked through me like I was a shop window.

Her compact closed like a shot just as we stepped up onto the crude platform that served as the floor of the makeup tent. That raised wood should be right useful once the sky started falling again, as it inevitably would.

Black stretched his long self up, peering over things. It must have been like being atop a fire tower up there. He spotted whatever he was looking for, and was just about to move toward it—you could see him thinking with his whole body, just as a horse does—when his momentum was interrupted by a female-type raised voice from back the way we'd come.

And *that* was the ruckus.

I looked, because everybody was looking—Black included—and peering out through the raised tent wall I weren't too surprised to realize that the source of the voice was Miss Roman. She was remonstrating—a woman with her pretense to quality would certainly never shout—none too gently with Mike Evans—the tall man in the gray suit and a city hat, a gold watch chain stretched a little taut over his plum-colored waistcoat, that I'd seen earlier talking to Otis Kindness.

"I don't care about that," the woman said, with a kind of sweet venom. My awe of her crumpled into a little sadness. Maybe she was just having a bad day, but I've never liked it when folk take that superior tone with anybody. If she was a filly, and mine, I would have sold her, at a discount, on the spot.

Evans rubbed his temple under the hat. "You realize that caravan has the lowest step," he said reasonably. "Mister Steele does not enjoy the resilience of youth anymore, Helene. His knees and hips—"

"So build him a ramp or something," she scoffed. "It will be easier on him anyway. I was promised the best caravan, Michael." She pouted prettily with her lacquered lips. "It is in my contract."

I could tell he was going to give it to her. No horse race is all that interesting when you're forewarned of the result, so I turned to Black and said, in a low voice, "So what's that?"

"I'm sure you recognize the star of the show," he said with infinite tiredness.

"I'm not also doubling for her, am I?"

I must have sounded dubious, but in honesty it was because I was mentally comparing my own sturdy self to her sylphlike one.

But Black laughed sympathetically. "Oh, no," he said. "I'm not sure Miss Roman knows which end of a pistol to point at the person she don't like. And she doesn't like anybody for long, so that's to the best for all of us. You're only doubling Annie. Annie, I think you'll like."

Phoebe Ann Mosey was in makeup still, which was the reason we had come here. And she weren't no better match for me size-wise than that Helene Roman. But Black was right: personality-wise, we were gonna get on fine.

So how does a body describe Miss Annie Mosey?

She's famous, of course. If she weren't already famous then—and she were, plenty famous, though mostly back East where the Wild West shows played, them not having what you call cachet for those of us who just has to walk out the kitchen door to find wilderness, and the West—well, if she weren't already famous then she would be by now, what with all that transpired after that moment. But as we came up on her, what struck me was how still and quiet she was. She was holding her head perfectly motionless. That made a big difference to the man dressing her hair and the girl doing her paint, let me tell you, having been on both ends of that operation.

She looked like she felt some distaste at it, but she didn't budge. It weren't no passive stillness, though. It was the patient kind. Her expression was that of somebody doing a necessary but mildly tedious job: the washing up. They was putting a lot less lacquer on her than they had on Miss Roman. She was young—about my own age, I'd guess it—and they was painting her younger.

She was a spare little thing, and she weren't in no Calamity Jane leathers or even dungarees the way I wore. She had a shirtwaist and a gray skirt short enough to show her boots but no shorter, under the smock they'd put on her while they fixed her up. Her little hands were folded in her lap.

Black cleared his throat.

She didn't turn, or even speak until the folk helping her stepped back. She balanced her head on her long neck like she was on horseback with an egg in a kitchen spoon, as we used to do when we were sprats to prove how smooth we could sit the gaits.

"Mister Black?" she said, when it was safe to move her lips again.

"Miss Mosey." He walked around front, and gestured me to join him. "This is Miss Karen Memery. She'll be stunt doubling for you in the horseback scenes."

"I can ride," she said, but it was mildly. There was bone under the softness, though.

"And I can shoot," I said, with equal mildness. "But I wouldn't challenge you."

That got a little smile.

"Miss Memery here," Black said. "She knows horses the way you know guns."

"Is that so," Miss Mosey said. She turned, finally, and looked over at the beautician and the hairdresser. "Am I ready for the Kinematoscope?"

"Yes, miss," the beautician said.

Miss Mosey held out her arms and let the man pull the smock off her before she stood. She dusted herself off. There was so much starch in her shirtwaist I swore I could hear it crinkle when she moved.

"Well then." She smiled at me with some real warmth and extended a delicate hand. Her hair was as dark as mine, but piled up a lot higher. "I guess I better let Miss Memery here have my chair."

Chapter Six

And that was where Black the wrangler up and abandoned me. I sat in the chair, which were still warm from Miss Mosey, and I got poked and prodded and prettified in ways I had not at all expected when I signed on as a wrangler on a motion picture shoot. I still didn't look a thing like Miss Mosey when they was done with me, but I guessed they had some kind of motion picture magic to make it all work out, and they'd duplicated her hairstyle exactly.

I admired their work in no fewer than three mirrors at once, and they finally told me their names. Hazel was the makeup artist, a tall brunette slip. Caleb—a lean young man with cultivated hands—was hair.

All in all, it was actually a bit fun. Besides, while they weren't paying me quite what I still could have made working on my back, even at the ripe old age of seventeen, it was a damned sight better wages than horsebreaking.

After that, Hazel and Caleb sent me on to the costume department, which come to find out was actually the other side of this tent. That was where I figured out that Miss Mosey didn't starch her own shirtwaists, at least not here on the motion picture set. What she did at home, of course, was her own lookout.

For an even bigger wonder, the clothes they had for her double was more than big enough, though I wouldn't go so far as to say they fitted me. At least not before Amber, the wardrobe mistress, was done with them.

Grinning and mumbling around a mouthful of pins, Amber explained it all while she sewed me into the inside-out clothes. According to her, they usually just used men in women's clothing to double for the female stars. So getting me to double Miss Mosey—and probably, I guessed despite what Walker Black said, Miss Roman eventually, once the dust around her settled—was a real coup.

I weren't looking forward to pins sticking me in the scalp under no honey-blonde wig. But I would take the money and I wouldn't complain.

What was amazing was how fast Amber got me fitted into that shirtwaist so it hung on me like I was a dressmaker's dummy. Now, I can sew, don't get me wrong. I make all Priya's clothes and most of my own. But my sewing bore the same resemblance to Amber's as Priya's did to mine.

The best part was that Amber had a big industrial Singer sewing armature back there. It was newer than the one we had at home, and not all Priya'd up like ours, but otherwise not too different. It was making a bit of a rubbing sound I knowed it weren't supposed to. So I struck up a conversation over that, and allowed as how my partner was an engineer, and she'd just signed on the crew as well, and maybe she could come over and see if she could fix up that noise. It never hurt to make friends, and that conversation passed the scant fifteen minutes it took Amber to get me kitted up like a 200 percent scale model of Miss Mosey, striped shirtwaist and gray skirt and all.

She let me keep my own boots on—they were more practical, and nobody was going to notice whether the stunt double was wearing buttoned girl boots in a chase scene in black and white—and told me to come back for my real clothes when the shoot was done.

Then she told me where to go—in the friendly rather than the blasphemous fashion—and sent me on my way.

So that, willy-nilly, was how I came to walk onto a motion picture set for the first time in my life—dressed as a lady shootist and totally unprepared for what I was getting into.

Really, I probably hadn't needed Amber's directions. All I had to do was follow the noise.

Reader, making a silent film apparently involves an awful lot of clatter, and a fuss such as God can hear above. Even and He's got His earmuffs on.

So what I saw when I came up was, first, a lot of people. There was *two* Kinematoscopes set up now, one just on a tripod and one on top of a tripod on top of a thing that looked like a miniature railroad tender. The railroad tender was on a tiny set of rails, but rather than two burly gentlemen pumping up and down and up again while keeping in time with off-key rendition of "Someone's in the Kitchen with Dinah," it had hand poles on the side so a man or two could pull it along the railing.

And here was Miss Mosey, on a flashy piebald with one blue eye, and there was Cowboy, the mechanical, currently standing at parade rest with his arms behind his back while the whole world swirled around him. Honest, I would have thought he was dozing, he was so still, 'ceptin' I was pretty sure mechanicals didn't doze.

Miss Mosey definitely weren't dozing. She was wide awake and saying nothing. She had that stillness on her as before, like she was just waiting for everybody to be done with their silliness so we could all get back to work and she could get on with getting her job done.

I told you I liked her.

What appeared to my uneducated eye to be the source of the delay—because there was obviously a ruction imminent—was a tall, good-looking man with dark hair and a Roman profile who was having what I will charitably refer to as a conniption in the general direction of a fellow who weren't nearly so handsome as the first, but who had a real air of being in charge of everything.

If there had been a soul around I knew to ask what to do next, I would have asked them. But Miss Mosey was up on that gelding, and Cowboy was down on the ground but I was a little too nervous to just go right up and ask him, and anyway he was in the middle of a ring of folk who looked like they had business on their minds and who was swinging a whole lot of intimidating technology around. So I just stood there in my pin-striped shirtwaist and my fancy hair and my good plain gray skirt—none of which things was actually mine rather than being on loan for the while—probably looking as lost as I felt. And eavesdropping.

"I don't believe you gave that trollop my caravan!" the saturnine fellow was bellowing over the soft speech of the more average-looking fellow in his black worsted. "You know my knee hasn't been right since the war!"

"It was Mister Evans who gave her the caravan," the average-looking fellow said soothingly. "Look, her old caravan is bigger, anyway. And we will build you a ramp."

"You'll make me a laughingstock, Forth!" The bigger man brandished a cane and I had a peculiar sense that I recognized him from somewhere, though I knew I'd never heard his voice before. "As if this weren't bad enough. Word will go around that Matthan Steele needs a *ramp* to climb into his caravan on a set, and the next thing you know it'll be the end of my marquees." He was lowering his voice, though. The soothing man was pretty good at soothing things. Even large, angry actors.

Matthan Steele. I *had* heard of him. He looked better in the motion pictures.

"A war wound is an honorable thing," the smaller man said. "In any case, Mister Steele—*Matthan,* my old friend—you know if Evans hadn't given her the caravan, she'd just make your life miserable in a thousand petty ways until you gave it to her yourself."

Steele harrumphed, but seemed to get a wrap on his temper and pulled it down a bit. "I haven't the foggiest why you hired that woman, Mister Forth."

"The producers still like her as a headliner," the man in the worsted suit—who I guessed was Mr. Forth, who I had also heard of. At least, I had heard of him if he was Mr. Max Forth, who was a motion picture director whose name I'd seen in the papers and up on the silver screen once or twice. "Look, can we discuss this later? We're burning daylight, and I'd like to shoot while my cast is assembled."

I could see that Mr. Steele pull up his dignity like a man who's gone hungry recently hitching up his pants. He strapped a belt of self-control around his professionalism and got it tied on tight enough to take his hands off it and say, "Oh, very well."

About then was when a young man in shirtsleeves and tweed trousers came up to me. He had those straps on his sleeves like accountants use to keep 'em out of the ink. "Excuse me. Are you Miss Mosey's double?"

"I'm Miss Memery," I said, and stuck out my paw.

He took it gently. "I'm Vernon," he said. "Chief Kinemato-scoper. As you can see, Mister Forth is just settling some ruffled feathers. He'll be along in a moment to direct you. Can I take you to a seat?"

I leaned on his arm somewhat, and let his elbow brush my blouse.

"Would you tell me what the scene we're shooting is?" I asked, wondering if I had got the parlance right. Everybody's got some kind of specialized dialect outsiders can't hardly penetrate. Whores and horse people are just the same.

He glanced over at me, and he seemed to approve of what he saw, because he smiled. "How brave a girl are you, Miss Memery?"

"Bravest girl in Rapid City, so they say." I dropped that in a light tone, so he would think it was teasing.

"You've come to the right place, then."

He proceeded to detail a thoroughly unpleasant line of opera-tions, in which the piebald would be replaced by a stunt horse—I assumed a less valuable one—and Miss Mosey would be replaced by a less valuable… er, me. The scenario was that Cowboy was playing a mechanical who had come to "life," whatever that means, and was terrorizing the local populace.

Cowboy and Miss Mosey were both supposed to be affiliated with the same Wild West show. Cowboy supposedly had gone haywire in just the way a mechanical couldn't, and was fully devoted to the business of pursuing Miss Mosey in order to capture her and carry her off to his lair with the evil Mad Scientist who had built him.

Why a mechanical would have a lair was left as an exercise to the student. Maybe it was supposed to be the Scientist's lair.

"Why do the monsters always seem to want a pretty girl?" I asked him. "Surely we're no good to them."

I blinked at him innocently, and he laughed.

I waved to Miss Mosey. "Is she going to do the carried-off-by-the-monster part?"

"No, ma'am," Vernon said.

I looked at Cowboy and tried not to think too hard about those cold metal arms pressing into my body. I was too proud to want to show a shiver, even though I flinched like a fly-bit horse. It weren't no reflection on Cowboy—or at least I sure didn't mean it that way—but I couldn't rightly help it that he gave me a feeling like a spider done crawled up my spine.

I did jump when Vernon spoke again, because it disturbed my reverie. "Looks like Max is done with Mister Steele. Guess I'll take you on over."

"That *is* Mister Max Forth?" I was swept up in his wake and hustling to keep up.

"The director. I say, you really did just fall off a flatcar, didn't you?"

Maybe I should have been sore at that, but there didn't look to be any malice in him, and the truth was I *felt* like I *had* just fallen off a flatcar. Possibly one hauling a load of turnips. So he weren't far wrong.

"*Max Forth,*" I said, disbelieving. I'd never heard the name out loud before, and I guess I'd missed it, just reading it here and there.

"It's a stage name." The grin didn't falter.

"Has anybody seen Evans?" Max Forth said after Mr. Steele had huffed away. He turned around. I got a sense from looking at his expression that maybe he wished to remonstrate gently with Mr. Evans for putting him in such a difficult spot.

Vernon strode toward the man. I followed on, but not too close.

I admit if I weren't more than half nervous to be presenting myself to the gentleman when he was fresh off soothing a wounded self-image of those proportions, well, I would have had to consider myself a born fool. Men is funny creatures with funnier ways of being, and an inordinacy of them expect a body to drop everything to sweep up after their messes, while denying they make any messes at all. I suspect as many of them as not don't even notice the messes, until the women around them get tired of cleaning that stuff up, and then they stomp around blaming everybody but themselves.

"God dammit," Forth blasphemed. "He's used up a good twenty minutes of my daylight sorting that. I'd like to—"

So I was apprehensive coming up on that Mr. Forth, and more than just possibly expecting him to take his humiliation out on Vernon or me. But Vernon shook his head and said, "Max, in that case, maybe save the rawhiding until the sun goes down."

I could not have been more pleasantly surprised when this powerful man turned around, looked from Vernon to me, and visibly settled himself in an attempt to be gracious.

"This is Miss Karen Memery." Vernon was all business and no prologue, once he had Max Forth's attention. "She's your new stunt rider what Black sent over."

Mr. Forth looked me up and down critically. I puffed myself up a little, then caught myself doing it and made myself settle.

He stuck a hand out. "Karen."

"Mister Forth." I put my hand in his.

"Max," he said, giving mine a vaudeville pump before releasing it. "We're too much in each other's pockets to stand on much ceremony here. Have you ever worked a motion picture set before?"

"No, sir," I said, and blushed to my eyebrows when I heard myself. "No, Max."

His eyebrows grinned at me, even though the rest of his face didn't do nothing. "Just follow directions and hit your marks, and don't get yourself hurt. We'll get along just fine."

You get a sense about people in my old line of work, especially you get a sense of whether they got any interest in what you're peddling, and Mr. Code Name Forth couldn't have cared less about what I had under my wardrobe, or in anything else about me other than whether I could ride, and look more like Miss Mosey shot from the back than a six-foot wrangler in a corset and a dress.

I decided not to tell him I didn't know what my marks was, or how to hit 'em.

A wrangler brought the new horse over. I was surprised to see how well they'd matched the paint patterns, because paint horses in general is pretty characteristic and individualistic. Then I got a mite closer and snorted to realize that the horse they'd brought me was actually a pale gray, done up with black dye to look like a paint. He was also much bigger than the gelding Miss Mosey was still up on, and I laughed out loud at the cleverness of all this. I'd look the same size on Bill—because that was the gray gelding's name—as Miss Mosey did on her piebald.

Bill was a friendly old thing, too, and even though I didn't have any carrots he whuffed my hand and lowered his head so I could scratch behind his ears under the mane where it's always itchy.

I was still making friends with him when I felt somebody come up behind me. I turned my head slow, trying not to look spooked, and saw Black standing on my left.

"You ever worked with a fall horse?"

People around this place sure didn't go in much for preambles.

I mutely shook my head. I didn't even know what a fall horse was, and I was hoping I might figure it out before I had to admit to even more and deeper ignorance.

My silence worked out to my advantage, more or less. Because Black explained that any stunt horse who'd been taught to fall over on command was a special commodity—so I guessed I had been wrong about the paint being replaced by a less valuable animal for the stunt—and that horse generally would only fall in one particular way and no other.

That helped keep the horse from hurting itself. But also from hurting the rider, because the rider always knew what to expect.

Bill's fall was a fun one. Black would point his finger and say "Bang!" and old Bill, he'd toss his head up, as if he had been shot, whinny sharply, and fall over on his right side. You just had to make sure you had your foot good and clear before he did it, and

Black told me if I were comfortable with it they'd take the stirrup off that side so Bill wouldn't fall on it and maybe bruise his ribs.

"Oh wait," Black said. "Right, you'll be sidesaddle. So you won't have to worry about your feet, at least."

It had been years since I had ridden that way. I reckoned I could survive it, though, if so many fancy folk learned to do it and from a youthful age and rode over fences. *We need the money,* I told the knot of apprehension in my belly.

Sidesaddle made things easier on Bill, at least.

The stunt we were going for would look like Bill was being tripped and falling from a canter, and me being thrown and knocked out. Most of that would be motion picture magic, of course, and I was thankful I didn't have to take a fall with a sixteen-hand pony at a lope.

Still, it occurred to me that I must have made a pretty decent impression on Black if I was being trusted with a prize like Bill on my first day on the set, and I had to remind myself twice not to be too damn impressed with myself. I had a job to do, and I was that determined to make my mark as a professional.

It *also* occurred to me that this might just be a little something-something of a test.

Black showed me how to get Bill to lay himself down, and we practiced it from the ground while Miss Mosey and her paint, whose name was Merrimack, got their close-ups shot. Those would be cut in with Bill and my work, as I understood it, to make it seem like Cowboy was in hot pursuit and overtaking the hapless Miss Mosey. Then I got up on Bill's back and we did it a few times standing still, mostly for practice, while Vernon cranked the Kinematoscope and everybody else stood around.

That was the day I learned just how much of the work that gets done on motion picture sets is the work of standing around waiting for it to be your turn to do some work, while other people are waiting for whatever it is that they need to be able to finish *their* work. I learned that Miss Mosey, as I would have expected, was a fine competent rider with quiet hands and an upright spine. The horse respected her authority, so I knew she was paying close attention whenever he tested her. I would have put her on one of my own ponies. And that's not something I'll offer just anybody.

Honestly, what Miss Mosey was doing looked hard, and boring as hell. There was a lot of careful posing, and carefuller filming of even more careful angles. Then Max would come in and re-pose her, and they'd do it all over again. There was more fussing about the light and how long it would last and whether it might get lost (don't ask me where you might lose the daylight to other than to China as the world went 'round) and Merrimack—her paint horse—got his natural blacks re-blacked with shoe polish twice over.

Miss Mosey thought it was all nonsense. I mean, I don't know that for a fact, but I felt reasonably confident in guessing. For one thing, I could see the way Merrimack's tail switched and figured he had to be feeling her irritation. And for another, she just seemed a little... taut. Frayed, like, or on the edge of it.

Whatever she was feeling, though, Miss Mosey never let on with her face. She just registered what she was meant to, fear or horror or what have you.

Then Miss Mosey climbed down and somebody led Merrimack away, and she let Cowboy scoop her up and toss her around—across both arms, over his shoulder, and so on—while Vernon shot some more close-ups. That gave me chills, especially when I figured I was probably going to be doing those same poses in a minute or two.

I'm sure Cowboy had no harm in him. I just couldn't like the idea of getting picked up by him no matter what story I told myself.

I wished Priya was here.

Vernon moved the Kinematoscope around, and Bill and me did a few falls for keeps, with him cantering so slowly it seemed like a walk from on top him. Vernon said they were overcranking the Kinematoscope to make the action look faster. Everybody seemed happy after and I felt like the falls probably looked pretty good.

And the sidesaddle weren't as much of a problem as I'd been afraid. The heads bruised up my thighs something awful, but that's how the biscuit breaks. And I was happy to be earning the money.

The hard part was staying loose as Bill went down, not tensing up when I knew what was coming. Vernon told me I'd be able to see the "footage" if I showed up to watch what he called the "dailies," and I thought I just might, at least once or twice. Priya'd be fascinated by it, anyway, and probably try to learn how to develop film.

So then it was down to me and the mechanical.

I didn't want Max and Vernon to think I was chicken-livered, and I sure didn't want Cowboy to twig that he gave me fits just by existing, and I *really* didn't want to give Black a reason to regret giving me a chance before the end of my first day. Because I guess I don't know any other way to do things, smart or not, it didn't occur to me until a whole lot later that they was expecting an awful lot of me on my first day, and maybe even expecting me to balk at something.

All my life, I've done what I've done because the world ain't given me no options to refuse. It never occurs to me that I could just say no until it's way too late in the process to get out of it orderly.

Some mares just don't know any better than to run themselves into a thicket, and the ones who don't expect help got no way out except to push on through.

So I kicked my courage up into a canter and took it at the fence.

By which I mean, when they called me over, I walked right up to Cowboy and stuck out my hand. "We met earlier," I said. "My name's Karen. I'm not sure I introduced myself proper enough for somebody who's gonna manhandle me."

Or machinehandle, I thought, and wondered if I was being unkind to Cowboy's sensibilities. Did Cowboy *have* sensibilities?

He once again took my hand as gravely as a child shaking a strange grown-up's, as if aware of and impressed by the signification of the ritual. "I apologize for the impropriety, Miss Karen."

Being called Miss Karen was a strange sensation. It was what we called the older girls at the parlor house I used to work at—the ones who was established, and as had a stake in the place. Full members, I guess you'd say. But it made me feel surprisingly grown-up and responsible, which as you know is pretty silly for a woman who owned a little house of her own and weren't beholden to nobody except for Priya, and that went both ways.

"Oh, don't worrit on it none," I told it, recollecting the thread of the conversation. "It's a job of work is all, and when it's done we'll draw our pay."

He cocked his metal head at me, and I didn't know why he seemed to find that comment amusing. If he were gonna answer, though, he got interrupted by Max coming over and subjecting us both to a bewildering array of instructions, which I didn't follow at all though I smiled and nodded and frowned and said "No sir-I-mean-Max" as it seemed appropriate.

Cowboy said, "As you wish," at intervals and not much more.

When Max was done, he looked from one of us to the other and said, "Did all that get through?"

I was about to admit it hadn't, which would have no doubt gotten me another incomprehensible set of directions, but Cowboy said, "Yes sir," and rattled it all back just about—near as I could tell—word for word, but edited for clarity and brevity, as they say. When the mechanical said it, I understood what we was meant to do.

And then we did it.

Cowboy scooped me up, first across his arms and later over one shoulder, and didn't seem to have any problems at all carrying that weight. Leaning on the mechanical's arm was like leaning on a tree limb; maybe it dipped a little under me, but maybe it didn't, and he certainly didn't struggle to hold me up.

"Kick a little!" Max yelled over the whirr of Vernon winding the Kinematoscope. "The motion picture–going public likes to see a good flurry of petticoats!"

The motion picture–going public apparently liked all sort of things I wouldn't have anticipated, including watching me accidentally bruising the hell out of my toes when they connected with Cowboy's chassis and biting my lip to keep from whimpering when I jarred my sore leg. I began to suspect that just possibly Miss Mosey weren't doing this part not because it was dangerous, but because it was an affront to her dignity. What reasonable woman would fight that way, with tiny little kicks of her toes? If I was to find myself actually abducted by a metal man, I would take a pipe-fitter wrench or some such to it and go down fighting.

"Sorry," I said, when the take was over.

"Think nothing of it," the mechanical responded. "You are unlikely to fracture my carapace. It is very strongly constructed."

He had me draped right over his shoulder then. I looked down and thumped it lightly with my fist, about as hard as you'd punch a pony in the rump to get it to move.

"Ha," Cowboy said, just like that. The perforated belts inside him rolled back and forth under the formed crystal. "Ha. That tickles."

Was he *joking*?

Did mechanicals *joke*?

Then Max called us over to where Vernon was standing on top of that thing that looked like a railroad tender, and lined us up, and told Cowboy to run.

It turned out that Vernon needed the railroad tender to keep Cowboy in the shot, because that mechanical is about as fast as a quarter horse when he gets moving. His legs were some kind of hydraulic and piston arrangement not too different from my old friend the Singer, and they seemed to snap from front to back without covering the space in between.

It weren't no easy gait to ride.

We did six or seven takes, with him holding me in slightly different ways and me hiding my face so I could be mistaken for Miss Mosey from a distance and moving past. Did you know that them unpadded metal arms and shoulders are pretty bruising? Like sitting down over a trot in a saddle made of steel. By the time we called it quits, I was numb in places I hadn't known you could go numb in. Cowboy had to steady me with those long jointed arms of his when he finally put me down.

I leaned on his shoulder while Max came over.

Max said, "I hope this metal fellow was a gentleman."

"He was a grand dance partner," I answered, trying to get my breath around ribs that felt like they was bruised or maybe cracked. A year of practice in the parlor house was the only thing had me keeping a bold face on now. I found myself realizing with a bit of surprise as I said it that I'd started thinking of Cowboy as a him and not an it.

"The young lady is well within load capacity," Cowboy intoned, to much shuffling of his tapes. They were silk, I realized on closer inspection. The light was failing, and I could see that some static charge built up inside him and gave him a pretty blue glow. Pretty, if you'd never seen Peter Bantle's mind control machine.

"Well," Max said, "fair job for your first day."

I was real glad, one way and another, when they announced I wouldn't be needed for the next scene they was shooting and I could have a break to eat and rest a little.

Chapter Seven

I found the machine shop, but there was no sign of Priya in there, so since I was off duty and all, I went to get some food and introduce myself to Angel Maker. Sure, I wondered where Priya had gotten herself off to, and I was a little minded to go find out what she was and had been doing and how she was liking her new role. But she was working, wherever she was, and either I'd distract her from that, or I'd get nothing from her but grunts because her mind was caught up in a mess of gears and pistons.

Her job was her job, and my job didn't have nothing to do with that. And it did have to do with Angel Maker, especially if I was going to be expected to ride him bucking. Wrangler was my job, I justified. I needed to know the stock. So I found what they called "craft services"—which it turned out was just a real good chuckwagon and mess tent—and got myself around some kind of lunch, about three hours late by my stomach's reckoning. There was fried oysters and mashed potatoes and early spinach and I did it all rough justice. Once that was inside me, I got my costume back to Amber the wardrobe mistress and pulled my own dungarees and boots back on.

It was a flat relief to think I wasn't going to have to be the one to launder and iron that skirt and shirtwaist, given what all it had been through.

I blinked as I came out. The sun was westering. I caught a glint off Cowboy, walking away toward the outbuildings. He seemed like he was going somewhere he needed to be. The dazzle died down in a couple of moments, and I walked down the line of corrals back toward the ranch house and the stable where I'd left Molly.

Well, I palmed another apple slice to my bay dun friend while I went past, since she came over and mumbled at me. Maybe she remembered that I'd given her a hand.

Copper had that black stripe down her back, and the big bar on her withers, and tiger stripes on both front legs above the white splashes, like she was designed to be a type drawing of how to tell a dun. She seemed sound, despite our adventure, and she got another scritch for not caving in my head with her big cart-horse hooves instead of just leaving that smarting gash in my shin.

When I went in to check on Molly, she was fine, and munching a fresh pile of hay for her wages so I thought probably Priya had been in there. I gave her another slice of apple I'd pocketed from my lunch plate. She whuffed and lipped my hand to see if I had extra. I did, but I was hiding them and didn't show her any more. She would have thought I was terribly disloyal if she found out, I know.

I gave her one last scratch under the forelock, and she made a little eager moaning noise under her breath and lipped at me again. It was good to have her back. I hated walking away.

But the big buckskin was out in the paddock, waiting, and I could fuss over Molly at home.

And then I walked on down the line, to Angel Maker.

———

I'd thought before that he didn't look like a mean horse. Wary, sure. But bucking horses got reasons to feel wary about folk. Your average horse, even one that's been worn down to ride by being ridden till he quits bucking, is going to accept after a while that the rider is the boss of him, at least until the next time they have an argument about something. My da raised me to consider that it were better to make the horse think your ideas was his ideas, too, and that means a different take than just bossing a horse. Takes longer, but you get a better result, and an animal you can relax around a little instead of always having to watch out for the next trick.

Don't argue unless you have to, and if you have to argue, make damned sure you win. So he said, and so I believe to this day.

Pretty good advice for how to deal with a human, too. Except sometimes, with humans, winning arguments doesn't get you what you want in the long run.

So what does a mean horse look like?

Some folk say they got a snaky head, or small ears, or big ears, or small eyes. I don't think it's any of those, though, any more than you can tell for real if a man is a criminal by his bushy eyebrows or low forehead or any other damn fool thing. What you can tell is the way they hold themselves, though. And Angel Maker, sure thing, held himself like he thought he ruled the place, and like he was looking for an opportunity to prove it... but he weren't *mean* looking. His ears weren't pinned; they was up and listening at me.

He didn't bother with all the pawing and stomping this time, either, just eyed me cautious like as I leaned on his top rail. He had a wisp of hay in one corner of his mouth and it protruded just a little and bobbed in circles as he chewed like he was thinking about something.

"Hey there, beauty." I hopped up on the bottom bar of the gate, and put one flat hand with a slice of apple on it over the top rail. "Want to make friends?"

He inspected me, and he arched his neck and inspected the apple. Then he minced over with tiny steps like a Spanish barb, stopped half his own length away, and stretched out his ridiculous stallion neck, all muscles and mane, until his lip brushed the apple and his whiskers brushed my skin. There was a whuff, and he danced back two steps so fast it seemed like the damned horse had teleported before he started to chew.

Now, I'm out of practice. But I've known me a lot of horses, and ain't one out of ten as is made out by folk to be vicious that's actually got a mean bone in its body. That don't mean those horses won't kill you, once they get turned unreliable. It just means that killing you ain't the most important thing on their minds, though they ain't gonna consider on it if you might be collateral damage on their way through.

Angel Maker was watching me, sizing me up with a real worried kind of comprehensiveness. He was trying to decide in advance who might come out on top in an argument.

Well, I knew right then that I needed make sure that we never managed to get into that kind of an argument. Because if I ever got into it with him bad enough that Angel Maker started to fight me, I was gonna have to make sure I didn't lose. This horse had an astute eye. If he ever once beat me, he would never forget that I was beatable, and never quit trying to beat me again.

...Reader, I ducked down under the top rail and slithered into that paddock with that unbroke stud like I didn't have a single sensible particle in my brain. Which Priya would be the first one lined up to tell you was the God's honest truth.

Angel Maker didn't rush me while I was bent over, which was good for two reasons. One, because it meant I was right that he hadn't just been biding his moment to murder me. And two, because I would have been pretty bruised up and muddy and ridiculous rolling in the dirt after I lunged out of his way. Which I had been prepared to do, albeit not gracefully.

I was, however, downright ecstatic not to have to resort to that.

Instead, I was standing inside Angel Maker's paddock, sweat and horse spit drying on my palms in the cool air because I didn't dare move enough to wipe them on my trousers.

I was close enough to the fence still to vault it or roll under it if he charged me. I made myself trust that my instincts would take care of me if it came to it, and carry me in the right direction. I couldn't afford to think about it right now, because I couldn't afford to be scared around Angel Maker.

He was scared enough for the both of us. He had backed away until he was almost rumped up against the far fence. I was glad he seemed to know where that fence was, because with those nervous ears and that nervous tail, an unexpected contact on his haunches might have been enough to spook him into a bolt. And I didn't really care to be in a little square paddock with eleven hundred pounds of stud horse experiencing a brain fever.

So I stood real still and didn't stare directly at him, and let him stamp and snort and swish that long black tail, glad that at least he'd untucked it from against his backside, where he'd at first had it clamped. I stood there long enough to get good and bored, but more importantly, I also stood there long enough for Angel Maker to get good and bored.

He eventually got bored enough to decide that maybe today wasn't the day I was likely to eat him—not right that second, anyhow. His ears, which had been pricked sharp like he was thinking about a startle, relaxed a little and his head came down. And he started looking at me a little more serious like, as if he were trying to figure me out.

Well, while he was looking at me, I was looking at him. He'd started off all warhorse but as he settled, he stomped again. It was a warning, but I didn't budge. I was right. This weren't no vicious stud.

This animal was scared of me.

I stood there long enough that I was struggling with wanting to shuffle the pins and needles out of my feet, and long enough that my back was getting sore. Angel Maker watched me real intent for a little and when I didn't do nothing interesting, eventually his ears relaxed a little more and his head dropped down some again.

This weren't gonna be a horse I could just teach to trust folk. This was a horse that already knew too many folk, and knew too much about what rotten wretches and poor horsemen folk generally was. But I might be able to teach him to trust *me*.

It was while we was standing there eyeballing each other without admitting we was eyeballing each other that I noticed the scars all over him.

They wasn't the scars from stallion fighting, though he had some of those. These was rowel scars—all along his flanks and ribs—and there was other marks over his shoulders and crest that looked like maybe whip cuts and maybe something else. Sure, he could have won a fight with a cougar and walked away with those. But I didn't think so.

Plenty of folk spur a bucking horse to get a showier ride out of him. And plenty of folk whip a horse hard enough to make any animal mean. I'd thought better of Black, though, and I felt a burst of frustrated rage that I'd agreed to take the man's money.

I was stewing on that when I realized that the scars weren't fresh, and it was perfectly possible they'd been purchased along with Angel Maker rather than having been installed here. And maybe I should get a checkrein on my temper (I got a temper) and figure out my facts before I made any big decisions based on speculation.

I dug another apple slice out of my pocket, moving slow. As soon as I twitched, all the relaxation went out of the horse and he was up on tiptoe again. I held the apple out flat on my palm.

Angel Maker eyed me with sublime suspiciousness, and didn't budge for a good five or ten minutes. That whole time I stood there with my hand out, that slice of apple (and my arm) got heavier and heavier and heavier, until they weighed the whole earth. My muscles ached and trembled. Sweat beaded on my forehead and ran down my ribs.

Angel Maker whuffed, catching the apple scent. Then he stretched his neck out until he was leaning forward on tippy toes, his upper lip questing after the juicy snack like a velvet-gloved finger.

"Karen," Black said, low and urgent behind me. "Just take two steps off and you'll be at the fence."

I knew what he'd seen: me in the paddock with a horse he thought was unhinged, seeming to be frozen in my boots with fear and being menaced. If he'd been right about that, what he did after he spoke to me wouldn't have been wrong. And he kept his voice level and soft, for talking to horses.

"Black, wait—" I started to say.

Black landed with a thump in the paddock with us. He appeared to have used his height and long legs to just vault over the top rail.

It was all too much for Angel Maker, who blew his top like the blowing of tops had just now been invented and he was trying to get in on the ground floor.

He went straight up in the air, spooked like a bunny. I expected his next step would be lighting out at a hard bolt and maybe crashing into the paddock rail and ripping himself right open.

But that weren't Angel Maker.

Angel Maker charged.

I jumped out of the way before I realized I weren't in his way, exactly: he was coming *by* me, not *at* me. He was aiming right past me, and right at Black.

Black was trying to draw Angel Maker off me, except Angel Maker weren't *on* me. He was just trying to stomp Black.

Black was spry, though, and would have gotten away with it if not for that constant hazard of the stable yard: a big pile of horse apples.

Black yelped as his ankle twisted and his foot slid out from under him. I had a vision of brains splashed on a black hoof and squealed like a mad mare. As Angel Maker surged past me, I reached out with both hands and punched him in the rump.

Honestly, it was more of a shove than a punch, but it was what I had in me just at that instant. And one has to make do.

Horses move away from pressure. This is why it's easy to teach them to neck rein. Well, when I thumped Angel Maker on his powerful haunches, the stallion danced sideways. It knocked him off his line of attack on Black, who took advantage of the distraction to roll under the low rail as Angel Maker staggered into the fence. He didn't fall, but recovered in time to stomp after Black. By then I was over the top rail on the other side.

I scurried around the outside of the paddock and was relieved to find that Black was already sitting up. He slid one hand down his boot and felt around his ankle.

"How is it?" I crouched down beside him.

"Not busted," said he.

"Are you hurt otherwise?"

"I ought to be asking you that. What possessed you to go into that corral with Angel Maker?"

"I can tame him," I said without thinking about it.

"You can *what*?"

"I can tame him," I said, trying to feel confident so I would sound confident. "He ain't mean, Black. He's scared, and he's learned to fight what scares him, is all."

Black looked at me with pursed lips.

"I want this stud. I can fix him."

"Don't get too attached to things you can't have." Black wiped the sweat out of his eyes along with a healthy forelock. "You'll break your heart."

I said, "I bet you. If I can tame him, will you give him to me?"

"Depends. If you can't tame him, what do I get?" Black didn't leer it at me, so I took it at face value.

I know I should think before I talk. I know I shouldn't jump in. I know I should be more aware of the consequences.

"You can pay me half," I said. "If I can't ride Angel Maker tamely by the end of the shoot."

If the shoot ran four weeks, I had just given Black enough money back to buy two or three Angel Makers. Priya was gonna kill me.

Oh, but I wanted that stud.

And as I looked over Black at the big yellow horse snorting and pawing beyond the fence, I didn't feel like I was going to be losing.

Black said, "He ain't mine to trade. He belongs to the production studio."

"Sure, but ain't they gonna sell the stock at the end of the picture?"

"Some of 'em, maybe," Black said. "Depends on if they get the right offers."

"So you make 'em an offer on my behalf. If I can ride him."

"And if you both survive," said Black darkly.

———————————

I helped Black over to the infirmary, and they didn't even think they needed to wrap his ankle up—though they did it anyway—so it couldn't have been too bad. I was surprised to notice that the person in charge was a nurse. Then I was even more surprised that people were referring to her as "Doc."

Don't get me wrong. I know there's women doctors, and I know some of them is even colored folk. I just never expected to *meet* one, as they ain't nohow common. But I figured it was probably like anything else—horsebreaking, for example. That if a woman was doing it, she was probably twice as good as a man in the same position and line of work would have been. She'd have to be, just to stay in business.

Doctor Swan was a sturdy woman about my height, with a purposeful walk and black hair swept back in a braided bun. Not only was she a woman who was a real doctor of medicine, judging by the little black bag at her hand, but she was at least partways a Celestial, with pale olive skin and pretty Asian eyes.

She sure didn't take any of Black's nonsense. When he started teasing about going to see that faith healer in town she offered to get him a cane and hold the door.

He laughed, and I felt easier realizing there was some camaraderie between the two of them.

Her voice startled me, especially given what I had assumed to be her background. It had that Midwestern sound where the vowels don't blur together so much as they do in folk who hie from other places. She sounded like she was from Chicago or Minneapolis or some such place, all of which seemed just as exotic to me then as the Celestial Empire might.

I guess you shouldn't presume you know all about people just from their appearances.

There was a nurse, too, and she was named Marie.

When Doc Swan's mechanical surgeon—a different model than the one Miss Lizzie ran back at the Cherry Hotel—acted up she pulled a wrench out of her coat pocket and tightened a belt with efficiency. I wanted to introduce her to Miss Lizzie, I decided after knowing her for about five minutes, and to Priya also.

Anyway, I left her and her assistant and the kerosene-powered Doctopus binding Black up and tried to go back to work.

But when I walked back onto the set to see if they needed me again, they was just "wrapping" for the day, as they called it. Which made two kinds of wrapping, I guess.

Max said we had run out of light. And now I was starting to figure out what he meant. I mean, I knew about sunset, obviously. I didn't grow up in a cave nurtured by bats and mice. Though I'm sure there's a few people in and out of Rapid City who would make an opposite case, seeing as how I've managed to make myself one or two little enemies.

But we'd had a bright, soft, angled glow all over everything for most of the afternoon, and now it was fading sharply into the kind of half-translucent blue gloaming that some of those poets Miss Bethel likes so much would have waxed—well, poetical about. It was beautiful. But a Kinematoscope probably would have found it transparent as a big bowl of mud.

It made me sad to think that none of these wonderful colors would translate onto the screen when this motion picture was printed and shown. It would just be black and white and shades of gray.

There were ways of tinting plates. I wondered if anybody would ever come up with a way of tinting motion picture film.

Maybe a process like a printing press, where the colors were broken down onto masters and then recombined.

I should suggest it to Priya. If I ever saw her again. She was still not in evidence.

She wasn't over by the Kinematoscope crew, anyway. I also didn't see Evans, Cowboy, or any of the stars of this little production that I had met or at least stood near earlier. Right now, my impression was that the only actor I'd give a plugged nickel for was Phoebe Ann Mosey, whose practicality I admired.

I wasn't in costume any more, and I could see the momentary confusion in Max's face when I presented myself. As soon as I spoke, though, his countenance unclouded. "Miss Memery! We were just talking about you."

"Were you now?" I tried to sound cheery rather than suspicious. Lord only knows if I succeeded, but at least he didn't jump back from me as if I might bite. "Only good things, I hope."

"Well." He lowered his voice conspiratorially. "How would you like to double for Miss Roman as well as Miss Mosey?"

I thought of the petite blonde with the bad lipstick and frowned. "Will she be doing chase scenes also?"

"Celia is still working on those pages," Max admitted. "We sent the draft back to her to be punched up a little. But it seems as if we have one woman having daring adventures, well, why not have two?"

Was being carried off ineffectually kicking the chassis of a mechanical all it took to count as having a daring adventure? If I'd known that, I wouldn't have gone to such pains to get in trouble in years previous!

"It pays extra, of course," Max said. "There will be additional hours."

I'd have to arrange things so that *that* income didn't get halved if I lost my bet to Black. Of course, I didn't intend to lose it, but it never hurt to have a contingency plan. Whereas I was living proof that sometimes it hurt very badly *not* to have one.

Miss Roman was returning from somewhere as we spoke. She had a determined little march on. It was very pretty, and very stagy. That's the problem with actors, of course. They're always playing a scene.

My back went up at just the sight of her coming over. Her makeup was still impeccable, albeit heavily reinforced. She had some mud on her boots and I tried not to enjoy it. She weren't going to have to be the one to clean it off, anyway, so I supposed I should really hold off on wishing that unpleasant job on whoever she paid and browbeat to clean her shoes. It's never the terrible people who suffer the way they ought.

"Have you found a stunt double for me?" Miss Roman demanded of Max, without wasting no time on the pleasantries. All at once the plot came clear to me. Miss Roman, who was the biggest star on the set, was demanding that Miss Mosey not get to do anything that would make Miss Roman seem less appealing to her motion picture public. But of course Miss Mosey had been brought on particular because she could shoot, and I had been brought on particular because I could ride. And so Miss Roman couldn't demand that Miss Mosey be given a more boring job.

But she could demand that she be given a more interesting one.

"We have," Max said, soothingly. "Miss Memery here will double for you as well as for Miss Mosey."

Miss Helene Roman turned to me with a sniff. I topped her by a head—why were these motion picture women so tiny?—and I was probably twice as broad through the torso.

"I'm sure Miss Memery is a very fine rider," Miss Roman said. "But I don't think anybody in the audience will be fooled into believing that this person is me. No matter how much corsetry you strap her into."

Oh.

Was *that* how it was going to be, then?

"That's all right, Mister Fo—"

He looked at me. It shouldn't have been much of a look, but he had some real authority when he wanted to uncork it.

"—Max," I finished weakly.

"What's all right?"

Miss Roman was glaring such daggers at me that I almost clammed up and beat feet, but I'll be damned if I'm going to let a mean filly like that run me out of my herd. "Well, to be quite honest, doubling for two leads would be an awful lot of work for one rider. And are there going to be any scenes they're both in where they'll need doubles?"

"Oh." Max's back was to Miss Roman as he gave me a wink so quick I was half-sure I'd imagined it. "Most likely not, Karen. But I don't know where we're going to find a second girl who can ride like you one, and has your guts. And even if we could, I don't know if the production can afford it. I'll have to talk it over with Mike Evans."

He sighed, not too dramatically. Did you have to be a good actor to be able to direct?

He turned his attention back to Miss Roman. "It would be a blow to my artistic vision if we couldn't find a way to have two equestriennes in the film, now that you've convinced me of the merit of the idea." Then, brightening: "Perhaps you would consent to do your own stunts? You are such a fine rider. And of course there's always the Peace brothers."

Maybe you didn't have to be a good actor. But you had to be a good bald-faced liar, I could see. Which amounted to the same thing, once it was down with the hogs in the mud.

Miss Roman tossed her head prettily. Her voice was treacle as she said, "Permit me the latitude of a little time to think it over."

"But of course," Max said. "I know you'll make the right decision. And we wouldn't be shooting any stunt scenes with you until Thursday, at the earliest. Celia and I need to work them out, and we need to talk to Black about the logistics."

Black, I was gathering, was the stunt coordinator as much as anything else.

"Where is Black?" I asked.

Max made a face. "Miss Mosey got locked out of her trailer. He's getting her back in again."

Miss Roman whisked off, head just exactly as high as if she had won that round. Perhaps she thought she had.

"Say," I said to Max, once she was out of earshot, "You haven't seen my partner, have you? She went off to talk to whoever handles your machinery, and I haven't seen her since. Only we came on one horse, and I need to get home to care for our stock" —our stock was Molly, and that one milk cow who was at least part Jersey and would be calving any day now, and some chickens, but it wasn't *technically* a fib— "so if she's done with work, it would be just swell if I could collect her."

"Go ask Cowboy," he said.

I didn't know where Cowboy was, so I turned back to ask him. He had gotten busy explaining something technical to somebody in the intervening five and a half seconds, however, so a lad who seemed to operate like a cabin boy or page led me off. He was a young man of about twelve, bubbling over with the sort of energy that don't survive your fifteenth birthday.

We hadn't gone but ten steps, though, when we was interrupted by a great noise, like a horseless carriage whirring down the street or a steam locomotive blowing through a flag stop without being called to halt. I whipped around like a mare who's heard a snake rattle and I was greeted by the sight of Cowboy running toward us, so much faster than when he'd carried me that it was like the difference between a collected canter and a flat-out gallop. He left a line of tore up sod behind him, and he was making a beeline for all of us, and for a mad moment I thought the scenarist was a precognitive and he was going to barrel right into the lot of us and start slaying.

He didn't, though. His run turned into big, bounding leaps, as if you was skittering down a rocky hill and wanted to keep your balance by moving fast. Each one was a little slower than the last, and each one shook the earth with a thud of impact that I felt in the bones of my legs, all the way up to my knees. He came to a perfect, balanced stop right in front of Max.

A human would have paused, out of breath or searching for the right way to say something. Cowboy's tapes didn't even scrape; he'd had his sentence cued up before he even got to us.

"There has been an incident, Mister Forth," he said in his slightly-too-clipped words. "You must come quickly."

"Is someone hurt?"

"No," Cowboy said. "Someone is dead."

Chapter Eight

Sure, I'd been thinking of rounding Priya up and heading off, but Cowboy having just announced a death on the set, it seemed a little insensitive to run home to my wife's cooking and leave these folk all to deal with the mess. Besides, I'd seen bodies before, and that made me think I was probably pretty capable to handle another one if it needed handling. Max sent for Doctor Swan and most of the crew followed Cowboy in a hushed, worried clump.

So I figured I would be all right going along as well, and look responsible to boot. As long as there weren't a lot of blood.

I limped along after, because by then my shin was right painful, and I tried not to complain out loud. I assumed we would be finding someone who had fallen down from a bum ticker or the stroke, or who had gotten hurt in an accident. We came through a little copse of trees and over some blackberry bushes that looked trampled flat. I wondered if Cowboy had done that on his way through, or if there was some more sinister explanation. Then we saw the dead men laid out on the grass, and I stopped dead. They looked like dolls in suits, tumbled any which way like a careless God had dropped 'em from too high up and their china limbs had busted.

Reader, there was plenty of blood, after all.

I will scruple the details of my reaction, but suffice it to say, I had to go away from the scene a bit so as not to ruin any evidence of who might have done it. Because this was that obvious a murder. A whole bunch of other folk who'd followed us over from the shooting location was gathered around murmuring, and I had to shove through them on my way out and then edge through again when I came back, because the gap I'd made had closed behind me like honey behind a knife.

I looked again, and it weren't any better this time. But I knew what to expect, and besides, all that lovely lunch wasn't with me any more, so I managed not to disgrace myself a second time.

It was Mr. Evans and Mr. Kindness, and they was both dead as dead can be. I recognized 'em by their clothes, not their faces, let me put it to you that way. Because they looked like they'd been stamped on by a herd of buffalo, and then the buffalo had turned around and come back over them the other way.

The funny thing was that the turf weren't tore up around them. I could see where Cowboy had run through—on the outbound leg, because he must have been walking softer on the way in. I considered going over and checking them for... I wasn't sure what. But fortunately by that time Black had arrived, and he grabbed my arm and said, "The doctor is coming. Just leave them be."

"But they—"

"They're past helping, Karen. You stay here with me."

He was right, of course. No breath stirred their chests. They was as far past helping as it was possible to be. Past last rites, even, though I supposed prayers might still have a chance of reaching them.

We waited.

Waiting is the hardest thing. Maybe not for other folk, but for me for certain. And it seemed like we was waiting for a long, long time. But it was sunset when we found the dead men, and it wasn't even full dark yet when the doctor arrived.

Doctor Swan came up on a bay mare, cantering out of the gloaming. She had a practiced seat, but when she swung out of the saddle in a flurry of skirts she moved stiffly as if something pained her. I winced in sympathy, as somebody who was just starting to collect those kind of aches and pains of my own. She ground-tied the mare, who quivered for a moment or two at the scent of blood and then seemed to calm down enough to drop her head and crop grass.

I guess a doctor's horse gets used to all sorts of things.

Doctor Swan caught my eye, and Black's, as she walked past, and she nodded.

She paused a little ways past me. Cowboy had switched on the lights built into his chassis, and they was sure dazzling—but they also lit up all the macabre detail of those dead men like... well, like it was on film, on a motion picture screen. So it all looked black-and-white, and a little unreal.

Max hurried over to her. "Doctor."

I heard her suck her lips from ten feet away. "Well, Max, I don't know what all you expect me to do with this lot. They're past my assistance."

"Just make sure they're dead, Swan," Max said softly. "Let's just be sure."

"All right." She moved with him. He kept up beside her. I followed along a little bit behind them both with Black right there with me. I'm not rightly sure if we was eavesdroppin' or if we was hoverin', but either way we was real available. There was a couple dozen right behind us, too, who didn't seem like they had the fortitude to step past Black and me. Like as if we had some kind of a right to be out front, other than having set ourselves there—but those folk, or the folk behind them, had a pressure in them to push forward as far as they could without actually—in some kind of way—*involving* themselves in the crime.

I wanted Priya, and I wanted to know Priya was safe. And I wanted to pitch a fit about it, but I knew I could do no such thing. In the first place, because I had no reason to be pitching a fit about the safety of my business partner when there was no indication that she was in any trouble. And in the second place, two men were dead and I didn't want to draw any extra attention to me. Or to Priya.

Swan crouched a few feet from Mr. Kindness. She reached out and took his wrist. "He's cooling," she said. "No pulse."

She repeated the process with Mr. Evans. This time she just made a face and shook her head. "My preliminary diagnosis is that they're dead." She didn't say it callous like. More gentle, as if the black humor were there to balance out her sympathy so it didn't topple her or anybody else over into inconsolable upset. "How were they discovered?"

"Cowboy found them," Black said, when nobody else answered.

Doc Swan stood up and beckoned him over. She shielded her eyes from the bobbing glare of his lamps until he seemed to realize they weren't needed anymore and shut them off. My eyes was so dazzled the contrast made the blue twilight seem like black midnight for a minute or three, until my vision adjusted.

"Cowboy," Dr. Swan said, "did you witness this crime?"

"I did," Cowboy confirmed.

She folded her hands, one inside the other. "Who did this?"

"I may not comment," Cowboy said.

Max spat. Those faceless folk from the crowd scene behind us shifted and sighed.

"You may not comment," the doctor said patiently. "Is that because it would incriminate somebody, and that incrimination would bring them harm?"

"It is," Cowboy said.

"He can't," Doc Swan said aside to Max. "He really, physically can't. I built him so he can't do anything that might cause a human being harm, you see."

"Sure, getting somebody hanged might be construed as caus-ing 'em harm," Black muttered.

"It's hard-punched into his tapes. Woven right in there. I'd have to wipe his memory to take it out. Which would not solve the problem."

"Cowboy," Max said, "did you kill these men? Mister Evans and Otis here?"

"I did not," Cowboy said, after some whirring. "That would be contrary to my programming."

Max shook his head helplessly. "I'm not really sure how to proceed here."

"We should put a tarpaulin or some kind of canvas over the bodies," Doctor Swan said.

Black moved forward, leaving me standing alone between the people right on the scene and the people gathered behind us. "To protect evidence?"

"And keep the scavengers off," the doctor said. "And assuming this ranch doesn't have a telephone—"

"It don't," I answered, then blushed when I found everybody looking at me. "No lines run this far up the mountain."

It was local knowledge, and I was the only local here. Also the Kindnesses—just the one Kindness now, I reckoned, and I hoped that Otis' wife, Mourning, could make the finances work out and wouldn't have to sell the place, or worse, surrender it to the mortgage holder—didn't have the kind of money a telephone cost, especially not to have the wires run all the way up here. The Hôtel Ma Cherie down in Rapid had a telephone, but it was right in the center of the red-light district. Some people would say it *was* the red-light district. Priya and me sure didn't have a phone up where we lived, though, and we were a damned sight closer to Rapid than the Kindness place was.

"All right," Doctor Swan said. Her alert dark gaze rested on my face a moment. I could feel her noticing me. "So somebody needs to go for the sheriff. And somebody should guard the bodies until they get here."

Priya walked up just then, so I was saved from volunteering. I am so glorious bad at telling people no. But just as I was about to offer my services, I felt a strong little hand on my elbow, and Priya turned me around to look her in the face.

She pitched her voice just for me. "I deduce that I have arrived in the nick of time to preserve you from your folly."

"I need to hide those Poe stories," I replied, just to see her smile. She forced one for me, but I could tell her heart weren't in it. She looked strained, and exhausted, and there was scratches on her cheek and on both her forearms and wrists, once I started looking for 'em. She was wearing a man's calico shirt with the sleeves rolled up to just below her elbows. And I had a habit of looking at her forearms any chance I got.

What can I say? They was appealingly muscular.

She extended the hand attached to one of 'em to take my elbow and start steering me away. I followed willing, like. Black didn't seem to notice us going, or if he did he must have thought we deserved to be let go, because he didn't say anything and neither did Max Forth.

"Where've you been all day?" I asked.

"Machine shop," she said.

"I stopped by around lunch time and didn't find you. Nobody seemed to know where you'd gone off to."

"Well. I was probably at lunch, then." She paused and touched my shoulder. Through the gathering night, I heard Walker Black in a low tone say to Max, "...and somebody's stolen a revolver from the armory. Or at the very least, one's missing."

"Get the Peace boys and Jodi looking for it," Max said, back.

Well that was unsettling. But at least it weren't the murder weapon, I reckoned. These two had not been shot.

Priya guided me through the darkness and over the trampled bramble as much by feel and intuition as being able to see a damned thing, I suspected. I got my calves a little tangled up and stung, but nothing much to speak of. My hem got snagged, and Priya bent down and tugged it loose. When she straightened she had her thumb stuck in her mouth.

"Don't look," she said. "It's bloody."

I wondered if I was as finished with reacting to blood that night as Doctor Swan's mare, or if a little bit more would push me over the edge again. I didn't care to find out so I didn't look as she pulled out her pocket handkerchief to wrap it, even though it was so dark by then I could mostly see her as an outline.

"Take me home," I said weakly.

"Good thing you taught me to tack Molly up," she said cheerfully. "You look done in."

Chapter Nine

We got Molly home and I rubbed her down and picked her hooves and got her and the cow and chickens fed while Priya started on dinner. I was done in, Priya was right about that. But Priya was done in, too. And we had to be back on set for sunrise, which meant we all needed a good feed and a rest. The kitchen was warm when I went in, and Priya was bent over the top of the stove. She'd put all the stove lids on it and was using the whole surface to spread out... some kind of batter, swirling it around with the back of a ladle and then peeling it in big round sheets right back off again. Molly had hay and a ration of oats and a clean bucket of water from the pump in the yard. I had...

I don't even quite know what to call it. There was these thin, papery rolls the size of a wagon wheel, but so much more delicious. And they was stuffed with potatoes, and the first spring spinach, and chopped egg and cooked lentils, and all kind and manner of spices. Priya kept apologizing about them, saying they was supposed to have peas in but the first peas wasn't ready yet—and wouldn't be until June, I reminded her, so I would have to be happy to eat these the way she was making them until then.

And I would have been, too, without stopping for air. The pancakes they was rolled up in weren't quite like pancakes at all, but crisp and soft all at once. I'd expected them chewy, like those French crepes they resembled. But they was a whole different texture, one especially their own. And they kept the saucy bits inside something admirable, without getting soggy or leaking all over the plate.

I probably could have eaten two, but I contented myself with one because I didn't want to put Priya to the trouble of making more. I did get another scoop of the potato mixture from the pot where it had been cooking all day, nestled beside the coals, and I snuck a dab of butter on top of it when Priya weren't looking. Don't get me incorrect, there weren't nothing wrong with Priya's cooking. But have you ever tasted a single thing in your life that wasn't improved by a dab of butter?

It seemed like a good time to have a conversation—not that any time is a good time to have a conversation that needs timing to be had, but I felt the pressure of what I needed to say in me and it was making that good food not quite settle.

So I cleared my throat to get her attention, and when she looked at me I said slow, "Were you avoiding me because you were mad I was stunt riding?"

"Not mad," she said, having thought it over. "Plenty scared, though."

"Priya, I love you. But if I got to respect that we're a family and what I do reflects on you... well, you have to respect that I'm a person, and I gotta be who I am. And some of that is riding horses."

"You can't just cut me out," she said.

I touched her face. "And you can't just suffocate me, either."

She frowned at me, that little line between her eyes like it was drawn on with the pointy end of a draftsman's compass. "I don't aim to put you on a chain, Karen."

"That's good," I said. "Because I ain't no hound."

The frown turned into a pinch of distress. "I don't mean to smother you. Or run your life."

"I know you ain't your father," I said.

"Aren't," she said, automatically, and then smiled, and I thought things were likely all right between us. "I know you worry about my Mad Science, too."

"You're the bravest thing I ever met and I think it's beautiful," I said. She leaned into my arms and kissed me, and I told myself that the niggle between us was healed.

People is like horses, in more ways than one. Folk bolt, too, if you hit 'em right, get 'em in the place where the irrational takes over and they just want to run.

There's some that, even when they're bolting, can feel a friendly hand on the rein and adjust themselves. Some, though—they get started bolting and once they're gone, they're so busy bolting they don't notice anything that ain't the bolt. They'll run right off a cliff and never be able to stop themselves, they get running hard enough.

Them, there ain't much you can do for except leave the stall door open and pretend not to notice anything happened once they exhaust themselves and come limping back all shame-tailed. Spirits break easy if you hit 'em right. And some do it out of ignorance, and some out of spite. And some think being broken-spirited is what's best for a nag or a jade, for that matter.

I don't hold with that. It's a plumb mean way to be, for one thing.

Getting a marriage to work out all right may be mostly about finding people you like enough to put up with the fits they give you. And also finding out who people really are, and forgiving them for not being who you expected them to be when you was deluded by love, and also learning how to love who they really is.

You can't get into a relationship with the person you expect to change your partner into. But contrariwise, you got to expect that your lover is gonna change while you're in that relationship, over time. Probably even change in ways you're gonna hate, or that are gonna make you work hard to meet the challenges of. Ways that are gonna be miserable and hard to live with, at least for a while.

If nothing else they're going to change by getting old. And so are you. And that is gonna be hard on everybody.

Priya went to put to her nightgown, after, and I scraped the plates and washed 'em and set the covered pot with the last of the potatoes in it in the pantry, next to the stone wall where it would keep cool.

"We should get a dog," I said as Priya came back and set the kettle on.

"Another mouth to feed," she said, but she was laughing. Her nightgown was paisley flannel, gathered at the wrists to puff the sleeves out, by far the most womanly thing she owned. "A dog, and three cats, seventeen ducks—not too many, since we have a few chickens also—and perhaps a flock of shee—"

Her mocking me might have gone on indefinite like. But she was interrupted just as she was winding up by a tromp of boots up onto the porch—two or three pair—and a real assertive banging on the door. It didn't quite rattle in its frame, but the outhouse seat hung up on its peg near the stove to stay warm until needed trembled against the wall.

Priya jumped back so hard she nearly fell against the hot stove.

"Get the shotgun," I said, and turned toward the door. There was no point in pretending we weren't home, because anybody could see that lamps were lit inside and the stove was smoking.

The shotgun rattled as Priya cocked it.

"Who's there?" I called out.

"Constables," came a familiar voice. It was a constable, all right—Waterson, my old sort-of-friend. "Open up, Miss Memery."

I looked at Priya. Priya shook her head, but it didn't mean *Don't let 'em in* so much as *I don't trust this.*

"Not much we can do to keep 'em out," I said in a low voice.

She sighed and uncocked the shotgun. "I dislike this."

"You and me both." I moved toward the door.

"I'm opening the door," I called. "Don't shoot the place up, Constable."

It crossed my mind that I was overreacting, but that knock hadn't sounded friendly. Nor, when I unlatched and opened the door, was the sight that greeted me. There was Constable Waterson, sure, and behind him was a man I'd never met and knew by reputation: Josiah MacGregor. Sheriff of Rain County, for whom I wouldn't have voted even if I was a man and could vote.

I hear me some things from friends of mine, let's say, like Merry Lee and Crispin Hayden, about how you don't want to get noticed by the law in Rain County if you ain't white.

So seeing as how Priya is Priya, and seeing the apologetic look on Constable Waterson's face (and the apocalyptic one on MacGregor's) a chill of apprehension crept through me. I stood aside and let them come into the house, and I was real glad Priya'd already set down that gun.

Waterson opened the door the rest of the way, then closed it behind the sheriff. Waterson was a thin colorless man with a bit of a pinched face, like he was always one meal behind and one cup of coffee ahead of where he ought to have been.

That apologetic look turned into grade-A dog-caught-in-the-pig-trough, and I think he would have slunk away into the underbrush if MacGregor hadn't had a firm grip on his leash right then. Waterson isn't a bad feller, and he's got some real personal courage in him for physical dangers and such. I couldn't speak to his spiritual courage, because I ain't never seen the man tempted.

But he ain't got no moral courage, to stand up for what's right even when he knows it could come down on his head and where he lives. He'll put a word in your ear, sure, but he won't stand up for you.

I got a special place in my heart for folk as will.

I guess I can't judge, because if he ain't got no moral courage, I ain't got no spiritual courage. Or maybe I just ain't got no spiritual convictions, which I suppose might amount to the same thing. Anyway, there's worse men in the world than Constable Waterston. And I ain't without sin to throw that first stone.

That's what I'm saying, and when you got something to say you might as well say it plain as contemporize at it.

"My apologies about the mess, Miss Swati, Miss Memery," Waterson said. It must have started to rain again, because he was wearing oilcloth and the edge was dripping mud all over our clean redwood.

Well, MacGregor—it sticks in my craw to call him sheriff—didn't waste no time once that door was shut. He pulled a writ out of the inside of his own duster—he had an oilcloth on over everything, too, so the writ was dry except where his damp gloves touched it—and said, "This here is a warrant for Miss Priya Swati as a material witness in the murder of Mike Evans."

"That's ridiculous!" I was still stepped between Priya and the men, and I didn't step out of between 'em, neither. "Priya never even met that man."

"That's not so, is it, Miss Swati?" MacGregor asked with that leading softness lawmen get when they think they know something you don't want them to.

Don't get me wrong, some of my best friends is lawmen. I guess technically I'm one myself, having been deputized by a U.S. Marshal not six months past. But they have got a way about them, and I'm sure if you've met a couple you'll admit I ain't wrong.

Priya looked at me, and then looked at MacGregor, and clammed right up. She got that blank look on her face that I was coming to know as her refusing to give away anything, and she drew herself up as tall as she got in her stocking feet, and she took a big breath before she spoke, then let that one out and took another one for good measure.

"May I at least put on some clothing?" Priya asked, with formal dignity.

"Your friend can bring you some," MacGregor said, with a wave in my direction. "In the morning."

But Waterson, I noticed, handed Priya her boots and socks from where they was drying beside the stove. And he held her coat for her to shrug into before MacGregor put the cuffs on her, despite MacGregor's huffing like a hungry hog impatient for its dinner.

"Takes a big man to handcuff a slip of a girl," I muttered.

MacGregor gave me a look that promised mayhem, but he didn't say anything. And I didn't say any more, because I was afraid of it getting taken out on Priya.

"I'll wake the mayor," I told Priya under my breath as they walked her past me. Her mouth was a grim line and her complexion was yellow. She'd spent her time in chains before, and I couldn't imagine what this was like for her.

She still managed a nod for me, though, and I went to get my own boots before they was even out of the kitchen. I was glad I hadn't had a chance to undress yet. Molly wasn't going to be best pleased by being tacked up again on a night like this when the rain had closed back in, and coldly. She'd manage.

The kettle began to whistle as they hurried Priya out the door.

I was right about Molly not much liking the rain, and not much liking the ride down the mountain in the darkness. Her night vision was better than mine, though, and she was sure-footed in the road mud as long as I let her put her head down and inspect her passage. We didn't move as fast as the lawmen and Priya, so we wasn't gaining on them. That scared me half to death because if one of their horses slipped in the muck...

Well, there wouldn't be much my beloved could do to protect herself, with her hands chained up behind her.

Still, there was three of them and only one of me. And nobody was coming to help me or Priya if Molly and me went down, so it was up to us to make sure we didn't.

The cold rain flattened Molly's mane, which looked more pale than streaky in the dark. She was just a big, mottled, slightly-less-shadowy shadow under me. Water would have dripped down my coat collar like a live thing trying to get my goat if my second-hand Boss of the Plains hadn't been such a good hat, even if maybe it were a touch unbecoming.

To make a long, damp, slippery, boring story short, we made it down the mountain in one largish lump and only left every nerve we had along the roadside, which is why this ain't coming to you as a piece of automatic writing via a Spiritualist. I rode Molly right up to the front porch of the mayor's house, which were still all ablaze with light—the habits of a lifetime don't fade easy, and it was really only maybe nine at night, even though my ride felt like it had lasted a lifetime. Maybe two—Molly and I might both be on borrowed time after that stunt.

Anyway, the door was already opening as I thumped across the boards to it, and the butler looked out at the rain, squinted, sighed, and said, "Good evening, Miss Memery. I'll send Jack out to see to your horse."

I don't know why it is that all stable lads and grooms is named Jack, but it's so. I imagined Mr. Dirk would send an unlucky footman out into the rain to wake the groom in the stable, and Molly would be under a roof in warm straw before I was fully inside.

"Much obliged, Mister Dirk," I said. "You got someplace I can leave these boots? The state they're in is a disgrace, and I wouldn't want to tromple all over your parquet."

I wanted to prove my moral superiority in the matter of muddy footprints.

Mister Dirk came with the mayor's house, but I imagine he was probably getting used to the kinds of visitors his new boss sometimes entertained. He simply ushered me inside and fetched a maid to help me off with my boots and my own oilcloth, and on with a pair of sheepskin slippers that had been warmed up before the fire. They was too big for me, especially once I peeled my wet socks off.

I could not make myself care too much about it. The fleece was so springy and warm under my toes I nearly forgot how distraught I was. It all came back in a rush as Mr. Dirk turned back to me—he'd turned away politely while my boots was coming off, lest he spot a flash of ankle or something else only half of Rapid City had paid to see before him—and said, "May I inform Madame of the purpose of your visit, Miss Memery?"

I saw him look sadly at the little silver tray on the table in the hall beside the bench I was just getting up from, but fantasies of becoming a personage aside, visiting cards weren't a thing I stocked, in general, and if I had done I would have pulled a soggy mess of wood pulp out of my pocket if I'd been carrying them around on a night like this.

"It's about the murders up at the Kindness place," I told him, because there weren't no point in lying to Madame and so there weren't no point in lying to anybody who reported to her. "My Priya's been arrested for them."

"What a shame, Miss," he said, and swept off in a crisp rustle of pin-striped gray flannel.

———

Well, I hadn't long to wait from that point. I was ushered into a library with a roaring fire and settled in front of it, on one silk love seat facing another one. There was a tray on the table already with a brandy decanter, two snifters, and a teapot and its associated technologies. I'm not too proud to say I went for the brandy. I only poured a little, though, which was a good thing because it went to my head as straight as if I hadn't eaten anything. After two sips I set it down and poured myself some tea.

A door behind the other love seat opened—not the one I had come in through, which was behind me—and there was Madame Damnable. She was a battleship of a woman, and I mean that as the sincerest form of flattery. Her iron hair was swept up like a turret and her iron-gray dupioni silk shimmered mauve when she moved in it, even though it only had the firelight to work with. Now that she was mayor, she did not affect the décolletage she once would have, but the pigeon breast of her corset was still enough to give a strong man pause for contemplation.

I poured a second cup of tea as she limped over, moving quick despite the liberal use of her cane. The brew smelled like a rose congou, so I left it plain. She could doctor it up with milk and sugar on her own if she chose to. I was a little surprised to find no coffee, but I suppose it was a mite late in the day.

She settled across from me and I handed her her own good tea. A shocking breach of manners, but for a year and some months

I lived in her house and worked for her. And we'd saved each other's lives at least once each.

We was more or less beyond etiquette, Madame Damnable and me.

The tea made a whirlpool noise of irritability between her teeth when she sipped it. "Now," she said. "What's this I hear about our Priya getting fixed up for a murder?"

"I'm gonna go out on a limb and suggest that weren't your doing."

"You reckon right."

"Fixed up is what it's got to be." I shook my head. I could imagine Priya killing somebody, maybe, but it would have to be somebody like Peter Goddamn Bantle, somebody evil to the core and just plain mean beside it.

I wondered why it was so much easier for me to believe in basic evil from a man than from a horse. But horses were in a state of innocence, weren't they? A beast that has no reason couldn't fall—

Well, I supposed I weren't qualified to speculate on issues of theology. Not that that ever stopped me.

But if the sheriff was fixing up a murder charge against somebody who was more or less under the mayor's protection, and he weren't including her in that decision, there was only two reasons that could explain it that I could see. Either he was that sure she'd done it... or he was playing at politics and Madame had best watch her back.

Maybe both. It weren't like those things was exclusive.

It bothered me that Madame couldn't trust her people. It bothered me that they weren't telling her everything.

"That sheriff is a problem." It could have rung like a mild observation if you weren't somebody who knew her.

I sipped my tea. It *was* rose congou, and it was good and warm and settled me more than I expected. Maybe that was why she put out tea instead of coffee. Or Mr. Dirk did. Maybe I looked like I needed settling.

Madame would have made a good horsewoman if she'd cared to be one.

"Sadly," she said, "he's also a duly elected representative of the law for Rain County. So I can't just up and fire him, no matter how richly he deserves it. And he doesn't owe me any loyalty."

"What would it cost us to get Priya out?"

Madame cupped her tea between ringed hands, the saucer balanced on her knee. She let the steam bathe her face, her hooded eyes half-closed while she thought on it. It was strange to see her without paint—maybe just a bit of blacking on her lashes, but nothing that a man would comment on—but she didn't look tired, or pale, or anything like she couldn't handle herself.

When she looked back up, her mouth was firm. The little softness along her jaw set with the muscle behind it. "She's going to have to go before a judge. The circuit is due after Easter. Today's Tuesday, so that's about six or seven days. Can she take that long?"

"I can ask her," I said. "If they'll let me see her in the morning."

"I can vouch for her character, and I'm willing to take the risk to do it. She might have to stay here with me, and you might have to post bond. Can you do that?"

I'd have to stake the ranch, for bond on a murder charge. But it was Priya's ranch, too. And she wouldn't cut and run if it was my life and livelihood on the line, would she?

I told myself my hesitation was unworthy of me, and that if our places was reversed she wouldn't flinch. I reminded myself of the four hundred dollars I had handed her once, in the aftermath of a fire, and which she had handed back to me untouched a few weeks later.

"I can do that." I tried to sound grown-up and confident. My voice wobbled at the end.

Madame, bless her, made like she hadn't noticed. This from a woman who notices everything.

She poured me more tea. Somehow I'd got through what was in my cup, despite feeling like I was too queasy to swallow anything.

"Karen, I'm going to ask you something," she said. "I know your temper, and I want you to take as long as you need to answer honestly without getting mad at me, all right?"

I almost got mad at her right then, I'll tell you what. I drank my new tea off in a draft, and was grateful that Miss Bethel weren't there to frown over my failure to take tiny, ladylike sips. Madame didn't say a word about it.

"All right," I said when I had swallowed it, and my anger along with.

"How well do you know Priya?"

Reader, I got fired up all over again. But it was good that Madame had made me practice, or maybe I was learning a thing or two. Because I got mad, and then I realized I was getting mad, and then I thought about it and realized it was a good question, even though I hated it.

Maybe I hated it *because* it was a good question.

"I think I know her pretty well," I said.

"Just between you and me, could she kill somebody?"

I smiled. I set my teacup down on the notional table. It clinked. Madame looked at it, then refilled it.

"Just between you and me," I answered back. "Could you?"

She frowned at me a minute, her mouth twisted up in a knot on one side of her face. Then she laughed. "Point taken."

"That's a thing that bothers me," I said. "I don't know why she'd know this Evans fellow, or that Kindness, either—though I guess the Kindnesses is neighbors, or near enough—or far enough, up where we live—but the law don't seem to care too much about him—but I said to MacGregor that she didn't even know Evans, and MacGregor smirked at me something ferocious and hinted that she did. So how would he know that? And if she did, why didn't she tell me when she saw him?"

I tried not to think of her stiffening up at the sound of his voice, or how she'd smoothed her face self-conscious like for a minute after. Priya was a bottler. She didn't care to burden folk. So there was things in her past I might never know, unless she chose to unbottle about it someday, and I tried real hard to be at peace with that. I figured it were mostly things I was happier not knowing, as it happened.

Madame watched my face for a minute, then sighed. "I guess I better get her a lawyer."

"I don't know if I can afford no lawyer. Especially not if I got to stand bail." It stung to admit, but this was Madame.

Her rings flashed by her face. "She's still one of my girls. And so are you. Your legal troubles are mine."

"Madame—"

The finger that had been waving so airily an instant before pointed direct at my face. "You did part of what you did to protect my interests, Karen Memery. Don't you turn down my help now after you came to me for it."

"All right." I settled back on the silk. "Do you know why they suspected her?"

"I have some rumors about reasons," Madame allowed. "Some of those reasons might just be that she is Indian, and nobody seems to know where she was when it happened."

"MacGregor hinted she had some history with Evans. But I don't know how she could," I said bitterly. "She got right off the boat and got locked in a crib down by the docks until Merry Lee busted her out. And she ain't got no reason to know nobody from San Diego, no, nor Chicago, either."

Madame nodded judiciously. "Have you heard the cause of death?"

"I saw the bodies," I admitted. "Not up close!"

Her expression twitched toward sympathy. "I heard they looked pretty terrible."

"Smashed up," I said. "Like somebody had beat them up with clubs."

"More than one someone?"

"How could a little girl like Priya do that to two grown men, each one twice her size?" I demanded. "If they was shot with a rifle, I'd say, sure, a small woman could have did it."

"Priya ain't that small—"

"She's tall," I said, "and purty near the strongest thing her size I've ever heard tell of. And you know I'm the last person on earth who would say a woman can't do a thing just because she's a woman. But can you see all hundred thirty pounds of Priya overpowering two men, one of them over six foot tall and two hundred thirty if he was an ounce, the other accustomed to hard labor? And Otis Kindness had a reputation as a brawler, didn't he?"

"I've heard he was hard on his wife," Madame admitted. "Maybe she knows something about it."

"Are you suggesting I interview her?"

"You was still deputized, the last I checked."

"Marshals don't investigate crimes," I said. "They just enact warrants."

Her nose wrinkled like she was smelling what I was full of.

"All right," I said, relaxing back on the cushions. "Can I tell Miz Kindness the mayor sent me?"

"Some folks think that it don't matter how large or strong the person who murdered Evans and Kindness was, if they had a big machine."

"Oh," I said.

Madame Damnable sipped her tea.

"You think I ought to look at the Singer."

"I think you ought to lock it up. If you want to impound it here, we can keep it under key. That is, if you trust me."

I hesitated. It weren't a question of who I trusted—and I trusted Madame with my life, brazen and harsh as she could be—but a question of whose honor would be considered unimpeachable if it came to a court of law. Because it weren't my life on the line. It was Priya's.

"Can we get it photographed?" I asked.

"That's smart," she said. "Yes, once the sun is up, I daresay we can get it photographed."

"I'll pay—"

"You'll do no such thing," she said. "If it's being photographed for evidence, then the city or the county will pay for the pictures. Not you."

The tea had gotten cool. I sipped at what was in my cup still before Madame warmed it from the pot.

"I'm worried," I said. "Because Priya and me have been quibbling at one another and I'm worried she's alone and scared. And she don't take to stall rest at the best of times."

"Karen," the mayor said. "She is alone and scared. But we're doing what we can for her. Sometimes you just gotta sit with the scared because there ain't much you can do to fix what's scaring you."

I said, "I can bring the Singer down tonight. For safekeeping."

She relaxed enough to smile. "Get on home with you, Karen. I'll get a word taken in to Priya so she don't think she's been abandoned and forgot. If you bring the Singer by, do it tomorrow. Mister Dirk will lock it in the cellar where he keeps the spirits. He's the only one with that key. There's nothing else we can do until the morning, so we might as well be rested for the fight."

"Thank you, Madame," I said, and stood. She rang a little bell, then stood up, too. She came around that low table and hit me with a quick, hard hug that I was too shocked to return before Mr. Dirk came in and showed me out again.

I stood on the front porch, watching the rain fall cold as strings of diamonds and waiting for Jack (they was all named Jack) to bring my Molly around.

I missed the old Hôtel Mon Cherie something fierce right then. Just the women, and the warmth, and the plushness of it all. And being surrounded by my friends, and knowing they was my allies if the world weren't. But it was almost eleven, and the renamed the Hôtel Ma Cherie would be jumping this time of night, even on a Tuesday. They didn't need me showing up and being a distraction while they was trying to get a spot of work done. Anyway, it weren't my home anymore.

Maybe I would go by after shooting ended the next day, though. They might have some solutions I could share when I visited Priya.

Chapter Ten

As it turned out, I didn't have to go back into town that evening or even the next morning before dawn. Because I got back to our barn, which was also Molly's—and the milk cow's—stable, and I got Molly rubbed down and her hooves picked out and gave her a slice of turnip as the best I could do right then for a treat. Then I took the lantern I'd lit so I could see to tend to my mare, and I walked down to the far end where Priya's workshop was. I unlocked the big old padlock on the hasp and went in to where the Singer lived in a shadowy corner.

I lifted the lantern.

The huge, heavily modified industrial sewing machine that should have been right there—

—was gone.

I was late on set that morning following, because I had to go and see Priya first and bring her some food and clothes she'd be comfortable in. I hadn't slept a wink thinking of how somebody had gotten into the locked barn and taken the Singer. Had it been MacGregor confiscating it as evidence already? Was he going to do something to it to make Priya look guilty?

Or had somebody else stolen it for reasons of their own?

I had spent my sleepless night baking, and while I was baking I had tried real damn hard not to think about whether somebody had come into our barn earlier that day and taken the Singer and used it to do what had been done to Otis and Mike.

I was glad Madame had gotten a word to Priya, because I hated to think of her alone in the county jail, thinking she'd been abandoned or forgotten or worse. I knew she wouldn't *choose* to believe that—but what we want to think and what we think in the dark of the night when nobody ain't looking are two separate thinks, and the second one ain't got a lot of mercy or self-love in it.

At least Rapid City was the Rain County seat, so I didn't have far to go.

I saw a few folk as I was acquainted with on the way in. They waved and I waved back, and they didn't avoid my gaze, so I knew the public opinion hadn't turned against Priya yet. We still had some goodwill in the bank, I guessed. That could end quick, though. Opinion could turn on a silver penny and give you a halfpenny change. Molly poked along, thinking her own thoughts—probably about the hay I'd taken her away from before she'd managed to get more than a mouthful of it, though I'd let her get through her oats while I was tacking her. She seemed to be enjoying the cool and fly-free morning, and it had stopped raining, though the road was sloppy still.

Something terrible had happened to the old jailhouse, and it weren't deemed structurally whatsis after. So the county lockup was a new timber building, because in Rapid City most buildings were. It was rectangular and two stories, and whitewashed, and upstairs and in the front half was the sheriff's office, and offices for his two deputies, and the constables they'd added on as Rapid outgrew the ability of a three-man squad to police. In the back, opening on to a yard with a brick wall around it, was the jail with its barred windows and reinforced walls.

I rode up to the front.

I won't lie and say my knees wasn't knocking as I swung down out the saddle. Honest beast Molly were, she stood calm and easy when I hitched her outside. She must have picked up on my mood, but she weren't going to let it rattle her none. She had bigger fish to fry, I supposed. Like her lack of hay.

Horses spend a damned lot of their lives eating. You would, too, if you were that big and obligated to grind up straw between your molars to get your sustenance from it.

I gave her a pat, unhooked the basket from my saddle, knocked my boots clean on a handy curb, and walked up to the porch. The door was on the latch, which made me wonder what sort of a sorry law it was that locked itself in overnight. I rapped stoutly and the door rattled a moment later, preceded by the tread of bootheels across a well-sprung, rugless floor. When it opened, it opened on somebody who was neither MacGregor nor Waterson, but a big man in plaid flannel and red suspenders, with a silver star pinned to the left one. The sheriff had a gold star, and the constables got copper ones, so I guessed this was one of the deputies and I was ashamed to say I could not remember his name.

I reckon it made sense that the sheriff weren't in yet, if he'd been up all night. But I'd been up all night, and I was here in my own boots and even fresh linens, so you might say my sense of Christian charity was limited by the circumstances.

I might have lost track of the local law, but I hadn't lost all my professional skills. I met the deputy's eye through my lashes, and pinned a little coy smile on my kisser tight as if I planned to appliqué it there, with a little batting behind so it would stand up once I quilted it. That reminded me that I could quilt, and I thought I should start picking through the scrap basket so I could piece something and maybe give it to Priya when I got her home.

I pushed that thought away, because my face wanted to scrunch up like a walnut when I contemplated Priya being gone long enough for me to get a good start on a quilt—even a machine quilt, which I couldn't do without the Singer anyway—and while a little lip quiver was pretty, men generally panicked when confronted with a woman crying for keeps. Since if I started in to wailing I weren't likely to stop, I bit my cheek real firmly and in so doing I got my teeth into that sob. Maybe I'd be lucky and it would look like a brave smile to old what's-his-name.

"Deputy Sheriff," I said.

He had a long face and a sallow complexion, and hair that brown where later you can't remember what color it exactly was, and he'd shaved his chin yesterday or the day before but his upper lip wore a luxurious soup-strainer that was red in the middle and grizzled at the sides.

His mouth started to form some other shape, but he corrected it, and what came out was easy and proper. "Miss Memery," he said.

There are hazards to being well-known in a small city. The voice was a mite familiar, but he had the advantage of me.

"I'm afraid you got the advantage of me," I said.

His mustache wriggled at the ends. "Sam. Sam Beam. I knew you when you was... when you used a different name, Miss."

That was what he'd been stopping himself from saying. Prairie Dove, which was my old house name when I was a parlor girl. And I remembered him all of a sudden, but he'd had a lot less face scraped when he'd been working timber, which was how I'd met him. I wonder how old hell-raising Sam wound up a deputy sheriff.

But I'd wound up a deputy U.S. Marshal. It's a weird old world, and the Lord works mysterious, they say.

"Ain't no shame in that," I said. Then I flirted. "Less'n you're ashamed, of course."

"No, ma'am." He reached to tip his hat and realized he weren't wearing one.

"Sam Beam! I didn't recognize you with a chin. What a pleasure to get acquainted with it!"

He laughed, and stepped aside to let me in, and I lugged my basket on my hip through the door. It looked like he'd been having coffee at the desk in the front of the office. There was two more desks behind it, unoccupied, and an open door behind them that I got a glimpse of the sheriff's office through. There was a closed door, too, solid oak plank with a little barred window in it, that I figured was like to be the door into the cells.

I plumped my basket down on his desk and said, "Deputy Beam, would you care to get your teeth into a carrot muffin?"

It was that and onions, potatoes, and rutabagas left in the root cellar this time of year, and I didn't hold much for the chances of a rutabaga muffin. We were even out of mince, and dried apples for dried apple pies. If anybody could stomach one more dried apple pie by April.

As the song goes,

> *Give me a toothache or sore eyes*
> *In preference to such kind of pies.*

He looked at me, and he looked at my basket of muffins. They was still warm, even after the ride, and a little steam was coming off them when I flipped back the towels. I ain't the cook Priya is, but I can heat muffin molds on the stovetop and spoon an alum soda and sour cream batter in. I'd brought butter and sour cherry jam too, because I meant to feed Priya and bribe the lawman on duty both. And here was my opportunity.

"Miss Memery, I didn't know you was a chef d'cuisine." He accepted the split and buttered muffin reverently. I'd brought a tin spoon instead of a knife, because I thought they wouldn't let me give Priya even a butter knife.

"Oh, I ain't," I said. "But I can cook a muffin." I hooked a thumb over my shoulder. "I'd like to bring my partner breakfast, if I may."

He licked the butter off his mustache. "I can't abide waste," he said with a grin. "I'll walk you back, Miss Memery."

Well, that were a relief and a half, and I don't mind saying. I'd been afeared that MacGregor or whoever he had on duty would fight me on seeing Priya, because I weren't her lawyer and I had no legal rights as family, like I would if we could have got churched. But it was just my luck to run into an old customer who remembered me fondly and was willing to play the rules as they lay. He even let me go in alone, after he searched my basket and the bundle of clothes and confiscated one more muffin. The best one, that I'd got perfectly golden brown on both sides.

I should have hid it in my corset, but I'd have never got rid of the crumbs.

There was three cells in the back, and two of them occupied. I had no eyes for the big figure slumped on the bench in the end one, though—just the pretty, haggard girl in the middle.

Priya was awake, of course, and I'd lay good money and a pair of muffins that she hadn't been down in the straw once all night. Her trap didn't look too bad, as cells went: she had a straw tick on a bench that was part of the wall so you couldn't bean somebody with it, and she also had a cane stool. There was a pot with a lid and a shelf built like the bench but at belly height, so you could sit on the stool and eat your dinner or write a letter. The floor was wood and it wasn't foul, and there was sawdust strewn on it that could be swept up with any spills. It smelled like clean pine.

If my sewing machine tax had to be spend on jails, I guess I minded less if they was jails like this.

I didn't think Priya was smelling the pine dust, though. She looked haggard, though it had been a few hours only. There were tired bruises in her eye sockets and her hair was staring and ungroomed.

She whirled around like a wild cat when I came in, and it was long moments before she relaxed enough to lower clawed hands to her sides.

"I brought your breakfast," I said, and held the basket up. "And some trousers."

"Did you bring my bail?"

"It ain't set yet." There was a stool for visitors. I plumped on it and began opening up a muffin with the handle of the spoon. That's basically a butter knife, and yet nobody ever worries you might slit somebody's throat with it. "They need the circuit judge to come through before it can be done."

She looked away and down. "I can't stay in here, Karen. It's too much like the crib."

I spread butter and jam on the muffin and made a sandwich of it, then held it up to her. "Anybody bring you stuffed muffins when you was Peter Bantle's captive?"

"Peter Goddamn Bantle," she said, but accepted the muffin. She sniffed it. "You bake this?"

"Ye of little faith." I split and buttered and jammed up another one.

Priya was still eyeing hers dubiously. "What's this orange thing?"

"Carrot," I said.

Her head tilted.

"Oh, don't look so damned confused." I took a bite out of my own muffin. It weren't so bad, if I do say so myself. "What about that carrot sweet you make sometimes? It can't be that strange an idea."

"I had no idea," she said, "that English people also made sweets out of carrot."

"American," I corrected.

She shrugged like it weren't no account to her what nice and irrelevant distinctions I wanted to make about species of white people. Her cheek bulged out with muffin a minute later and she smiled.

"It's good." Then she swallowed with difficulty. "A little dry."

"Got a cup?" I held up a vacuum flask I'd borrowed from Madame. "This won't fit through the bars."

"Oh, Karen." She sighed. "Tea?"

"I do love you."

She had a tin cup with water in, and being Priya she swallowed the mouthful instead of waste it before she gave me the cup for the tea. That fit between the bars, as I guessed it was intended to.

She took one long sip and sighed. I'd already milked and sugared it the way she liked.

She pulled her cane stool over, and looked a little easier. "I can't stay in here. You'll get me out."

"Priya."

Her face fell. "You won't even try."

"Priya, listen to me, and not the monsters in your head for just a minute. I'm already trying. I'll clear your name or die in the attempt. But it may take a little while. I can't just steal a key and spring you. You own property. If we was to light out, we'd be losing everything."

Her mouth went grim. She balanced the rest of the muffin on her knee as if her appetite had deserted her.

"Drink your tea, sweet," I said.

She sighed and did. The sugar or the heat put some color back in her. She picked her breakfast up to nibble on again.

"All right," she said. "We've been in worse scrapes."

"That's my girl."

"So. What happens now?"

"I talked to Madame last night. She says bail can't be set until the circuit judge comes through, but we're going to try to find you a lawyer. You're safe in here and nobody in town thinks you actually did it. It'd help if you could tell me where you was when the murder happened."

"If I knew when the murder happened, I might," she allowed.

That was an excellent point. I tried to think back to when I'd seen Kindness and Evans on the porch together, and what time it might have been. I'd seen Evans after, though, with Miss Mosey giving him a piece of her mind. And maybe—

"Do they know what killed them?" she asked. "I mean, aside from the obvious."

"You mean how they died?"

She nodded.

"Priya," I said. "Where's your keys?"

"You're not answering my question."

"You're not answering mine."

"If they're not in the house," she said with irritation, "I can only guess MacGregor has them. Did you lose yours?"

"No," I said. "But the Singer's missing. Did you take it some-where?"

"Somebody stole the *Singer*?"

"Apparently." And annoyance not just because it was a mystery and a potential murder weapon. But because it was money on the hoof, so to speak, if it came right down to it. Those industrial machines did not come cheap.

"But—" She paused, and her face went that green color it went instead of paling. "Oh bless me. Is that what Evans and Kindness were killed with?"

"I don't know," I said, honestly. "They was beaten to death. Bludgeoned, Madame said."

"Sister's dick," she cursed, awed. Priya don't usually conversate so rough, but I guess it all sank in on her of a sudden. She slumped over her tin cup. "I can't spend years in here, Karen."

Make no mistake, I felt on the narrow end of the horn right then as I rarely have before. I weaseled a hand between the bars and took her cold fingers. "I know, love."

I didn't tell her that she wouldn't be, however things came out. Because murder was for hanging.

Next to us, the hatted man in the flannel shirt raised his head, and from the clicking sound I realized at once that he weren't a man at all. Cowboy looked over with his unsettling, glassy, almost-human eyes and said, "The murderer was not Miss Priya."

I looked at him through the bars. "You can say that, but you can't say who it was."

He straightened up, rattling faintly. "It is a dilemma."

I tried not to feel angry at him. It wasn't his fault how he was built, and there were good reasons for building him that way. "If you tell what you know a human will be killed. And if you don't tell what you know—"

"A human will be killed," Cowboy agreed. "It is a dilemma."

I was still chewing on the fact that Cowboy was in jail too—also as a "material witness," as if he couldn't just walk through the wall if he had no regard for the law—when the cross-grained oak door behind me with its little barred window swung open. I jerked my hand out through the bars of the cell, which I guess was more suspicious than just holding Priya's hand like any friend might. We'd all make a lot fewer mistakes if we was omniscient, I suppose.

The good news was, it weren't anybody who was gonna be shocked by a little hand-holding.

My eyes bugged out when Miss Francina Wilde—I guess I ought to call her Madame Francina now—filled the doorway with about two cubic yards of pewter lavender warp-and-weft tiered skirts and a waterfall of impeccable golden ringlets.

"Fear not, ducklets," she purred. "Your legal counsel is here."

Chapter Eleven

Miss Francina was tall as a man even before her bootheels lifted her up that little more. She was blond and stately and utterly impeccable. My heart cheered the moment I clapped eyes on her. I stood up to greet her, and Priya inside her cell stood, too. She waited until the door to the office closed and the bolt loudly shot before she reached out and took my hand again.

That bolt's rattle was as ominous as the rattle of the bolt on a repeating rifle.

I didn't go over to hug Miss Francine, because I didn't want to step away from Priya. It was all right, because she came over and quickly hugged me.

I gave her a muffin and said, "You're a *lawyer?*"

"Well," she admitted. "I don't have an *official* diploma. And the Washington Territory doesn't have a bar. But the best thing about the West, Miss Karen, is if you got the skills, ain't nobody check your paperwork."

She broke off a little piece of muffin and popped it between rouged lips.

"Miss Bethel would turn white to hear you talk like that."

She winked. "I won't tell on me if you don't."

———————

Now it was still too early to go by the Cherry Hotel, because the girls would all be sleeping off the night before. It was amazing that Miss Francina was up as early as she was. And it told me how highly she regarded Priya.

And if we was going to be trying Priya in court, I was going to need all the money I could get my hands on.

So I went to work at the motion picture set instead. Rehearsing first, because you do a stunt the safe way fifty-hundred times for nobody in particular before you do it the spectacular way for the Kinematoscopes.

Now it might seem strange to you that we was shooting despite the producer being murdered that very day previous. I'd asked Black about it, because I felt like I could ask Black about things. He already knowed I weren't educated about Chicago or San Diego matters. And I didn't feel like he was gonna use my ignorance against me.

I badly needed an ally on that set. I was just that desperate, I figured, that I would take anybody who seemed kind. Especially when the rest of 'em was either giving me the side-eye and a wide berth since I got there that morning, or coming up to pump me about Priya, who she was and what she might have had in for Evans.

Nobody asked about the Singer, but then maybe they didn't know we had a Singer. And nobody asked about Mr. Kindness.

It was all right. I had half-expected to be fired, though I don't rightly know as I had admitted it to myself until I walked on set that morning and heard the conversations stop like my approach was striking men and women dumb. I watched the little knots of whisperers break up and shake themselves apart when I approached.

I weren't getting the benefit of the doubt from this lot, and that was for sure.

I was this close to turning myself around, Molly and all, and riding right back out of there when Max Forth detached himself from his little knot—his was with Vernon the cameraman and Celia, that redheaded scenarist—and strode on over just as if he was happy to see me. I expected that the big smile on his face was a lie, given his purposeful walk, and that when he caught up he'd tell me to go on home and maybe if I was lucky pay me and Priya off for the previous day.

Instead he patted Molly on her spotted neck, looked up at me, and said, "Glad you're here, Karen. Do you feel up to a stagecoach stunt?"

Well, when he put it like that, I couldn't see how I could say no. No matter how ominous "stagecoach stunt" sounded.

"I'm glad to find out you still want me." I put my hand over my mouth; I hadn't intended to be quite so forthright. He'd taken me by surprise and got the unvarnished Karen in return. Not sanded down even a little and full of splinters.

I was not sure I'd ever let a man who wasn't my da see that much of me before.

He was just looking at me. I hemmed and said, "Sorry I'm late, Mister Forth. I ain't got no excuse."

He said, "I wouldn't hold you accountable for your partner's actions even if I believed for a second she had anything to do with such a garish misdeed. Now, about the stunt. Black will coach you through it. He's got a horse picked out—"

This man was not a damned thing like motion picture directors was supposed to be.

Which made me wonder. If he was so sure Priya hadn't done it, was that because he knew who had?

I didn't used to be such a suspicious type.

I was pleased to find the mare was the same one who I'd met to start this all off. Copper wasn't bright copper—not like a new penny, but more like an old roof flashing, with a sooty mane and tail and a lot of white splashed on her face and on her legs below the tiger stripes. If she was a stunt horse, that explained why she'd been so calm when things inexplicably started going wrong around her. And how ready she'd been to accept my help.

The second wheel horse's name was Baldy, on account of his white face, which I would have gone with something a little more creative maybe. Horses do labor under a selection of terrible names.

At least it weren't "Diamond."

Anyway, either Copper recollected me, or she was just that friendly with everybody who showed up with treats and petting.

Black harnessed her up, and showed me how her rig was fitted out with handholds and a stirrup that I could use to get over her back while she was moving. He said the trick was to use the mare's own speed to pull myself up.

They rosined up my hands. I already knew that my costume for the day would have split skirts with a drape over them so they would look like one piece even when I forked the mare, so my trousers were fine for now.

Then we practiced it a lot.

First with her standing still. Then with Black walking her, and it wasn't as bad as it might have been because they put me in one of those rigs the circus riders use when they're rehearsing because it ain't good for nobody's well-being to hit the ground as often, hard, and fast as you would be otherwise. The rig was basically a counterweighted pole on a pivot, with cloth-covered India rubber tubes that hung down and hooked to an elastic belt that went around me under my jacket. The pole was hooked onto me; I held on to the mare; and if I fell off, I fell softly and landed—theoretically—on my feet.

It was a silly-looking object to be sure. But after I'd failed at the trick three or four hundred times, my barked shin throbbing a little worse under the bandage and the stockings, I started to be able to do it every time. Grab the harness as the mare jogged past—Black said they'd speed it up on film to make it look crazy dangerous and like she was at full flight—swing myself up astride, get the reins, and rein her down.

It didn't take much reining, honestly. She responded to seat and legs just as well, which weren't something I'd been expecting of a cart horse.

These motion picture horses was full of surprises and specialized skills.

So I hopped on her back for the fourth time running, swung a leg over—that concealed stirrup helped!—and settled her right down to a nice walk and then a whoa. She was fired up and wanted to go again, her upper lip quivering and questing for the apple bits Black fed her every time she let me do some fool-ass thing up on her back.

Now I just had to do it without the rig, with three other horses hooked up and the bright red Concord stage that was parked just over by the chuck tent. The red wouldn't read on film, of course—the stage would look black.

But it sure was shiny.

"Miss Memery, you're bleeding."

I looked down. It was the leg where Copper had kicked me—was it only two days before?—and it had a bright red, sticky, nauseating streak of crimson soaking down my stocking.

"Oh, it's just a cut from Monday," I said, looking away fast. I hadn't had Priya to help me change the wraps this morning, or any real time to do a proper job myself. I guess they had come loose on their own, and rough enough to take the scab with them. Or I might have pulled a stitch out—

I gagged, and stopped thinking about it.

"Well, go to the infirmary and get that looked at," Max said. "Get your costume on and get yourself some lunch, come back, and we'll shoot for real. One take."

"One take," I said, and ferreted off. Once he mentioned food he didn't have to tell me twice. It had been a real long time since I ate that muffin. And I knew I was going to be hungry... just as soon as my ridiculous aversion to blood wore off and I could contemplate eating again.

———

The infirmary folk didn't act none too surprised to see me, though they did seem a wee bit bemused that I wasn't coming in for something I'd just incurred while falling off a horse but rather an old wound from two days before. There was another gentleman there, a skinny redhead, not too tall and just about my own age, with a mop of curls. He was holding an ice pack on his hand and introduced himself to me as "Justin Peace, don't mind if I don't shake."

Nurse Marie, plump and with gentle hands, helped me take off my stockings and soaked the bandage loose while I didn't watch.

"I don't meet many Celestials with a Midwest accent," I said, because curiosity makes me nosy.

"Doctor Swan?"

I nodded.

The Doctor's dry voice interrupted from over my shoulder. "My father was a missionary in China. He came home with a bride. I went to medical school in France, before you ask the next question."

I winced when she glowered at me. "You're probably real tired of people being curious."

She didn't say anything, just bent over to frown at my leg. "Well, it hasn't gotten infected. And the stitches aren't the prettiest, but they're working. Don't let another cut like this go by without treating it, though."

"Listen to her." The redheaded boy swung his legs around on his cot to sit up with both feet flat on the floor. He rested his elbows on his knees and gave me a pretty good charming grin. "She hates doing amputations, so you know her advice is good."

"You're a bossy— Ssss!" The hiss as Doctor Swan plied my kicked shin with carbolic defeated whatever clever thing I'd been about to say. Presuming it were actually clever, which was always a consideration.

"You're the new stunt girl," he said. "You took my job."

I looked over. He was skinnier than me, for sure. Heck, he might have looked more like Miss Roman in skirts than I did, with a bit of padding in the right place. No wonder it was taking a while to get the costumes fitted.

"If you want Miss Roman back, you can have her."

He spread his hands in a shrug, that smile widening. He might have been flirting with me. Or maybe he was just a charismatic sort of person.

"You're a stunt rider?" I asked.

"A clumsy one," Doctor Swan said tartly, before Justin Peace could answer.

"Are you actually going to ride Angel Maker?" Justin asked.

"That's what they tell me." I sighed as Marie greased up my leg with petroleum jelly to keep the gauze from sticking in my scab again, then wrapped a new bandage comfortably tight.

"You can sit up," she said. She handed me a paper sack. "Here's your stockings."

The air was chill on my bare legs, so I smoothed my skirts over them. I was going to wardrobe next anyway. "Thank you."

I'd been hoping to talk with Doctor Swan privately. But it didn't seem as if Justin was about to leave, or Marie, either. And I really hadn't got a thing to hide.

"Doctor Swan," I said as she was sweeping dirty bandages up. "You know the person as was arrested along with Cowboy for the murders is my partner. We own a ranch together."

"I hadn't known." She didn't look up. "I met her. We worked together yesterday."

"That's right," I said. "You're the local Mad Scientist." I *really* needed to introduce her to Miss Lizzie.

"Mechanic at best," she said. "I never apprenticed."

I thought about Cowboy and weren't so sure. Maybe all these formal qualifications weren't nothing but a way of keeping folk who didn't have money to begin with from making any money going forward.

I probably couldn't convince Priya that if Doc Swan didn't need no Mad Science license, neither did Pree. You want what you want, and that's fine. But I want what I want, too, and it occurred to me with a big pile of worry that nowhere in the universe is it written that you get to *have* what you want just because it happens to be you that's wanting it.

Still and anyway, I done owed Priya a pile of forgiving from a couple of things I done. And what she wanted weren't all that unreasonable, even if it scared me.

Peter Goddamn Bantle had this machine that let him run people's minds. And that was the thing about Bantle's machine.

It could be subtle enough that you thought what was going on was your own idea, at least until you started to think it through a little. And a lot of folk, they don't think stuff through. They just feel it and do it without wondering why they're doing it.

So with that thing, you could tell afterward that your mind had been being run for you. And this was like that. Except if Priya had decided to do it, and do it right, I probably never would have known that she was making my mind up for me.

So that was a kind of trust she was giving me, weren't it, letting me ride stunts when I knowed me riding stunts scared her to hell and gone? Could I figure out how to give that trust back?

Maybe I could.

Anyway, the first thing I needed to do was get Priya out of jail.

Anyway, I might be digressin'. If Doc Swan wanted to put her hat on modestly, I weren't the one to tilt it all rakish for her. I said, "I saw Cowboy and Priya at the jail this morning. He asked me to tell you he was all right."

"I've got a lawyer coming in for him from Indiana," she said.

"A lawyer for a mechanical?"

"Do you think he's not going to need one?"

No, actually, I rather thought he would. And much as I loved Miss Francina—

"Would your lawyer be willing to work with Priya's lawyer, do you think?"

"Oh," she said. "Probably. He's pretty well known for doing work for mechanicals and colored folk even when nobody else will stick up for them. And I saved his life a few years back, so he owes me."

She had the air of somebody chewing over a juicy surprise, so I didn't press her. "When will he be here?"

"I telegraphed him as soon as they took Cowboy away yesterday. He might be here tonight or tomorrow, if he got a fast train."

"Good," I said. "You examined the bodies."

She nodded tightly. I knew I was pushing my luck, but I needed help. And then there was the desire to just say what was on my mind and have it out.

I have the same relationship to speaking out as a drunk does to his coffin lacquer.

I cleared my throat and my voice came out soft and quizzical. "Can you—"

"I'm not the sheriff!" Then she pushed an escaped lock of hair off her forehead and said, "I am sorry. I shouldn't have snapped at you."

"It gives me heart," I said.

She looked at me.

"Knowing you're frustrated by it, too."

"They'll probably pin it on Cowboy," she said. "When your partner gets cleared."

"If she gets cleared." I hated myself for saying it. "I don't think the constable would railroad her. But that sheriff. I don't know. He likes his reputation for keeping a law-abiding town."

Then I did a double take. "How come you care so much about Cowboy? Ain't he just a machine?"

"I feel a bit proprietary. And you've met him. Do you think he's 'just a machine'?"

The question shamed me.

"Wouldn't you like to know who really did it?" Marie asked.

"Sure would," I said.

Doctor Swan sighed. "I'd like to know nobody innocent is going to get hanged. Or disassembled."

"That, too," I agreed. "Maybe we can find out something useful if we investigate."

She looked dubious and gestured to my leg. "I'd tell you to stay off that but I know what you do for a living."

"As one does." As I tested my weight on the leg, the tent flap was pushed aside. Two more redheads came in, identical to the first except for lacking the ice pack and having some different colors to their shirt plaids. They went over to the first one.

"Hello," the one in the front, who was now in the middle, said to the man who was obviously his brother. "Did it fall off yet?"

You know how sometimes you just open your mouth, and for no reason at all except having been caught by surprise, the stupidest thing in the world just falls right out?

I said, "Holy cow, you're triplets."

"Shit," said the one on the right. Turning to his matched opposite on the left, who was holding the ice pack—Justin, at least I knew that—the one on the right continued, "Now how is it we never noticed?"

My face scorched like I'd been sitting too close to the fire.

"Any luck?" that first Peace brother asked the other two. Looks were exchanged, and a slight shake of the head. I remembered what Max had said about the missing revolver and bit my lip.

The one in the middle caught the look on my face and re-arranged his instantly into a caricature of flirtation.

"Marie, Marie," he said. "No kiss for your beau Justin?"

"That's Justin," she said tartly. "And I've already kissed him. You're Joshua. Your cowlick goes in the other direction."

"What about me?" the one on the right asked.

"You're Jonah," Doctor Swan said.

I was impressed. I couldn't have told them apart unless I was invited to paint numbers on 'em. "How do you know?"

"He ain't got no cowlick at all," said Marie, waving her hands so vigorously her little cap slipped in its pins. "Now out, the lot of you. And back to work."

I didn't think she was shooing me, because she gave me a wink, and the gestures of her hands was directed at the Peace brothers, but it seemed as good a time as any to make my escape. Besides, they was waiting for me at the wardrobe tent.

Still, it seemed like I might have got lucky, and like Doctor Swan and Nurse Marie might be allies. And I felt I needed all the help I could get.

Chapter Twelve

The problem with sitting in the stylist's chair or standing on the dressmaker's stage, was while getting my hair made over with an assortment of falls and curls to match Annie's, or getting my costume fitted, was that I had too much time think about everything. And in particular, too much time to think about Priya fretting in jail.

Even though I knew Miss Francina was going to take very, very good care of her. And the girls from the Cherry would be in and out all day with food and books and paper and pens and anything else they thought they could get past the deputy. Miss Lizzie would probably sit there and help her draw up plans for a steam engine.

But I still felt helpless and useless, my fingers curled in fists while Amber sewed the day's dress around me. I tried not to stare at the industrial Singer she was wearing. There was no trace of blood or whatnot on its big manipulators, and I couldn't see no dents or nothing that might indicate it had been misused.

But one Singer was surely as good a murder weapon as another, weren't it? Except in that case, why had somebody liberated ours?

Miss Francina's face had gone all grave when I told her the Singer was missing, and Priya had been furious. "Now I know I am being framed," she had said, with the particular emphasis she sometimes gave a word which she had heard used but with which she wasn't completely familiar.

I made up my mind to have a look at this one, and moreso to check it over much more closely for... I didn't know. Bits of hair. Spattered blood. What you'd expect, I suppose.

We finished fitting the dress that matched Miss Mosey, and started on the one that I would wear the next day, to double Miss Roman. I was glad I was being paid, because I wouldn't have done nothing for that... horrible woman on credit except maybe shove her into a stagecoach on its rough way out of town.

My anger was as much feeling helpless about Priya. But I really didn't like Helene. Pity, because I'd been hot for her films before I met her.

"I hear you met the Peace brothers," Amber said. At least, that's what I think she said around the habitual mouthful of pins. She was a plump pretty thing with dark hair cut in a fringe across her forehead. Very à la mode.

She mumbled something else, but I couldn't make it out.

"Sorry," I said. "I can't follow."

She sighed overdramatically and stuck the pins into the ribbon she wore around her neck. Then she spoke clearly: "Did they give you a hard time?"

"Not really," I said. "One of them hassled me a little about having this dress let out."

"Well, there's more than enough work for them still." She fussed with the hem. "There, that's straight, more or less. Can you wiggle it off?"

"I can." And did.

She gave me that day's costume and stockings to go with it, and promised to launder mine and give 'em back the next day, which I wouldn't have asked her for but she pointed out she was likely to just throw them in with all that night's linens to be washed, and they even already had a tape sewn in with my name on it, because I'd had them back at the Cherry Hotel.

———

Luncheon was a pair of chops—pork or lamb, as you liked it—fried potatoes, bread, butter, oysters baked under breadcrumbs, coffee, pickled beets, and sauerkraut. There was dessert, too, but in all modesty I just didn't have room for trifle *and* for oysters, and at this running the oysters won. Maybe tomorrow there would be a rematch.

The cook tent was chaos, and the coordination of a hundred or so folk devoted to making a motion picture film while they all got in one another's biscuit batter was a sight to behold. I wasn't sure if wrangling the people weren't more of a struggle than wrangling the stock. I saw that woman again, the straw-blond with the mechanical arm, and I went to sit down with her because I was interested and if I was going to be playing Pinkerton I guessed I'd better get it under me. She had a plate of pork chops and a tin coffee mug, and a mess of fried onions that smelled like heaven and she was sitting all by herself on a picnic table bench.

I won't say but that it occurred to me you could beat somebody to death with a mechanical arm. Such as Miss Lizzie had.

Such as this trail boss was sporting.

I walked up before her, bold as brass, and said, "Pardon me, ma'am, but is this seat took?"

She looked up at me, startling pale eyes in a sun-coppered face, that blond hair sticking out every which way under her hat. She said, "You're the local talent. Or should I say, fresh meat?"

"You're what I want to be when I grow up."

"Sit, kid," she said, and pushed her hat back on her brow so her metal hand glinted. "Me is not somebody you want to be."

I sat, fussing my skirts over the bench. I had a big napkin to spread over my front while I ate so I wouldn't get mess on the costume, and I had a mug of coffee of my own. "I'm Karen Memery."

"Squalene Jones," she said, and drained her coffee.

I was going to offer to go get her another cup, but she pointed a mechanical finger at the opening and fanned her thumb like she was cocking a gun. There was a grinding sound, and then a hiss, before a steaming stream of brown fluid jetted from her finger into the cup.

It smelled much better than what I was drinking. I will not lie.

"That's genius," I said. "My partner would love to look at that."

"Ain't your partner in jail?"

I took a bite of my chop. It had mustard in the sauce. I felt bad enjoying my groceries while Priya's life was in the balance. On the other hand, I would bring her dinner that night, and she had the rest of the basket of muffins until then. And whatever our fallen sisters brought her, which was likely to be a lot.

"I might not mind losing a limb if I got a replacement like that."

"Blood is caffeine. I suck the coffee of my enemies. This here can brew you the finest bellywash west of the Mississippi and shoot someone's eye out from seventy paces. At the same time." She winked and pushed bread through the juices on her plate. "Can't guarantee I'll hit both targets, though."

"I'm trying to keep myself from making steam and froth jokes," I said.

"I bet you're just a martyr to your better nature there." She pulled a flask out of her hip pocket, under the leather vest she had over her check shirt, and measured a dollop into her coffee with a squinted eye.

I could have said something about drinking on the job, and I noticed she didn't offer me any. The pale sun creases around her eyes seemed to ease a little after she drank half the tin mug off, however. I ate my pork chop and my potatoes and I chewed them carefully.

"So you're the trail boss."

"I'm the help."

"How's a woman wind up with a job like that?"

She rattled her tin fork on her tin plate. "I used to have a ranch of my own. We fell on some hard times. These film folks—well, you might have noticed they're not real fussed about who you are if you can do the work. They're all pretty marginal their own selves. Jews and queers and other folk you don't mention in polite company."

She didn't say "queers" like she meant anything by it, so I tried not to bristle about it. "Did you know Evans well?"

She looked at me over the rim of her coffee mug. Even her eyelashes were startling blond.

"Don't let the velvet waistcoats fool you. Or the gold watch chain, neither."

"You didn't like him?"

"We've all got our eye on the main chance." She eyed me up and own. "You do, too, or you wouldn't be here."

Fair.

"Evans was marginal?" Even frontier society had its class divisions. But they ain't the same as the way things is back East, or so I've heard. Fortunes are easier to come by out here, and easier to lose. Getting one still all seems to involve stealing something from somebody, though.

Nobody was clean. Priya and my ranch was on what had used to be Skokomish land. I thought about that more than I used to, for a couple reasons.

"There's money in it. But it ain't like steel money. It ain't even like gold money, and boy howdy would I like me some of that. You won't ever be seen even as nouveau riche, no matter how successful you are. You don't wind up making motion pictures if you're respectable."

I wanted to ask her some more questions, but the lads were going around calling up the folk who was going to be in the stagecoach scene, and that was me, so I got myself around the rest of my luncheon as fast as I could. I didn't quite get to finish, but I figured it weren't going to be great to be too heavy loaded when I was jumping over horses and trying not get crushed under a stage.

A young man with a blond ponytail, Jodi, was holding the stock when I got there. Copper was the near wheel horse and that fast-talking, hardmouthed gelding Baldy was in beside her.

Copper grumbled cheerfully in her throat when she saw me, her upper lip reaching for apple slices like the fingers on the tip of an elephant's trunk. People who ain't around horses a lot don't realize how much they can do with that lip. Shoot bolts, if they figure out how. Open gates. Pick pockets, too. Pick grass, which is what it grows that way for in accordance with God's plan, but horses don't feel no more reason to limit their adventures to what the Almighty anticipated than we humans do.

Black was standing beside her. He gave me a steadying grin as I came up. I tried not to let on that I was buzzing full of coffee.

"Where's Miss Mosey?" I asked. I'd seen her at lunch—she had been eating lamb with an appetite that belied her slender frame.

"She'll do the closeups later," Black said. "We want to get this now, while the horses are fresh."

Copper *did* look like she'd bounced back from this morning's exertions all right. She was groomed shining under her harness, her hide the color of a good piece of raw liver or an old penny, and she looked pleased to be at work. She weren't going to be a very convincing runaway with those happy ears, but my experience in motion pictures was that most of the wolves was Alsatian dogs, and most of the mustangs was Justin Morgans.

Anyway, Copper weren't a Justin Morgan *or* an Alsatian dog. I was apprehensive, sure, but I hoped we'd make an acceptable team. I went to say hello to Baldy and make friends with the other two on the team. They was both geldings, a bay and another dark dun, all with flashy white. They'd look like a matched team on film, which made me chortle up my sleeve for three reasons. One, because I was getting a real crash-course edification in the magic of the Kinematoscope and how things you saw in the Odeon might be pretty different from how they had looked from the ground behind them.

Nobody in real life would try to run a Concord stage with only four up. They were too heavy, fully loaded with mail and people and carpet bags. Four horses would barely move them; six was what you ran them with.

But four horses was more than enough for an empty stage, so that was what we were using.

And three, because who ever saw a matched team in a real overland stage? We still had one running through Hay Camp when I was a girl, and my da ostlered for them. Them stage horses weren't picked for how pretty they looked, or their even temperaments. They was picked for guts and endurance, size and strength, hammer-hard hooves and—to deal five cards straight with you—they was picked for having even less sense of self-preservation than the stagecoach drivers had.

At least the drivers was getting paid for it. The horses got hay, and oats, and the lash.

Course, the horses got to rest after ten miles if they made it that far. The drivers, not so much.

My da liked to say there was no horse handler like a stage driver. Some was good on the stock and some was bad, but they all had the confidence in their hands.

If they didn't, they died.

And sometimes they took a lot of passengers and a few hundred-pound bundles of U.S. Mail along with them.

So you might not know this, but moving pictures ain't shot the way they're run in the theatre. They do the scenes any which way, as is convenient for the cast and the director, with such logistics to make 'em go as I wasn't surprised when I learned later that the set manager used to be an Army quartermaster for the North. Then they edit those scenes together in an order that makes sense.

If you're lucky.

I know we've all seen a few films that don't have a lick of story you could follow, scene cards or no.

Then the scene cards and the dialogue cards get put in, and it all gets set to a music score, and it's printed on a bunch of reels and off it goes to the projectionist and the organist—or in some cases these days, a player piano reel goes with it, at least to the theatres that got a player piano.

Well, Copper was jealous of the attention I was paying the others, and even more jealous of the apples, so I had to go back and give her that one last pat. And by then Vernon was showing up and pointing his Kinematoscopes where Max told him to, and there was a complete overwhelm of people—Caleb fixing my hair, and Amber checking my costume, and Black was showing me my marks, which I had to hit because of the Kinematoscopes.

"You don't want to have to do this twice," he said.

"You ain't got to remind me."

He grinned and I grinned and he gave me a little pat and said, "You'll do fine."

What happened next was all a swirl and I'm not sure I can rightly relate it. I found myself on my mark, and Max came over to check on me and make sure I was ready. Black was driving the stage, so I didn't have to worry about whether the person doing that was going to cause me a problem. There was a crowd scene going on in the background, because the stage was supposed to be running away from the Dread mechanical.

That would be Cowboy, in this instance, who should have been over by the Peace brothers, or at least two out of three of them. Since he was rusting in jail with my darling Priya, the third Peace brother was wearing the Cowboy suit. He didn't look too convincing but maybe it would read better on film, and he only had to be in the background anyway. We'd shoot the close-ups and his mechanical expressions once we got him sprung.

I didn't scruple to think that we might not be getting Cowboy back, nor Priya, neither. I would not allow that to be.

The bravery of Miss Mosey (or her alter ego) in stopping the stage before it crashed into the crowd of onlookers—and thwarting Cowboy's evil plans, or rather the evil plans of his owner, Professor Killjoy—was what got the mechanical's attention and made him fall in love with her.

That got me wondering if mechanicals could fall in love, and if they did, wouldn't they be more likely to go sweet on a nice locomotive or somewhat? *Then* I started wondering whether you could put a mechanical's tape brain in a locomotive. And whether it would be a terrible idea.

I wished Priya was here to share my terrible ideas with.

I could tell I was agitated, I guess you could say, because I was thinking of anything except what had to happen next, and I kept wiping my palms on my skirts even though I was wearing gloves.

Matthan Steele was on set too, because he was playing the Wild West Hero (retired) whose Wild West show Killjoy and Cowboy was supposed to be terrorizing. We all knew who he was supposed to be, with his handlebar mustache and rugged profile and his long gray coat. He looked right dashing, though—that I have to grant.

The outfit didn't look half bad on Walker Black, either, who was also a long drink of water and a better match for Steele than I would ever be for Mosey.

I got to meet the other principal actor, Alphonse Bugera—Al—a saturnine fellow in a black frock coat who was playing Professor Killjoy. Nobody had to double the Mad Scientist behind Cowboy's depredations in this scene because he wasn't supposed to do anything dangerous, just stand around and rub his hands menacingly.

I had finally, I thought, figured out the plot.

Anyway the next thing I recollect was that I was all by myself in the middle of the pasture with a ring of crowd around me. We was on turf to slow the stage and keep the dust down, and to give me something softer than rock under me if I fell. The extras all around me moved in groups, like a flock, because they'd been drilled all morning, too.

Max shouted "ACTION!" and Vernon shouted "ROLLING!" and then the earth was trembling under my feet as the stage came up on me. It was a canter and I knowed it was a canter, and it was a canter on grass, even. But I have never in my life seen anything so big and coming so fast.

You gotta let the lead horses go by, I told myself.

And I told myself again that the carriage weren't run away, that Black wasn't going to run me down, that this wasn't the mad stampede it looked like. The extras was peeling off, running in little groups that made them look even more like flocks of passenger pigeons, and I hoped Vernon was getting the shot because even from my angle it looked pretty spectacular.

I gave my skirts a flick to make sure they'd settle right when I swung a leg over Copper, and got myself in position to sprint.

All my practice has taught me that I had to be running—I had to have some *oomph* of my own—in order to be able to get my foot in the stirrup and my leg over the mare without being dragged. Being dragged was bad enough when it was just me and the mare and I could shove myself clear. With the stagecoach rattling and bounding behind me, it was like to get me killed.

So as the horses and the coach came up on me, I broke away from my standing start like some kind of professional.

My split skirts whipped around my legs. The fabric felt light and fluid without the weight of petticoats, and molded to my body in ways that were probably as distracting to the onlooker as they was to me. I almost overbalanced because of it, but the leather of my boot shafts around my ankles saved me. Then I was running as fast as I could, pelting along like a little dog chasing a mail wagon and trusting Black to bring the team up beside me. That, and trusting the horses not to trample me.

They really do prefer not to stomp all over human beings if they can possibly help it. We make damned uncertain footing.

The lively three-beat of the team's steady cantering en-loudened off to my right. *Second horse,* I told myself. *Second horse, second horse, second horse.*

The first horse drew up alongside me even, snorted, and passed. Black was talking to his team, keeping them in line and pulling and listening. No matter how chowderheaded this thing we was doing was, it was his job to keep it calm and everyday for the horses.

Horses are not masters of breaks in routine.

I was running hell for leather now. My little costume hat flopped on the pin holding it to my twisted-up hair. My boots was bruising up my heels.

"On your right," Black shouted over the thunder of hooves and the rattle of the equipage. I'd been straining for that yell and I still nearly didn't hear it.

I heard Copper, though. And saw her surging head making long uneven ovals on the end of her neck as she loped along beside me. She overtook me with every step, and I could see the collar. And then the surcingle with its brass and leather handholds worked right in. She snorted with joy, those happy ears flipped toward me, and I knew she thought she'd finally found her a two-legs with enough sense to just tear around beside her for the sheer joy of it.

I hated to disappoint her.

I reached across my body and grabbed for the handles with both hands simultaneous.

The brass was cold through my thin suede gloves. And the mare nearly yanked my arms out of their sockets and my feet right off the ground. I used that, though, and leaped along with her. My foot banged off the stirrup, which even in a boot let me tell you hurts like hell.

She kept on smooth and steady, beautifully trained, while I dragged my left foot in the dust, leaped again, barked the hell out of my cut-up shin, and almost went down under her hind hooves and the wheels of the carriage.

It occurred to me that if Black was the murderer, I was giving him a hell of an excuse to do away with me.

Panic gave me strength as I hauled on those handles. The mare's hind hoof clipped my boot—*That's two I owe you*—but she didn't stumble and I didn't get tore loose. And then I had a good grip and my balance, and I hopped one more time, letting the mare provide all the *forward*.

My foot found the stirrup then. Just the toe, but I jammed it in and with Copper's next stride let her toss me up onto her back. I landed with the rein guide on the surcingle right in my girly bits and that ain't no nice feeling, let me tell you what. If I'd been able to get a breath it would have come out tinged blue with all sorts of words young ladies ain't supposed to be able to deploy, much less with authority, so it's probably best I couldn't.

But I kept my head and I kept my seat, though it weren't easy and I didn't always want to.

Copper was a good old thing, and while I was bouncing around up there she was adjusting her gait to catch me. Black was keeping that whole conglomeration rolling like a trail boss. It was all going real well.

And that was how I wound up on the back of my new-old bay dun friend, who was supposed to be running away with a stagecoach and three of her cohorts. My much larger copy of Miss Mosey' costume was admirably fitted, thanks to Amber, and I could move freely in it because of the cunning way she'd attached the sleeves and slit that skirt.

I grabbed a handful of mane with one hand and pulled myself off the surcingle. I didn't have much time: the Kinematoscope was rumbling alongside us on its rails and people were scattering out of our path in every direction. There were the reins. I snatched at them and the next thing I knew I was easing her up, gentle on the heavy stage bit, and all the other horses had stopped running, too. We came up three feet shy of the end of the Kinematoscope track, and I sat on that good mare and hugged her and giggled for at least five minutes by the watch before I could find the balance and strength to slide down.

Walker steadied me off her. Then I stood there panting and fed Copper most of a carrot, with bites for the other three. It'll be our little secret what I was really doing, which were clinging surreptitiously to the harness until I had the wobbles out of my knees enough to walk away without crawling.

———

That finished my call sheet for the day, so I went to tend stock and spend a snip of time with Angel Maker. He was trotting circles in his little corral when I got there, which made me wonder if I could get him to go on a longe line. Or just treat his corral like a pen and ask him to move for me.

I guessed from his prancing and the arch of his neck that he was half showing off for the mares and half going stir. So when he was on the far side, I slipped through the fence with a buggy whip in my hand and went to the center of the ring.

I ached to ride into town and check on Priya. But I had to do this first: now I really couldn't fail to ride him. Frivolous as it seemed.

Priya wasn't getting paid for her time in jail.

I didn't snap the whip at him or any of that foolery. He looked like he'd been cut enough that he might take that as a threat that needed defending from, and I didn't want to be on the receiving end of those big hooves.

Instead, I just stood there quiet like until he noticed me. It took another couple of circles, me following him, the whip folded up in my hand, until he looked over. He took two more strutting steps, tossing his head. And he looked over again.

"You are pretty," I said. "I won't contest it."

He snorted at my voice and took off again, a canter around the edges of the pen that had my teeth sucked back into my mouth in fear he was going to crash through the fence or just topple over on one of the tight angled turns. But I made myself breathe and kept my body quiet, and after two breathtaking turns around the corral he slowed again.

He had a flashy action. He was sound, and he was watching me.

He made one darting movement toward me—not quite a charge, but the threat of one, to see what I would do—and quick as the devil I snapped that whip tip under his nose and pulled it back again. He half-reared—not to lash out, but to pull back—and went back to his calamitous galloping for about another two circles.

Then I managed to use the whip to guide him to his less-favored direction. He squealed at me and showed me his heels, but he changed for me. So I took the pressure off, and—wonder—he slowed his crazy racing to a considered trot.

We were communicating!

I stayed in the ring, turning him back and forth—with less drama each time—until he finally trotted to a stop and stood there, ears up, looking at me with his tail swishing.

"Hey," I said, letting the whip rest in the dirt.

He stretched his lip at me, which I hadn't been expecting yet. The sooty smudges on his face caught the evening light, finally revealing his sharp cheekbones and finely modeled head. But the head was still up, and I wasn't leaving the corral until it came down. Today wasn't the day to try to touch him. Tomorrow I might.

We stood there, sizing each other up. And finally he gave me a gigantic sigh, dropped his head, and turned away to go eat some of the hay piled by the water trough.

Without turning my back, I edged to the fence and slipped through. When I straightened up on the other side, I realized I was standing next to Walker Black.

With pursed lips, he looked at me. "You know your horse taming, Miss Memery."

I smiled, warm inside from acceptance and the respect in the address. "Thank you," I said. "I grew up in corrals and was on a horse before I walked, so my ma told me."

Chapter Thirteen

As I was packing up my saddlebags, a woman I knew from town wandered into the stable. Cora Darling, in her cotton print dress ragged around the bottom, with a pistol strapped on over it and her hair in a faded kerchief. She was thin as a whippet and drawn as a bow, and she blinked twice when she saw me in the barn gloom.

"I wasn't expecting you, Karen Memery."

A voice came from one of the two empty stalls. "I'm in here, Cora."

It was Squalene Jones, creaking to her feet from a pile of hay that just matched her yellow hair. She dusted herself all ineffectual like and stomped out into the aisle, smelling faintly of cigar smoke. "Was just catching a few bees," she said. "You got my poison?"

"One hundred percent grade A coffin varnish," Cora said, holding up a canvas sack. Something clinked in there.

I guess I ought to mention that Cora is the local moonshiner, and has been since time immemorial. Or since as long as I've known her, anyway, which is about two years.

"Umm," said Squalene, looking at Molly and looking at me.

"Oh don't mind me, I was just leaving," I said, as Cora, talking on top of me, said, "Karen's not gonna squeal on anybody."

Money changed hands, and Cora winked at me. I winked back, led Molly outside, and swung into the saddle. My heart was already racing with the expectation of seeing Priya. My bed had been cold and wide the night before, and I hoped maybe Doc Swan's lawyer friend would arrive tonight, and that he might make a difference.

Next day was the funeral for Otis Kindness—Mike Evans was being shipped home to Chicago by train—and I figured I should go to watch people and see what they did. I wished I could figure out how to get Priya sprung in time for it. Priya should go, too, so as to look grief-stricken.

I meant to pitch the idea to her when I took her her dinner, but it occurred to me that the Hôtel Ma Cherie happened to have a much bigger kitchen than Priya's and mine, and it were an awful lot closer to the jail than my ranch house. And it occurred to me likewise that the Hôtel Ma Cherie was the place to go to see Priya's lawyer, Miss Francina Wilde, and that as part of my radical plan to get into fewer terrible scrapes that made for funny stories later, and also to keep my Priya happy, possibly I should talk through things with her and let her know about Cowboy's lawyer.

So with that in mind, I took Molly down the long switch-backed road from the Kindness place—and past our little ranch, too, though I only blew it a kiss in passing and hoped I'd be back in time to milk my poor cow. Fortunately she hadn't calved yet, and it was late enough in her cycle that she was barely producing a trickle.

Rapid City was mostly wood buildings, and once you got through the outlying farms and ranches that clung to the hillsides over the Sound that had already been cleared by logging, you quickly found yourself riding along one bank of the river or the other.

There weren't a horse crossing below Logtown, where they had a barge ferry on a rope set up, until you got into Rapid proper—and the river was too rough to ford even if it hadn't been full of redwood and hardwood logs being floated down to the splitting mills.

Rapid City came by its name honestly, even if it had been changed from the original Rain City to drum up business, immigration, and tourism. So you'd find yourself riding along parallel with some wagonload of turnips or tired prospector on a tireder mule on the other side of the canyon, and over the roar of the water all you could manage was a wave.

Or possibly a bullet, if you had a rifle along and spotted somebody you didn't like much.

Then you'd come past the railroad tracks, and that trestle had a footbridge slung under it for people who was so all-fired to get across they didn't mind a cinder in their hair or possibly a tie spike rattling loose and bouncing off their noggin. Current hairstyles and hats for ladies might afford a little protection, but even a Stetson hat ain't gonna shed a hot clinker the way it sheds rain. Anyway, you couldn't get a horse across it, less'n it were a little foal you could carry in your arms.

So I went on past.

Molly was grumpy for whatever horsy reason she had—probably because I'd just ridden her right past her barn and her nice warm clean straw and her oats and her hay, and I'd probably be a little miffed about that also. And she didn't know there'd be a bran mash for her at l'Hôtel Ma Cherie to make up for my perfidiousness. So I had my hands full keeping her on the rein and on the road, especially when we passed a patch of new spring grass just poking up all greeny-yellow and delicious out of the roadside mud. She wanted that grass pretty bad, and I had to thump her in the ribs to keep her going. She did, though not without an ear twist that told me what she thought of me.

Still, she was being a good mare, despite all her own inclinations, and so I reached up under her streaky red-and-gray mane and scratched her around the spots at the top of her neck that are always sweaty and itchy. There's no creature on this earth as has got ears that don't like to be scratched behind 'em, my ma would say, and I ain't never found evidence to contradict her.

Also I never get tired of marveling at Molly's spots and her variegated hide. It's downright magical how complicated she is, being—

Well, picture a red horse. A nice sorrel. Now, picture a red horse somebody has dumped a whole bucket of white paint over. Two buckets. And then ridden through a river of white paint. And *then* blown more white paint around the face and legs through a hollow straw, and then another layer of red over that, and then dabbed with big oval polka dots all over the withers and rump. Paint yellow and gray streaks on her hooves, and white and red streaks in her mane, and that's pretty much my Molly.

She was busy as a patchwork dress, is what I'm saying. I think if she could have figured out a way to get some tiger stripes in there also she probably would have.

After the trestle bridge, there was a stand of trees, and then there was the start of the houses. Lots of houses, cheek by jowl houses by ranch standards, close enough so you could see one another's windows and wave from porch to porch. They started off modest, but street by street got better until I was in the neighborhood where the mayor's house stood, with all its yellow scalloped siding and lavender-and-mauve trim. It would have been nice to veer off there and see Madame, but I didn't have the time and I needed to get downtown to the Hôtel Ma Cherie before business started booming. Wednesday nights were slow. But there was slow and there was slow, and a slow night in a whorehouse still means the person you want to talk to might be entertaining a client for an hour or two.

It weren't far. A city without streetcars—yet, Madame Mayor's got plans—ain't gonna be bigger than you can walk across in a half hour or maybe a whole one. Once you got off the bumpy part and onto the level, where the bowl of the rising hills turned into the dish that cupped the cream of the city, to stretch a metaphor past recognition, it wouldn't have taken me fifteen minutes to ride Molly right up to the waters of the Sound.

Traffic increased, picking up from one or two riders or walkers to a steady stream of pedestrians, and some wagons, and mules and handcarts and God knows what. There was the smells, too. Fires and baked bread and the aromas of Chinatown I couldn't put a name to. Horse dung and human piss and rotting food, too, less appetizing than the other smells. Well, horse manure ain't too bad. You get used to it. And horses themselves smell kind of pleasant, if'n you ask me.

I avoided Skid Road as I descended. I didn't want to deal with Molly *and* skidded logs, though it were late in the day for that business. So my road took me past the exhibition grounds and the airfield. There was an airship in or two, but nothing going on at the grounds today except what must have been a Mad Science duel, except it was more of a Mad Science breakdown. From Molly's back, I could see two comparatively tiny figures poking around the feet of a couple of giant Megarms. One was brass-colored, and arched way backward with its forelimbs upraised to the heavens as if it were crying out in outrage at early morning back pain. The other one was bent full forward, and folded in half with its forehead resting on the ground between its feet and its arms splayed limp around it. That one was enameled fawn-colored and in place of hands it had two great augurs that glittered along the spiral edge.

Well, at least the articulation was flexible.

I recognized the beige one from the other day. It belonged to Dr. von Hammerstein. But she'd made some changes to it since then.

Like Priya and the Singer. Mad Scientists, you can't leave them alone with a wrench and a screwdriver unless you plan to come home and find everything in the house disassembled and put back together in different combinations.

I was glad they wasn't fighting this time, for Molly's sake. I tried to let her feel how unconcerned I was about giant Mega-Armatures in my seat. She seemed utterly unconcerned about giant Mega-Armatures, at least busted ones, whether my seat was telling her so or not.

Good mare. She don't worry overmuch. And she'd seen the damned things before.

She was less fond of that revival tent, which seemed to be doing a booming business for an operation that wasn't supposed to open until tomorrow, by the flyer we'd had. There was a lot of people packed into and around it, and a lot of shouting going on. But we managed.

They was closing up the streets downtown, which I suspected was a direct result of Madame leaning on people.

When I say closing up the streets, mind, I don't mean that they're not letting traffic through. So there's a peculiarity about Rapid, which I hear has been a problem in Seattle and Chicago and Boston and other places, too, where the lowest level of the streets was too low, and prone to flooding when the tide came in. And so what they did was just raised the whole city up on fill. Excepting where there was already a few hundred buildings built, you ain't gonna just pull them down and fill and start building all over. No, what you do is you raise the streets and leave the old plank walk beside the buildings as a buffer, and then you roof it over with a new plank walk and skylights in it. They use those crystals you put in the decks of ships to let daylight into the hold.

They could work worse, I suppose. But I'd be stretching the truth if I claimed it weren't shadowy and dark down there. At night when the lamps was lit—if the property holder on that block in particular sprang for lamps, anyway—it was a little brighter.

Folk who had to use those passages still generally brought torches and torchbearers, though.

Anyway, when I first came to Rapid, a lot of those ditches hadn't been covered over, and the trenches had a well-known tendency to claim a few lives every year. And more than a few broken ankles. And peeped-up petticoats.

We was all pretty glad when Madame Mayor kicked the chamber of commerce in the rump a few times and got them moving on a project that had been what you call languishing for years. The next step was supposed to be building stairs in place of all them treacherous ladders. I weren't sure, though, if the sort of stairs those folk were likely to build weren't more likely to be deadly than a ladder. A ladder, you're a mite cautious on. Stairs, even the neck-breaking type, people get careless. And a careless or a drunk person on a steep wet stair ain't gonna have no good result.

I was thinking that as I rode past the jail and saw Miss Francina coming out, her face a mask of professional politeness I knew meant she were beyond angry. Well, that was going to delay my visit to the Cherry Hotel. I reined Molly out of traffic and stopped beside her. Standing up on the plank walk out of the road, Miss Francina was tall enough to come up past Molly's withers.

"Wat's wrong?" I said, not even certain what I was fearing. Molly stepped sideways under the weight of my emotion.

She reached out and patted my knee. "Are you going inside right now?"

"I was going to head over to the Cherry Hotel first and see if I could rustle up some grub for Priya's supper."

"As it happens, I'm going that way myself."

She suited stride to words, covering the ground in an angry swish of green taffeta. I reined Molly alongside. She went easy now, neck long and nose leading.

"Problem with the sheriff?" I asked.

"Problem with your wife," she said tartly.

"Oh, no." I pictured half a dozen catastrophes.

"The sheriff I can handle. 'Oh, sheriff, you don't think that little slip of a girl could really have beaten two grown men to hash, do you honey?'" she mocked. Then she lowered her voice, glancing about to see if anybody was close before she continued. "The sheriff, let's say, has certain proclivities he might not wish lauded about. That, and the bond on your ranch, was enough to get her sprung."

"That's a dangerous game," I murmured back, letting the clop of hooves cover my words. "Men who's ashamed of themselves take it out on the women they blame for feeling shamed."

"Oh, don't I know it," she answered. "Feel bad for hitting a woman, the solution is to hit her harder. Like they got to prove to themselves you deserved the hitting in the first place and you ain't really a person anyhow."

I had expected bravada from Miss Francina—but she laid her hand on my knee once more and finished, "Karen honey. But Priya's worth the risk, now, isn't she?"

"So what's the problem?"

We came up on the whorehouse stable then, and Miss Francina said, "I'll tell you inside."

I swung down, feeling weirdly out of place in my ranch-wife sprigged cotton. I still had my whoring clothes, packed away in a chest with cedar, and it occurred to me that I could sell those, too.

But it felt strange to be standing in the courtyard of the rebuilt Hôtel Ma Cherie and wearing buttons up to my chin.

Jack (all grooms is named Jack) came out and took Molly for me. I told him I wouldn't be long, but to take off her tack and give her her supper. He nodded and patted her on the shoulder cheerily. "All hospitality of the house for Miss Molly!"

We went inside, and I asked the new cook, a short, muscular woman named Emily, if she could put together a basket for Priya. Emily winked, flexed an arm like a circus strongman, and said, "I hope she likes cornpone."

Because we went in through the kitchen, I had the delight of surprising Crispin Hayden at the front door. He swept me up in a hug the likes of which I hadn't felt since Da died, then set me down very gently and said, "Miss Karen, I do apologize. I was overcome."

"Oh hush up, Crispin," I said, and threw myself at him again.

When we was done hugging, he stroked my hair—in the side, where the hatpin wouldn't get him—and said, "I'm so sorry about Miss Priya."

"We'll have her out in a minute," Miss Francina said, steel in her voice. "Come, Karen. Sit and have tea."

She took me into the private parlor, the one the girls don't show the custom, and we sat on big white brocade couches while Emily brought in tea and biscuits and cream. Signor the white cat came in and hopped right up on my lap like I had never been gone, purring his fool deaf head off. I felt something unkink in my chest.

"So what are you so all-fired furious about on the jail steps," I said. "You said you got Priya out? Where is she?"

"Still in the jail." She sighed, swirling the tea in its willow-patterned china. "Saying she won't leave without that mechanical."

"Oh, Priya," I said. Even though I was secretly proud of her.

"This could be a big problem," Miss Francina said. "I don't know if I can make it all go away."

"We'll think of something. I ain't scared," I said.

"Karen, honey." Miss Francina tossed her ringlets at me. "Nobody is more scared than somebody who can't admit it."

"Oh," I said. "I ain't saying I ain't *been* scared. You know I have. Or that I ain't gonna be scared again. Or even that I ain't scared for Priya and what might happen to her. Because you know and I know that that would all be just bluster. I been orphaned and starved and thrown from horses. I've whored. I been electrocuted and mind-controlled and kidnapped and shot at and caught in bar brawls and I been set on fire. You know I was scared as a coyote through all them things. But I ain't gonna *live* scared, all mured up in guns and posturing and telling people all the time what an asskicker I aim to be and how scared they oughta be of me."

Her eyes sparkled as she poured the tea. "Why do I have the sense you might be thinking of somebody in particular?"

I helped myself to another biscuit. They weren't Connie's biscuits, but they were damned fine. And Connie's biscuits had the advantage of being a nostalgic memory.

"Why Miss Francina," I replied. "I surely do not have any idea what you mean by that. And here's to Sheriff MacGregor, wherever he may be."

Her laughter was interrupted by a sharp rap on the front door. We had left the parlor door open, and I turned to see Crispin slide the peephole open.

"I'm sorry," he called through it. "House is closed until candletime."

A crisp Eastern voice came back, "Thank you, but I'm here professionally. Doc Swan sent me."

I jumped to my feet and it's a good thing my teacup was empty or I would have spilled it everywhere. "That's the lawyer!"

"Lawyer?" said Miss Francina, setting *her* cup down with neat precision before rising like a graceful tide.

"I came here to tell you, Cowboy's owner called a lawyer in from back East."

"Oh boy," said Miss Francina. "This, I cannot wait to see."

Chapter Fourteen

When the door swung wide, I saw silhouetted a very tall narrow man all in somber black like a Quaker, made even taller by his beaver hat. A gentle hissing sound accompanied him, and the faint whiff of machine oil. When he stepped inside, I heard the rattle of mechanicals, and he moved stiffly on one side of his body.

Then he stepped one step farther into the light, and Crispin dropped a startled bow. I about wet myself, and Miss Francina emitted a mouse squeak she would have denied unto death.

"Greetings and felicitations," the tall man said.

The rattle and hiss, I could see, was because a mechanical armature mostly concealed under his coat supported his frame and moved for him. A metal cradle cupped his skull on the left side, and his hazel-gray right eye looked out from a sculptured plate replacing the upper half of his face on that side. He wore a thick graying beard but no mustache, and when he reached up to take off his hat the chassis gave a click and hummed faintly.

"Abraham Lincoln, Esquire. At your service, ladies, gentleman."

This was the man whose life Doc Swan had saved? No wonder she had been so amused by her secret.

I stood there, swoggled, and stared like a poleaxed nanny goat into the ruined, ugly, sainted face of the man who freed the slaves and saved the Union and came within a quarter inch of dying a martyr for it. If it wasn't for him, I thought, Crispin might still be in chains somewhere. My friend Marshal Reeves would be a hunted runaway.

I had been three years old when he was shot, but my ma and da had been abolitionists and they had worshipped this man. If he'd died, Ma said, that might have been the end of Reconstruction, and Andrew Johnson of all the blackguards on earth would have been President.

I knew my friend Tomoatooah might have a different impression of him. Lincoln hadn't stopped the resettlements or the massacres, and there had been the Mankato hangings of thirty-eight Dakota men accused of war crimes, back during the war when I was just new born. Until I spent time with the Comanche warrior who'd saved my life I am ashamed to say I hadn't thought much about the Indian side of all that. So I froze up like my namesake dove when the hawk is circling, caught between two different impulses.

Luckily, Miss Francina collected her wits and lunged into hospitality. "Please sir, come in and sit. Make yourself at home."

"Excellent," he said, handing his hat to Crispin. "Miss Wilde, I presume? I understand you're representing young Miss Swati. We better get this wrapped up before Good Friday, I think, or it'll be another week before our clients have a chance of being released."

I blinked, having plumb forgotten that Easter was on Sunday. This is the sort of corruption of the spirit that overtakes you when you're shacked up without benefit of matrimony with a heathen fallen woman, I suppose.

"So we've got to do this tomorrow," said Miss Francina. "Sir, please sit. Will you take tea? Or a nice cup of coffee?"

"Oh yes," he said. "A cup of coffee would be capital. Shall we get to work at once?"

The silence upstairs was a dead giveaway. All the little noises of the house had stopped. I raised my eyes to the landing of the grand stair and saw Miss Bethel, Miss Lizzie, Beatrice, and half a dozen other girls all lined up behind the balustrade, peeking down with eyes as big as cats.

"Maybe we'd better go into my office," Miss Francina said, never glancing upward. "Karen, honey, why don't you come along?"

Crispin carried the tray up the stairs for us, and Miss Francina and Mr. Lincoln and me settled in on the velvet chairs by the coffee table in the office that used to be Madame Damnable's. Miss Francina had redecorated a little, but the big carved desk was the same, though it had a new shell-pink blotter. The chairs were the same but had been reupholstered. The same shell pink, and the curtains were now pale gold.

It lightened up the heavy dark wood, and I decided I liked it.

We sat and ate cookies—Mr. Lincoln lived up to his reputation for abstemiousness, having only two of Emily's butter cookies though they was so good I had to sit on my hands to keep from stuffing them all down. Nutmeg and a little vanilla. Delicious.

"Miss Francina got Priya sprung," I said. "but she says Priya won't leave until Cowboy is released also."

"Miss Swati sounds like a woman of principle," Mr. Lincoln said. "What is your relationship to her?"

"We're partners," I said, and let him make of it what he would. "We own a little ranch together. We're just getting started."

"And you were both working on the motion picture to make ends meet?"

I remembered he grew up poor on a farm. I imagined he knew all about it. I nodded.

His chassis hissed gently as he sipped his coffee. "Do they have any evidence that you're aware of?"

"No," I said. "Just picking up the Indian girl and the mechanical because they was standing there, I imagine." I paused and stared at him for a moment before I decided to trust him. He was who he was, after all. "My partner and I own an industrial Singer chassis. It's missing."

"That's not good," he said. "Where was it before?"

So I told him all about the padlocked barn, and Priya's desire to be a Mad Scientist, and halfway through it occurred to me that the Mad Science chassis that helped Mr. Lincoln walk and drink tea wasn't all that different to the Singer.

His unassuming manner made it easy to forget myself. I rattled on at a snake's length until Miss Francina caught my eye, and then I stopped, blushing. "Anyway, Priya was a little weird about Mister Evans when she caught sight of him and won't tell me why. But that's not a reason to murder somebody. And it ain't a reason to murder Mister Kindness, neither!"

"Your partner is going to have to reveal what troubled her," said Mr. Lincoln formally. "To us, at least, and possibly to the court when the judge gets here—if not to the sheriff. But the question is, of course, what did Mister Evans and Mister Kindness have in common that led them to that place and time? And we will need to find the missing sewing machine."

"There's another sewing machine, too. And I'd imagine there are some armatures they use for loading and unloading and setting up and whatnot. Drivable ones, I mean. Not mechanicals like Cowboy."

Miss Francina steepled her fingers under her chin. "Karen, you're on set—and Priya will be, too, once we convince her that the best way to help Cowboy is to go back to work and help you investigate."

"You're gonna get me fired," I said. "But that would not stop me."

"The motion picture director has a vested interest in getting his property back, especially as Cowboy is vital to the scenario of the motion picture," Mr. Lincoln said. A little tightness squeezed his voice when he said "property."

So the man was still an abolitionist. That was good to know. "And unless he's the killer, he has a vested interest in finding out who murdered his producer, don't you think?"

I weren't completely sure what a vested interest was—I guessed it was legal speak—but I nodded. "I'm pretty sure it weren't him as did for Mister Evans and Mister Kindness, as I had eyes on him when they bit the ground."

"Can you swear to that in a court of law?"

I thought about it. "We was shooting a stunt, and I guess he could of snuck off while I was busy with something else, but I can't imagine him having the time to do it without somebody noticing he was gone. And Cowboy wasn't around, but he ain't supposed to be able to hurt somebody nohow."

I remembered the map Evans and Kindness had been smirking over like a couple of broody hens. And how at pains they had been to either hide that they was up to something, or... or pretend they was hiding that they was up to something?

Would I give odds they hadn't been baiting a hook with that performance? Reader, I would not swear that on a California prayer book, let alone the Holy Bible.

Where *had* that map got off to? And why was a motion picture filming all the way up here in Rain County? I understood the industry was moving from Chicago to San Diego because of the need for sun—but sun was not a commodity we had a lot of here. And I've seen enough of the desert in California in motion pictures to know it made a perfectly fine Wild West town. Unless we were supposed to be back East, but why not use Chicago then?

The Kindness ranch had some beautiful cliffs overlooking the Sound. But I imagined San Diego had sea cliffs, too, from what I remembered from Da teaching me geography. It was right on the ocean, wasn't it?

None of that made any sense, and whatever was going on, I was all of a sudden certain that map was kissing cousin to it.

"Mister Lincoln," I said. "Miss Francina. There's something I ought to tell you. Was there a map found on either of the bodies?"

"Not that I heard," said Miss Francina.

Just then, Emily came in with a wicker basket that smelled of every good thing and put it on the table by the door. Miss

Francina stood, with a rustle, and Mr. Lincoln stood a moment behind her. "It's getting late. Tell us on the way to the jail, Karen?"

I filled them in along the walk, talking low and fast so nobody would overhear me. Pleasant people passed the time of day with me and with Miss Francina. A few nice ones commiserated with me about Priya behind arrested, and a few nosy ones pried for details. There was more than a few double takes aimed at Mr. Lincoln, and all that slowed down our progress until I was fretting.

But, "Keep people on your side," Miss Francina whispered. And so I smiled and was polite.

To our bad fortune, Sheriff MacGregor was minding the store himself when we got there. Miss Francina touched my arm as we entered—ahead of Mr. Lincoln, because he was a gentleman—and whispered, "Let Mister Lincoln do the talking, Karen," as if she could read the look on my face like a book.

I stepped to the side, and Mr. Lincoln came up beside Miss Francina and said, "Allow me to introduce myself, Sheriff. I'm Abraham Lincoln, attorney. I'm here to see about the release of Miss Swati and the mechanical known as Cowboy."

Sheriff MacGregor blinked at him, set his pipe aside, and rose slowly, still blinking. I guess it's not every day a living legend creaks into your place of business and demands to see the owner.

For a hot second I thought he was going to snub Lincoln, but after a meditative chaw he thrust his flipper out and shook Mr.

Lincoln's extended hand. The dainty finger rings on the ex-president's armature curled carefully around MacGregor's hand, and I could see from the look down that MacGregor was thinking about whether those long-fingered fists could be used to beat somebody to death.

Probably, I thought, but not without leaving you with some bloodied knuckles.

And that was another thing. How had the killer gotten both men down so fast and furious? While you dealt with one, wouldn't the other try to run?

Then I realized that of course the first thing you would do is break one's legs, before you did down the other one. I managed not to retch or make a face, thinking on it, but it ain't always a kindness being possessed of a good imagination.

I'd missed some of the conversation. When I brought myself back from my terrible thoughts, I heard, "...That little Hindu girl is free to go and has been since this afternoon. I want her ass out of here, not to put too fine a point on it."

He winked at Lincoln.

Lincoln regarded him stolidly.

Macgregor cleared his throat. "We could remand the mechanical to the custody of its owner."

"I'm his owner's lawyer," said Mr. Lincoln. "I'll see to that."

That little twitch of the hooded eye again, this time on the word "owner." If MacGregor noticed it, I should never play poker with the man, because his expression was as placid as a milked cow.

Which made me wonder if I should play poker with Lincoln. Maybe his eye weren't doing that on accident.

One thing and another, Priya and Cowboy walked out of that jail half an hour later as more or less temporarily free personages, in the company of me, Miss Francina, and Mr. Lincoln.

"So we can get back to work tomorrow," I said to Priya. "And get back to being nosy parkers."

Cowboy said, "I would enjoy, if I might, assisting you in your efforts to solve the crime."

"You are very much welcome to," Priya said. "The only good thing about our detention, Cowboy, is that we got to know one another better."

My wife, there, treating a machine like a human being. I felt my jealousy kick up, but reminded itself that childish displays were beneath me, a grown woman of seventeen. And maybe she knew something I didn't.

When it came to machines and mechanicals and Mad Science, she *definitely* knew something I didn't.

"Well," I said. "I imagine we all need the wages."

"I am not paid wages, Miss Memery," Cowboy said.

I looked at him. "You work as hard as anybody on that set. Maybe harder." Mostly, other than me, folk on the set was talent or they was manual labor. Cowboy and me split the difference, along with Black and Jodi.

Cowboy said, "My owner is compensated for my labor."

"Mister Cowboy," Mr. Lincoln said. "Your owner is still Doc Swan, is that right?"

"She built me," Cowboy said. "Mister Forth holds my license for the duration of this motion picture."

"I am surprised," said Mr. Lincoln, stepping deftly around an ox pie in the road, "that Doc Swan would license you out."

"Maintenance is expensive both for humans and mechanicals."

I said, "So you don't get paid, and you're considered property. Didn't we fight a war about that?"

Lincoln chortled, his dour ugly face sweetened by a grin. "Don't I know it."

All of my previous apprehension about Cowboy seemed to have fled into moral outrage. "Why are you letting Doc Swan get away with that?" I asked Lincoln.

Yes, gentle reader. I got so het up about robot rights that I went right up into Abraham Lincoln's chin whiskers.

"Can we argue later?" Priya said. "I want to go home."

I looked over at her. She seemed worn down to the bootlaces, and it hadn't even been twenty-four hours. And she knew more about slavery than I ever would, and might not want to hear my righteous outrage on the subject. I looked down at the picnic basket I was still carrying, because we hadn't needed it. "Let's take this back to the Cherry Hotel and eat it in the kitchen with Emily. And then we'll get Molly and do just what you suggest, Priya dear."

"To answer your earlier question now that everybody is fed, I am letting her get away with it," Lincoln said, setting down a fried chicken bone, "because by law, somebody has to own Cowboy. If Doc Swan didn't, then somebody else who might not consider him a thinking creature would."

"That's the law?" Priya asked, horrified.

Lincoln nodded.

I wasn't sure I considered Cowboy a thinking creature. I mean, everybody said mechanicals were just automatons with complicated tapes in them, right? They could do things—chores, stunts—but they didn't really have souls. Man made them, not God, so how could they?

Except maybe God gave it to Man to make them, and then—

"They used to say women didn't have souls," Priya said. "Or heathens like me."

I looked at her. "You read that off my face?"

"Your face talks more than your mouth does," she said around her chicken. It was perfect chicken, too, fried crisp and drizzled with honey and red pepper. I only managed not to take a second piece because I was hoping Priya would eat more. "And that's saying something!"

"Priya!" I yelped, scandalized—but she said it with love, and worse, she weren't wrong.

"I believe I have a mind," Cowboy said quietly from his place in the corner. "As for a soul, well. Who can prove the existence or lack of such in anyone?"

"I've been meaning to ask you," I said to Mr. Lincoln, feeling emboldened, "why did you have them Sioux men hanged?"

If everything I'm thinking passes across my face, reader, you can't say the same for Honest Abe. His countenance stilled as stone, bushy eyebrows drawing together only a little.

Then he said, "Because I thought I had to. We commuted as many sentences as we could, you know."

I hadn't known. "Do you think that mattered to the ones who died, and to their families?"

He shook his head, a tick of the gears as he moved. "No."

____

Priya and me rode Molly double back to the ranch, and to prove I love her I let her sit in my lap the whole way, even though my legs got numb. She proved her love for me by getting the saddle horn right in the pink bits, so I guessed we was evens.

By the time we got home the sun was set and that old cow was standing in the dooryard, lowing. "You get the horse taken care of," Priya said. "I'll milk the cow."

I would have protested but both things needed doing with equal urgency, so I got on my half of the bargain, finished up, and was inside with the lamp and hearth lit, making tea by the time Priya tottered in, lugging the bucket with both hands.

"She'd better calve soon," Priya said. "She looks like a blown-up sheep bladder."

I was sorting the mail, which I'd picked up at General Delivery on our way back to the Cherry Hotel. There was a letter from Bass Reeves' wife, Jennie—she being the lettered one in that family—and a letter that I made a face over before I handed it to Priya. "Your da wrote."

"Appa," she corrected absently, taking the letter with a reluctant hand. The address was in English but I knew the words inside would be in that boxy curlicue script that looked to me like a real elegant bit of tablet weaving.

"I'll fix you some of that tea," I said.

When I came back with the tea, Priya was sitting with her chin on her hand, the letter resting on the table beside the lamp. She'd draped a clean cloth over the milk bucket, so I knew she weren't too shattered... but she didn't look ready to get up and go put it in the cold room, so I knew she also weren't perfectly all right.

"What did he say?"

"He said," Priya said tonelessly, "that there's a man who wants to marry me, and that I should come home at once."

"Oh," I said. "What do you think about that?"

"I think he's going to be very disappointed to learn I can't come because I'm under suspicion of murder," Priya said brightly, and tossed the letter onto the fire.

––––––––––

There's that old saw about how if you love something you gotta set it free, and you know I always did have some questions regarding that one. Because it ain't no kindness to kick your collie dog out to run on the hills. Man made that animal and man had the raising of it, and that poor dog's most merciful fate under such circumstances is to get eaten by the coyotes.

I guess there's my answer as to whether something mankind made can have a soul. I've known preachers as said dogs had no souls, and we all know that's hogwash, don't we?

What dogs ain't got is original sin. They're just dogs. Like horses is just horses. Dogs don't need no redemption because dogs ain't never fell.

The curse of the tree of knowledge is being made overconscious and overanxious of yourself and everything you take up. Dogs ain't worried they're sniffing butts wrong.

Dogs at least got that over a child that ain't yet got its judgment nor reason grown. That child might be born a sinner, but it can be raised up in grace. Let it run loose with no schooling nor discipline though and there won't, I promise you, be no good result.

But then there's Priya and her da, where he's hell-bent on pruning her to fit his trellis without no regard for whether it suits the natural shape she's bound to grow to or not. And you don't get good fruit that way, if I may torture a metaphor.

At least what you get is something stunted and misshaped, all twisted up and gnarled inside from being bent in deviations one weren't never meant to grow toward.

So maybe what that old saw means is that you gotta respect the right of the things you love to grown into what they is meant to be. And while you're in there, you gotta find ways to get your own wild heart respected, which ain't no easy trick, neither.

But if you do everything you do out of getting out of other people's way, you're pruning *yourself* to fit their trellis. Which will get you all gnarled and stunted also. Whereas if you go in the other direction and try to lop every bough off your friends that you feel grows into your light, well, after a good few years of that you may not have many friends or much shade to enjoy.

I wondered if that was what had happened to Miss Roman to make her so mean.

It's complicated and it ain't easy, this game of leaving the people you love to become themselves and hoping they still have regard for you. And also allowing yourself to be who you are, but having regard for them.

I wish everybody could be as carelessly certain of herself as Miss Francina.

You marry somebody, sure, and you think that's the package you're getting for life. But you unwrap that package and there's another wrapped package inside. Then one more, and then another. And so on.

You gotta keep your heels down and keep on adjusting.

Being married is a lot like riding. You start thinking what is is what is always gonna be and it ain't gonna change, and you wind up in the bushes or riding a bolt a long way from home.

All that is a long way of saying I was pretty nervous the next morning, when I asked Priya about Evans.

She looked me in the eye and said, "What makes you think I knew anything about Mister Evans?"

"I saw your face, darlin'," I said. Then I stopped. "You didn't know him from... from the crib, did you?"

"No," she said. "Men like that don't come down among the cribs. They patronize places such as the Hôtel Ma Cherie."

Unless their tastes run to hurting, I thought, but had the wits not to say.

Priya rubbed her lean hands together. "I knew him from the ship on the way over. He was one of the procurers who hired us as 'domestics.' And then sold us as slaves. He also stole technology from my homeland and sold it to Peter Bantle as 'inventions.'"

She looked like she wanted to spit, but she wouldn't on our clean split log floor.

"I wouldn't blame you a whit if you had killed him," I said fervently. "Squalene did say he was after the main chance, and not half so charming as he could appear. I guess he got his stake for motion picture producing kidnapping girls out of the Far East, then."

"Your Far East is west of here," Priya said pedantically, and I loved her so much I thought my heart might pop my chest wide open.

"Why did you pretend you didn't know him?"

She laughed. "You said it yourself, Karen. First, because I did not care to lose us the job. Then, after he was dead, because I did not wish to be blamed for his dying. And once I was blamed for his dying I did not wish to make it worse for myself."

Well, I couldn't argue that.

"Come on, honey," I said. "Drink up your tea and let's go to bed."

Chapter Fifteen

The whole moving picture crew turned out for Otis Kindness' funeral. It seemed a strange thing, so many white folk at a black man's graveside, but Miz Kindness was having him buried at the ranch, in a little plot not too far from the cabin window. And it seemed rude not to attend.

Besides, Priya had made her famous curried potato salad for Mourning, so we was obligated. You can't just shove a bowl of salad into someone's hands and skedaddle when they just had their husband brutally murdered and your wife is suspected of the crime. You have to leave it on the table with the other good things, and then you have to stay for the funeral and a decent interval of the wake also.

It was raining, of course—a miserable little drizzle. We motion picture folk all sort of clumped together and tried to stay out of the way, so we had a good view of the other side of the grave during the service. I recognized the faces of a lot of folk from the Baptist church. The tall, dignified Pastor Elwyn Ryan had a voice that carried. He gave a sermon of so much hellfire I wondered if it was always like that in his church or if he had saved it up special for Mr. Kindness.

Crispin Hayden caught my eye from the colored side. I nodded in return, then went back to try to study all the faces around me for evidence of guilt. Now, this might be a mite surprising, given how often those penny dreadfuls say things like "Guilt shone out of his eyes," but nobody's eyes on either side of the grave was a beacon.

There were two white men standing behind the pastor, which surprised me. One was Sheriff MacGregor, who was giving Priya the hairy eyeball the whole time.

The other one was not too big, and not too wide. He wore a white robe over a frock coat and a cleric's collar, and was all pink-faced and scrubbed with his hair greased down tight as a beaver's tail.

Priya nudged my shoulder when my eyes lit on him. I leaned toward her, and she whispered, "Since I am not lying to you any more, Karen, I also know that man. He was a missionary in Tamil Nadu. He worked with Mister Evans."

"Now what are the odds on that?"

"Rapid City is not big," she said. "People who come here mostly bump elbows."

"Or uglies," I quipped, just to watch her cheeks turn red.

Squalene, standing on my other side, nudged me about the whispering and I shut up, so I didn't get to ask the white preacher's name.

The brimstone had continued unabated for ten to fifteen minutes when it gave way, finally, to the hope of redemption in Christ. By then, Pastor Ryan was nearly singing, his big voice rising and falling along with his arms. Each pronouncement was met by a hearty "Amen!," which I joined in on after looking around and seeing a few of the other white folk doing it. I didn't want to seem rude, nor like no spectator.

The widow was easy to pick out. She stood front and center, her narrow hands folded in front of her narrow hips, her black dress a little weathered and dusty at the hem. Her face was a little weathered, too, but scrubbed bright, and her hair was graying at the temples and twisted back into a good tight bun.

That black face had an even blacker bruise on one cheekbone, and she didn't look transported with grief. She just looked tired.

My heart went out to her. There were three crude little wooden grave markers next to the big one at Otis Kindness' head. Had any children survived? Would they come home if she sent for them?

How was she going to run this big old place alone?

Four strong men—one of them Crispin—stepped up as the preacher wound down his eulogy. One stood at each corner of the coffin. They picked up the ropes slung under it and shuffled themselves around the grave before carefully lowering that pine box down.

Miz Mourning stood for a long minute, watching as they snaked the ropes out. Then she bent down and with an air of finalism picked up a handful of dirt which was just about mud, and dribbled it over the grave like she was sugaring a cake-top.

It was a gentle gesture. Even if the dirt was so wet it fell down in spatters rather than as a soft earthy rain.

And I thought, and said to Priya, "Maybe we can offer to help out with her farm chores until she can get somebody permanent in."

"We've only got one horse," Priya said. "And I'm no cow-puncher."

"Maybe we could get another horse," I said, thinking of Angel Maker—and thinking of the bay dun mare, who Priya could ride with no trouble. I'd never put her on that stud. Not that she would get up there, being a mite more on the sensible side than the other half of this partnership.

"I'm going to talk to her," I said, and moved forward.

There was a ring of well-wishers around Miz Mourning. Pastor Ryan had headed toward the outhouse—briefly, I assumed, and probably to answer Nature's call—and I wasn't going to push through a bunch of church ladies to offer up my harebrained scheme.

It only takes one mistake to scare a horse or a human in ways that can take ages to unkink, and I didn't want to scare Mourning Kindness.

Not everybody had my scruples, though. Because as I waited politely at the end of Miz Kindness's reception line, that other preacher shoved past us and everybody else and inserted himself at the head of the line.

Some people's children ain't got no raising, I tell you what.

"Wait," I said as he bent urgently over Miz Kindness, who was wiping the mud off her hands on a rag, "that's... what's-his-name, Father Postlethwait, isn't it? The faith healer that's done pitched his tent down by the fairground."

"Pulsifer Postlethwait. That is what I was trying to tell you," Priya whispered back. "But you had to make a joke about it."

It smarted like a whack on the nose, but she wasn't wrong about me. And so I didn't even point out that she hadn't told me she knew this man, either, when that lad handed us the advertising sheet about the tent revival.

I felt guilty for feeling suspicious, so I touched her arm in apology and bent my ear toward Father Postlethwait and Miz Kindness.

He was saying, "...I would assume the debts, of course. And you'd be free of this place. You could go somewhere else and start over. You're not old yet, you know—"

"I need to think on it," she said, in a voice that suggested she sure *felt* old. Or maybe that she was old enough to know better.

"If I can't find land for a church, I must move on after Easter." He leaned in closer. "I don't have much time, Miz Mourning. This offer won't stand and you'll be left high and dry."

In the crowd, I saw Crispin's mouth twitch, and made a note to myself to call her Miz Kindness no matter what.

"Sign the deed over to me," he urged. "It'd be a good work, and lighten the burden on your soul."

She was turned half away from him, her hand raised, and that was enough for me—no man of the cloth was so godly he had the right to hassle a widow on her husband's funeral day. And if he was Mike Evans' old business partner, and by extension connected to Peter Bantle, well that just made me all the more dubious.

As far as I knew, nobody had found that map, and as far as I knew, nobody but me and Priya was looking for it.

"Miz Mourning—" He put a hand on her shoulder, and I saw her flinch with her whole body at the touch.

I stepped forward, squaring my shoulders while Priya murmured, "Here we go again," and let go of my arm.

"Excuse me, Father," I said to Postlethwait. "But the lady said no."

He looked at me down his nose, which was pretty funny because he weren't no taller'n me. "Who are you?"

"I'm Miss Memery," I said, deciding right then and there he didn't get my Christian name. "I own the next ranch down the mountain, the Bent D. Miz Kindness here just said she needed some time, and I'll appreciate it if you let my neighbor alone for a mite. She is just right now burying her husband."

I was starting to suspect there was a reason Mike Evans and Pulsifer Postlethwait had come to this out-of-the-way place on their various excuses. And I was starting to suspect as well that it had something to do with that map that had vanished. Or maybe it hadn't vanished. Maybe I just didn't know where to look for it.

I felt the steady presence of Crispin breathing at my back, which made me a little bolder than I might have been. And I was a white woman, something I knew from working with Crispin for a year and some gave me latitude in dealing with the unruly that he didn't have, always. I said, in my calmest voice, "I think you should let the lady alone."

"Aren't you the famous whore?" Postlethwait asked, drawing himself up to his full five foot seven or so. "I've heard your name around town. You ought to be ashamed to show your face where decent people are."

And suddenly I was the eye of a hurricane, as Squalene Jones blew up beside and said, in ringing tones, "You shut your cock holster, preacher man."

Gasps, hands over mouths. People took a step back all around us. Postlethwait got red starting from his collar and rising up to his thick brown curls. "Well," he said, "I never."

He spun on the ball of his foot and stalked away.

"Language, young lady," said Miz Kindness gently to Squalene.

Squalene blushed, pulled her hat off, and scuffed the earth like a schoolboy.

Miz Kindness turned to me. "They're telling me your woman did the killing on my man. Is that so, Miss Memery?"

"No," I said. "I do not think so. Ma'am, we're neighbors, as I said, though we haven't much met yet. You just give me'n Priya a yell if you need anything at all, and I mean anything. I can bring in your stock, or whatever."

She put her hand to her mouth. Her eyes went a little wet just at the edges, when they had stayed dry this whole funeral. "That's very sweet, young miss," she said. "I got my church folk to help out, but that's very sweet of you."

"Nevertheless," I said. "Nevertheless."

And that was how I met Mourning Kindness, who did not seem to be in mourning.

But that wasn't the end of the fun at the funeral. Because as Priya and me was walking away, MacGregor caught Priya by the elbow. He swung her around, and I stepped in between them so he and me was nose to nose and Priya was pressed up against my back.

He let go of her and loomed over me. "You've got a lot of brass showing up for this funeral."

Rain was running down my face and ruining my hair, and I wasn't in no mood for any of this man's shenanigans. "We work here, Sheriff. And it's polite. But I don't expect you would know about politeness."

Priya stepped out from behind me and stood at my right hand.

"I want to know where your fancy lawyer came from. And why the hell he's cluttering up my life with his paperwork."

"Why Sheriff," said a sweet voice, "He's here because he's an old friend of mine, and I'm Cowboy's owner. Thank you for releasing my property, by the way."

It was Doc Swan. And the look on MacGregor's face from being confronted by an Indian woman, a part-Celestial one, and a white one simultaneously was worth it.

"You don't fool me, you little Hindu whore," he snarled at Priya. "You lied about knowing that Evans man. You worked for Peter Bantle, and he worked with Peter Bantle."

"Peter Bantle kidnapped me," Priya said, "I think you will find is the correct construction. And Mister Evans was his partner in that kidnapping." She smiled. "So was Father Postlethwait, if you weren't aware. Maybe Postlethwait had a reason to kill Mike Evans. I would look into that, if I were you."

Chapter Sixteen

There would be no filming that morning, because of the rain, so I took up the stock work and Priya went off to the machine shop. Cowboy hadn't attended the funeral, but I saw him moving around set with loads of scenery, and when he saw me in the distance he waved.

When I had finished with the other horses, I went to spend a half hour before lunch gentling Angel Maker.

The big horse stood in the mud, head down, letting the rain roll down his face from his mane. My Boss of the Plains was keeping my head dry, even though my shoulders and my lower half was drenched. He didn't have the advantage of a hat and I didn't think he'd thank me to offer him one.

I slipped through the fence—getting more wet in the process—and stood beside it. I knowed he'd noticed me: the head came up ever so slightly and the ears twitched my way—but I guessed he was too wet to have much interest in histrionics. I had a pocket full of dried apples—well, they used to be dried, before the weather got to them—and I pulled one out and held it on an open hand as I approached. Not too direct, and not staring at him like a hunting dog. But at an angle, the way a friendly horse would come up on him. I'd watched my da do it this way a thousand times, and for a second my breath caught in my chest on how much I missed him.

I stood there, the apple outstretched, until the paddock mud about washed through my boots and my fingertips shriveled like I'd been in a bath. Angel Maker eyed me, eyed the apple—and turned his head away.

Now that were a request for space, and I decided to let him have it. I stepped back into deeper mud, squelching like to drown a frog, and he swung oward me again. He had a big eye over those high cheekbones, and right now for the first time it was brown and soft.

"Hey fella," I said. "You been through a lot, ain't you?"

Hesitantly, he stretched toward me and sniffed that apple bit. His whiskers tickled my palm and his neck went so long if you saw him in one of them there zoological gardens, he could have passed for a giraffe. Big lips brushed my palm, and the apple bit disappeared. He reeled his head back, but took a step toward me.

I fished out another apple bit.

So it went for maybe a quarter hour, with me getting wetter and wetter and him getting calmer and calmer. Finally, with the last apple bit, he let me put my hand against his cheek. We stood like that for a minute, his eyes half-closed, and then he snorted and stepped back.

"All right, lad," I told him. "I think that's enough for one day."

When I turned around to go get a pitchfork and clean up his paddock, I saw somebody leaning against the gate, indistinct in the pouring rain. As I came up I saw it was Max Forth, looking as dour as I felt with the drenching.

"Miss Memery," he said, touching his hat but not tipping it. I wouldn't have, either, in that weather. "Walker was right about your way with horses."

I blushed up to my eyebrows to think Walker Black spoke highly of me. "Thank you kindly, sir."

"Don't get too attached to the stunt horses though," he said. "It's not always good, what happens to them. And without Evans' money, we may be wrapping shooting faster than we planned."

It was meant kindly, I knew, but I still felt a chill in my heart. "That's a good stud," I said. "It would be a shame to waste him."

Max shrugged. "There's another money man on the way up from San Diego. I don't know what he's going to tell me to do."

He looked defeated. I said, "Evans got out of your way?"

"Mostly. Not always. Still, a rare good quality in a producer." He rolled his head to one side as if his neck hurt him. "Course, days like this don't help the bottom line."

"It might break this afternoon," I said. It wasn't just hogwash. The sky looked a little lighter off to the west. You live in Rain County, you get used to reading the rain. "Actually, I meant to ask you. I'm grateful for my job, and Priya's. But considering that rain is what we got here in Rain County, why on earth did you come all the way up here to shoot a motion picture you could have done in the desert, where it's dry?"

"Evans," said Max disgustedly. "He insisted it would look more like the East."

"Hmm," said I.

—————————

I went and found Priya before lunchtime. She was just finishing up in the maintenance tent tightening bolts on Cowboy's left leg when I walked in. "I hope you haven't lamed my noble steed!"

"Quite the opposite, I assure you, Miss Memery." Cowboy stood up, testing the leg. "That should be very adequate, Miss Swati."

"Priya," said Priya, with her usual refusal to stand on ceremony.

"You'll never be a Mad Scientist to strike fear into the hearts of rivals if you don't market yourself better than that," I told her. "Are you hungry?"

"Starved," she said, and put her tools neatly back in the tool belt, which she hung on a peg. "Cowboy, you want to come along with us? Just for company?"

The mechanical, who had seemed just about to protest that he didn't need grub, froze in mid-gesture, reset, and nodded. "That would be delightful, Miss Swati."

Priya rolled her eyes but didn't correct him about her name again.

When we trundled into the mess tent it looked like the line had just died down. Rain drummed on the canvas but it was dry underneath. We grabbed plates and stacked food on them while Cowboy saved us seats at a table with Doc Swan, Squalene, and Miss Mosey.

Miss Mosey won my heart over a little, out eating with the hoi polloi again when she could have had meals brought to her caravan. She picked over a pheasant salad but downed coffee like a wrangler. I sat down between her and Doc Swan, who had pushed her plate away and was writing something on a glue pad.

"Sorry," said Doc Swan. "Just writing to my friend Doctor Crumpler back East. She's working on a book about child-birthing."

Of course, I thought, all the women doctors knew each other. I had heard about Dr. Rebecca Crumpler: not just a woman, but a colored woman, who'd earned her degree during the War. I thought I would have liked to meet her, and I bet Priya would have liked to meet her even more.

For a moment, I felt a tight feeling in my chest that I wasn't ever going to run away to make motion pictures. Stunt riding was even harder on my body than gentling horses. And we owned our ranch and had a life here, family of a sort, a future together. And Rapid City was the place for Priya and her Mad Sciencing, unless we went all the way back East to Boston or Kansas City. People came here to learn the trade: it would be damfoolish to leave.

But damfoolish or not, I felt that welcoming embrace of the odd folk, the folk that didn't quite squeak into the peg holes expected of 'em, the freaks and strange ones, and I realized I had missed it. I didn't miss the work at the whorehouse—I preferred backing horses to being on my back for cowboys any day—but I missed the *women.* I missed the culture of it, and the acceptance of who you were as long as you treated others decently.

I was musing on that when the Peace brothers and Alphonse Bugera came by and sat down at the other end of the long table. Now we was full up, and Doc Swan put her letter away.

The Peace brothers sure ate like young men. I was surprised that end of the table weren't groaning under the weight of their plates. Mr. Bugera, his silver hair immaculate despite the rain, cut his food into tiny bites and chewed them carefully. Was he Fletcherizing? I decided I didn't want to know, but I admired his ability to eat and drink without smudging his lipstick.

Somehow the topic of conversation got to shooting, and I said I had never seen Miss Mosey shoot yet. She looked over at me, little scrap of a thing that she was, and said "We could arrange a demonstration after lunch. It's clearing up."

"We have never shot together, Miss Mosey," Cowboy said. "Would you accept my friendly challenge to a shooting match?"

Miss Mosey regarded the clanking mechanical with a smile. "You bet your britches, Cowboy."

"I require my britches," he replied. "Also, I do not wager. But I would be delighted to shoot with you."

Miss Mosey looked over at Squalene. "You in?"

"Oh, I don't know now," Squalene said. "I ain't in the league with the likes of you all."

"It will be fun," Miss Mosey pronounced, and that was settled.

"We should roll cameras on it," said one of the Peace brothers—Justin, I thought.

Squalene, blushing, looked past Miss Mosey, and I followed her gaze to see Cora Darling loitering just under the edge of the canopy. Already? They met eyes, and Cora nodded and stepped back into the shadows, obviously waiting for Squalene to be able to break away.

What surprised me was that Squalene and Mr. Bugera traded a glance afterward, and he nodded. Miss Mosey caught the exchange and looked dour. I had heard she was teetotal and I guessed she didn't approve of the cast and crew drinking.

But her lips got real tight and a sharp line creased her pretty forehead when Matthan Steele came out of the mist—the rain was, as I had thought, moving past us—and walked right up behind Cora Darling and put his hands on her waist. She jumped and shrieked, so the whole tent turned and looked. Then, without hesitation, she slapped him.

I jumped to my feet, rocking the bench. But before I could clamber over it and go to her rescue, she had stalked off—and Steele just stood there cupping his slapped cheek and grinning like it was a victory.

I blew out hard, like a filly full of feelings. Priya reached across the table and tugged my skirt to suggest I oughta sit down.

I did. I didn't think anybody had noticed, though. All eyes were on Steele as he walked back into the mist.

I looked over at Priya and said, "Men. The pretty ones are always a problem after a couple of hours. Just like shoes."

"Just like women, too," Jonah Peace said, unless'n it was Justin.

"Oh, I don't know about that," I answered, looking at Priya. "I like to think some of us wear in all right."

"Miss Memery," Joshua Peace said, and I was sure it was Joshua because he had been wearing the blue neckcloth since that morning. Unless they'd changed their clothes around. "I do believe you're fishing for a compliment."

I smiled, and turned my attention back to the men. They can be mighty oblivious when it comes to what women actually think, and they're mostly all susceptible to a little flattery. "If it suits you to think so," I said, and used my dimples, "of course I would not say no."

Lunch wrapped up pretty quick after that because everybody was eager for the shootin' contest. The Peace brothers went and got the backup camera from Vernon, and Miss Mosey, Squalene, and Cowboy set up out on the north side of the house where there was a bit of a meadow and a hill for backstop in case anybody missed.

I didn't expect anybody to miss.

We was drawing some interest by the time it was all arranged, and Priya'n me grabbed a rope from the equipment tent and flagged it up to keep the crowd back. I even saw Miz Kindness come out, her black dress faded but immaculate under a gingham apron daubed with flour.

Life must go on.

For a target, the Peace boys set up a trestle with three pyramids of seven beer bottles each on it. The idea was that each contestant would start at the top of their stack, and shoot their way down to the bottom without disturbing the lower rows.

I wouldn't want to try it. Not at ten yards, and definitely not at fifty. But I'd heard Phoebe Mosey could shoot a silver dime tossed into the air at a hundred yards, so I guess she weren't too concerned about it.

Cowboy went first, having won the coin toss—which nobody shot out of the air. He had a Spencer repeater, and he worked the lever like a pro. The Spencer holds seven cartridges, so he wouldn't have no bullet to spare.

He worked top to bottom and left to right, methodical as a type-writer. Each bottle disappeared with a bang, a curl of smoke, and the tinkle of glass shattering, and I didn't see no way Miss Mosey could beat him.

Phoebe Mosey stepped up to the line, all five foot nothing of her immaculate in a little gray dress and cock-brim hat, her dark curls all atumble. She was such a pretty little thing I wanted to pick her up and put her in my pocket, but that would only be possible in a world without Priya. And a world without Priya didn't bear thinking about.

I suddenly wanted to slide my arm around my wife's waist and hug her close, and if we'd just been friends I think I might have done it. But we wasn't just friends. And we needed these jobs more than I needed a hug right then.

Priya was distracted, picking at one of the scabs on her arm. "How'd you get hurt?" I asked.

"Oh, I just scratched myself on some gears and wire. MacGregor tried to say I got all scratched up fighting Otis Kindness and Evans, but you know as well as I do that the Singer is padded too well to cut anybody that way."

"Well, don't pick at it. You'll get blood poisoning."

Priya looked at me with a smile and pushed her sleeve down.

Meanwhile, with a twinkle in her eye, Miss Mosey loaded up her lever-action Marlin, which she did with the tiniest, cutest little cartridges you ever did see. Those might not be sufficient for a bear or a steer, I thought, but they sure would motivate a difference of attitude in any human person who might be troubling one.

I didn't see how Miss Mosey could do better than Cowboy. We were going to have to call it a draw—

She pulled a mirror and a little clip from her pocket, and mounted them on the stock of the rifle. Then she turned her back on the bottles, rested the rifle over her shoulder, and repeated Cowboy's precision. Backward, in little kid boots, and without messing her curls.

While the smoke drifted away, we all stood silent. Then one person clapped, and another, and pretty soon all assembled was aroar with applause. I clapped so hard my hands stung in their kid gloves, and Priya whooped beside me.

"Well damn," said Squalene, when the noise died down a little. She stepped up, but she wasn't holding no rifle. She leveled her mechanical arm at the remaining target and propped it with her other hand. I watched her squint down the pointing length of her first two fingers and held my breath.

The only sound was the steady whirr of the Kinematoscope, Jonah Peace presiding. I could see Celia the redheaded scenarist beside him, rapidly scribbling in her notebook with a pencil. Her hair had gotten loose and she was oblivious to the fact, too busy writing. I reckoned this scene was going to find a way into the motion picture.

Someday, I thought, I'd tell my grandchildren about witnessing this contest.

How I was gonna get my hands on any grandchildren, I would figure out in due time.

Squalene drew in a breath loud enough to hear over the silence. She let it out again, and at the bottom of the exhalation, whispered, "Bang."

Her arm twitched, and a jet of hot black coffee squirted five feet easy to fall into the meadow grass.

"Damn," she said to the general laughter. "Waste of good joe. Somebody get me a tin cup. And a towel."

Chapter Seventeen

The sun had come out as predicted, and so I went to the costume department to get outfitted. Amber had done a perfect job tailoring the dress and pinning that blond wig on, and I felt like a princess as I got ready to mock-fight Cowboy. The way things was supposed to end up was that Cowboy, having carried Miss Mosey off to his lair (secretly at the behest of Mr. Bugera), encountered the fictional Wild West show's trick roper and Miss Mosey's rival for Mr. Steele's affection. The roper was played by Miss Roman, of course.

Miss Roman was supposed to try to rope Cowboy and tie him to a tree, but of course Cowboy would break loose and come after her. That was when Matthan Steele would arrive, dressed in a labor mech, to do battle and save the girls.

I'd tried to argue with Max and Celia that it was more fun if the girls saved themselves, but Celia just rolled her pretty eyes and said, "It's silly, but the public expects women to be rescued."

And Max shrugged and murmured, just for me, "Do you want to tell Steele he's gotta get saved by a girl?"

I did not. "Well," I said, "I know how to wrangle a mech, if you change your mind."

Walker Black, still limping on his sprained ankle, was already dressed up to double Steele. They got him strapped into the mech and his ankle braced up. I felt bad for him, wincing like that, but as somebody said, the show must go on.

Why must it?

Because, I guess, people put their lives on hold for entertainment. They spend money and they spend time, and even as I was literally the person shoveling horse shit in the joke about quitting show business, I could see how you might get the fever. Might feel like all this moving picture magic had a kind of importance.

I say might get the fever like I didn't have it. I also, lucky for me, had the sense to see it weren't permanent like. What I had was an infatuation, and I knew I ought to enjoy it for what it was and not let it turn into a bad love affair that was bound to break my heart.

I weren't the trick roper. That was Jonah Peace, but this scene didn't require any tricks. I can drop a loop over a cayuse if he don't make it too complicated. So I was warming up my arm and minding my own business while Miss Roman did her close-ups, which mostly involved fainting melodramatically as Cowboy clutched at her.

Between takes, she complained.

"I don't see why Annie has to win the man," Miss Roman whined, pursing her over-rouged lips in a bee-stung pout. "I'm prettier. And everybody knows gentlemen prefer blondes."

That, I thought, was a matter of opinion, and one I did not share. Being a dark-haired girl myself, and besides, there wasn't nobody prettier than my Priya, and her hair was near as dark and shiny as a crow's wing.

Speaking of Priya, I spotted her off to the left, in the crowd watching the stunt, and I winked to her and roped her a tree branch special. Her smile made my whole world light up warm and cozy.

Lordy, I hoped we was done fighting.

"Besides—" Miss Roman started to say, but Max looked up from his notes and smoothly interrupted her.

"Miss Mosey is the ingenue," he said. "She's eighteen and you're twenty-nine, Helene. It will surprise the audience a little that the brunette gets the happy ending. And you, my dear"—he smiled at her, his tone mollifying now that he'd delivered the bad news—"have the pathos to show a broken heart and sell it to the punters. I promise they will never forget this performance."

They went back and forth like that for a while, but it was all chasing in circles: Miss Roman trying to get her way and Max standing dead firm on everything. Finally she threw her hands up and stormed off toward the costume department, her dainty steps calculated to show her great restraint by not stomping.

Max Forth pulled his watch out of his pocket, looked at it, and sighed. "That's twenty minutes of daylight we're never getting back. All right. Places, people."

I hoped they'd gotten all the close-ups with her they needed. That hope was dashed when Max said, "Miss Memery, after we shoot your part of the stunt please stay in costume. I'll need you to double Miss Roman with Mister Steele, I think."

Well that sounded like no fun at all, but I'd been paid to do more intimate things with men who smelled worse. I could handle it.

Cowboy and I got our stunt in six shots, two takes each, and we was both pretty proud of it. I roped him—they shot that from a rear angle, so my face was hidden—and ran around him to "tie" him to the tree. Then he snapped the rope—we'd used twine clothesline rope to make it easy and not waste a good braided lariat. He came after me and I ran. I fell. He grabbed me and shook me—very gently, but I flopped around like a landed fish.

Miss Roman's close-ups would get spliced in later.

I heard the *thump-thump* of Black, in Steele's costume, approaching in the labor mech. I couldn't see him, but when Max shouted, "Mark!" I knew to go limp so when Cowboy dropped me—gently—I wouldn't get hurt when I hit the ground. We'd picked a soft and grassy spot on purpose, and Cowboy knew his business. He might as well have laid me down on a featherbed for all the bruises I collected.

Then my job was just to lay there while Cowboy and the Wild West show's headman fought over me and tried not to step on my head.

I had to lie still and trust they wouldn't hurt me. Which weren't the easiest thing I ever did.

Mr. Bugera stepped from behind the tree and revealed himself as the villain when all seemed lost for our hero. But somehow Walker wriggled free from the mechanical's clutches and disabled him with a mighty blow.

Cowboy staggered backward and sat down hard, head cocked to one side as if the punch—which in real life had only swished air—had broken something. He wobbled for a moment and then fell over sideways. Defeated!

Mr. Bugera ran away. According to the scenario, back to his lair where he was holding Miss Mosey captive. Walker wriggled out of the mech—and the camera was stopped while he was replaced by Matthan, who crouched over me and pulled me into his arms.

With one hand, he tenderly cupped my face—incidentally hiding it from the camera. With his other hand, though, he was squeezing parts of my body men usually pay to squeeze, and it took all my discipline to lie still, pretend unconsciousness, and not kick him in the goodness' sake when he scooped me into his arms and got one hand right up my skirting.

"Cut!" Max yelled, not a moment too soon.

I wriggled out of Steele's grip and smoothed myself down, not caring who saw me glare at him.

"No wonder Miss Roman walked off set if this is the way you treat a lady." I turned away.

Steele looked like he was like to follow, but all of a sudden Mr. Bugera was right there beside me, offering his elbow.

"Miss Memery," he said. "I had a question about stunt riding." He looked tired, and not in a bodily way. Tired in his soul.

Given who he had to work with, I couldn't blame him. But I appreciated him walking me back to Priya, and the wink he gave me when he turned away.

He hadn't asked me a single thing about horses.

———

"I'll break his fingers," Priya said as we walked across the Kind-ness' dooryard toward the barn to fetch out Molly.

"You'll do no such thing—"

"Miss Swati," a soft voice interrupted. "Miss Memery."

We looked up to see Miz Kindness leaning out her door onto the porch. She looked from side to side, but the yard was deserted. Everybody was still over at the caravans or tents, I guessed, or at the location wrapping up.

"What is it, Miz Kindness?"

"Would you come inside?" she asked shyly. "I've got something to show you."

We looked at each other and trooped up the steps. She led us inside, to the darkness of the one-room cabin—just one window beside the door, and one lamp lit on the table, and evening was coming on. And then, to our surprise, she led us right out the back door again. Because the cabin was on a little slope, the back door didn't have no steps up to it, and the woodshed was right beside it. She opened the woodshed door—there weren't no lock on it—and threw it wide.

Just inside was something that weren't no woodpile. The Singer—*our* Singer—stood in front of split logs of maple and pine, something dark on its metal hands and the little brass plaque that read *Presented to Miss Priyadarshini Swati and Miss Karen Memery by the grateful people of Rapid City*—Madame Damnable's idea of a joke—plainly visible if not readable even in the fading light.

"Holy Jesus," I whispered.

Priya touched my arm. "That looks bad, doesn't it?"

"We need to tell Mister Lincoln," I said.

"That ain't all," said Miz Kindness. She shut the door. "Quick, come back inside."

We followed her in, this time spending long enough that my eyes adjusted to the dark. It was a clean, spare place, not much in it but a bed, a scrubbed trestle table, a cupboard, and a couple of benches. A bentwood chair stood beside the fire, and two pots, a coffeepot, and a pan rested on the hearthstone.

Some clothes hung from pegs behind the bedstead, and a little trunk stood beside it. Half the pegs was empty, I saw: Miz Kindness must have already put away or given away her husband's things.

The bruise on her cheekbone and her stiff way of moving made me glad she'd done that.

I ought to bring her a basket, I thought. Some of Priya's baking, and we still had some wizened storage apples in the cold cellar that could be worse. They'd do for a pie.

"Let me offer you some coffee," Miz Kindness said. She fetched three tin cups from the cupboard, and the coffeepot from beside the fire. She poured for all three of us. It was cowboy coffee, and I could taste the eggshell she'd settled it with. It was hot and I felt it sizzle along my bones.

"Somebody's trying to fix you up for killing my husband," she said. "That much is plain as my nose."

"I think you're right," I said.

Miz Kindness reached into her apron pocket and pulled out a little chamois bag, the kind the gold panners use. She put it on the table. "You look in there."

I picked it up, and knew what it was from the weight of it before I ever worried the drawstrings open. It felt like a bag of sand, but no bag of sand was ever that heavy. I stuck a finger in, and when I pulled it out, even in the dim light of the lamp my finger glittered like a thousand stars.

"Whew," I said.

Priya looked at the bag, her mouth tight. "I think we do not understand at all what is going on here."

"I found that," said Miz Kindness, "going through my husband's things. It ain't enough to pay the debts." She sighed heavy. "Maybe with the studio money."

It would have been enough to go Priya's bail, if they put her back in because of the Singer. Or to go mine, for that matter. But it occurred to me that it was probably evidence. And it wasn't mine.

I dusted the powder off my fingertip onto the sueded inside of the bag and gave it back to her, first tying a careful knot in the suede drawstrings.

"I don't know why you're showing us that," I said. "You shouldn't just trust people."

"The good Lord provides." Miz Kindness pursed out her lips, showing the thin rich band of purple-red inside their darkness. "Miss Memery, I did not know my husband had that in the house. I do not know even now why himself would have *still* had it, wherever it came from, unless he got it recent. Because otherwise I can't not have seen him spending it on drink or steers."

"Do you think there's gold on your land?" It occurred to me that if there was gold on her land there might be gold on our land, too. The same stream ran through both of them.

"There's a couple of caves up the mountain," she said. "But I ain't never heard there was anything of value in there."

I said, "I could ask my tommy-knocker."

She cocked her head at me. "What?"

Priya kicked me gently under the table.

"Never mind." Stone Mad probably thought he was well quit of me, anyway. And if I gave him a gold mine, he wouldn't want to give it back. Instead I said, "We ought to tell Mister Lincoln."

"We ought to nose around a little more," said Priya. "With your permission, Miz Kindness."

"You got my permission," she said. "I think somebody is trying to get you girls in a mite of trouble, and I would hate to see them succeeding. Even if they did do me a favor after a fashion." Her teeth flashed. "My husband used to spend a lot of time in that woodshed."

I thought about the dark stains on the Singer, and shuddered. Then I looked at the bag of gold dust in her hand, and another thought took me. "Those pegs over the door. Did he have a gun?"

"A shotgun," Miz Kindness agreed. "I put it in his trunk, with the loads. Do you want to see it?"

"I do."

She got up, crossed the room, and in a minute came back with the gun and the paper cartridges. She put them on the table like she was handling a dead rat.

I pulled a shell out of the box, looked at the paper wrapper, and weighed the thing in my hand. "Priya, are these blanks?"

"I don't know," she said, also taking one. "I don't see shot or a slug and they feel light, don't they? I should take Miss Mosey up on her offer to teach me to shoot."

"Miss Mosey offered to teach you to shoot?" asked Miz Kindness, while I reminded myself that jealousy was a sin.

"She says," said Priya, "that every woman ought to know how to handle a gun. But I think you're right, Karen. I think these are blanks." She grinned impishly and pointed at the box. "Look, it says on the box, *blank shells*."

"Wicked girl," I told her.

"Now why would he have a box of blanks?" asked Miz Kindness.

"Ain't that a good question?" I broke the gun to make sure it was empty, then peered down the barrel and ran my finger around the inside. "Well look at that. I guess your husband didn't always clean his gun."

The finger I pulled back glittered the same way the dust in the little bag had.

Miz Kindness kissed her teeth and sipped her coffee and said nothing for a good long time. When she looked up, she said, "He was salting a mine."

I nodded. "I think we got to assume so."

"Well, that would provide a reason for somebody to murder him," Priya said in her musical accent.

"Sure," I said. "You think Evans just got unlucky?"

She sniffed. "I think Mister Evans was likely to have been involved. That was the sort of man he was."

I stood up. "You want me to put these back in the trunk, Miz Kindness?"

Miz Kindness shook her head. "They bother me less than they did a minute ago. I wonder if Miss Mosey would teach *me* to shoot."

"I imagine she would be delighted," Priya said. "But right now those are evidence. We're going to have to tell Mister Lincoln about them, and send him to collect them. Along with the sewing machine."

Miz Kindness put a hand to her cheek. "I wouldn't mind meeting Mister Lincoln," she said. "But this place ain't nohow grand enough—"

"You know he grew up in a cabin smaller than this one," I said. "I don't think you're going to shock him with your straw tick and your clean cupboard and tin plates, ma'am."

She put both hands to her cheeks then, and looked down.

It was time to change the subject. I pointed out the window at the little graveyard. "You kept him close."

Miz Kindness had the most beautiful smile. "I wanted to keep an eye on him."

Chapter Eighteen

We walked out into the dooryard past darkness, and headed straight for the barn. I'd drop Priya off at the Bent D and go right into Rapid to tell Mr. Lincoln and Miss Francina what we'd found while she took care of the cow and rustled up some dinner.

Molly nickered when we came in. She was out of hay, and ready to go home. I went into the next stall to get her saddle, and tripped right over something in the hay and measured my length before I even realized I was falling.

"Ouch!" I said.

And, "Fuck, ouch," said the thing I'd tripped over.

I rolled over and found myself face-to-face in the near-pitch blackness with a semiconscious Squalene Jones. She was beyond three sheets and well-nigh into legless, and her breath reeked with it. Priya stood in the stall door. I could just about make out her silhouette in the shaded dark. Her hand was over her mouth in that way she had of holding in laughter.

"Are you hurt, Karen?" she asked.

"Only my dignity." I clambered to my feet, and spent a minute picking hay out of all sorts of places. "It's Squalene, she's passed out."

"M'not passed out," said Squalene. "M'resting."

"You should be resting in your own bed," Priya said with all that primness she got when people wasn't measuring up to her expectations. "Come on, Miss Jones. We probably can't carry you."

"Just leave me here," she mumbled. "My arm's broken and I don't want to go home."

"If your arm is broken you need to see a doctor." Priya put a hand on my arm. "Go get Doc Swan?"

"I think she means her metal arm," I said. "Remember earlier when the gun didn't work? Come on, Squalene."

I got my arms under her armpits and hauled. She weighed a lot for such a split rail of a woman. Maybe she was made out of hickory.

"I need to get out of this business," Squalene said. "I'm gonna get rich and quit."

"That makes two of us," I told her, getting under one of her arms. Priya propped her up on the other side. I needed the help, because Squalene was dead weight and reeling.

"Do you know where she sleeps?" I asked Priya.

"She's in one of the crew tents," Priya said. "With Amber and Celia, I think."

"I hate to wake them up—"

"No," Priya said, correctly intuiting that I was contemplating just laying Squalene back down in the straw and sawdust. "She's too drunk to be left here alone."

"Jus' leave me to die," said Squalene.

"See?" said Priya.

We weren't the most popular people with Amber and Celia when we brought Squalene back, but they didn't hate us too much, and they helped us get her stripped down to her underthings and lain to bed with a bucket beside her in case of necessaries. We all tried to be as quiet about it as possible, so as not to wake the neighbors, though Amber lit a kerosene lamp.

"Get on home, girls," Celia said. "We'll see to her."

With admixed reluctance and relief, Priya and I went back into the night. The waning gibbous moon was just a-rising, so it must have been gone nearly nine, and I heaved a heavy sigh as I contemplated the ride into Rapid City.

"If only we had a telephone," I muttered.

"I'd settle for a messenger pigeon," Priya replied.

We walked through the caravans arm in arm, keeping to the trampled path so we didn't trip over a guy wire or walk face-first into a clothesline. Instead, we almost tripped over Helene Roman, and just might have if it weren't for her bleached yellow hair. She was crouched down outside a caravan, and for a moment I thought she must have lost an earring or something before I realized the caravan in question belonged to Miss Mosey.

I wanted to smack her snooping face. Instead I said, "Oh hello, Miss Roman. Did you lose an earring? Should we get you a lamp?"

She shot upright with gratifying speed. Then she saw who had caught her and her consternation turned to fury. "How dare you," she said, with a rage that seemed to come out of nowhere. "You know as well as I do that this little hussy is up to something." Miss Roman sniffed. "She's probably a deviant like you."

For three beats of my heart I stayed utterly still. Then I smiled wide and said, "A guilty mind sees sin everywhere!" in my most cheerfullest tone.

Priya grabbed my arm and spirited me toward the barn before Miss Roman could rip my throat out with her fangs, which, given the expression on her moonlit face, was a more than slight possibility.

Molly didn't nicker the second time we came in, but just eyed us suspiciously as if to ask if we were going to make her stay in this strange stall all night with no hay.

"There, girl," Priya said, and fed her an apple she must have liberated from the mess tent. Priya pretends I'm the only one in the family who loves animals, but Priya ain't always very convincing.

I fetched Molly's saddle and bridle. She stood nicely for it, and took her bit in exchange for a piece of molasses candy. Some people spend all day getting a horse to open its mouth. Some people jam their thumb in there to get it open.

Me, I believe in bribery.

"Come on," I told Priya, once I was in the saddle. "I still got to ride into town and back tonight."

She used my hands and the stirrup to swing up in front of me. "You could stay at the Hôtel Ma Cherie."

"I could," I said, "But tomorrow's Good Friday. The joint is going to be jumping and I'll be in the way. Never mind that I won't get no rest at all. And—" I leaned forward to kiss her on the ear. "—there's no bed there as good as the one I got at home."

Chapter Nineteen

The next morning was Good Friday but the motion picture people didn't seem to care. They was up bright and early, already moving around when Priya and me rode in beside Mr. Lincoln, who had rented a livery horse in town, and a little cart driven by Constable Waterson. We were lucky: the sheriff was at church that morning, and Mr. Lincoln hadn't seen fit to disturb him when he stopped by the jailhouse looking for a representative of the law.

We put the saddle horses in a corral and hung their tack on the fence, under the little roof meant to keep the leather dry. The paddock gate was guarded by Squalene, who looked like she'd been washed in lye and then run through a mangle. But she was upright, at least as long as she was clinging to the posts, which was more than I would have been in her position.

As I walked past her she put a hand on my arm. "Celia told me you got me home last night. Thank you."

"You ought to lay off that stuff," I said, just as quietly. "It'll kill you. And it was Priya insisted we didn't leave you to sleep it off in the straw. Even though you were determined to stay there."

Squalene blushed behind the green. "Well, Miss Priya, I owe you a debt as well. If old Squalene can ever do anything for either of you, you let me know."

"Thank you," Priya said. "Now, if you would not mind excusing us—"

We made our way to the front door of the house, with everyone we passed turning to ogle Mr. Lincoln's tall, clanking frame as if he were a Good Friday miracle. Come to think of it, I suppose he did more or less rise from the dead. And hadn't he been shot on Good Friday and risen from his deathbed on Easter Sunday, too?

I reckoned it was kindest not to remind him of the anniversary. And safest not to blaspheme any more, even inside the privacy of my own thoughts. God knows our private sins just as well as the public ones.

We led the men up to the house and introduced them to Miz Kindness, who offered everybody coffee and didn't seem too upset when they refused. Especially the lawman. But she let them in, and Priya and I went to work, because it wouldn't do no good to have us hovering while the constable was impounding the Singer and Mr. Kindness' gun. He'd brought the cart along so he could haul it all back with him, and brought cart and horse both around the back toward that woodshed. Mr. Lincoln and Cowboy between them bundled the Singer into the back of the cart. I frowned at it. That hunk of metal had saved my life and Priya's more than once, not to mention who knew how many dozen other people. It felt wrong to just hand it over without a fight.

"Where's it usually kept?" Waterson asked.

"Our barn," said Priya. "Which we padlock."

"Could somebody shimmy in, say, the hayloft window?"

"They couldn't shimmy back out again," I said. "Not wearing that thing. The loft ladder wouldn't hold them. So they had to pick the lock."

"Or have a key," said Waterson, but he sounded more like somebody repeating from a sermon than somebody statin' a conviction of fact.

Around us, everybody was staring at the loading process, and murmurs broke out when Miz Kindness came out of the house with the gun in a sack. You can always kind of tell when the thing in a sack is a long gun, and this weren't no exception.

She handled it like a dead possum, arm's-length and nose wrinkled up. Miss Mosey was going to have some work cut out for her getting Miz Kindness comfortable with guns.

Or maybe it was just the evidence that her husband had been up to some kind of shenanigans and it had most likely gotten him killed.

Once the cart was loaded, Mr. Lincoln stopped to whisper in my ear. "Keep an eye peeled for that map," he said. "Whoever's got it might be a pretty good suspect. And be careful. Don't go anywhere alone if you can help it. Or let Miss Swati go anywhere alone, either."

"We're not going to make real convincing alibis for each other," I said. "Folks know we hang together."

"Just don't literalize that metaphor," Lincoln said. "Surely you have other friends."

We had, I thought, a whole city full of them. Or had done, before this latest trouble arose.

Well, brazen it out—that was the only way I knew how.

"Anything else?" I asked.

"They found crumbs of grit and a few flecks of dust that might have been from a gold-salted rock in Evans' pocket," he said. "It looks like the bodies was robbed. So if you should happen to locate the map, be cautious. The person holding it might be a murderer."

I watched the cart pull out, and Cowboy came up beside me. "Hello," I said.

"Hello, Miss Memery."

I swallowed the acid taste in my throat. "Cowboy, you handled that thing up close. Was it blood on the gauntlets?"

"I believe it was."

"Crickets on crackers," I said, because I was trying to blaspheme less. "We're being framed. But we ain't got no motive, and Priya ain't got no alibi."

"I know Priya is not the killer," Cowboy said.

"Cowboy, can you lie?"

"I am not programmed to lie."

Well now that weren't exactly definitive, were it? I thought of the long scratches on Priya's arms, and I thought of the look on her face when she saw Evans.

"Cowboy, would you lie to protect a human life? If she had done it?"

His tapes purred back and forth. "Would you believe me if I told you no?"

"You'd just hold your silence."

"As I am doing," he said. "Yes. I would hold my silence, Miss Memery. But I am not holding my silence on Miss Swati. You need have no concerns about her."

I felt the worse for having felt the need to ask Cowboy about Priya. But the better for having done it.

Though I supposed Cowboy could lie about lying, if he could lie at all. But that was a rabbit hole I wasn't gonna climb into, because deep as it was, it was as likely to end in Wonderland as answers.

So I was walking toward Angel Maker's paddock, enjoying the rare spring sunshine, when Matthan Steele came up beside me, smoking a slim cigarette with dandyish flair. He put an over-proprietary hand on the small of my back, making me glad of my corset and its armor. I wasn't prepared when he said, small-voiced, "I think I owe you an apology."

I stepped away. "You can start making me believe you're sincere by keeping your hands to yourself when a lady ain't volunteering to be manhandled."

"I can't help myself," he said. "You're so beautiful. And I'm an awful person. I'm bad and worthless and I ruin everything I touch."

He was limping more than he usually did.

Maybe my work at the Hôtel Ma Cherie weren't something I wanted to keep doing indefinite, but I had to give the experience this: my younger self might have been moved to pity by Matthan Steele's self-flagellation.

But at the ripe—even wizened—age of seventeen, I was wise to how his kind used self-loathing as an excuse. And how they took that self-hatred out on any woman they could get their hands on.

"Apologies ain't about you," I said.

He touched my shoulder again, massaging. I stepped away. "You're so pretty and innocent looking," he whined. "Give me a chance, Karen. I could help you get real roles, starring roles. You're beautiful enough and the camera loves you. It would be a lot more money, and fame."

I couldn't pretend I hadn't peddled what I got to keep a roof over my head, nor was there anything wrong with it. But I would have hesitated to go upstairs with Steele even when I was on the job. And I wasn't on the job no more.

"You take your hand off me," I said. "And if you put it on me again without my permission, or anyplace it oughtn't be when we're running a stunt together, and there's gonna be a third murder."

"Now Karen," he said, and I wanted to snap in his face that my name was Miss Memery to him, but by the time I'd gathered my wits he'd moved on to the threats. "You know I can help your friend if you help me. Nobody really cares about that Negro buck, and Evans—there was plenty of people who wanted to see the back of Evans. Life is cheap to some of them. It's possible I saw somebody going into your barn to steal that sewing machine, isn't it?"

I was so swoggled, dear reader, I just lifted up my chin and stared at him, struck dumb by the bald audacity of it.

He must have taken my silence for interest, because he purred, "I heard you used to work in the best cathouse in town. You must have some good tricks. Show me a few of them and I not only will remember witnessing that thievery, I also *won't* tell that police constable where I saw your mignette on Tuesday."

That son of a bitch. I wanted to wallop him right in the fajitas, but I held my temper and said, "Mister Steele, you had better go."

"I think you ought to consider this decision for a day or two," he said.

I said, "Mister Steele. You ought to go."

"You're an unnatural woman," he said, and stalked away.

I wanted a bath as much as anything.

Priya came up behind me a minute later. "What was that all about?"

"Never be alone with that man," I said. "He's one of the kind as don't think women are people."

Priya put her arm through mine. "You're only noticing that now?"

———

When folk compliment you and run themselves down in the process, that's just a way of either making you feel guilty for the compliment, or a way of making the conversation about them after all. It ain't that they *mean* to do those bad things, when they does it. It's just that they're bent that way from mistreatment, and they don't know anymore how to just ask for what they need, and they don't know how to be generous without being kicked, so they'll kick themselves if ain't nobody else will.

And they'll kick everybody else around them, too, because if you hate yourself so much you ain't got no self-respect, you don't know how to respect anybody.

If you can manage most of your mess just fine, bump along pretty good, get past bobbles and the like with friends and family without anybody getting disowned, work stuff out with talking and maybe a little bit of shouting, and there's still that one person with whom you can't ever get along with no matter what you do, well, it's possible you two just wasn't meant to get along.

On the other hoof, if that person seems to be having some dad-blamed fight with every sorry son of a bitch who wanders along, well. The problem probably ain't you.

On the other hand, if you're the one who finds *yourself* always having the same dad-blamed fight with every sorry son of a bitch who wanders along, the problem most likely ain't *them,* in that case. And maybe you ought to look to your own way of doing things and relatin' to the world for the cure.

Sure, there's people as have got to be managed because they can't manage themselves—where if you got one of those in your life you got to gauge how every interaction is gonna affect them, and whether you want to deal with the consequences when they blow up or fall over or do whatever they're going to do. Some of 'em is scared and need to feel like they got control over everything and everyone that they let close to 'em. And some of 'em is just fragile, due to breeding or to consequences, and they need to be protected and it ain't no fault of their own. Some of them is going through a bad patch or a busted heart and need a little shoring up, and that's the same but temporary.

You always got to be on your guard, though, and you can't ever put too much of your own self into your relations with a person like that, because they ain't a grown-up and they won't take care of any precious thing you hand them. They're a little kid, even if they're wearing a big man's boots, and you might get love out of 'em one minute and pure selfishness the next and you can't rely on either, because they're performing their idea of who they want to think they are for an audience of them. And they rely on you to tell 'em they're that good person at every turning.

I knowed a lot of girls in the trade like that. Madame didn't allow that kind in her house long; they always made trouble with the others, because you had to treat them just the way they liked being treated and they never gave a damn about how they treated you.

You just got to know you can't ever let yourself need a person like that, because their vanity will lead them astray at every turning.

So Matthan Steele's offer wasn't all that attractive to me—I knowed he'd leave me high and dry even if I was to take him up on it.

But then there's the other sort, who think they ought to think that the sun rises and sets up their own ass but just can't quite manage it, and so they're always on edge. Some people think well enough of themselves and it's fine; they owned their own regard by earning it. Those ain't usually the ones who run around making you tell them all the time how pretty they is.

These ones, they need constant shoring up, praise and petting and coddling and management because they don't got no bottom, as Da used to say, and they don't feel no conviction that their accomplishments was earned by them. They never learned to stand on their own feet despite the boat being rocking.

So they got this idea in their heads who they ought to be, but because they ain't really accepted who they *is,* and because that somebody they think they ought to be is somebody, deep down, they know they ain't—they get a little frantic about it. I knowed some girls like me—ladies who prefer the company of other ladies, in a sapphic way, I mean—who about go crazy chasing after men, as if they got something to prove by avoiding the love of a good woman.

Some of 'em get better in the end.

Anyway, folk like Mr. Steele—and Miss Roman, come to think on it—need you to agree with them constantly that they is who they think they ought to be, and ain't got no developing to do. And if you ain't busy all the time shoring them up, they pitch a fit like a cat whose breakfast didn't arrive on schedule and exactly to her liking.

They got to control everybody and they can't let nobody be free.

Now, I ain't talking about maintaining your obligations, here. That's good to do and it's got to be done.

Priya's Appa is one of this other kind, and let me tell you, even from some eight thousand miles away as the airship glides, that man is plumb exhausting. All them folk is exhausting. They cause real harm, and they don't do much good, either, and they sure do make some extra work for everybody.

So if you got one of them in your life and you can't get them out, you got to make plans and coordinate actions, because otherwise you will spend all your time standing around with a mop. And probably getting made to feel bad for no reason and set up against other folk just so whoever it is can feel important and like they're the hand on the reins.

So all that's bad enough when you got to do it. But doing it *ain't* the same thing as being conniving. And I can't tell you exactly what the difference is... wait, I can, actually. Because managing somebody as needs managing is like managing a horse with no manners. It's all about getting a little peace and quiet so you can get some steady work done.

But conniving... well, if you're a conniver, that's like being a mean horse all by yourself with no help from anybody. It's all about getting what you want when you want it, and not respecting what other people have a right to or a need for because you're busy finding out ways to make them do your will, and there ain't no thought there at all for your fellow creatures or what anybody else needs to have in their basket by day's end.

Mr. Matthan Steele, oh my sisters and my brothers... he was a conniver.

And I was worried to tarnation what he might do next.

Chapter Twenty

Hair and makeup beckoned, and the coral silk dress I was going to wear to double for Miss Mosey on her daring escape from the clutches of Mr. Bugera. Once Amber buttoned me up, I sat in the chair for Caleb and Hazel.

Priya stopped by to see me all gussied up. "We ought to buy that dress for you," she said, ducking over my shoulder to plant a dry, sisterly kiss on my powdered cheek.

I winked at her.

"If it survives," Amber said dubiously. She adopted a schoolmarmish voice. "Miss Memery is a lovely girl, but she is hard on her uniforms."

I laughed. "You got me dead to rights, pardner."

Celia looked up from where she had silently been hunched over a table in the corner of the tent, scribbling on her pages of scenario.

"Tell me you're not changing today's stunt," I said. "It's bad enough already."

"What is bad enough?" Priya asked, her hand tightening on my shoulder.

"Don't fret," I said. "It's much less dangerous than the horse stunts. I just got to jump out a window into the hero's arms."

"Not Matthan!" she whispered.

"Walker Black," I said. "I wouldn't trust Matthan not to strain something. Or drop me on camera and pretend it was an accident."

We all looked at one another, five women and Caleb. Caleb cleared his throat. "Do you think Steele... you know. Did it?"

Celia tossed her flaming hair. "Christ, I'm starting to think *I* might be the murderer."

Caleb laughed. "Of course you're the villain. You're a redhead and this is the West."

"I don't know," I said, "if it's anybody from the shoot. They wouldn't have had to come here to kill Evans."

"He didn't join us until we reached Seattle," said Amber. "Most of us came out from Chicago. He came up from San Diego with Max."

"Huh," I said.

Priya said, "You're assuming Evans was the target?"

"Who had reason to beat that poor colored man like that?" said Amber.

I said, "Maybe lots of people. I've heard he wasn't too honest in his business dealings."

Let them think I was talking about the cattle ranch.

"I want it to be Steele," Hazel said, putting the final touches on my false eyelashes.

"I want it to be Helene," Caleb said, with a glance over his shoulder. "But we all know Miss Princess would never get *her* hands dirty."

"Anyway," I said. "We found the bodies one day after the medicine show came into town. And that Father Postlethwait fellow was hassling Miz Kindness at the funeral about selling her land. I want to go talk to that preacher."

Not until after work, though, which meant sunset at the earliest.

I left Priya in the costume tent and killed the time before my call doing a little more to make friends with Angel Maker. I wasn't going into his muddy paddock in my long dress and little kid boots, and that was no mistaking. But I leaned up against the fence and stood very still and patient while I held out an apple from the mess tent. I'd even taken a bite out of it so the smell was strong, and it was a real good apple.

If Angel Maker didn't hurry up I was going to eat the whole thing and leave him the core only.

He stood warily for some time, looking at me with pricked ears and head lifted. I made a kissing noise and stretched the apple out a little more.

He pawed one big sooty foot, then stepped forward and stepped back again. He wanted that apple, and he wanted to come to me, but he'd been betrayed by the world before.

"Buddy, don't I know it," I muttered.

I made myself look away, studying the horizon behind the farmhouse, over toward where the sea cliffs were—invisible behind the fields and the line of trees, and then the seagrass meadow that ran right up to their rim, where we had been doing most of the photography—the Pacific standing in for the wild Atlantic. I'd never seen the Atlantic, but I wondered how convincing it would be to somebody who had.

It took a while, but eventually I felt whiskers tickle my palm. I hadn't even heard the stud come up; he was like a cat when he wanted to be. The apple vanished into his mouth and I felt him turning it around, looking for the place to bite it. He crunched down delicately, with measured strength.

I kept my hand where it was, supporting the other half where he could slurp it up, and a moment later he obliged me.

I thought he'd walk away again, but he didn't. He stood companionably beside me, staring lazily off in the same direction I was. Then he snorted, as if to say, "Don't worry, there's nothing dangerous," and nudged my hand before he turned away to roll in the hoof-deep mud.

I was standing there watching him heave himself to his feet again when Squalene walked up to me. She looked brighter than she had that morning, but still a little green at the gills. "Karen, can you hold this for me?"

She shoved a packet into my hands.

"I—" I looked at her, startled. "Just hold it?"

"Stick it in your saddlebag," she said, gesturing to where Molly's saddle still hung. "I have an errand I need to run and I'll be right back for it."

"All right," I said, and did as she asked. I wondered how safe it was leaving it there if it was valuable. But nobody seemed to be around—

When I turned back, Squalene was vanishing toward the cliff meadow. So of course, seeing as I was a nosy parker, I decided to follow.

———————

Squalene didn't seem to notice that she was being followed. And she wasn't headed for the shooting location but upmountain and back from the road.

Following the trail boss was easy. Her woodcraft weren't bad, on the face of it, but I knowed this mountain pretty well by now, though I aimed with time to learn it better. And I could stay back along the shadowy tree line while she walked up the clear meadow edge with the ocean far below.

The seagrass tossed, rippling gold. It had these flat blades that sparkled in that hard, slanted light bright as if somebody turned the facets of a diamond in the sun. I had harder going in the mossy shade of the big pines, avoiding the tumbled nurse logs, but I was also sober and a lot younger, so I kilted my skirts around my knees and kept up.

Half-wild cattle dotted the high meadow, answering the question of where the Kindness' beef stock had gotten off to. Squalene had to pick her way around them. We had been walking for a good fifteen minutes and I was starting to worry about missing my call when I heard somebody call, "Hey, Squalene!" and step out of the long grass.

He must have been standing in the shadow of some rocks that jutted up along the drop, because I almost screamed and jumped out of my hide when he appeareated.

I bit my tongue though, and I was glad of it, because a minute later I recognized the rangy fella in the Stetson hat as that Brent Bolan, the careless so-and-so that nearly got me and Copper killed. He came striding up to Squalene, and at first I thought he was going to haul off and paste her one right in the cakehole. But she put her hand up and he stopped maybe fifteen feet off.

There was a shore breeze and I ain't no lip-reader, so I couldn't make out a single word they was saying. Bolan kept pointing into the rocks and Squalene kept shrugging off whatever his point was. They was at it for five, ten minutes though, and neither one of them looked happy about the results. Eventually, Bolan threw his hands up in the air and stomped on past her. And Squalene shook her head up to heaven and kept going the way she had been.

I waited until she was a bit up the cliff, then slipped into the long grass and down by where he had been pointing. I had to see what he had been on about.

It was a campsite. A little rough and ready but fit enough for purpose, with an oilcloth to keep the rain off, backed up to some big rocks to break the wind. There was a low banked fire, a mess kit, and a saddle with saddlebags, but no horse and no food—and no sign of either.

I hadn't thought, in my anger, that somebody getting fired this far from home wouldn't have noplace to go and no resources to travel on with. Not that I'd exactly *gotten* him fired. He'd done that his own self. But I certainly hadn't been quiet about my opinion that he *ought* to be fired.

Just as I thought the word *fired,* as if I'd summoned it, a flat crack of gunfire echoed down the mountain. My first urge was to run out, but instead I peeled myself against one of those big rocks and fought off the urge to peek around it. My pulse hit so hard it made my ears hurt. *If I get murdered up here Priya's gonna kill me.*

The, what d'ya call it, irony of the thought didn't sink in until much later.

I didn't hear anybody cry out, which weren't no good sign. If a bullet misses you or wings you, you're like to yelp. If it does worse than that you go down fast and quiet.

I was still deciding what to do when I heard running feet among the rocks. I looked up to see Brent Bolan squinting at me over the barrel of a rifle.

"What the hell are you doing here?" he said.

"Just leaving," I said, raising my hands to head height. "I didn't know you was staying here. My apologies, I'll just be on my way."

"That wasn't your gunshot?" he asked.

"It wasn't yours?"

We regarded each other for a long minute, and then both of us simultaneous like squawked, "Squalene!" and legged it up the cliff edge, staying in among the boulders and trying to stay low.

I expected bullets zinging around us, but not one single gunshot threatened. There was just the sound of our panting and the crunch of stones and grass underfoot.

We found Squalene on her back about a hundred yards up the mountain, a tiny neat hole drilled through the front of her plaid shirt. I couldn't see the back, and I was glad, because the grass and ground all around her was soaked black-red and the flies was already buzzing around her nostrils and her open eyes.

I edged back into the rocks for cover before I blew my breakfast down the mountainside.

"Shit," said Bolan. "Ain't nobody gonna believe I didn't do this."

"The shot came from up there—" I pointed to the tree line up above. "And you was downmountain from me. Come on, let's get out of here before whoever did that decides they don't want any witnesses."

We legged it back down the mountain, feeling an itch between our shoulder blades and imagining a malevolent stare that prickled the backs of our necks. When we burst into Miz Kindness's dooryard, scaring the chickens, we was staggering and out of breath.

I collapsed against the fence and looked wildly around. Two of the Peace brothers and Lucas, another one of the wranglers, were turning toward us. Walker Black came out of the tents, a rifle in his own hand, a medium-sized, brown-haired white man in an expensive suit and shined shoes following behind him.

"What are you doing back here?" he snapped at Bolan, raising his gun. "I told you to get clear, Brent Bolan."

"Black, don't," I said, stepping in front of Brent. "Somebody get Doc Swan. Squalene's been shot."

Bolan took Walker, Doc, and Nurse Marie back up the hill with Justin and Jonah Peace and Lucas, all armed except for Doc and Marie, who was carrying the litter. I didn't think they would be able to do anything for her. My one brief look had suggested she was past helping. But I was just as happy to not have to go back up there with them.

I leaned on Angel Maker's corral, and the man with the shiny city shoes leaned up beside me.

"Alexander Oster," he said. "I'm the producer on this over-budget mess."

"Karen Memery," I said, and stuck out my hand. He shook it ceremoniously. "I'm the stunt double for Miss Mosey and Miss Roman."

Footsteps crunched up behind me. I turned to see Max Forth walking toward us, his hands in his pockets with as much fake casualness as anybody could want to muster.

"Mister Oster," Max said.

Oster put his hand out to Max, so Max had to take his out of his pocket. Max didn't look like he wanted to be shaking hands.

Oster jerked his chin at Angel Maker. "What's that one do?"

"Bucks," said Max. "We're going to shoot some footage this afternoon of him."

"You could do a spectacular fall with that horse and a running wire and the sea cliff," said Oster, and it was only Max's fingers digging into my elbow that kept me from coldcocking him.

"Dangerous for the rider," Max blandly said.

"Oh, you stunt riders live for adventure, don't you, Miss Memery?"

"Besides, if Miss Memery here can fork him, we're going to use him for the chase at the climax of act three. When she escapes from the dastardly Doctor Killjoy."

"I might have some notes on that chase," Oster said. He took his hat off, ran his hands through his thick brown hair, and settled the hat firmly back down again. "Well, off to placate the stars!"

Max held his breath until Oster was out of earshot, then let it out in a low whistle. "Well, this is going to be fun."

"You really want to use Angel Maker for the climax?"

"Can you ride him?"

I looked over. "I'll move faster. If I have to, I'll stick him until he quits bucking. It won't be in a sidesaddle though."

Horses don't generally like sidesaddles any better than I do. They can feel your balance isn't centered, and they have to be trained special not to worry themselves about it.

Max's face did something he probably intended to be a smile. "Miss Mosey will cope with the affront to her femininity, I'm sure."

"I won't ride him at a trip wire, though."

"It might mean your job and mine."

"You're not going to let Oster kill him!"

"If I *were* gonna run somebody of my choosing at a trip wire," Max murmured, "I'd pick Oster instead. But he's the boss, Miss Memery. I did warn you not to get attached."

———

The afternoon stunt was postponed while somebody went for the sheriff, which was what Max had been coming to tell me when we was interrupted. So I had a good two hours in which to work with Angel Maker. (I buttoned a duster on over that coral dress first, kilted it up, and changed into slop boots.) By the end of it, he let me reach over his back and scratch the dock of his tail, and hang on him with my arm while I scratched his belly. He even reached around with his long neck and nibbled on my shoulder.

I figured I might be able to lie across his back tomorrow. Was the motion picture going to stop filming for Easter Sunday? One way or another, I would be here to feed stock and muck corrals.

I looked up to find Priya leaning over the corral rail, looking at Angel Maker. Her pretty features wore a pinched frown.

"What are you thinking?" I asked her.

She made a face. "I don't necessarily feel safe telling you everything I think, Karen."

"Why ever not?"

"You're very judgmental."

"But I'm right!"

"See?" she said. "That right there is what makes you judgmental." She smiled at me and waved away the argument. "Anyway, I must admit that you have the magic touch."

I looked left and right to make sure nobody was watching, then hopped up on the bottom fence rail and kissed her. Playfully, she pushed me, then froze as Angel Maker came over to see what the roughhousing was about.

Gently, she reached out a flat hand in greeting, as I'd showed her to do with Molly. And gently, he lipped her fingers.

Somebody cleared their throat just then, and I flushed hot and hopped off the fence rail. When I looked up, Walker Black was giving us all a considering expression. He'd seen me kiss Priya, I just knew it. I was as headstrong as that stud horse and I was a much, much bigger fool—

Black said, "The sheriff wants to talk to both of you."

Chapter Twenty-One

I folded up my duster and unkilted my skirt before we went to see the sheriff. I didn't have time to do much about the boots, but I did knock the muck off them before MacGregor took us into Evans' caravan. That was the space he was using to question us, much to the annoyance of Mr. Oster, who wanted to be moving in. The sheriff pulled in Priya and me together, which I thought was poor police work, but I weren't gonna correct him.

"So," said MacGregor, "You, Miss Swati, was *where* when the shooting occurred?"

"I have been in the machine shop all day," Priya said. "Except the last fifteen minutes when I was by the horse corrals. I do not know when the shooting occurred, exactly."

"That lady doctor backs you up." He didn't sound none too happy about it.

I wanted to squeeze Priya's hand so I knotted my fingers in my skirting.

"Well," he said, "maybe you two was working together."

I shook my head. "I didn't kill Squalene. That Bolan will attest I didn't have no rifle."

"You could have tossed it off the cliff."

"I look like I could afford to waste a gun?"

"Then what was you doing up the mountainside?"

"I went for a walk," I said. "I saw Squalene headed out and it seemed like a fine idea to stretch my legs and blow the cobwebs out a little. That's all."

"Matthan Steele said you threatened his life," the sheriff said.

I choked. "Mister Steele made an advance to me," I said primly. "I told him no."

I didn't tell the Sheriff about the package in my saddlebags I hadn't had time to inspect. I didn't tell him about what Squalene had said the other night, drunk, about having a plan to make her fortune.

"Did she have a map on her?" I asked.

"You didn't notice when you... *found* her?"

"I didn't get close. I can't abide the sight of blood, Sheriff. Makes me toss my cookies. I definitely didn't go through her pockets."

"This the same map you're claiming you saw Mister Evans and Otis Kindness looking over?" He snorted. "Should we put out that it's all a mine-salting plot, in your *professional estimation,* Miss Memery?"

"It might save a few lives," I said. "If folks are really being killed over the gold."

"The gold," Priya said, "that isn't there."

He looked from me to her, his big meaty fingers curling like he was just itching to manacle the both of us. But he stepped off and said, "I ought to run that Kindness woman in for questioning, too. I heard her husband beat her."

"Why would she kill Mister Evans?" I asked, temperate in manner. I learned acting in Rapid City's best whorehouse. "Why would she kill Squalene?"

He snorted, shrugged. "Who knows why women do anything? Anyway, I ain't gonna arrest you today. And I hear from the clanking outside that your gimp lawyer is here."

———

We went outside to—indeed—find Mr. Lincoln pacing back and forth, his armature ticking away, his hand scribbling with a stub of pencil in his little black notebook. He looked up when he heard our tread on the steps. "Is he arresting you?"

"Not today," Priya said. "He might be working himself up to arrest Miz Kindness, though."

"On what grounds? That she's a colored woman?" Lincoln scoffed. "If I have to I'll pro bono this whole town."

I asked, "What's a pro nono?" just to watch Priya put her hand over her eyes. "Anyway, we've got bigger trouble."

"We have somehow bigger trouble than a murder charge?" Priya asked, incredulous.

"Oster, that new producer." I lowered my voice. "He wants to add a fall stunt that's likely to kill Angel Maker. And maybe me. And if I won't ride it you know he'll fire both of us and there won't be no severance, either."

"Karen," Priya said, her deep voice rich in concern.

"Wait," I said to her and Mr. Lincoln. I'd spotted Walker Black moving toward his caravan. "I'll be right back."

And picking up my skirts, I sprinted after him.

I caught him by the door of the stable. He looked over at me, and I said, "We've got to stop Oster from killing the horses."

He put a hand over his mouth, pinched his upper lip, and blew into his fingers. "I've got no power over that man."

"Christ doing cartwheels," I said. Then I remembered that he had like to seen me and Priya canoodling, and my face got hot again. I should have kept my mouth shut, I knowed, but keeping my mouth shut has never exactly been the core of my abilities.

I got it so wound about me that I purely couldn't stand it anymore. I just squared up my shoulders and gritted up and said, "Can we step inside your caravan?"

"Miss Memery," he said. And led me the last few feet, and held the door open. I was afraid to go inside, but I could feel Priya and Mr. Lincoln watching. So I set my haunches and dusted up the steps, feeling like a horse that ain't sure if it's just nearly stepped on a rope, or a snake.

I was still prancing and head-tossing when Black, from the doorway, gestured to a chair and said, real friendly, "Please sit down. With what can I help you, Miss Memery?"

Well, I tromped up those hanging steps and heaved myself into the caravan, then swung the door shut behind me and set myself up square. "Are you going to fire me?"

His eyes got big. "You done something I don't know about?"

"I done something you know about," I said, and let it hang.

He gave a long few seconds of attention to his chaw, then turned and spat delicately into a tin mug. No hawk and goober, thank the good Lord.

"You're good with the stock," he said, having tongued the lump back into his cheek pocket. "You're good with the stunts. You're good with the other crew, more or less. Your Priya's a whiz at machines."

He stared at me and I stared at him. "My Priya?" I asked, when he didn't give an inch.

He had a good shrug on him, for an American. "The way I see it," he said, "mares get with mares, you leave 'em out in the field together. Heifers get with heifers. Now, they're dumb beasts ain't never suffered the fall of man, so I reckon they're closer to the Lord's intent than some bishop somewhere as is fed fat on setting his touch on Bible stories that people could just as well read and figure for themselves."

I just gawked at him. It was like he'd reached into my own head and said out loud what I had been thinking.

He continued, "I ain't no blackmailer. Not like some folk around here."

I said, "Who do you mean?" because I ain't got no rein on my tongue.

He chawed again, spat again, and must have decided he wasn't going to answer that question, because he gave me a serious eyebrow and continued on, "You're good with my stock, you're good with me, Miss Memery. Now, don't you have work to be getting on with?" He pulled his watch out. "You've got some time before evening light, and we're going to try to get your jump in the can."

"You're catching me, right?" I asked. "Not Steele?"

From the flick of his eyes I knew he noticed I ain't said "Mister."

"I'm catching you," he agreed.

———————————

I sure wasn't going to look in my saddlebag—or move it, or do anything to draw attention to it—until Priya and me was home and dry in our own kitchen. So I invited Mr. Lincoln to the mess tent, since Priya said she'd already eaten and anyway she needed to get back because Doc Swan was teaching her welding.

Or apparently she'd been taught, because after lunch when I walked into the machine shop she was singing "Lily of the West" to herself and making a fierce arc of sparks fly across the trod earth floor.

Now, I got my opinions about "Lily of the West," and they're not complimentary, though I've heard it sung by folk—all right, I've heard it sung by women—who obviously have figured out that the narrator ain't no nice man and he's been dogging after poor Flora without her say-so, like some men is want to do.

Men like that is dangerous and Flora the Lily got off lightly, just losing her beau. Because men such as won't stand off—men as think they own women—they're a rough ride all around.

Anyway, I was smart enough to keep the literary criticism inside my own head.

"How's the mad science, honey?" I asked her.

She set her welding torch aside and smudged her goggles up. "I don't have a control group, so technically it's mad engineering."

Her tone told me it was a joke, so I laughed, because that's how domestic harmony is maintained.

She grinned at me, as happy in her welding gloves as I've ever seen her, and she said, "You didn't understand that joke at all, did you?"

"Nary a slice of it," I agreed cheerfully. "What's a control group?"

"Something I just invented," she shot back, and I knew I wasn't getting more out of her until she was ready.

I said, "Look, I came to tell you Walker Black done saw us smooching earlier, and he don't mind."

"I should hope not. You know that director likes young men. Jodi's been going into his caravan at night and nobody seems too het up about it. So I think he's a... sissy, is that the word?"

"Sissy ain't no polite word," I said. "Actually I ain't sure there is a polite word. But that explains why I ain't felt him staring down my dress. And that explains I guess why these people feel like home. Even despite Matthan Christ-damned Steele."

Priya put down her tools and came around the workbench to give me a hug, then stepped back and studied me at arm's length. "You miss the brothel sometimes."

"I miss..." I shook my head. "I ain't missing the work, and that's for sure. I miss the women. It was full of my sisters and now I can visit but I don't belong there anymore and I miss having a place for just... belonging."

"It's a whorehouse, Karen my love."

"...can't it be both? Anyway, Pree, they're going to be at your back and have been with this ridiculous murder accusation. You're a sister, too, even if you didn't choose it."

"What if I don't want to be a sister?" Her expression was critical. More of herself than of me, I reckoned.

"Well," I said slow. "Then I suppose they're like to love you in your own way, Priya darlin'. But don't think Miss Francina and Miss Lizzie and the rest won't be there for you no matter what befalls. Whether you want to think of yourself as their sister or something else entire."

"And you?" she asked in a small voice. "Will you be here for me? I don't make you lonely?"

"Oh Pree," I said, and pulled her into my arms, because there were either not enough words or far too many to explain what I was feeling.

We was shooting the escape scene down in Rapid proper, at one of the big Queen Anne houses on the edge of town that was standing in for the evil kidnapper's castle. The scenario called for me to wiggle out a tower window, reverse-Rapunzel, and climb two stories down a knotted bedsheet into Walker's arms, dropping the last few feet so he could catch me.

We'd shoot the horses running away from Cowboy and the final cliff-edge confrontation Monday. There was still three weeks of shooting to go after that, and I was just hoping there would be enough work for me.

There was the stock work if nothing else. But I wasn't sure I could stay on here if Oster killed Angel Maker.

I left Molly with Priya and told her I'd meet her at home, and rode down shotgun in the cart with Walker Black driving. In addition to the crew for the stunt, Miss Mosey rode along beside us on her own piebald horse. She was, she told us, going to a meeting at the Friends House for Good Friday evening.

I am an idiot with a big mouth and I opened it up and said, "I thought the Friends considered the worship of the Christ Child to be idolatry."

She smiled at me. "We're obedient to our great pattern," she said. "Which he represents, and in which we as he are washed and sanctified."

Well, I wasn't sure what all that meant, but it didn't sound bad. And as she didn't seem inclined to hold who I was or what I'd been against me, I was inclined in turn to let her have her religion.

Not that, you understand, I thought I could have stopped her.

Chapter Twenty-Two

Reader, I skedaddled down that bedsheet three separate times so Vernon could get it from an assortment of angles. The whole time I was grateful moving pictures was silent, because I was grunting and cursing and if it weren't for the kid gloves I would have been rubbing blisters onto my palms. The welts from my earlier adventures had nearly healed, but this was enough to make 'em sting.

Still, it was my job of work to get done, and I managed it. The bedsheets had a rope knotted through the center, but I didn't have no rope for safety because it would have to be scraped off each negative with a razorblade to hide it, and that was a lot of work and would leave a scratch in the final print you could see.

The third time down was the last, because my hands gave out and I purely fell off, and the only reason I didn't break an ankle was because Walker Black stepped in and really did catch me, easy as if he were catching a baseball. He was gentlemanly about it, too, setting me on my feet without a hair out of place except the ones stuck in my neck sweat.

When we wrapped up for the night it was mostly because the light was going, and because I was too tired to climb down that stinking bedsheet again. At least Vernon assured me he'd got the shot of me falling and being caught, so the bruises on my shoulders wasn't wasted.

Then I caught the cart most of the way back up to the Kindness place, and hopped off at the end of our lane. I hiked in the half mile to the ranch house thinking I'd bring the costume back to Amber tomorrow. She was probably eating her supper by now anyway and would prefer not to be distracted from it.

Speaking of supper, I could smell cooking as I came up the lane, and our little house was bright with lamps and spilling light out the windows. Molly nickered to me from the barn, and I went in and said hello to her and the cow before proceeding inside.

"Oh there you are," said Priya, looking up at me from a seat by the table where she was studying some ungainly sheets of paper. Blueprints, I thought. "Come and eat."

She popped up before I could protest, and when I tried to help told me to wash up and change my clothes. I was so tired I just naturally pulled on my slippers and a nightdress.

She dished out some savory stew of lentils and potatoes. I almost fell asleep in my bowl before eating it gave me a second wind. Then Priya cleared the dishes and plunked a pile of papers down in front of me. "Do you want the brandy?" she asked.

"No," I said. "I'm going to bed as soon as I look this over. What is it?"

"Look in the middle."

I flipped through the blueprints until I found the smaller but still overlarge piece of paper tucked inside them.

It was a map—a good map, probably traced from one of the survey maps in the town archive. I'd seen the one for the Bent D when Priya and me bought it, and I recognized the style.

"That was in your saddlebag," Priya said. "Did you put it there?"

"Squalene handed it to me," I said. "Right before she went up the mountain."

"Well I think I know where she was going." Priya tapped her finger on the crackling thin paper. An *X* literally marked a spot upmountain of the Kindness place and overlooking the Sound.

"We need to keep that hidden until we can get it to Mister Lincoln," I said. "I think three people have died for it. And it ain't even real, just a salted mine."

A wave of sadness threatened to suck me under when I contemplated that. Otis Kindness' flimflam to sell his ranch at a profit had ended in his own death, and the deaths of several others.

"It can stay in the stack of blueprints for now." Priya had cleared the dishes while I stared at the map. Now she took them all out of my hands, squared them up, and laid them on the little rough table she'd sanded down into a passable desk.

"We got to, I don't know," I said. "Publicize that there ain't no gold up there. We gotta get MacGregor to tell people that the mine was salted."

"Mister Lincoln and Miss Francina will know what to do," Priya said. "Now come to bed, my Karen Gertrude Memery."

I didn't sleep none too good knowing that map was in the house. Every little sound woke me—the cock crowing, the livestock moving around in the barn. Eventually I just gave up and slid out from under Priya's arm. She was snoring like a kitten, every breath moving a lock of her disarrayed hair.

It was getting long, I noticed. Pretty soon she'd want me to cut it.

The night was crystal clear and cold when I stepped outside, and I wished I'd brought a sweater. I wrapped a blanket from the porch rocker over my shoulders and stood, looking at the night, listening to the owls and the rustling of the chickens. Standing watch over my beloved.

This was my place, I thought. And nothing was going to take it, or Priya, from me.

In the morning we collected the week's pay, which was more than I had anticipated given all the stunt riding I'd been doing. I gave my share to Priya for safekeeping and went to hand in the dress to Amber for repairs and cleaning. Today was the day that I was going to have to try to back Angel Maker.

It was a pretty story, I thought. The wild horse that only one person can tame. But the truth of it is that there's nothing like that. There's just horses whose trust has been broken, and people willing to put the work in to win that trust back again.

Most people won't stand there for hours, waiting for that moment of connection. Most people grab, push their luck, get impatient. And that won't get you anywhere with a horse or a human that has learned to be afraid of folk playing rough.

I had to wait for Priya to come to me, too. I'm pretty good at waiting.

But now I had to hurry, because I had to prove to Oster that Angel Maker was a valuable stud, and not to be sacrificed on a whim.

If I could. If Alexander Oster was even half the sort of person to care.

I suspected I might be up against a brick wall there. But I had to try. And if I won my bet, then Angel Maker would be mine, right? And where Black would do whatever Oster wanted, I guessed, I could refuse to use him.

Except I couldn't. Because we needed the money.

Just, I realized, like Max Forth and Walker Black.

So once I'd mucked out and trundled my two or three wheelbarrows to the dung pile, I slipped off my work gloves and climbed into the paddock with Angel Maker.

He seemed eager and alert to my coming, his big eyes bright and his ears easy. That skin on the face that gets taut when a horse is worried or in pain was soft and supple, and I was flattered at his trust when he walked right over to me and shoved his nose into my middle.

I wasn't fool enough to just climb up on him, nor to try him with a saddle. Angel Maker weren't no virgin. All his naïveté had left him a long, long time ago. He knew all about what to do with a rider, and that was to put 'em in the dirt.

So I had to convince him that I was some other class of creature, and that he needed a whole different set of responses to me. I didn't know if I'd ever be able to make him safe to ride, but I knew he weren't going to progress if I didn't work with him. And me standing there worriting didn't get me any closer to saving his life.

And me standing there contemplating how that Alexander Oster had plumb *sparkled* at me didn't make me not want to reach for a knife.

Now Karen, there's been enough murders.

I went through the same rigamarole I had the day before, scratching his belly and weighting his back, scratching his tail dock and withers and under his jet-black mane and basically making him out to be the best thing ever. And slowly, bit by bit, I reached up over his back to scratch the other side of him.

At first the head came up and the ears weren't pinned but they was worried. Still I kept at it, hanging some weight on him and making it worth his while, then getting him to follow me around the corral for scritches and bits of bread. The bread made a difference, and I got him to line up by the fence rail over and over again. He weren't no pony that I could just jump up and lay over.

Once he'd come up beside me at the fence (more bread, more scratches) I started putting my arm over him. First he snorted and danced away, but the scratches and bread weren't moving, so he came back over and over. The poor horse was bored to death, I realized, all alone in his little dirt circle.

That boredom and loneliness played out to my advantage. If he wanted affection and grooming, he'd have to put up with me.

Once he'd stand for my weight on his back as I leaned on him, I sat on the fence and put one leg over him. Then I leaned over him belly down, and he stood like a rock for me.

I slid back off and he didn't do nothing. Three more times I leaned over him, and the most he did was turn his limber neck around and lip my hair a little. No saddle, no bridle. Nothing like what he'd experienced being ridden to break him.

I didn't want to break him.

I wanted to *enlist* him.

The fourth time he let me lean my whole weight on his back, I planted my hands on his withers, pushed up, and swung my leg over. He snorted and dance-stepped a little, but settled when I didn't do anything. He was big and warm and solid under me, breathing a little hard with agitation, but he weren't going anywhere.

And there I was, riding Angel Maker.

I didn't sit him more than thirty seconds, because I didn't want to push my luck and I didn't want him to remember that he had the option to start bucking. Before he could decide what he wanted to do with me, I put my weight back on my hands and slung my leg back over and slid right off him.

Then I turned right around and gave that big old stud a hug like he was a kid's pony. Walked right up under his head and threw my arms around his neck, aware that he could kill or cripple me if he chose to, and trusting him not to. I squeezed him around the muscular neck, so thick my arms barely reached... and Angel Maker lowered his head and pressed his chin against my shoulder, hugging me in return.

———————

Technically I'd won my bet, but Black hadn't been there and I suspected he'd want to see me put the horse to work a little. That would be a problem for tomorrow, though—Easter Sunday we wouldn't be shooting. And I'd be able to do some work with Angel Maker and show Black I could ride him without having too many people around to complicate matters.

As it was, I just patted him one more time for good luck and portioned out the hay and grain, making sure everybody got their share. There was the usual stomping and demanding nickers as I served up breakfast. Everybody's a critic. *And* a mite ungrateful.

I had finished shoveling out the corral with Copper and Baldy and their friends and was starting on Bill and Merrimack's, pushing my barrow through the rutted dirt, when a rustle in the haypile drew my attention. *Rats.*

I left my barrow and walked over quiet like, pitchfork still in my hand. That were a lot of rustling. More than just one or two rats. It occurred to me that I ought to investigate more thoroughly before I stabbed into it like Vlad the Impaler.

So I brushed the hay aside, and saw a woman's arm in a sprigged calico sleeve. For a horrible moment I thought I had just discovered another dead person, but the arm heaved and I heard sobbing. Not just normal sobbing, either, but the kind of curled-up wailing that was beyond heartbreak.

"Hey, it's okay, it's me, Karen," I said, not knowing who I was talking to or if they knew me from Eve and Adam. It was a white woman's wrist, and the hand below it was skinny. "Are you hurt? Were you sleeping rough, honey?"

"Karen?"

A face emerged from the haypile. It was Cora Darling, and she looked like she'd been through the War and fought both sides of it on her lonesome.

"Sweetie, what's wrong?" I asked, and reached out to touch her.

She flinched away harder than Angel Maker. "Don't see me," she whispered. "I don't want anybody to see me."

Oh, no.

"Okay," I said. "I'm just going to go sit over here by the fence for a bit, okay?"

"No, don't... don't go."

I closed my eyes. Then, in a fit of desperation, I turned my back on her. "Okay, honey, I can't see you now. And I ain't going anywhere. Will you talk to me?"

"I don't know what to say." Her voice was still so faint I had to strain after it.

"Did somebody hurt you?" I asked as quiet as I could.

A rustle of hay that was probably her nodding.

"How bad?"

"I don't know," she said. "There's blood. I got bruises."

"Can I take you to Doc Swan? Or in town to Miss Lizzie?"

"Who—who's Miss Lizzie?"

"She's a friend of mine. She's a medic for the girls at the Hôtel Ma Cherie."

It was a gamble, because I was pretty sure I knew how Cora had been hurt, and who had done the hurting. She might have been offended. She might have curled back into herself and not come out.

Instead she said, "I guess she knows about female troubles then."

"You could say that," I said, fighting all my instincts not to sneak a peek at her. "She can do you an abortion if you need one."

Cora ugly-laughed like she was going to cry. "I hope it won't come to that." Another rustle in the hay. Dusting noises, and a footstep as if she was moving forward. "God Almighty, am I really hiding in a haystack?"

Her voice sounded stronger. I knowed it was probably just one of the upswings and she'd crack apart again soon, but I aimed to use it while I got it.

"You really is."

"Well, I'm coming out." A moment later and I felt her hand on my elbow. I turned to peek at her. She tried to smile and didn't, quite.

She was all scratched up and one eye blackened. The little cotton socks over the top of her boots was stained red, and so was the front of her skirts, in streaks and patches. My gorge rose and I choked it down, fixing my lights on her eyebrows.

"You still bleeding?" I asked her.

She winced and nodded. "Don't think I can ride. So I guess it's gotta be Doc Swan, don't it? You think she'll treat me when I ain't part of the motion picture official like?"

"Come on," I said. "Lean on my elbow, Cora."

I wanted to be anywhere but in the medical tent while Doc took care of her, but Cora wouldn't have me anyplace but. So I held her hand and looked at her face and distracted her as best I could with bird chatter while Doc and Nurse looked after her. She had a split lip to go with the split eyebrow and she kept wincing while Doc stitched her, but she was braver than I would have been.

At least the lip weren't bleeding no more, which was a consolation to my stomach.

Finally she looked at me and said, "It wasn't my fault, was it?"

"Oh Cora," I said. "How could it be your fault that somebody hurt you?"

"I went off alone with him," she said. "He said I wouldn't have done that unless I wanted him to. But he said he wanted..." she paused. "What I been bringing for Miz Jones and Mister Bugera."

"What he said, that's poppycock," Doc said briskly from behind me. "And if you think you're the first girl he's done this to, well. You are not."

Cora bit her lip, then winced, because it was fat as a roll of nickels.

"Why don't nobody stop him?"

"If I knew how," said Nurse Marie, "if *we* knew how, we surely would. I know Max would love to fire him."

"Max is the boss man, ain't he?" Cora said. "Why can't he fire him?"

"Because Max ain't where the money is," I said, thinking of Mr. Oster. I looked over my shoulder, caught a glimpse of a blood-soaked rag, and quickly looked away again. "Ain't that right, Doc?"

Doc sighed. "I hate this."

"Just to be plain, so I'm sure," I said, "who are we talking about here?"

Cora Darling turned her head aside.

"Matthan Steele," said Doc, mercilessly.

Cora flinched.

Doc said, "I ain't wrong, am I?"

"No," Cora admitted. "You ain't."

"Let me tell Priya," I begged. "We'll come up with some way to get to him."

Chapter Twenty-Three

Just then, I heard somebody hollering my name outside the tent. One of the Peace boys, it sounded like. So I gave Cora one last squeeze, unpeeled my hand from her clasping fingers, told her, "We will figure out a way to get that son of a bitch," and squared my shoulders to face the next thing the day was gonna throw at me.

"Miss Memery," the Peace boy said—I thought it was Jonah, looking at his hair for cowlicks—"you're wanted on the set."

"Thank you," I said, and decided not to hazard a guess at the name. We ought to make 'em wear badges, but they would just swap those around. "Miss Darling got hurt, and Doc was just seeing to her. I'll be right along."

I'd plumb forgotten we was shooting a scene that afternoon. Or rather, that *I* was shooting a scene that afternoon.

Fortunately, this time I was doubling Miss Mosey again, because I didn't think I could take listening to Miss Roman whine about how fat I was and how my hips was going to destroy her career. I had made an entire career of my own on the strength of those hips. More than one man has compared my figure favorably to that of Miss Sarah Bernhardt, so I could have told her not to get too het up about it.

Amber, Hazel, and Caleb got me squeezed and slathered and serpentined into corset and dress, makeup, and hair in record time. Another reason I preferred doubling Annie Mosey was that her hair was even darker than mine, so I didn't have to wear a hot, scratchy wig.

I seethed with fury, grinding my jaw so tight a tooth might have cracked, and I braced myself before I came out of wardrobe in case I ran into Steele. Today wouldn't require too much of me; the fictional showman Wild Willy Fair was supposed to ride Angel Maker in the arena they'd faked up to look like a Wild West show, and since there was no way in Hell Matthan Steele was ever going to climb up on that horse, that meant Black had to ride him.

Which weren't gonna make my task of gentling him any easier, because bucking horses ain't exactly the model of restraint and affability.

My part in the stunt was to ride out on Bill—good old Bill—and pull Black onto the saddle with me after he got thrown. Because we all assumed he was gonna get thrown. And Angel Maker was playing a killer horse, so the script treated him like he was a rodeo bull and not a bronc. When let me tell you, broncs and bulls, they're real different.

A bucking horse bucks because he wants to get rid of you, sure, but also because he's trained for it. It ain't like riding a cayuse until they give up trying to unseat you so you can go and get a job of work done. The horse keeps bucking after you come off, because he's trying to get the gear off also.

The bull gets you off his back and then his next step is that he's coming to kill you. That's what the clowns is for—to distract him. And maybe keep the bull rider alive long enough to annoy the bull another day.

Anyway, the point of this scene—according to Celia the scenarist—was to show (she said "establish") that Angel Maker was a badass and that Wild Willy was, too.

I said, "So when Miss Snow"—that was Miss Mosey's character's name—"rides both of 'em, we'll know she's a badass too?"

"Karen!" Celia laughed, pleasantly scandalized.

Pleased with myself and not feeling quite so angry anymore, I went to check with Black before we mounted up. I'd need to be ready to go as soon as he and Angel Maker came out of the chute, because there was no telling how long Black could stick him.

Black was a good rider, but Angel Maker had a reputation, and I would be lying if I said I weren't eager to see him use his skills.

"Don't you rowel him," I said to Black. "I gotta ride that horse on Monday."

"Don't you worry, Miss Memery," he said to me. "I ain't gotta do nothing to this horse to make him angry."

And indeed, the stud in the chute was nothing like the doe-eyed innocent who'd let me climb all over him that morning. He knew his business and he knew what he was in for, and I hoped he'd be pleasantly surprised that at least he wasn't gonna get cut to ribbons by the spurs.

The object was for Black to stay on long enough for Vernon and his assistant to get a variety of shots, which meant Black had to ride Angel Maker for longer than usual at a Wild West show.

Or get back up after he came off and ride him again, and I didn't think any of us really wanted to go through that rigamarole. Especially not Angel Maker, and even more so not Walker Black's backside.

Jodi gave me a leg up on Bill and I settled into the sidesaddle while Miss Mosey shot her close-ups. She and her piebald Merrimack zipped around the arena with the verve of a barrel racer. At the end, she lifted the reins, and the horse skidded to a stop, set back on his haunches, and reared. I thought he would have hopped forward like a big ol' jumping rat if she'd asked for it, but she let him down and, laughing, slid to the ground. She gave that horse a big old hug and I liked her better than I had already—which was considerable.

Thinking that I liked her reminded me of Miss Roman poking around outside her caravan the other night, and then I got angry all over again.

Then it was Angel Maker's turn. The crew reset the cameras and dragged the arena—my old buddy Copper pulling the drag—and Jodi brought Angel Maker into the chute. Vernon and his Kinematoscope filmed Matthan Steele climbing up the boards beside the angry horse and I curled my nails into my palms so Bill danced sideways. I hoped Angel Maker would eat him.

No such luck. Matthan climbed down stiffly, favoring his knee, and I changed my hoping to that he was limping worse than usual because Cora had kicked him.

Vernon pulled the camera back to long range. Then Black climbed up, limber and clean, and I held my breath as he slung a leg over Angel Maker and got his hand into the loop good and solid.

Angel Maker's snorts and the thump of his hooves was so loud I could hear them from across the arena. Bill was still picking up on my tension, but he was a solid old guy and stood firm even when Jodi yanked the chute gate aside and Angel Maker exploded into the arena like a locomotive running off the tracks.

That horse could buck with the best of them. He was big, he was fit, and he had the talent that would have made him a fine jumper or cow horse if he'd led a different life up to that point. He seemed to spend seconds suspended in air on his first leap, though I knowed it weren't so. When he came down he landed on both forelegs, stiff and hard, and Black's head snapped as he took the shock of it.

I realized I was holding my breath but couldn't seem to let go of it as Angel Maker sunfished, twisted, and crow-hopped sideways three times. That was impressive enough, but he was just getting warmed up, and Black was already holding on to his hat.

Most bucking horses, they got one or two tricky moves, and they settle into a rhythm. If you can ride those tricks and find the rhythm, you can stay on better than you might to oughta. And Black could ride a bucker. I'd seen some bronc busting and this was the real deal, and I didn't think there was anything on God's green earth that Walker Black couldn't stick on until it quit.

Max yelled "Go, Walker!" and I saw him loose his grip on the loop. The next twist launched him sideways, and I already had old Bill moving forward at a jog that quickly turned into a lope. I reined him left then right, trying to stay well away from Angel Maker while still keeping him in the shot.

Angel Maker was still bucking, though not as hard now with Black off him. Black had tucked when he landed and rolled to his feet. Now he ran toward me, and I leaned forward to be out of the way when he threw himself up behind me.

Bill's saddle had a handhold screwed to the tree in the back, and as Walker came up to me I grabbed his right hand in mine and gave a good hard yank. The sidesaddle didn't hurt me none there because my legs were off the left, so when I hauled on Walker the weight of my lower half was distributed so I didn't get pulled over and neither did the saddle. I about stomped through the stirrup keeping my balance, and Bill snorted to let me know he weren't best pleased. But I felt the tug on the saddle as Black heaved, and the next thing I knew he was facedown across old Bill's rump. Then his hands was on my waist and all I had to do was rein the horse out of the arena and right at Vernon and his camera for the triumphant final shot.

We about charged over poor Vern in the process, because he just kept on cranking. But I managed to miss him and the Kinematoscope by about a sixteenth of an inch. And he got the shot, and that was all that mattered.

When I reined Bill up just outside the corral, I realized the whole crew that wasn't actively engaged in catching Angel Maker was standing around in a ring. Black let go my waist and slid down. I was about to follow him when the applause burst out all around us—two dozen men and women clapping and cheering and stomping their feet.

I laid a hand on Bill in case the ruckus made him nervous, but that silly old boy, he just dropped his head and stretched out a foot and sketched a bow like the campaigner he was. And I burst out laughing and, for the second time that day, gave a horse an exuberant hug.

For a moment it seemed like everybody in the world was cheering for us, and I basked in it. There was Max, and there was Miss Mosey, who grinned at me from Merrimack's back. And there was Priya, whooping and cheering despite the fact that I knew she thought I was a dad-blamed fool who was probably gonna get her head broken.

Well, we was a well-matched pair of fillies.

And there was Miss Roman, standing off to the side and looking foul weather enough that I wanted to warn her about getting mean wrinkles, and that if she wasn't careful her face might stick that way. I didn't care about Helene Roman, I decided. I didn't care what anybody thought. We had pulled this off, and it was all on film, and me and Black and Bill and Angel Maker was all unhurt.

So that made it the best day ever.

I was still thinking that when Miss Roman walked up behind Mr. Oster and took his elbow and led him aside, whispering in his ear, her long skirts swishing. And off they went together.

And then I remembered about Cora Darling, all stitched up in the infirmary, and Squalene lying dead, and my spirits weren't so high all of a sudden.

———————

When I came back from turning my dress into wardrobe, I followed the sound of gunshots out to the north meadow behind the Kindness place. It was still bright enough that I saw Miss Mosey standing with Priya, arms around her. My heart skipped an angry beat, but then I noticed Priya had a gun in her hands and Miss Mosey was steadying her aim.

I had to step over a spike of jealousy, but I didn't trip and fall on it, and that was enough to make me lift my head. Just because you got a feeling don't make you a bad person, just so long as you don't make it everybody else's problem.

I walked over to them, trying to make enough noise not to startle anybody with a gun in her hands. Miss Mosey was still wearing her coral dress, and it flattered her very well.

"Priya, I need to talk to you about something," I called, when I was close enough.

Both she and Miss Mosey turned, and I was glad to see Miss Mosey made Priya keep the gun barrel pointed at the ground. Miss Mosey stepped back, but I gestured her to stay. She might as well have the bad news.

"Steele raped Cora Darling," I said plainly. "And I don't know what the hell to do about it."

"Language!" Miss Mosey said, and then, "Who's Cora Darling?"

"The moonshiner," I said.

Miss Mosey grimaced. "I wish I could say I was surprised. It's not the worst I've heard of Mr. Steele. And I don't know what to do about it, either."

"You're powerful!" I said. "You're the star of this motion picture! Can't you... I don't know. Threaten to walk if Matthan don't get fired?"

"Even if I could do that, which I can't, he'd just go home and take it out on the next girl he got his hands on." She shook her head. "Look, Max has everything he needs from me. He could fire me tomorrow and make Helene Roman the romantic lead.

And I need this money as much as you do. I've got a widowed mother and sisters and brothers at home in Ohio."

I hadn't expected her to speak so plainly—but when it came down to it she was only a year or so older than Priya and me.

"Can you face kissing that man for the camera?" I asked her.

"No," she said. "But I done worse for money. When I was little my momma had to send me away to service because she had too many mouths to feed. Those people was downright animals."

"As bad as Steele?" I asked, before I rightly realized what I was asking.

"Maybe not as bad as," she admitted. "But bad enough, to a ten-year-old girl."

Priya didn't say nothing about what happened to her.

"I was orphaned," I said. "I went to the whorehouse. At least I got paid and I could make 'em take a bath if they weren't dainty enough to my liking." I shook my head. "This can't stand. He tore her up something awful."

"Where is she now?" Miss Mosey asked.

"At the infirmary, Miss Mosey."

"I'll go and talk with her. See if there's anything that can be done. And Karen, will you please call me Annie."

Priya went to return the gun to Miss Mosey's caravan. As I was walking back, I found Cowboy standing by the outhouse. He looked up as I approached, glass eyes flashing in the evening light, and I was pleased to realize I didn't feel no measure of apprehension at being close to him.

"Evening, Cowboy," I said.

"Evening, Miss Memery," he answered. "Are you all right out here alone?"

"I might ask the same of you. I know you ain't in need of a shithouse, so why so studious out beside one?"

He laughed, his tapes whirring quickly back between each *ha* so it sounded mighty sarcastic: "Ha. Ha. Ha." He finished and his tapes whirred again. He said, "I was contemplating the ironies of the universe, Miss Memery."

"I'm not sure I rightly know what that means, sir."

"It means," he said, "that I can't harm a person even to save a person. Even when I know what the first person did was wrong. But *you*"—his gesture condemned the whole human race—"hurt each other all the time for no reason and don't seem to think there's anything untoward about it."

I put my hand over my mouth. Over the whole bottom half of my face, truth to tell. He weren't wrong, and I didn't know what to say about it.

Just then, we heard the shouting.

Chapter Twenty-Four

It was getting dark, but Cowboy and I both legged it in the direction of the noise. He, being gentlemachinely, stayed beside me. I knowed we was both thinking the same thing—what if another body was discovered—and my heart was in my throat that I had not seen Priya.

No, but there she was, fine and dandy in the midst of a ring of people by Miss Mosey—by *Annie*'s caravan. And there was Miss Roman standing in front of Annie, pointing in her face and shaking her finger as if transported with rage. "You stole from me! Everybody knows you're a money-grubbing little hussy, but this is beyond belief!"

Annie just stood with her arms crossed, face like a solemn bust, shaking her head very gently. "Whatever you misplaced—"

"I didn't misplace anything! You stole it!"

I walked up beside Priya and touched her arm gently to let her know I was there. She favored me and Cowboy with a glance, her lips twisted in worry.

Mr. Oster came forward and placed a proprietary hand on Miss Roman's back, confirming my suspicions about the two of them. "Miss Mosey, I'm afraid we're going to have to search your caravan."

"For the love of Mike," she said, and rolled her eyes, but stepped aside. "You go ahead and look through my drawers, if it's that important to you."

I wondered if I was the only one who noticed the double entendre.

Jodi and the Peace brothers came forward, all of them looking reluctant and apologetic. Miss Roman smirked and held on to Oster's elbow, melting helplessly against him with a professionalism I might have admired under other circumstances.

Matthan Steel came limping up just then, and surveyed the scene with his usual arrogance. "What have we here?"

"That hussy stole from me," Miss Roman said. "And the proof is in her caravan somewhere!"

I stiffened, remembering almost tripping over her a couple of nights before. I didn't look at Cowboy, but I heard his tapes whirr, and wondered if he had made some similar connection. Not that he could say anything about it if he had.

I was going to have to intervene, I realized.

"Now Miss Roman, why would Miss Mosey need to steal from you?" Steele's voice was pretty poison as he said, "We all know she's paid higher than any of the rest of us."

Miss Roman's jaw dropped.

He smiled. "You think I don't know that Evans was blackmailing you into working for almost nothing?"

"Blackmailing me!" she said. "There's nothing to blackmail me with. You and your light-skirt women, on the other hand—"

"Oh, I think we both know that's not true, Miss Roman," he oozed. "Or should I say, Mrs. O'Neill."

She gasped. I gasped. Everybody around the whole circle gasped, except for Cowboy, who just whirred quietly.

"That's contumely," she said, pulling herself up and smoothing the shock off her face. "I have never been married."

"Never abandoned your husband in a sanatorium to die of consumption, either," Steele said. He swung his cane lightly. "You know the only reason you came to work on this... I can barely dignify it with the term... 'motion picture' was because Evans told you he'd destroy your career if you didn't."

Well, it looked like this argument might draw on for a geological era, and either Jodi or the Peace boys was going to come up with the bright idea of checking under the caravan sooner or later. And I was getting chilly now that the sun was setting.

I pushed forward and went to stand in the weeds where Miss Roman had been crouched the other night. I hunkered down, same as she had, and started feeling around the undercarriage of the caravan, remembering that her arms was somewhat shorter than mine.

I'd only been there for five or ten seconds when the arguing stopped, and I realized that everybody was staring at me. And then Miss Roman started to charge toward me, her hands outstretched.

Annie stepped in between us, her arms still folded. "Let's see what Miss Memery finds."

Just then my fingers brushed a bit of hide cord, and I tugged on it. A little suede bag fell into my fingers.

"Well I found this," I said, and held it out to Max, who had stepped forward out of the crowd. "I think you ought to open it."

He took it from my hand. His nimble fingers worked the knot loose, and he upended it over his palm.

A necklace winking with gold and diamonds spilled out like a short waterfall of light, and we all gasped again.

Except Miss Roman, who drew herself up and yelped, "See? I told you so!"

"Except," I said, "two nights ago I found you crouched down feeling around under Miss Mosey's caravan in the middle of the night. Which is why I knew exactly where to look for this."

"You're lying," Miss Roman spat.

"I ain't," I said. "And Miss Swati saw you, too."

"I deny it," Miss Roman said. "How do I know you two didn't hide that under here to throw suspicion on me *and* Miss Mosey?"

"Now I don't believe *that* for a hot second," said Annie. "The way I see it—"

"Hold on just a second, Miss Mosey," said Mr. Oster, smoothly interposing himself. He stepped up beside Miss Roman, and plucked the necklace off Max's hand. "Miss Roman, was this the only item that was missing?"

She nodded, her teeth prettily pinching her lower lip. Her eyelashes fluttered as he handed the necklace back to her.

"There, then," he said. "Whoever's mischief this was—and I think it was a terrible prank and you ought to be ashamed of yourself—it's all settled now. Now everybody go to dinner. Tomorrow is a day off for Easter and I want you all to contemplate how better to exemplify the spirit of Christ in your hearts. We don't have time for this nonsense."

I only heard Max mutter, "Jewish," because I was standing right next to him. But I let him know I heard him with a little sideways smile.

Mr. Oster—I marked him in my mind.

Because bearing false witness is in the Bible for a mortal sin. Selling what you sit down on to earn your bread ain't one of the Commandments that I ever heard, but folk will cross the street to avoid a whore that shakes the hand of a hypocrite.

The bit that smarts ain't having enemies lie about you. It's when somebody you thought was a friend and who knew you takes their word. Or at least doesn't argue, because they're too afraid of what the viper might do to them in turn.

Lord, what moral cowards these mortals be.

———————————

We ate at the mess tent because it was a hell-sight easier than going home to cook for ourselves. Then I got caught up talking to Walker while Priya went to tack Molly so we could ride home.

And if Priya hadn't gone on ahead, it never would have happened. but I was just going to meet her at the barn and my eye lit on Matthan Steele's caravan.

I'd managed to keep my tongue in my head earlier, because the important thing was protecting Annie from Miss Roman, but now there was nothing to stop me. The door was open, and I could see him moving around inside by the light of a kerosene lamp.

So I marched up that ramp and I came face-to-face with Matthan Steele and reader, my Irish got the better of me. I knowed I should keep walking. I knowed I shouldn't even turn an eye in his direction.

But I did, and he saw my sneer.

"Miss Memery," he said slickly, "you showing up at my caravan after dark like this. People will talk."

I had enough sense not to go inside. I stood on his threshold and hissed, "I know you raped Cora Darling, and you're going to pay for it. I'm going to see to it."

"That slattern?" He laughed. His hand moved toward me and I stepped back. You don't give ground to a pushy horse, but I wasn't going to let Matthan Steele drag me into his den. "You're a woman of the world, Miss Memery. You know what these girls are like. They want something, they come on to a man, and then when they get it they decide they didn't want it after all."

I shook my head and rolled my eyes. "Someday somebody is gonna pay you back for what you done."

He smirked. "Why don't you go tell Mister Oster about it?" Actorly, he spread his hands wide. "Or that Sheriff MacGregor. I wager he'd take your word over mine, don't you think?"

That fire inside me had to go somewhere and if I broke his handsome nose there would be Hell to pay. "You just can't stop playing to the cheap seats even when you got no audience but me," I said. "You're rich and you're white and you're a man. You've gotten away with everything forever, but that don't mean you *is* gonna get away with everything forever." I smiled. "So just remember that."

I stepped back, wishing the door was on my side so I could slam it.

Mostly people ain't got a lot of moral courage when it's their own friends or even just members of their community that's acting poorly. They may talk in private and have plenty to say, but when it comes to a public unpleasantness they won't stick up to a bully unless it's a bully none of their friends is in bed with.

So I mused on that while I stomped back to the barn, and I was all the way inside before I remembered that I had been meaning to pay a visit to that preacher man and find out exactly what he and Evans thought they were up to, with regard to Miz Kindness' land.

Chapter Twenty-Five

It was raining by the time we reached the ranch. I left Priya there to get a start on chores and rode into town on Molly.

Mr. Lincoln was not staying at the Cherry Hotel, which was prohibitive for overnight guests because of the other services involved—but at an actual hotel, and the best one in Rapid City: the Rain City Riverside. I wasn't keen to visit it, having experienced some misadventures there. But I girded myself up nevertheless and asked after him. The concierge seemed happy to see me, pointed out the fresh refurbishments in the lobby while I blushed, and told me I would find Mr. Lincoln in the lounge.

Now, ladies don't usually intrude upon such gentlemanly spaces, I concede. But I was there on business and it wasn't like women was *barred.* So I decided to be a tiny bit rude and go on in.

It was a dark room with little pools of electric light here and there—the Rain City Riverside were that fancy—and leather and red velvet on every surface that wasn't a Turkish rug or varnished walnut.

I didn't have much trouble spotting Mr. Lincoln. He sat facing the door across a low table from another wingback chair, and he was going over some papers and scribbling notes in his little black-backed pad.

Cowboy sat in the deep-seated chair right across from him.

I swished up, making sure my skirts and shoes made plenty of noise—I'd stopped off home to make myself presentable before riding into town, so it was convenient I still had that trunk of my seamstressin' clothes—and stopped alongside them. "Sorry to intrude, gentlemen."

Both Mr. Lincoln and Cowboy popped out of their chairs like corks, clanking slightly.

"Miss Memery!" said Lincoln. "Won't you sit?"

"Ain't I interrupting a conference with your client?" I said, indicating Cowboy.

"Your partner is also Mister Lincoln's client," Cowboy replied, in his particular staccato way of talking.

There was a third chair, red silk brocade, and I availed myself of it even though it clashed with my mauve-striped wool. Not for the first time, I contemplated that Priya needed to invent and patent a popular dye process, and then we'd be rolling in money.

"Brandy?" asked Lincoln.

I was chilled through, so I accepted even though he weren't drinking. And neither, obviously, was Cowboy. It was pleasant to be treated not as an interloper but as somebody who had every right to be there.

I had shrugged out of my pelisse but not surrendered it, and now I reached into the pocket to produce the packet of maps and blueprints. "Squalene Jones gave me these right before she was killed," I told Lincoln, handing them over. "I thought they might be useful to the case."

"Hmm," he said, sorting through them. He looked at Cowboy. "Do you want to tell her?"

"I suppose there is no reason not to," the mechanical intoned. He fixed his eerie gaze on me, his metal eyelids blinking like the Kinematoscope's shutter. "Now that no further harm can come to her, I have informed Mister Lincoln that Miz Jones was the person who murdered Otis Kindness and Michael Evans."

"Well I never," I said, because I had not. "Don't that solve all our problems then?"

"Unfortunately, no," said Mr. Lincoln. "MacGregor is going to say it's a convenient lie that absolves Cowboy and Miss Swati. And there's the still the question of Miz Jones' own murder. And her motives."

"You think," I said uneasily, "we got a criminal conspiracy here."

"I am afraid so," said Mr. Lincoln. "Miz Jones may have given you those papers in order to additionally frame you."

I rubbed my eyes. "How did she know to frame Priya and me in the first place? I mean, she's new in town, how did she even know about the Singer?"

Cowboy said, "She did not use the Singer. I would guess the blood on the armature was chicken blood, or from some other farm animal."

"Miss Memery," said Lincoln, "you forget that all these United States"—I detected a tiny bit of pride as he said it—"knows about the Singer. You have been in the newspapers and there was your delightful recounting of the events surrounding the Russian plot, which was widely serialized."

I put a palm to my forehead. Sometimes a woman can be just plain oblivious to what's right in front of her.

I asked Cowboy, "So she used her own arm to do the beating?"

He nodded. "I assume that is why it was not working properly afterward."

I said, "All right then. But why was she following that map when we had already discovered that Otis was salting? I guess... it ain't like we made a point of telling anyone. In fact MacGregor made a point of *not* telling anyone."

Lincoln looked up over the rim of his reading glasses. "Word got around."

"Maybe word didn't get to Squalene," I said.

"Perhaps. But if it did, there must be something else valuable up the mountain," Cowboy said. "Logically speaking."

"Wait," I said. "Hand me that map, would you?"

Lincoln gave it over without a qualm. I studied it. "Do we think the blueprints was just for camouflage?"

"It seems likely," Lincoln said, thumbing through them. "These look old, and I think some of them are schematics for Miz Jones' mechanical arm. They might also have been to make it look like you and Priya were stealing important-looking paperwork."

"Cowboy," I said, the fumes of the brandy going to my head a little, "I don't suppose you know who murdered Squalene?"

"I do not have that knowledge," he said formally.

I tried not to feel angry at this person who I barely knew but had liked, somewhat, even if she was a drinking woman. Maybe she'd been drinking to ease her conscience.

I remembered what Walker Black had said about blackmailers, and Steele's revelation that Evans had been blackmailing Miss Roman. That made me curious if Evans had been blackmailing Squalene, too, and if that was why she was so desperate for money.

But I was angry, and it didn't matter that she was facing God's judgment now and far beyond that of me or the Circuit Court judge who, with any luck, would be along on Monday or Tuesday.

Maybe he would take Cowboy's testimony serious, even if MacGregor wouldn't.

Anyway, I told them my blackmail theory and the evidence behind it, and they both nodded and looked serious. Mr. Lincoln said, "Do you think, based on his comment, that Evans might have had his hooks into Mister Black, as well?"

"I don't know," I admitted. "It seems like almost certainly he was milking Steele. Maybe half the cast and crew was under his thumb. But if Squalene killed him—" I shook my head.

"Did she have any next of kin who ought to be notified?" Cowboy was apparently the one among us with the refined sensibilities.

"I don't know," I said. "I guess Max would have to send them a telegram. If he hasn't already."

I spread the map out in the puddle of light under the table lamp. It was really astonishing how bright that glowed. A girl could work all night on sewing or writing or Mad Science with a light like that without ruining her eyes.

Someday I would know our mountain like the back of my hand. I did not yet, quite, but as I was staring at the hand-traced lines something struck me.

"Most of the property ain't on here," I said. "This is just the line up along the bluffs and where the sea caves are."

"Correct me if I am wrong," said Mr. Lincoln, "but aren't sea caves an unusual venue for a gold discovery?"

"Maybe Mister Kindness weren't too aware of geology." I noticed that the map drew a boundary that left off the inland portion of the Lazy B, and Miz Kindness' cabin. And the stream that ran through both our properties. So he hadn't been planning on selling the whole ranch. If selling was what he had been planning.

I lowered my voice. "There's got to be a real gold deposit up there somewhere, don't there just about? Otherwise where did Otis get that little bag of dust?"

"Miss Memery," Lincoln said. "I do think you might be on to something. May I hold on to this map?"

"I think it's safest with you," I agreed, and handed it over. The brandy had warmed me up, and I hid a yawn. "I think maybe I should head on home now. I still want to stop by and chat up that tent-revival fellow a mite, just to find out what he thinks he's buying."

Mr. Lincoln and Cowboy exchanged glances. "May I accompany you, Miss Memery?" Cowboy asked. "I fear that man may be dangerous."

"That's right chivalrous of you, Cowboy," I said, and patted him on the metal arm. "You won't have no problem keeping up with Molly?"

———————————

I bundled up and Cowboy and me departed. I was all atwitter with excitement, frankly: if there was gold in the stream up by the Kindness place, there might be gold in the stream where it ran through our stake, too. And even if it were only a little, that would pay the bills, most like, and maybe even a bit left over.

The rain had even let up some, and Molly was cheerful to be headed home. She'd been a saint all week, with the toing and froing and walking past home in either direction. I guessed maybe I was benefitting because she was lonely with nobody but a cow for company, and I did keep taking her places with other horses at least. Winning with livestock ain't too different from winning at poker, excepting nobody considers it cheating if you stack the deck.

They just think it's witchcraft when it works out.

The revival tent was lit up with some lanterns when we got there, but there only seemed to be a few people about outside. At least everybody hadn't yet gone to bed: I could hear plenty of voices coming from inside the tent and see shapes moving around behind the canvas. I tied Molly to the rail and swung down, Cowboy flanking me as I headed closer.

I paused outside the tent flap, because there were a full-blown prayer meeting in session. Father Postlethwait was up on a plank scaffold with a Holy Bible in his right hand and a satin stole around his shoulders. He was all a-going on the fire and brimstone—a bit more than I thought seemly on Easter Eve, which is supposed to be about the hope of redemption and such—and as I listened a kind of unease dawned in me.

I could only catch about two words in three but he was talking about those unchurched aliens as had washed up on American shores and was bringing their heathen and murderous ways with 'em.

He was talking about Priya. And given what our people had done to the native inhabitants of these "American shores," I didn't think he had a leg to stand on in calling anybody else murderous.

I might not have realized it before I met Tomoatooah and got to know him so well. Or Priya, and heard about what the English got up to in China and India. But weren't nobody's hands clean; we just liked to pretend to ourselves that we has some manifest destiny and that ordained right to other people's places.

People don't like to think about such as makes 'em uncomfortable.

I put a hand on Cowboy's elbow and edged him back. We tiptoed through the dark until we was far enough away that I felt comfortable whispering. "Let's go around back and see if we can meet the Reverend Father Whatever on his way back to his tent for the night, shall we?"

"That should not be too hard," said Cowboy. "I can see in the dark."

––––––––

The alleluias rang out for another good half hour or more while I watched the moon peer through the clouds and was grateful for the warmth of my pelisse. My feet started to ache in my boots and I was filled with thanks for Cowboy standing beside me when the hoot owls moaned in the trees and the coyotes set up a howl along the side of the mountain. Those sounds made me feel warm and safe when I was home in bed with Priya and the stove burned down to embers. Out here in the chilly night, they made me feel as if I was like to wind up dinner.

Cowboy and I waited in a companionable silence, mostly. He wound himself up at one point. I hadn't realized until he pulled the key out of somewhere and inserted it in a little lock on his chest that his clockworks ran on a mainspring, but I suppose it made sense. I wondered what it felt like, having a spring for a heart. I wondered if he felt anything at all, but it seemed rude to ask of him, so I kept my curiosity under my hat.

We just stood near the lantern outside the biggest of the sleeping tents after that, him listening to me breathe and me listening to him tick softly. The faint hiss of his speaking tapes had stilled. I guess he wasn't even considering vocalizing.

Finally, the voices in the revival tent went quieter and folk started milling around outside. A shape came out of the darkness toward us. I recognized the Reverend Father Postlethwait as he emerged from the dark, and I stepped up into the light of the lantern. Cowboy clanked up two steps behind me.

"Father," I said, "I was wondering if you had a few minutes to talk to us."

"Us?" he said, then looked over my shoulder. "That thing is a mockery of God's work in man. How dare you bring this *thing* to my church?"

Well that got my back up and no mistaking. "I thought Miz Kindness' place was going to be your church."

And then I realized, he'd been asking after her house, not the cliff-line property. Which meant, I bet a stack of Necco Wafers, that he knew perfectly well where the gold was. Or least he knew perfectly well where it weren't.

I wonder if he'd bothered to tell Evans or if he'd planned to cheat Evans, too.

The realization was writ all over my face, and I knowed it because I could see the dueling realization writ all over *his* face.

Postlethwait raised his voice. "Get away from me, you... abomination!"

I stepped back, closer to Cowboy, as if I could shield the big mechanical with my little parcel of flesh and bones. I nearly protested Postlethwait's choice of words, which would have been a waste of breath. Instead, I used it to whisper to Cowboy, "Can you fight your way out of here if we gotta?"

"I cannot allow a human being to come to harm, Miss Memery," he said, and I got the sense that just this once he regretted it.

I was still thinking on that when what to my watering eyes should appear out of the darkness except fifteen or sixteen big strong men, solid citizens of Rapid City who must have been there for the tent revival, and a few I didn't recognize that must have been the Reverend's roustabouts. There was some women behind them, too, which was bad. Men hate to look weak in front of a woman.

"Children of God!" declaimed Postlethwait in a voice that about rang off the overhanging mountainside. "This fallen woman and this unholy, murderous automaton have threatened me. Please remove them from the premises!"

I heard a woman say, "Ain't that the mechanical as killed that colored fellow?" so I knowed it wasn't gonna get any less dangerous anytime soon.

One man, braver than the rest, moved toward me, and I turned and looked him full in the face. "Junior Cartwright," I said. "Don't you lay a hand on me without my say-so. I was just going."

The crown was murmuring and surging, getting ugly. But Junior stepped back, and that held 'em for a minute. I looked at Cowboy.

With a click, he nodded. He tipped his hat to the reverend—a saucy touch—and turned on his heels like they had ball bearings in 'em. I don't know: maybe they did.

They parted around us as I walked back to Molly. "Don't run," Cowboy muttered.

"Don't worry," I said. "This ain't my first rodeo."

"I've seen you ride," he agreed. I almost busted out laughing and I don't know if that would have been good or bad.

They stayed back as I untied Molly from the picket, but the line was rippling. I swung up into the saddle, Cowboy pacing beside me, and looked over the crowd to see Postlethwait's smirk.

"And a blessed Easter to you, Father," I called over the crowd, because I got no idea when to keep my mouth shut.

Then I wheeled Molly and put her to a trot, which she accepted despite being tired because she didn't like that crowd any better than I did. I didn't know if they was gonna follow me up the mountain. If they didn't, all was well. Or as well as it could be with Postlethwait gathering a flock and telling them Cowboy and probably Priya was the killers.

If they *did* follow... well then what I had on my hands was a good old-fashioned mob, and I couldn't go back to the ranch house. Priya was there. Because if they marched all the way up the mountain they wouldn't hesitate to lynch one or both of us and burn the whole place to the ground, too. And probably yank off Cowboy's arms and legs and take a hammer to him, just for gravy.

Then I thought, what would Tomoatooah and Miss Merry Lee do?

They would take to the rooftops, and while I wasn't as nimble as either of them, I was nimble enough. But they wouldn't have had Molly and Cowboy to worry about, and I weren't going to abandon neither one of them.

And there wasn't much in the way of rooftops where we was going.

"We need to step off the road," I told Cowboy. "Once we're out of town, and see if they follow."

"I understand," he said.

We could hear voices and some other noise coming up the mountainside at first, but then we got next to the river and that drowned out everything. When we found a place to step off the road, we waited a half hour and then a quarter hour more—Cowboy also functioned as an accurate timepiece, it turned out—and nobody followed.

Thank the rain for quelling a riot, I guess.

"I'll walk you home," Cowboy said. And I let him.

Chapter Twenty-Six

Cowboy left me and Molly at the bottom of the lane. I got the horse put up for the night with a double measure of feed as a sort of apology and took myself into the house, where a gentle lamplight was still burning. I didn't expect Priya to have waited up for me, but it was nice that she kept a candle in the window, so to speak. I left my muddy boots by the door.

I was feeling cold and sorry for myself and anxious as a filly in fly season and grateful for the dinner Priya had left to warm, covered on the woodstove. Potatoes and lentils in a seasoned gravy, and some rounds of delicious flaky unleavened bread that looked a bit like flapjacks but didn't taste like flapjacks in any particular.

I ate as quiet as I could, and then I padded in sock feet over to the bed and was about to lift the covers and snuggle in next to the warmth of my wife when I realized the covers was flat and the bed weren't warm at all.

It was empty and Priya was nowhere to be found.

There was no note, no nothing, and I searched the cabin five times to see that all that was missing of Priya's things was her coat, her boots, and a suit of clothes and two extra shirts and underthings. The cow had been milked and all the chores taken care of, but...

No Priya.

Reader, I did not sleep that night, and it was only the knowledge that Molly was done in and so was I—and that there was very little effective searching we could do in the dark—that kept me from riding right back into town and gathering up a posse of Mr. Lincoln and all the girls from the Cherry Hotel. So I sat in the bentwood chair by the fire all bundled up in the bedclothes and rocked myself back and forth with anxiety, waiting for sunrise.

It was about the darkest night of my life and two of the longest. Surely Priya hadn't left me? Things had been uneven between us for a while, and we'd had our troubles and disagreements for certain. But she wouldn't just have up and gone without a word, leaving my dinner to warm beside the fire. That weren't like my beautiful, bullheaded Priya. She wouldn't slink away from a fight, and she wouldn't sneak out in the middle of the night.

Especially not with our ranch house dependent on her not bail jumping.

The sky was just getting bright and I was just wondering what to do first and getting a clean pair of socks on when a bang on the door made me jump straight up about sixteen inches. Ain't nobody ever compared me to a cat, but I felt like one as I walked to the door, my heart pounding and my hackles standing on end. If I had a tail it would have been lashing.

It took all my courage to pull that pine door open. My eyes must have been wild and I knowed my hair was.

I don't know what I was expecting, but it weren't Jodi from the film set, looking shamefaced and apologetic in the gloaming. "Miss Memery?" he said. "Sorry to wake you so early."

"I wasn't sleeping," I said. "Come in, coffee's about boilt."

He toed out of his boots and stepped over the threshold. "I wanted to catch you before you went to church."

That's right, it was Easter Sunday. I said, "Catch me for what?" and poured him a measure of joe in the guest cup. I'd nearly finished mine, and it looked like I might have time to drink another, so I topped off my enameled tin mug and hugged it in both hands.

"I got a message for you." He held out a folded and sealed piece of paper. I put my coffee down to take it.

It had my name on the outside, in Priya's handwriting:

Miss Karen Morning Memery.

I blinked. Why would she use Miz Kindness's first name for me, and spell it wrong to boot? Sure, she loved to add bits and bobs to my name—but that was a strange one. And why would she send me a note via Jodi rather than leaving it in the house? Had she been at the camp all night dealing with some kind of mechanical emergency?

I asked, "Where did you get this?"

"It was in my tent this morning." Jodi shook his head. "I don't know who slipped it under the flap, though."

"Rude." I was trying to make light and I knowed it. Hands shaking, I picked the letter open.

The note was also in Priya's writing. It said:

Dear Karen,
I can't stay and face trial. You know as well as I do that I would be convicted.
So the best thing for me to do is vanish. I hope you do good running the ranch without me. Tell my Da I said I was sorry.
Also it's safest for both of us if you stay out of the business at the Kindness ranch. Just let it be.
Your humble etc,
Priya

I stared at it, hands shaking more and more and until the paper rattled and I had to set it down on the table. The first thing that hit me was that wall of loneliness, a feeling like I ain't never should have trusted nobody and like I never could again. It rose up my gorge like the sight of blood, burning in my throat, and I had to grab my coffee and gulp it down to settle the sensation.

Remorse can be a rein. A rein and a mean heavy curb. Something somebody can use to jerk your head around any way they choose to, and cut you bloody-mouthed doing it.

I wouldn't do that to a horse. I ain't gonna do it to no woman—no. No, this letter was in Priya's writing. But it weren't *from* Priya, if you take my meaning.

I said as much to Jodi. "This ain't from Priya. Or it is from Priya, rather, but Priya's in a heap of trouble somehow."

"What do you mean Miss Swati is in trouble?"

"I think she must be." I showed him the letter. "She don't call her da 'Da.' She calls him 'Appa.' And she knows full well I staked this ranch on her bail, so if she vanishes I ain't gonna keep it. Anyway, somebody made her write this. Can you ride into town for me and fetch Mister Lincoln, Jodi? I can pay for your time."

He *tsk*ed. "Miss Memery, if Miss Swati is in trouble, ain't nohow I'm going to take your money."

"Tell him to meet me at the Kindness place," I said.

———

Sheriff MacGregor rode up on his big gray while I was saddling Molly. He didn't bother to swing down, just looked at me from his seat on high and said, "Where's Miss Swati?"

"Up at the motion picture set, I reckon," I said. "I ain't seen her this morning."

Only half a lie, and the latter part was dead true.

He waved a piece of paper at me. "Well this is a court summons," he said, then stuffed it back inside his coat pocket. "I've had a telegram from the Territorial Associate Judge Alliene. He's diverted his circuit to come to Rapid City, since a murder charge is more pressing than insanity, probate, and Indian matters. He will be here tomorrow. If Miss Swati does not present herself, make sure she knows this ranch is forfeit."

"Oh," I said, my hands shaking on the saddle cinch. "She knows, I'm sure."

———

The motion picture was taking the day off for Easter, though I'd gathered Max Forth himself was Jewish and them folk don't have no truck with the Resurrection. Still, most of his crew did, and if he didn't take his own Sabbath, he let them have theirs. I rode right in, stabled Molly, and waved to my colleagues as I tromped up the steps to Mourning Kindness's porch.

I rapped on the door, hoping I'd caught her in time, and found her with her church clothes on—that black dress (I gathered she only had two or three) with a big black straw hat pinned on and a printed shawl to dress it up a little.

"Miz Kindness," I said. "Can I come in a moment? I have some things to tell you before you head on into town."

"Well." She glanced down the lane. "I don't see the wagon coming."

I went in and she poured me coffee, though I was already nearly floating. I drank a sip anyway. Her coffee, I am sorry to admit, was a sight better'n mine.

Then I launched right in: "Whatever you do, Miz Kindness, don't you sell this house or any of the land."

Miz Kindness sucked her lips against her teeth. "It's barely an hour past sunup and you're my already my second visitor, Miss Memery. That preacher man came up to me on *Easter Sunday* and told me he was going to buy the mortgage to this farm and foreclose on me if I didn't sell it to him. There's no gold. Why does everybody want this place?"

"Maybe there is gold," I said. "Just not where Mister Kindness was telling folks there is."

Her jaw dropped. "How do you know that?"

I held my hand up. "I can't believe it took me this long to figure it out, Miz Kindness. But Otis... that map was only the part of the property overlooking the ocean. Where the motion picture is shooting. And that gold he was salting with had to come from somewhere, didn't it?"

"It would be like him," she said thoughtfully, "to try to sell a fake gold mine and keep the real one for himself."

I nodded, feeling my chest tighten. This was explosive, in more ways than one.

"Oh we have to keep this quiet," Miz Kindness said. "Or there's going to be a gold rush all up and down this mountain. Who knows about this?"

"Just us," I said. "And Mister Lincoln. And Cowboy. And… look, Miz Kindness. I think that preacher man has my Priya locked up somewhere, and he's going to use her not showing in court tomorrow to get the sheriff to seize our ranch and then buy that as well."

"Your Miss Swati is missing?" With long, steady fingers, Miz Kindness reached up and unpinned her hat. "Do you know she's alive?"

I handed her the letter.

"I can't read that," said Miz Kindness. "My daddy and my husband didn't hold with women being too educated."

"Well, look here." I pointed. "She gave me your name on the front, but spelled like 'dawn' rather than like 'grief.'"

"Wait," she said. "Those ain't spelled the same?"

"English is a cantankerous beast," I said. "And see here inside she said some things that ain't how she would have said them, or that she would have knowed weren't true. And she ain't never once called herself my obedient servant. Also, why would she warn me away from your business like this here—" I read her the bit about the Kindness ranch. "—unless somebody was making her."

Miz Kindness squinted at the paper. "Miss Memery, would you teach me to read?"

I met her gaze. "Assuming we all survive this, and we keep our ranches and I don't have to go back to the Hôtel Ma Cherie."

She nodded. "At least to sign my own name?"

"I can do *that* today," I said. "Cowboy told us it was Squalene Jones as killed your husband and that motion picture producer, by the way. Now that Squalene is dead, I guess he ain't got nothing keeping him from talking about it."

"Pity she's dead," said Miz Kindness. "So I can't thank her. Did he say who killed Miz Jones?"

"I don't think he knows. I've got to find Priya," I said. "Or we're both going to lose our farms. And I have no idea where to start looking."

"I got to pay that mortgage," said Miz Kindness. She laid the letter on the table. "Before the bank can sell it."

"It'll take them until tomorrow," I said. "Today is Easter Sunday. Let's practice your name a little until that wagon comes."

We did it on the fire shovel with a bit of charcoal, just like Lincoln had done as a boy. It was a good distraction from my worry, and she was a quick study. I wrote down the alphabet for her and taught her how to sound out some words. She already knew her numbers.

She asked again about the difference between "mourning" and "morning" and seemed downright tickled that two words pronounced the same could be spelt different and have such different meanings.

A map could have two different meanings as well, I realized. It could be a portrait that included a place. Or one that excluded everything *but* a place. I put my coal-smirched hand to my mouth.

"Miz Kindness. I think I just figured out where your gold might be. Things is quiet here right now. The church wagon ain't yet come. I asked Jodi to fetch Mr. Lincoln, and I guess after church it's likely he'll be on his way up here. What if... you and me, we go pan that stream a little? Just to see if anything turns up?"

"On the Lord's Day?" Miz Kindness said, scandalized. Then her face relaxed. "Actually. Under the circumstances, having offered us this providence... I think he might understand."

Neither me nor Miz Kindness had more than a theoretical understanding of how to pan a stream for gold, but we did at least have a theoretical understanding. She sent me out when the church wagon showed up to tell them she was poorly, and the black woman driving it smiled and said, "And no wonder with all she's been through. You tell her we'll pray a little extra for her today."

Then Miz Mourning left her shawl behind and changed her church shoes for barefoot—in that cold morning!—and we snuck out the back door past the woodshed and outhouse and around the little graveyard and into the trees, me carrying her cook-pan done up in a sack to be a little less obvious about it. We picked our way up about a half mile, out of sight, and I took my boots off while she kilted her skirts. She walked into that icy snowmelt without a flinch. I made sad, small gasping noises.

The rocks was slick underfoot and minnows nibbled my toes, but pretty soon I went numb. We waded up to a pool with a sandy bottom where the water slowed, and I unbundled the pan and the tin cup we'd brought along to use as a scooper. The shovel would have been too obvious, we reckoned.

It weren't no fun dipping our hands in that cold water, and even kilted up the hems of our skirts got soaked and stuck to our legs. I had to work hard and steady to keep my teeth from chattering.

Miz Kindness picked up scoopfuls of sand and mud from various places around the pool, plunging her arms in deep with no more hesitation than she'd showed wading out here. She plopped them in the pan, and I dipped and swirled, dipped and swirled until the sand and mud washed clean and only some pebbles was left in the bottom.

A half hour went past, and I didn't find nothing that sparkled except some flecks of mica—but I knowed those weren't gold because they were light, and washed right out of the pan with every swirl. After that time, though, I was getting the hang of it.

"Maybe it ain't here," I said, shivering and desperate.

"If it ain't here we ain't got a better idea," she told me.

Miz Kindness was wading out deeper and deeper. She came back finally with a mug full of black mud, herself wet all the way to her bosom. "If this ain't it I don't know where else to look."

She plopped it in the pan.

Even looking at it I could tell this cup was different. It was thick and heavy, sticky almost, and it took a lot of water to thin it out and move it. I almost missed the first flash because I had drifted into a sort of mesmerism. It caught my eye though, and snapped me back to where I was (knee-deep in a river) and what I was doing (freezing my fool ass off). The second flash, through the murky water, was more definite.

I was blue and I was shivering and my hands wanted to shake so bad it was hard keeping the pan swirling. But I kept washing, because I wanted to be sure. And once the water ran clear, there it was in the bottom of the pan. Almost a whole pinch of gold dust, sparkling in the Easter sunshine that only just then filtered over the tops of the trees.

"Miz Kindness," I said, "I think we got something."

She splashed over to me with her wet skirts and her little tin mug and peered into the pan, tilting her head so she didn't block the sunlight.

"Miss Memery," she said, "I think you had better call me Mourning."

Chapter Twenty-Seven

It's hard to know when to drop a winning streak. You get antsy and have to keep proving to yourself you're hot, and you find out too late that you ain't. Miz Kindness went back two or three times for another mug full of mud as black as my da's coffee, and in each one we found a hefty pinch of color.

That didn't, of course, find me Priya. But maybe it got us one step closer to learning who had her, and finding something to bargain with.

We snuck back into the house, avoiding the San Diego and Chicago folk as best we could. Being dripping wet, we wasn't exactly subtle, but people walk around a motion picture set in all stages of disarray, so we stayed away from people, waved from a distance, and mostly hoped we wasn't as obvious as we would have been walking down Amity Street in Rapid.

Come to think of it, sopping wet and muddy folk ain't such an unfamiliar sight in Rain County, but that particular morning was unseasonably dry and sunny. I bet Max was chewing his toenails off over it being a holiday and him losing that good shooting weather.

Miz Kindness and me warmed up in front of her fire—she didn't have a proper Franklin stove, though I guessed if the gold held out she might soon—and we was nearly dried off by the time Mr. Lincoln arrived.

I heard him on the porch before he come in, thanking Jodi and sending him off. Then a sharp rap on the door, and Miz Kindness called, "It ain't on the latch, sir!"

The string pull lifted the little bar, the door creaked open, and Lincoln stood framed against the day. "Come on in," said Miz Kindness, standing. "Can I get you a cup of coffee?"

"That would be a pure kindness," Mr. Lincoln said in his famously folksy tones.

He closed the door behind him. "Now what's this Jodi tells me about Priya being missing?"

I showed him the letter, which I had managed to keep dry in my bosom, and told him the whole story of our morning, including the gold. He sat on the hearth, there not being enough chairs, and nodded, long legs stretched out like a harvestman spider. Over the letter, he stroked his chin. "And you're confident Miss Swati must have written this under duress?"

I went over what I had told Jodi already, about Priya's Appa and that she weren't likely to apologize to him. And the odd thing about combining my name and Mourning's, and misspelling Mourning's, though I blushed to tell the two of them about it.

Miz Kindness said, "I kind of like that it's a different spelling. Don't you think Morning is a prettier name? It ain't so sad, anyway."

I patted her arm in agreement and said to Mr. Lincoln, "That has to be a clue of some kind, don't it?"

"The problem with a person as brilliant as your Miss Swati," he said with some tiredness leaking into his voice, "is that they tend to assume everybody else is as smart as they is."

"Well if you're telling me I got to be as smart as Priya to figure this out"—I shook my head—"we ain't never going to find her." Then I said the thing that was pulling at me worst. "What reason do we got to assume she's still alive when they have already kilt three people, Mister Lincoln? And please tell me we got a reason."

"Well," he said, "they want her framed for these murders it seems like, and if somebody were to shoot her then that would open up some questions. That doesn't stop them from arranging something that looks like an accident," he added. "But we lose nothing, right now, by operating as if Miss Swati is alive and well and awaiting our rescue."

"Oh, she ain't waiting for it," I said, grateful for the permission to assume Priya was just fine somewhere and as pissed off as Angel Maker. "She's prying herself loose with her fingernails as we speak on it. But Mister Lincoln, we *got* to search for her. I can't just sit still. I've got to find her by breakfast tomorrow or we're going to lose the ranch."

"Good point," he said. "And that might be the point of the whole operation. That revival preacher might be the best place to start looking." He reached out and tapped the table next to the paper that held our tiny stake of dust. "I can ask the sheriff for help in finding her."

"How do we know the sheriff ain't in on the plot to get our land, and Miz Kindness'?" I asked. "He's sure been instrumental to the process."

Lincoln's mouth twisted. "We don't."

"If I tell him Priya's missing he's going to claim she lit out, whether he was party to the shenanigans or not, and then I'm going to lose my ranch as well."

Miz Kindness and I shared a bleak look. I reached out and put my hand over her long, work-weary fingers.

Miz Kindness said, "And we know what Miz Jones did, but we still don't know who shot Miz Jones."

I said, "I wouldn't say Postlethwait is the sort to do his own dirty business."

Lincoln supped coffee and rearranged his legs. "Well, without MacGregor we can't exactly ride in and demand to see Father Postlethwait's premises."

I thought of Constable Waterston, and my old friend Deputy Beam. "I might have a way to get around MacGregor."

It went against my every instinct, but Mr. Lincoln told me and Miz Kindness to wait up the mountain while he rode back into town and talked things over with Deputy Beam, Miss Francina, and Mayor Damnable. If there was a chance the sheriff was corrupt—and there was more than a chance, we all reckoned—then they was the only folk in Rapid City who stood a chance of doing anything about it.

What a pity the sheriff was elected rather than appointed, I thought.

That left me high and dry and picking away at exactly what Priya had meant by calling me "Karen Morning." Had she meant that I needed to bring Miz Kindness in to my confidence to find her? Had she meant to tell me that Miz Kindness was also at risk?

I just didn't know.

I went to fill Cowboy and Doc Swan in on the situation, them being intimately involved, and Cowboy instantly volunteered to search all the motion picture locations for any sign of her. Nobody would notice the mechanical poking around toting loads and shifting gear, and if he happened to go into every tent and caravan in the place in the process, well, that was just his job of work to be getting on with.

I didn't think they would keep Priya in so public a space as the set or the location, but I also didn't know what else to tell him, so I nodded. And then I had done everything I knew how to do. So, sitting in Doc Swan's infirmary, I finally started to cry.

They weren't no ladylike tears neither, but big old sobs and gasping, while Doc Swan rubbed my shoulders and patted my hair. I must have sobbed for a solid twenty minutes before it was all out of my system. When it was over I felt wrung out and not sad anymore, just plumb angry and determined, so I guessed that was an improvement overall.

I had nothing better to do after lunch, for which I didn't have no appetite. And I know it ain't always a great idea to be around a horse you don't know like the palm of your hand when you're in turmoil. But sitting and chewing myself open weren't working, and tearing into town wouldn't garner me nothing and might queer up Mr. Lincoln's more subtle approach.

And I still had my bet with Walker to win, which was going to be even more important if we lost the ranch. So I got myself gathered up, collected some carrots, changed into trousers, and went to see Angel Maker.

I didn't approach him, just stood inside his corral and waited for him to come over to me. Bored as he was, it didn't take long, and pretty soon he was letting me scratch his belly button and chest like he was a big dog.

He draped his head over my shoulder, letting me carry the weight of it. That was a mite dangerous—horse heads are darn big and mostly made of bone—but he seemed in a cuddly mood and I frankly needed the love.

I put a neck rope on him—he sniffed it suspiciously—and eased myself up on his back using the same process I'd pioneered last time, This time, bareback, I rode him around the corral on seat and leg pressure, using the neck rope only for a little guidance when he seemed confused.

He was ready to accept me, and the intellectual challenge of what I was asking him to figure out—how to listen to a rider who wasn't spurring him or jacking his head around—seemed like a welcome distraction from the stone boredom of his daily existence. He bucked a little, but it was just for sheer high spirits and he didn't get locked in. He weren't trying to get rid of me... and I held on to the mane and kept my seat, so he didn't, neither.

I looked up after a quarter hour, when my concentration was starting to go and Angel Maker was getting restless, to see Walker Black leaned over the gate watching us. "Not even a hackamore," he said.

"I thought he'd be easier with no reminders of his previous life, honestly," I said.

"I think you won your bet, Miss Memery," Walker said. "I admit, I didn't think you could do it. And I didn't think you could do it in just six days, neither."

"Thank you," I said, and slid off the horse.

Walker said, "Now you just have to keep him alive. Oster wants to shoot that stampede tomorrow."

"A stampede don't even make sense," I said. "How does that work into the scenario?"

"Celia's pulling out her red hair as we speak trying to figure that. But Oster's the only money man we have left, and what he wants, he's getting. Whether Max likes it or not. And Max don't like it."

"Mister Black," I said, the bit in my teeth, "was Mister Evans blackmailing you, too?"

"What a funny thing to ask," Black said, and spat tobacco juice through the fence rails.

Chapter Twenty-Eight

Mr. Lincoln didn't send no good news back from the tent revival. There weren't no sign of Priya down there. And Cowboy didn't find a thing, either, in all his perambulations. That left me picking over my dinner with Doc Swan, nerving myself up to go home to my empty house and do the milking.

I put the ride back off as long as I could, and it was all but dark out when I walked back across the encampment to kit up Molly.

Between it being Easter Sunday and that there was early call tomorrow, the camp was quiet, and I weren't making no fuss to attract attention when I caught sight of a slender figure moving around ahead of me.

The coral-colored silk looked slate blue in the dusk, only I knew it was coral-colored because I'd had the matching dress fitted earlier that week. The black hair was hidden under a bonnet, and she had a revolver in a cowboy holster in one hand.

I almost called out to Annie, but she seemed furtive, as if she were sneaking. And I was suspicious enough that I wanted to follow her.

So I did, and witnessed something I never thought to see: the woman in the coral dress opened the shutters on Miss Roman's caravan, then looked left, looked right, and leaned inside.

When she came back out again, the revolver wasn't in her hands.

I froze, not sure what to do. My inclination was to run after her—but if Annie was the killer, she could gun me down from five hundred yards and never bat an eyelash. Maybe, though, she was just taking revenge for Miss Roman trying to frame her about the necklace.

While I was panicking, I lost sight of her among the tents and caravans. I was still standing there staring when Max Forth came by with Vernon and Black, all of them yawning and rubbing their bellies like they'd just had a very satisfying dinner.

I put out a hand. "Max—"

He and Vernon looked over at me. "Miss Memery," said Vernon

And Max said, "Karen?"

I bit my lip. "Max, can I talk to you alone for a few minutes?"

"Of course," he said.

"Ooh la la," said Vernon, which unfairly made me want to hit him. What, after all, was he supposed to think? Except didn't everybody on set know that Max preferred gentlemen?

So maybe Vernon was just teasing, and I was on edge and taking everything real personal.

Max stepped aside with me. I lowered my voice. "Max, I just saw a woman in a coral dress put a gun inside Miss Roman's caravan."

He looked at me, lips pursing. "You aren't suggesting—"

"I didn't see her face," I said. "She was wearing a bonnet. But she weren't real big, and I can't figure out why Miss Roman would hide a weapon on herself."

He made a noise of despair. "Let's go find her," he said. "I shall not be searching that domicile without express permission."

"Go find who?" Miss Roman asked from right behind us, making us both squeak a little. She was coming from the direction of Oster's caravan, and her hair was a little mussed as if she'd pulled her dress on in a hurry. I was familiar with the evidence of deshabille from long experience at my former employment.

Max whirled, hands up. My own turn weren't much more dignified but at least I didn't land on my curvaceous derriere.

"Miss Roman," Max said. "I'd like permission to search your caravan."

Her pretty face hardened, the expression just about visible through the twilight. Around the camp, the lamps were being lit. "What nonsense is this trollop accusing me of now?"

"No one is accusing you of anything," said Max. "But somebody might have hidden evidence in there."

"What did you see?" asked Black, coming over.

He crossed over to the caravan. "This window is unlatched." He opened the same one the person in the dress had opened and stuck his upper body inside. His voice sounded hollow as he called back, "There's nobody in here."

I sighed.

"Don't you need a warrant?" Miss Roman asked.

"We're not the sheriff," I snapped, exhausted. "We're trying to help you. Unless you want to get blamed for the murder of Miz Jones, Miss Roman."

She sniffed. "Fine," she said. "You go right ahead and investigate. I'll wait here so there's no allegation that I might have *contaminated* the *scene*."

Black and Vern waited outside with Miss Roman while Max and I entered the caravan holding up his lantern. There were no lights inside, and it was dark as the belly of a whale. I wasn't sure how Black had been so certain it was empty.

It didn't take us long to search the place—even if Miss Roman had weaseled her way into the biggest one, it was still a tiny room on wheels, with a silk-covered daybed and a dressing table and a chest of drawers and not much else.

The bed doubled as a couch by rearranging the cushions, and was under the window where I'd seen the figure lean in. I dropped down to my knees to feel around under it. Nothing. But when I fluffed the cushions, almost instantly, I came up with a revolver. It had been tucked underneath.

"Well there it is," I said. "I guess the Mad Scientists can do some magic on it and the bullet that killed Squalene and see if they done match."

"Yes," Max said. "If the bullet was intact enough, I believe that's possible. But the sheriff has the bullet."

We stepped out of the caravan, and found Miss Roman standing there with one of the Peace brothers, Black, Vernon, Oster, Mr. Bugera, and of all people, Miz Kindness. Vernon and Bugera was sharing a cigarette, and the Peace boy had a hand-rolled stub between his teeth. I was glad as hell that Steele hadn't turned out for the ruckus, because I might have beat him to death with my shoe.

Miss Roman's eyes lit on the gun in Max's hand and she just about turned herself inside out with shrieking.

"I knew it!" she said. "That fallen woman is trying to put a frame around me! That is not my gun! I don't even know how to shoot a gun!"

Walker Black looked at me, lips twitching, and I wished I could read his expression.

She tugged on Oster's sleeve. "Alex, you must do something about these people. That Annie Mosey, she hid the gun in my caravan, I know it! Same as she stole from me and got this one"—her shaking finger pointed at me—"and her *friend* to lie about it! Maybe she and Annie and that Hindu girl all did it together. They're all unnatural women!"

I decided right there that I didn't for a second believe Annie Mosey hid that gun. Or that she shot Squalene, neither. Except—she needed money, didn't she? But no, she was getting paid plenty to make this movie. Steele said about Miss Roman not getting paid much because Evans had been blackmailing her into working for next to nothing?

But it didn't seem like Annie Mosey had ever done anything worth blackmailing her for.

Maybe Miss Roman *had* paid Squalene to kill Evans and Kindness. And maybe she was lying about not being able to shoot a gun.

Miz Kindness must have been thinking along the same lines, because she *tsk*ed and looked at Miss Roman with a jaundiced gaze. "My mama used to say, people keep singing their may-bes and pretty soon you are going to get stung by a whole *hive* of bee-bees."

"We need a proper certified Mad Scientist," Max Forth said.

I said, "If you can pay her fee, I might just know one."

There weren't no chance of getting Frau Doctor von Hammerstein that evening, nor probably the sheriff, either. And I didn't want to see the sheriff, since I was half-convinced he was the evil mastermind behind it all. But I did go and find Annie, and tell her what was being allegated, and what with one thing and another the two of us found ourselves at Miz Kindness' kitchen table.

"She must be very unhappy," said Annie, sipping her coffee. "I can't imagine putting that much work into hurting somebody else unless you were hurting yourself pretty bad."

Miz Kindness settled her skirts and harrumphed. "I can't say it trouble me in the slightest that that young girl is unhappy. She just about got to be part of trying to steal my land. I don't know if she had anything to do with the killing, but she got that revolver from somewhere. It don't matter that I didn't like my man much my own self, he was mine and he is gone and she got no right." She barely drew a breath. "So you won't mind if I say I got a satisfaction in me that she might get what is coming to her, and if that's some kind of a sin I'll answer to the Lord for it when the time comes, but I ain't gonna answer to no Miss Helene Roman."

I thought Miz Kindness was likely finished, because it was the longest speech I'd ever heard her give. I started to say something conciliatory, and in agreement, but Annie put a hand on my arm.

She'd noticed—and I hadn't—that Miz Kindness was just getting warmed up and lubricated.

"What does gripe me though is that she don't even got the knowledge about herself to have figured out that she's unhappy because she earned to be unhappy. She done set herself up for it and made all the choices that led to unhappy. And now she's standing up to her knees in miserable and blaming the map that was marked clear as anything, *here's the swamp*. Like it's my fault or your fault or anyone's fault but her own."

Miz Kindness was rocking back on the bench like a piston as she came up to speed, and it was a sight to behold. Awe-inspiring.

"If she could see her unhappiness as comeuppance for being such a blight on so many, she might find some redemption in it. As it is—" Miz Kindness turned her head and looked like she meant to spit on her own scrubbed pine floor. But she restrained herself at the last moment.

This time she paused long enough that I felt safe saying, "Miz Mourning, she ain't gonna learn no better so long as she's giving herself airs that folks just don't like her because she's so smart and pretty."

Miz Kindness laughed. "Nobody ever called me pretty, but I reckon I'm smart enough, and I got friends. Unexpected ones, even."

I basked in the compliment and the shy smile that went with it, but she didn't seem to want it acknowledged so I let it slide. Annie took the back of her hand away from my wrist.

Annie said, "Miss Roman's like a puppet of a person. She does things because she knows how people will respond to them, not because she understands why they're good for everybody involved."

Miz Kindness nodded, and continued, "Miss Karen, you and Miss Annie here got enough smart and pretty between you for three Helene Romans, and you seem to make friends all right too. So maybe that actress has better look into what else she's got that makes people sore if she doesn't want to be unhappy all her born days and into the afterlife. And making other folks unhappy too, because she doesn't know how to behave any better." Miz Kindness touched her cheek. "But I can't tell her that."

I looked at Annie. Annie smiled coolly and nodded, the lamplight bright on her pale cheek. "Maybe not," I said. "But maybe I can say it for you. If you want me to."

I only made myself go home because the cow and the chickens needed me. That poor cow was going to wind up with emotional problems from being left home alone like a farmwife to get on with it while everybody else in the household vanished for days on end.

Not to mention, she was used to being milked late, but by now she must be a mite uncomfortable.

It turned out I needn't have worried, because when I walked out to her pasture with a lantern to bring her in, I found her standing smug next to a little red-and-white-spotted heifer calf who was nursing away, tail going like a pump handle.

My heart swelled up and cracked, and all the grief of the day—and my own exhaustion—caught up with me. I leaned on the top rail of the fence—it needed whitewashing—and put my head down on my arms and sobbed over that tiny perfect calf, and the long road we had ahead of us.

"Priya," I muttered, wiping my top lights, "you better be all right. Because I can't do this all on my lonesome."

And that right there, I thought, was the heart of it. I was scared to let her be who she needed to be because what if she didn't want me any more after? And how did that make me different from Miss Roman, trying to ruin somebody else's life because her own was making her unhappy?

Now, I ain't saying that people all fit into one or two pigeonholes, mind. More that we come in breeds and grades and temperaments and categories, like horses. But Miss Roman was what you call a powerful cautionary tale, and no mistaking it.

Anyway, I brought that cow and her calf into their warm safe stall beside Molly, and chased the chickens into their roost, and locked them all in. Then I took myself into the house and straight to bed. As soon as dawn broke, I aimed to be out in the hills looking for Priya.

But though I was bone-tired, I was too restless to sleep, and that weren't going to do me no good at all. Nor Priya, either, come the morning.

Most folk is aware that there ain't too much most men like better than a good old-fashioned hand job. And most folk is aware that them same men can do for themselves when there ain't a woman handy. So to speak. What some folk ain't aware of is that women can do something similar with a less messy result. Well, when you get into a cold bed alone and you ain't got a bed warmer, ain't much works better to warm up your toes. And make you sleepy when you ain't. And clear your thoughts when they are racing.

So one way or another, I got to sleep in the end.

When I woke up in the chilly gray predawn, I knew where they was keeping Priya.

Chapter Twenty-Nine

I couldn't get Molly saddled fast enough, and it took all my willpower to let her get through her grain. It was Monday morning, and Priya had to present herself at the courthouse or we was gonna lose the farm for sure. And then that horrible Father Postlethwait and his surviving co-conspirators, if there was any, would have the claim on the gold in our stream. And we'd be out with nowhere to go.

Well, maybe Miz Kindness would take us on as ranch hands if it came down to it. At least, with the stream running through her property, she'd be able to pay off her mortgage.

Reader, I don't mind saying that I was hoping in my heart that terrible Mr. Oster was going to turn out to be his co-conspirator. Which train of thought reminded me that today was also the day I was going to have to ride Angel Maker if I wanted to save his life, and that got my heart beating so hard and my hands shaking so bad that Molly danced away from me the first time I tried to mount her.

So I had to calm myself with a few deep breaths and try again. This time she stood for me. As I settled into the saddle I realized something else: I was going to have to ride that stunt bareback and with no bridle, if I didn't want to find myself busting a bronc. And undoing all the work I'd done to make him rideable.

Well, it would look fancy on camera, I guessed. If'n I didn't die.

And if I did die, they could probably use that footage for something.

With all the toing-and-froing up and down the mountain, most of it with both me and Priya on her, Molly was dead fit. By the time we reached the bottom of the lane she was covering ground with a lope that fair ate it. We charged up the road like a one-horse cavalry, her digging in with her hind end and hurling us up. I rode into the Kindness place at a canter, and ran Molly right through the camp and past all the caravans and out the other side again.

The horses in the paddocks milled and whinnied, and Molly called back to them—but she were a good girl, and she kept on running.

Flat out we went up the mountainside, people pouring out behind us, clutching their nightclothes around them in the cold. I didn't stop, but kicked on past the shooting location. Molly and me cleared that railcar with the tripod on it with feet to spare. She took one stride before she jumped the equipment wagon, four feet high and eight feet broad.

She didn't even grunt on the landing.

We bolted up the seagrass meadow, past where Squalene got shot, farther than I had ever been before, until the whole Sound rolled out before us and the dawn, not yet breaking, colored the east. Far below, the ocean thundered its own response to the beat of Molly's hooves. But I had that map in my head, and I knew from it right where I was going.

I slid off Molly once the rocks closed in around us. There weren't room for a horse up here, so I ground-tied her in the seagrass—she wouldn't go nowhere with that banquet before her—and scrambled up to the caves I could just see peeking through a couple of scraggly fir trees.

By then I was yelling. "Priya?! Priya, are you in there?"

I heard no answer. The silence just made me climb faster.

A few minutes later, I barreled into the cave and realized in my haste that I hadn't brought no light with me. "Priya?" I called, softer now, feeling my way forward. I wouldn't do her no good if I slipped and broke my ankle.

Her, nor Angel Maker, either.

I strained my ears for an answer, and in the dark I heard a faint rustle, and a thumping.

I followed my ears, one hand on the wall, and found the figure lying on the ground because I nearly fell over her.

"Oof," she grunted, muffled beyond recognition.

I crouched down and felt around. I knowed in my bones it was Priya. Something—the smell of her, the sound of her breathing—was unmistakable even in the dark, dank cavern. Ropes wound her up like a mummy, and a gag was tied into her mouth. She was shivering, her skin too cool to the touch, and I felt an incoherent fury that she'd been left here, cold and alone, for a day and a half.

I pulled out my pocketknife and, acting by feel, cut the gag away from her head. I nicked myself in the process but I didn't get her, I thought, and I couldn't see the blood in the dark so it didn't matter.

I pulled the damp cloth wedging her mouth out and threw it into the darkness, furious and disgusted. "Don't try to talk," I said. "I'll get you out of here."

"Water," she whispered.

"Sorry," I said. "I didn't think of none of that. I just came at a gallop when I figured out what your secret code meant. Morning. Mourning's land, and the point you can see the sunrise from over the shoulder of the mountain. Right, my beautiful genius?"

"Love you," she whispered, and I took a second out from cutting rope to pet her hair.

"I'm just damn sorry it took me this long to figure it."

But she was alive, and that was what mattered.

I got her up, and she leaned on me, groaning with stiffness, as I led her out of the cavern at a snail's pace. It went faster once we got to where a little light filtered in, because our eyes was so adapted to the dark that even that grayness seemed like broad day. And once we broke out into the morning twilight, we was blinking.

I about had to carry Priya down the slope through the big rocks to Molly. Fortunately she didn't weigh much more than a bundle of twigs, but she wasn't much more articulable than a bundle of twigs right then, neither. Her voice was coming back as she worked some spit into her mouth, and though she was still shivering her skin was starting to warm.

She staggered, leaning on me—but she didn't stop, and it hurt me to see her feet was bare except for socks. She must have been so cold last night, when I was in our warm bed—

Stop it, Karen. I needed that sleep to be smart enough to figure out her riddle and strong enough to carry her down a mountainside.

As if to remind me not to study on my failings, Priya butted me gently with her head. Her hair was all sand and twigs, and she was wearing the same clothes she'd been in when I saw her last—and they reeked like it, too. Whoever had tied her up and left her hadn't provided no facilities.

I couldn't take her into court like this. I'd have to get the motion picture folk to help me get her cleaned up and presentable. And I didn't know but that one of them was behind this.

"Where's you boots?" I asked her.

"They took them." Now Priya was shaking instead of shivering, and had to lean back against one of the big rocks and gasp for breath for a minute. I could tell from the little sounds she was making that the kinks was finally working out of her muscles, and I could tell also that the cramps was setting in and she was regretting all of it.

"Did you see who it was?" I asked, when her cussing got a little more distinct.

"Bag over my head," she said. "And then a blindfold."

Well, that was goddamn inconvenient.

But we dragged ourselves down the rock field, Priya starting to move better on her own feet, and she hadn't bloodied up her toes despite being sock footed. The nick on my thumb had stopped bleeding, which was a blessing.

We broke out into the clear and found ourselves face-to-face with Mister Fucking Matthan Steele, who was holding Molly's reins and smirking at us.

"Miss Memery. I wondered why you tore through like your tail was on fire. Now ain't this interesting?" Menace dripped from his tone like molasses off a knife.

"Give me my horse, Matthan."

"I think I want something in return."

Priya shuddered. I set her down against a big rock and decided right then and there that I might be a fallen woman, but if Matthan Steele thought he was going to have his way with me, I was going to fight him for it.

"How's your acting career gonna proceed if I claw your pretty eyes out?"

He smirked wider and started toward me. I stepped sideways to get between him and Priya while she cussed in Chinese. I didn't speak it, but I knew the tone well enough. I flicked my pocketknife open in my hand, and grinned at Matthan.

"Come and get it," I said.

And just then, Cora Darling stepped out from behind a rock and got in between Matthan Steele and me. An unfolded straight razor glittered in her hand. "Don't you take one step."

"You want a little more, girlie?" he said with a grin. "I can oblige all three of you ladies."

He reached out, and I thought he was going to grab her wrist—but she moved like a clockwork, fast and true, and cut right across the palm of his reaching hand.

He reeled back, the blood starting fresh and red, and I bent over, gagging. He dropped Molly's rein to grab at his own hand, and she snorted and back away but didn't, thank the good Lord, bolt.

Cora Darling stepped forward. Steele turned and started to run—

—and Reader, she took that razorblade and she slashed deep and true as if she were slashing a bread loaf. As if she were gelding a colt and it was kindest done fast.

She cut right across his throat, and the razor went through his skin like shears through a bolt of thin gingham.

Doubled over, I watched. And when the blood welled up I turned my head and I tried to vomit, but there weren't nothing in my stomach but sourness.

Matthan Steele clutched at his throat as if he could stop the bleeding. The look on his face was disbelief. But it was done and I was glad as he toppled over.

Half to myself, standing up despite my cramping stomach, I murmured, "That ain't right."

Cora grinned over at me. "It ain't wrong, neither. And I ain't gonna pretend I'm sorry about it. Now do we want to explain to MacGregor that I was acting in self-defense, or do you want to help me roll him over the cliff and hope he gets cut up enough in the water to hide the slicing?"

"I don't think we can hide the blood on the grass," said Priya. "I guess it's option A."

The wind curried the long grass like she was running the mountain's hair through her fingers.

Priya managed to stay in Molly's saddle once I gave her a leg up, but only by clutching the saddle horn. Cora and me had to promise not to tell anybody.

"I hope I don't have to reshoot those scenes with Steele with whoever they get to replace him," I said when we were coming up on the costume tent.

Priya chuckled, sitting up straighter than she had been as her muscles warmed. She slid down on her own, and only staggered a little when she landed.

Amber and Hazel and Caleb came bustling out, rubbing their eyes and pulling their smocks on while I helped Priya over. She still weren't walking too straight. I explained the situation and the hurry. Hazel exclaimed over Priya and hustled her off to the bath while Amber went to rummage through the costumes for something suitable.

And Caleb looked Cora up and down and said, "You're all over blood. I'll go get Doc Swan—"

"Not for me," Cora said. "Get her for Priya though. But we need to send one of the boys for the sheriff, because I done kilt Matthan Steele."

Amber put Priya in a dress, and Priya weren't none too happy about it. But she looked nice, and she was going before the judge, and that was what was important. I borrowed the coral satin, since I was in dungarees and flannel, and there was blood on some of it. It turns out cutting a man's throat is as spectacular as cutting a hog's.

Cowboy and Doc Swan were coming down as well to offer testimony, and so all three of them went in a cart and Molly and me rode along beside or ahead, as the road permitted. We rolled into Rapid with the church towers only just striking nine-thirty, and Reader, if that morning hadn't been the longest four hours of my life then I didn't know when might be.

The Circuit judge, Alliende, had apparently ridden in around breakfast and was getting set up in the courthouse after a bath and a feed, so we had an hour or two to kill with Mr. Lincoln while we waited. I wound up telling him the whole story of finding Priya and Cora Darling killing Steele to protect us.

We'd all agreed to leave out the part where he tried to run away before she got her second cut in. Because if she wasn't defending us then and there, she sure as Hades was defending herself and us and God only knew how many other women in the future.

That wasn't today's problem, though. Though we figured it might have come up.

While we was waiting, Sheriff MacGregor rode up on a lathered chestnut. I thought a little better of him because he walked her for five minutes or so and took her down to the trough before he tied her to the picket. MacGregor looked over at Priya and me and frowned, and didn't tip his hat. Mr. Lincoln, Cowboy, and Doc Swan ignored him. I just concentrated on Priya, who badly wanted to sit down, so we rested a bit on the bench beside the steps.

Not too much later, Dr. von Hammerstein walked up, dust on her boots and her blonde hair done all up in a fancy chignon. She settled herself next to Priya and me. She had a case in her hand, and I suspected inside it was the gun that had killed Squalene Jones.

I was surprised that Miss Roman weren't in evidence.

Finally the big courthouse doors came open and we was ushered inside and it was all I could do not to clutch at Priya's fingers.

My heart was racing and my ears was ringing and everything went a little blurry around the edges of my vision.

People always say you ought to talk about your feelings, but if you do that you just got to deal with their feelings *about* your feelings while you're still having your own damn feelings in the first place.

Maybe it's my ma's Danish in me, but it just ain't worth it most times. But the truth is, I was as terrified as Angel Maker.

I frankly didn't hear much of what went on. Priya was tottering on her feet, and she showed the rope burns on her wrists and ankles to the judge, who wasn't near as old and hoary as I had envisaged. MacGregor tried to claim she could have done it to herself, and I had to testify that I'd found her done up like a fish in a net, and nobody could have tied themselves up like that.

Then Cowboy testified that he had witnessed Squalene killing Evans and Otis Kindness, and I testified that I had been nearby with a vagrant nobody could seem to locate when Squalene was shot. "It might have been a revenge killing," I said. "But I don't know who would shoot anybody for Mike Evans *or* Otis Kindness. Though she did have that map—"

"Can you produce the map?" the judge asked.

Mr. Lincoln produced it. That sparked a long discussion of the mine-salting plot, and I managed to get in edgewise that Pulsifer Postlethwait had been trying to extort Miz Mourning out of her land. Priya testified that Evans and Postlethwait had been business partners in India, and that they were engaged in kidnapping girls for the crib trade there.

The judge listened through pursed lips. My heart pounded and my hands shook. What reason did he have to believe us?

Mr. Lincoln waved to Dr. von Hammerstein. "Most interesting, we have the revolver that killed Miz Jones. Dr. von Hammerstein is a licensed Mad Scientist, and she's managed to establish that the bullet retrieved from Miz Jones was fired by this gun."

Dr. von Hammerstein laid the case on the table at the front of the courtroom and drew forth the gun. She produced a squashed-looking bullet from her pocket and said, "This is the bullet Sheriff MacGregor provided. You may not know that every rifled firearm leaves a unique pattern of marks on a bullet fired through its barrel, so you can conclusively link the bullet back to the gun."

"Fascinating," said the judge, leaning forward over his podium thing. "Where was this gun recovered?"

Doc Swan gave chapter and verse of that story.

"And where is Miss Roman now?"

"She's at the motion picture set," said MacGregor. "I didn't see any reason to arrest her. Somebody obviously hid it in her divan to frame her."

I hid my sigh pretty well, I thought. At least, nobody glared at me, though Priya nudged me with her boot. Well, if Miss Roman could only get one person fooled, I guess the sheriff was a useful one.

We weren't having no formal court proceeding, I finally realized, more like a fact-finding conversation.

Doc Swan also testified that Priya had been with her the whole time Squalene might have been shot, and Cowboy confirmed it. I wriggled my fingertips into my palms and prayed it would be enough.

"Well," said the judge finally, "I don't see any reason to keep Miss Swati in custody any longer. Sheriff MacGregor, I'm going to want to have a conversation with Miss Roman about the provenance of that revolver. Especially as Miss Memory seems to think she placed it there herself."

Doc said, "In fairness, we've got a lot of people dressing up as each other on set. It confuses the issue."

"Maybe," I interjected, "somebody should ask Miss Roman where she got the six-shooter."

"You still insist it was her hiding it in her own caravan despite seeing yourself that someone else put it in there?" MacGregor sounded a wee bit snappish. "As if that sweet child were the sort of hardened, scheming saloon girl you are no doubt *very* familiar with."

I pinched the bridge of my nose and Priya stood on my foot under the table until I got my temper under control.

She was free, and that was what mattered.

———

Sheriff MacGregor was so disheartened by the proceedings that he didn't even put up much of a fight when we stuck around to testify on behalf of Cora Darling in the case of the killing of Matthan Steele, and got her released on her own recognizance until such time as there was a trial.

It just weren't a good day to be a lawman.

Chapter Thirty

It was noon by the time the court was done with us, and I had to hightail it back to the set to ride in the stampede. Cowboy was gonna be wanted as well, and there was the unsettling possibility that Doc would be needed for her services, so Cowboy, Doc Swan, Mr. Lincoln, and me piled into the wagon. I hitched Molly on behind to give her a rest from my weight. She'd been hard used recently.

Priya followed along behind in the Singer, which the judge had de-impounded since he was satisfied neither it nor Cowboy was the murder weapon.

As we tromped up the hill, I started wondering again who could pick that padlock. Priya herself, of course. Dr. von Hammerstein, but that was a silly idea. Doc Swan, though I hated to think on it. Miss Lizzie, though that was ridiculous on the face of it for a whole passel of reasons.

"Pree," I called over, "can you remember anything at all about the person who grabbed you? Are you sure it was a man? Did they smell like anything?"

"Tobacco," she said promptly. Which didn't let out the majority of men in Rapid, but sadly precluded Father Postlethwait, who—belying his true nature—smelled of roses. "And I'm sure he was taller than me."

That was a narrower bundle of twigs, but still too big for me to snap.

———

When I got to the costume tent, Amber and her team were in an uproar. Hazel had just thrown her hands in the air and was saying, "Well, I never touched the silly thing!"

When I came in, every one of them turned to look at me and a weighty silence fell. "I can come back later," I said.

Amber heaved a sigh. "No, Karen, your costume is fine and Max wants to get this show on the road. Come over here and let me dress you."

"Wait," I said, climbing up onto the fitting stage, "what do you mean *my* costume?"

"Miss Mosey's dress has gone missing," Caleb said.

Amber was reaching for my buttons to undo them. I stepped back and nearly fell off the stage. "I might know where it is," I said. "Let me—"

"No you don't," Amber said firmly. "*You* need to get camera ready. Tell Caleb."

"I have hair to do!" Caleb protested.

I said, "Look up under the trees and axles of all the caravans in between Mister Oster's and Miss Mosey's, on a straight line." That got their attention. There was all three of them blinking at me, moon-eyed, as they figured out the implications of what I'd just said.

"That means the dress is evidence," Hazel said.

"If you find it where I think it is, it sure does."

Amber, not one to be diverted by a crisis, whisked my own dress off of me. "Well, we'll part that sea when we come to it. Arms up, Miss Memery. And Caleb, take one of the Peace brothers with you so if you find it, there's another witness."

———

Gussied up, I went to have it out with Miss Roman. She weren't in makeup—obviously—and she weren't in her caravan, though. So, at a loss, I went to inspect my tack for the stunt that day. I wouldn't have a saddle, but I'd be mounting Angel Maker while he was already moving, and he'd be wearing a surcingle with handholds on it like the circus trick riders use.

The stunt was supposed to involve me and Angel Maker running away from a posse of the evil professor's men. Then Angel Maker would hit the trip wire and fall right at the edge of the sea cliff. I was meant to fall clear of him and play at being knocked silly—and pray I wasn't really knocked silly. And didn't go over the edge. And that Angel Maker survived without permanent damage.

Then Wild Willy Fair—in the persona of Walker Black, wearing an armature, since Matthan Steele was deader than the proverbial doornail—would arrive in the nick of time to save me from Professor Killjoy's wicked horde.

I don't claim the scenario made much sense, but I had to agree with Oster and Max that if we pulled it off it was gonna be spectacular. I was determined, anyway, that I was going to have it out with Oster one last time, and that if he demanded to use the trip wire, I'd pull up short of it. We had the gold, at least until somebody else figured out we was mining and found the upstream source. I could afford to get fired to save Angel Maker.

Besides, where were they going to find another girl to ride stunts like me? Maybe I would get away with it.

I wasn't expecting to find Miss Roman, finally, walking toward her caravan as I got near the barn.

I like to think I handled the encounter as smooth as I do everything. The first words out of my mouth was, "That was you in Miss Mosey's dress, weren't it?"

Miss Roman lifted her chin. "You certainly have no proof of anything."

"No," I said. "But it wouldn't fit nobody but you or her, and you ain't got too much imagination. I can picture you trying the same flimflam twice."

"Get out of my way, you tramp." She meant for her voice to come out level and venomous, but it cracked on the word "tramp."

"I want to know where you came by that revolver," I said.

She said, "I never touched it."

"It matched the bullet they took from Squalene."

She looked at me blankly. "They can tell those things?"

"They can," I confirmed, "tell those things."

Her pale face went a little paler under the powder.

"Maybe we should talk in your caravan," I said. I knowed it was dangerous being alone with her, but I figured if worst came to worst I could probably beat her in a tussle.

So I went. She held the door open for me and closed it tightly behind us. The windows was open, though, so somebody would hear if I yelled.

I settled myself on her silk daybed and made a fuss of arranging my skirts around me.

"Look, Karen," she said. "Maybe we can make this up."

"You're like a wee baby copperhead, Miss Roman," I said. "You ain't no trouble to me sunning yourself on a rock over yonder, and you're cute enough on occasion. But I ain't gonna pick you up and put you in my pocket, and if you come into my barn I'll crush your head with a stick."

"I don't know who's been telling you what about me—" she started up, and I knew just from the sweet reason in her voice that she was gearing up to argue in bad faith and do that choplogic thing where she claims that A plus B equals X.

So I cut her off. "You're a nasty piece of work. You've been trying to get Miss Mosey fired, and when that didn't work you switched to trying to get her hanged."

She gasped. "That's not true at all! And now they want to blame me for the murder! I don't know why everybody hates me. I try so hard to be nice. Is there something wrong with me, Karen? Some reason everybody hates me? Is it because they're jealous?"

I looked at her. She was crumpled up in the corner on her dressing chair, and I could see just what a scrap of a thing she was. I probably made two of her, and her upper arms was like my wrists. Her nose was running and red and her lacy handkerchief was black at the edges with kohl.

I pitied her. I even felt some kind of compassion. But I didn't have a scrap of willing left in me for her. Not for the first time, I felt like a good roping horse must feel with a tyro on his back, getting us both tangled in his lariat because he's too excited to remember which tricks he can do and which he just plumb can't.

I wanted to quail, and mumble something and walk back out again. But I remembered Miz Kindness, thinking this hellcat might be moved to save herself—and everybody around her—and Miz Kindness not able to say something in her own defense because she was colored. And I found some courage in me and I said, "People mostly don't hate you, Helene."

She looked up me, hopeful that I was going to absolve her. And I wanted to; she had all the charm and magnetism anybody could want. But I knew by now there weren't much water under that thin ice, and her little-girl-lost routine was starting to chafe on me.

You can only let somebody off the same hook so many times before you start to wonder if maybe they shouldn't be staying on it.

Let her sort out her own problems. Maybe it would teach her to be a little more cautious about making such a big damn mess if she was the one who had to shovel the stable for a change.

"People mostly don't hate you," I said. "They just mostly don't like you much either, because you don't do much to make them like you, and you do plenty to make them not."

"I'm nice to people!"

"When you want something from 'em," I agreed. "You mostly is. Unless you don't get what you want as fast as you want it, even if what you want ain't yours or ain't deserved. Then you're a real savage bitch, pardon my saying. People notice that, and after a while they get tired of getting bitten just for going about their lives in a way that's inconvenient to you."

Her expression was crumpling further as she realized I wasn't going to take her side, or even make her feel better about what she'd done and who she'd been busy being.

She said, "You aren't always nice to people." It might have been honest confusion, but there was a nasty little twist to her voice that meant she was trying to get under my skin. Even now, despite everything.

I've known girls like her before. You give 'em slack, because you think maybe they feel powerless or they've been brought up to hate themselves. But half of 'em is just plain mean, and the other half is so empty inside they will take and take and take and never be full, even when they've taken everything you got. And then cut you when you ain't got no more to give.

They show you a softness once in a while, to lure you in, like a cat showing its belly. The instant you reach in, no matter how gentle you try to be, you find out it weren't never nothing but a trap.

"You're right," I said. "I ain't. But I try to be fair, and I try not be the one who isn't nice first."

"Well, you're not being fair to Black right now! You ought to tell him one thing, and stick to it. He deserves that. You oughtn't be stringing him along."

"I ain't stringing him along," I said, a number of things coming clear to me all of a sudden. "He's my boss, and we're friends, and I hope he's gonna get me a lot more work just like this work here, and he knows exactly how I feel about him."

"He's starry-eyed on you. How'd he feel if he knew about your dirty little Hindu tramp?"

It was a threat, plain as day. And Reader, I never knowed until that very moment what people meant when they said they saw red. But I did, just then, and I'm here to tell you it ain't no metaphor. Pink streamers shivered at the edge of my vision like tulle off a party dress, and I felt like I was looking at Miss Roman down a train tunnel, or through the barrel of a gun.

I am ashamed to say I lost my temper. "Ain't you riding that Oster fella?"

She did a pretty good impression of somebody who was shocked and taken aback. I guess she could act after all.

I went on, "So you want to know why people don't like you for long? I can fill you in on that in detail, you know. You don't have any friends, Miss Roman, because you treat your friends like hell. You are a selfish, scheming, manipulative child who plays people off against each other and humiliates them to feel powerful, and who doesn't feel real unless she's getting a load of attention and affection from somewhere, and who doesn't know how to get attention and affection unless she's taking it away from somebody else. You have no accountability and no regard for the feelings of others beyond a passel of lip service."

She drew a breath, but I was on a roll and I kept going, riding right over her when she started to argue.

"Black doesn't want you, not because he wants me but because he's too old and sensible to fall down in your bosom just because you're tossing yourself at his cock. You're vain, conceited, and so shallow you couldn't manage to drown yourself in a puddle of your own self-regard if you tripped and fell flat facedown in it. And another thing. You're damned mean. I came to talk to you because somebody thought you might be moved to treat people better. And be happier yourself. And I thought you might come clean about where you got that gun at. But you won't be moved and you won't come clean, and I am leaving."

"What do you mean by that?" She'd gone pale, and the two little blotched of crimson in her cheeks weren't no pretty spring roses. She had both fists balled against her belly.

"Just what I said. When you don't get what you want, you punish people. You're cutting and sly. Hell, I'm surprised you ain't the murdered one, the way you treat everybody around you."

"So you think I killed her, too." The lip quiver was a nice touch, I'll give her that. Whether I liked her or not, she wasn't the world's finest actress, so she probably was feeling a lot of upset right then. Even selfish people have feelings.

Madame Damnable would have run this one out of her house right quick, though. She liked arranging her chances at the spotlight a little too much, and at the expense of the health and safety of other folk.

"No."

She stared at me.

"I despise you, but I don't think you killed Squalene Jones."

She looked relieved, and started up, as if to come to me.

I stood up and took a step toward the door. She froze.

"I think your selfishness and playing people off against each other probably helped her to get killed, and your behavior since ain't helped a bit in finding out who did do it, but I don't think you killed her. And I gotta admit that she participated willingly in the circumstances that led to her demise, so you also got that going for you."

"You think I'm a monster." The noble lift of her chin was a nice touch.

"You ain't no bad person, Miss Roman," I said. "Well, I mean, you're pretty awful. But you're not a murderer. At least this time you ain't. You just ain't no better than you got to be, and you also ain't no problem of mine. If you won't tell me, though, and if you don't want to hang... maybe you ought to tell Sheriff MacGregor where you got that six-shooter from."

She pursed her lips, sighed, and said, "Fine. Fine, then. It was my ex-husband's revolver," she admitted. "I brought it with me for protection."

"I thought you couldn't shoot."

She scoffed at me. "How hard could it be to shoot somebody?"

I decided not to tell her. It wasn't like anything I said was going to shatter her illusions of her own competency.

"But I never shot anybody with it. And a funny thing—"

"Yes?" I said.

"The one I hid had pearl handles."

I thought back. "The one I found had a walnut grip."

"See?" she said. "Somebody *is* trying to frame me."

Chapter Thirty-One

I could have stayed and given her a piece of my mind for another hour, honestly. But I thought about something else, and just as I was about to *one more thing* her for the fifth or sixth time, I stopped myself, got up, and left the caravan.

She had her victim face on. I was the bully who was being unfair to her, and it made me want to sock her one. But that really would make me the bad guy. The power of victimhood is humbling. It should be humbling, because it's as seductive as any house girl after two hours of makeup and hair curling.

Miss Roman had a way of convincing well-meaning folk that they had harmed her. It didn't last forever: the charm wore off. But it lasted long enough that she could climb over them to the next sucker. She used their regret and remorse to make them give her rein for her bad behavior. So they—we—would contort themselves in expiation for our sins.

And I knew that power felt good to her. She was like any woman in the world: there weren't much freedom offered her, so she had to take her power where she might. It was even trickier for me to navigate because of that seductiveness, and because I understood where her cruelty and her pettiness came from. But I couldn't forgive her.

Because, as the preacher man says, it is not mete to offer forgiveness to somebody who has not made some atonement or reparations for their actions. Because that atonement and those reparations—at least some of them—are *owed*. There is a debt assumed in cruelty or thoughtlessness. And the one sinned against can demand penances and amends.

So I felt righteous anger, I thought, for Miss Roman usurping that victim role and using it to victimize others. Like Miss Mosey. Like Priya and me.

But that righteous anger is a hell of a thing.

Victimhood soon turns to a grave. If I stayed in it, I knew in my bones that I'd discover eventually that I'd died the day I laid down in it. That I hadn't growed or changed since.

No matter how many people heap flowers on it, a grave is still a grave.

You got to climb out of that grave while there is still time. While your arms are still strong enough. Before you get too damn cozy down there.

That was the thing I learned from not wanting to be Miss Roman.

As I left the caravan, I could hear Jodi calling for me. Priya waited at the bottom of the stairs, an anxious look on her pretty face, and caught my elbow as I descended.

"Sheriff MacGregor was just here." She dropped her mouth close to my ear. "He arrested Miz Mourning."

"On what grounds?!"

"The Singer was in her shed."

"She's the one who turned it in! And Cowboy testified that Squalene done murdered both those men." I knew I was arguing with thin air, but sometimes you got so much outrage in you it's gotta come out even if all you're doing is blasting blind.

"The sheriff," she said, with the coldness people generally reserved for silverfish and boll weevils, "seems to think that Cowboy would lie to protect somebody living at the expense of somebody dead. And I bet that Postlethwait fellow has him in his pocket. If Miz Mourning can't pay her mortgage, the ranch goes up to auction, and she can't very well pay it when she's in jail."

"That son of a bitch," I ejaculated, which was possibly no fair to MacGregor's mother, whoever and wherever she might be, but was an apropos of how I was feeling. I wanted to go get that selfsame Singer and bust up the new jailhouse the way I busted up the old, but I had just enough self-possession to realize that weren't gonna help nobody.

I uncurled my fists and said, "Well, guess we better go send one of the gofers to tell Mister Lincoln."

Priya nodded. "How did it go with Miss Roman?"

"Oh, I gave her a regular old piece of my mind."

"Do you feel the better for it?"

I thought about. "Not really. But I did learn, if she can be trusted, which she can't, that she brought the revolver she hid on herself with her. And just kind of held on to it until she decided to get up to mischief with it. She claims it wasn't the one that I found, however—the handles were different."

"Mmm." Priya walked me toward the machine shop. We were both keeping our eyes peeled for the flash of ginger hair. "I asked around with Doc Swan and Doctor von Hammerstein, and the pistol that killed Squalene *was* the pistol that went missing from the production armory."

"Miss Roman wouldn't pass up a chance to make mischief," I said. "And another thing," I added, remembering one more thing about which I had been incensed and offended. "She's got no idea how to wear that dark lipstick. You ain't supposed to just smear a big old red ring around your mouth. You got to taper it in in the corners, inside the line of your lips—what?"

"Nothing," Priya said to me, biting her laugh back in that way she had, her expression shining. "Just you're such a practical girl, mostly, but you do like your fripperies, and know all about the technicalities of 'em."

I snuggled into her grip on my elbow. "I got my fripperies education from Miss Francina and Miss Bethel."

"Study with the best," she allowed.

I grinned. "None finer."

And just then I heard Jodi calling my name. "Miss Memery, you're wanted on set."

When I came up, Walker Black had Angel Maker on a lead rope—proving he was a pretty fair horse wrangler—and everybody was giving the two of them a wide berth. The surcingle was fastened around his body and painted up to match the sooty splashes on his hide. It looked pretty obvious to me, but Vern said it wouldn't read on camera. And there was a braided rope around his neck.

"I wish you'd reconsider a hackamore," Black said. He looked nervously over at the Peace boys, already mounted and waiting to give chase. They was all dressed real different, with some merkins on their faces so it might not be completely obvious that what made up Professor Killjoy's posse was a passel of triplets. "He's tolerating the halter okay."

"I don't want to put pressure on his poll," I said. "I'm afraid any kind of messing with his head is like to set him bucking. Where's the trip wire?"

I had absolutely no intention of hitting it. I could see from the look Walker gave me that he knew it, too.

"I got Oster to back down," he said, and turned and spat tobacco.

You know how a penny drops sometimes, and it's such a long time falling you can see it going, going, and the pit of your stomach drops with it?

Walker Black was lying to me. And I didn't know if he was lying to me on his own sake, because he thought I was on to him, or because Oster had put him up to it. But nonetheless, lying he was.

I remembered Priya saying the man who took her was taller than her, and smelled of tobacco. I remembered Max saying that Walker was getting Miss Roman back into the caravan she'd gotten herself locked out of. That suggested he could slip a lock.

I knew who was working with Pulsifer Postlethwait. Who'd lifted that revolver from the armory, and used it to keep Squalene Jones from finding the real gold. Who'd swapped it for the gun Helene Roman had hidden on herself, knowing it might really incriminate her.

I never had any luck in keeping my whole soul off my face. And I saw in Black's face that I hadn't managed it this time, neither. "I liked you," I said, because it was all I could think to say.

"I never hurt anybody who didn't have it coming," Walker said. "You think about that, and we'll have a conversation when the stunt is ridden."

I didn't have any proof, that was the problem.

And of course he had hurt plenty of people who didn't have it coming. Me, Priya, Cowboy. Miz Mourning, who stood to lose her ranch and who was right now as we spoke in jail. But I had a stunt to ride, and a stunt to survive, and a horse who trusted me to keep alive through all of it.

I was not going to be the last person in his long life of disappointments to let Angel Maker down.

The stunt was this: I would catch Angel Maker in a round pen, and ride him out of the gate. Then we'd reset the shot, and the Peace Brothers would chase us past the cameras in their new positions. One would be on the trolley for the tracking shot.

I'd fall, and Wild Willy Fair would come to my rescue in a roustabout mech suit.

Simple and straightforward. Except Walker had lied to me about the tripwire, and now he knew I knew he'd killed Squalene Jones. If I fell, it would be way too easy for him to kill me by "accident." And solve all his problems at once.

Vernon and his assistant got their cameras set up first in the little prop corral. My stomach churned; I didn't have time to throw up. We were rolling.

Max Forth waved his thin cigarette and shouted, "Action," and I opened the gate of the corral and walked inside, leaving it gaping wide.

Angel Maker eyed me as I walked in, and started moving toward the tempting route to freedom. I hadn't practiced this stunt; it was one and done. I stepped toward him, took a running stride to match his pace, and leaped up to grab the handles on the surcingle.

All my practice with Copper paid off. One hard bounce and I was on his back before I even knew it, holding on for dear life while my left hand grabbed for the neck line. We charged past the camera and my hat went down my back on the cord, flapping against my hair.

Angel Maker wanted to run. He'd been cooped up in that muddy little paddock all week, and it took all my diplomacy and the insistence of my seat and knees to guide and settle him before he fair ran off the cliff edge.

I stayed up while the boys moved cameras around, not wanting to have to talk to Walker. And not wanting to have to get back up on Angel Maker, if I were honest. I let him crop the seagrass, and he was beside himself with delight to do so.

Then Jodi came and got me, looking grim. "You ready for this?" he said, so grave I knew he knew the wire was set, and that he thought I did also.

Well, at least Jodi and Max weren't plotting to kill me. That was a little comfort after all.

We lined up for the chase scene. I peered ahead, trying to see the trip wire. It wouldn't be high, I thought; just knee height on the big guy. An easy jump. If I could get Angel Maker to jump for me.

Max shouted, "Action," and we was off again. I strained my eyes. It wouldn't be all the way at the end of the trolley line for the cameras—they'd want the footage of Walker charging to my "rescue." There, maybe—a couple of posts sunk in the ground. Priya standing next to one of them, staring intently at me.

God love her.

We kicked forward.

The sun came out from behind the clouds. Something sparkled up ahead—

Black had told me there wasn't going to be a trip wire. But there it was. His treachery made manifest.

With my hands and my seat, I told Angel Maker, *You're going to have to jump.*

I felt his confusion. He didn't see any reason to shorten his stride and set himself. But I saw it: a shining wire, gleaming in the sun.

I didn't know if Angel Maker would trust me. What reason did he have to trust anyone? But he had to. He had to. Or we were both going to die, because there was no time to stop, the wire was right there—

We were going to run right into it. We were going to die—

Priya dived from her spot on the sidelines to her hands and knees right in front of the charging horse. Right under the deadly wire, as if it could shelter her.

Angel Maker gathered his body like a tremendous spring. I screamed out loud and lifted my hands, nothing to guide him up by but that neck rope. He lofted into the air with all the strength in him, knees tucked, back strong. Was it enough? Would he catch a trailing leg and go sprawling? Would he kick Priya as he went past?

Just as he jumped, the surcingle snapped around his barrel. I felt it slip out from under me, flopping loose around his neck and only held on by the chest band. If it weren't for the grip I had on his mane with one hand and the neck rope with the other, I would have gone flying off him to—probably—a broken collarbone if I was lucky, and if'n I weren't, a broken neck.

He struck the ground so smooth it felt like he hadn't even broke stride. We hadn't hit Priya. We hadn't hit the wire. I wheeled him, though, and took him right toward Walker Black in his armature. Black shouted something, incoherent, and turned to grab Priya up out of the dirt. The chasing horses with the Peace brothers on board pulled up shy of the trip wire, milling left and right.

The earth shook under their hooves, and under Angel Maker's, and under the heavy tread of Walker's exoskeleton as he hauled Priya around. I brought the horse to a halt, fast and gentle, and opened one hand.

"Let her go, Walker."

He snorted. He stepped back, dragging Priya by the arm. I thought if she'd had a wrench in her belt she would have disassembled him.

"Get off that horse," Walker said. "Or I'll do what I don't want to do and tear this little girl's arm right off her."

The rest of the crew and actors was circled around us. You could almost hear their hearts beating. Nobody moved and nobody said a word.

"All right." I dropped that neck rope and slid myself sideways off Angel Maker. "All right, Walker, just let Priya go."

"I guess we all know she's my only way out of here," he said, taking a step backward. The circle of people behind him pulled apart, opening. A gap he could slide through.

Priya twisted against his grip, but the machine was too much for her. She kicked him in the shin with one bootheel and must have got through the armature with it, because he winced. He didn't let go, though.

"I liked you, Walker." I snuffled up a tear, determined not to shed it. "But you framed my partner for murder, and killed somebody who maybe weren't altogether *good* but who still deserved better. And I wish I could say I thought it was a pity you're going to swing."

He smiled at me. "You could of let it slide."

"You framed my partner!" I said to Black.

He said, "I was hoping to frame her *and* Miz Kindness, actually. And I ain't too proud of it, neither. But we needed her land."

"And our land," I said.

He nodded.

I thought about how purblind he was and had been. About the vigilantes I had barely dodged in Rapid City, who hadn't cared about a poor black man at all but sure had been eager to turn some rough justice on a woman.

Walker said. "Are you going to tell me any one of those three didn't have it coming?"

"I think you can use vigilante justice to justify all kinds of killings," I said. "And most of them are going to be of people who was just the wrong kind of people and it don't matter if they really did anything wrong or not. It's just mob law. Anyway, you just confessed in front of all these people. Where you gonna go?"

I don't know what I was thinking. Maybe that if I stalled long enough, somebody could get Annie Mosey out there with her little .22 and she could drop old Walker with a bullet in the eye. Something. Anything. If I just bought enough time.

"It's a big country," Walker said, dragging Priya another step backward. She dropped in his arms, limp weight, and he winched one machine arm back to swipe at her in frustration.

I screamed. Angel Maker snorted and ducked back behind me.

Mr. Lincoln stepped out of the crowd, in front of the punch, and caught Walker Black's swinging mechanical fist in his open hand.

Chapter Thirty-Two

It weren't no even match, Mr. Lincoln and his mobility mech and Walker Black and his big roustabout machine. Lincoln's only advantage was that he was faster, and once those big hammer fists, shaped for driving metal tent stakes, got swinging they could have pulped his skull with a single blow.

But Walker had to drop Priya to fight. He tossed her away and she landed with an *oof,* but pushed herself to her knees immediately. Lincoln dodged a haymaker blow and came back with a solid poke in Walker's chassis. Walker grunted, but I caught a glimpse of red dripping down Lincoln's fist and had to look away real quick to keep my lunch down.

"Walker, stop!" I yelled. "It's already a hanging! Hurting more people won't make it none better!"

I lost track of Priya. I couldn't do much but hold Angel Maker; he still weren't wearing a halter and he weren't in any mood to be led. I had to skitter with him as he was backing away, that broken surcingle flapping around his neck from the chest band.

I really was lucky as a dog with two buttholes. That surcingle should have put me under his hooves when it broke.

"Get a halter!" I yelled to one of the Peace boys. A second later he was throwing me one.

That didn't help me get it on Angel Maker, though, and he weren't about to put his head down for me with two armatures crashing away at each other.

Distracted by the horse, I lost track of the fight for a second. A big circle of people was pulled in back from Lincoln and Walker. Walker's punches fell like rain, but so far Lincoln was ducking and weaving much better than you'd think a tall old man would be capable. He seemed to know he couldn't afford to get himself hit—

He got himself hit.

Walker's hook got Lincoln right along the side of the torso. He *oof*ed hard and went sidewise, sprawling in the dirt. Sparks flew from his armature as he crawled away, scrabbling to get his legs under him.

I'm pretty sure I screamed. I knowed other people did. Angel Maker reared up, his big hooves flashing, and I had to let go of the neck rope or get dragged under him. When he came down I grabbed his mane in both hands and hauled myself onto his back with some damfool idea of charging Walker—

Priya lunged out of the crowd with a tripod in her hands. I had just time to think, *Oh no,* and, *That's a mighty poor weapon against an armature,* when she shoved it, hard, through the knee joint. Walker staggered, metal grinding, and turned to swipe at Priya.

That was when Annie Mosey shot him through the other calf with her little rifle.

Walker Black pitched over like a turtle balanced on end, fortunately not on top of Priya or Mr. Lincoln.

———

I was panting with fear, and so was Angel Maker, but I managed to slide back off him. The sugar cubes in my pocket were just about ground to dust, but he bent his head and lipped the dust up and while he was distracted I got that headstall on him, which was a little better than a neck rope and a busted surcingle. While I was doing that, I looked over the surcingle and saw it had been cut nearly through, and I remembered Helen Roman coming away from the barn that morning.

Had she actually tried to kill me?

Probably. But I couldn't prove that, either.

I could see her now, pushing officiously through the crowd while other folk—Max Forth, the Peace lads—moved in to circle the incapacitated Walker Black. Alexander Oster followed her, a six-shooter in his hand, and behind *him* I saw Pulsifer Postlethwait with Sheriff MacGregor and a stout man in a bottle blue waistcoat I knew from town as Zenophon Charles, the banker.

They say if you sit by the river long enough, the bodies of your enemies gonna float on by. Well Lord, I brought a picnic basket and a bottle of that good French wine, but there seems to be some kind of logjam upstream and I'm starting to wonder if I oughtn't fetch the dynamite.

A leather folder flapped in Charles' hand, and I was pretty sure it held Miz Kindness's mortgage papers.

"The gang is all here," Priya said from beside me. I hadn't heard her come up.

Angel Maker snorted. He was still looming warily beside me, but he was down off his tiptoes. I felt warm at the trust. He was telling me he felt safe beside me.

My heart broke for him. He'd just been waiting his whole life for somebody to be kind to him, and nobody had ever bothered.

And now Oster stepped around Miss Roman, who pointed at me with an outraged dignity so convincing I nearly believed it, and said, "Miss Memery, get the hell off my set. You are fired."

With Walker Black lying on the ground bleeding from one of Annie's tiny perfect bullets, and the evidence of Helene's perfidy flapping around Angel Maker's neck, I could not help myself.

I just plumb busted out laughing. "I'll get my things. And good riddance to you, Alex Oster. I'd watch your back around that Miss Roman, by the way. You'll be the next one she sticks a knife into."

"You can't fire her," said Annie Mosey, stepping toward me. "If you fire her I quit also."

Miss Roman filled up with so much steam she about doubled in size. She tugged Oster's arm. "And if you keep her, I quit!"

"Well," said Max. "If Annie goes I go." He shrugged, like it wasn't anything. "So I guess you got some decisions to make, Mister Oster."

"Hmm," Priya said. "Dumped by all your friends again? Curious how that keeps on happening."

Miss Roman drew herself up. "Are you insinuating something?"

"A repeated pattern of evidence suggests a common cause," Priya remarked with a shrug.

"Unbelievable." Oster looked at Miss Roman. "Sorry, sweetheart, but Annie here is more important to the film."

She gaped, her pretty face crumpling. "But I'm the star of the show. And this tramp—" she stopped herself, as if she found herself about to say some words a lady weren't supposed to know.

One thing I've discovered for my own self, tramp or no tramp, is that the better known you get around town, the more lies people are gonna tell about you. Just make them up, because you ain't real to them and your feeling ain't real to them, either.

I felt a moment of pity for Helene Roman. She was better known and had more people telling themselves and one another lies about her than I was ever gonna know.

A moment of pity. It passed on.

Oster clapped his hand to his head and seemed to remember at the last minute that he was holding a gun. He looked at it curiously.

"What's the six-shooter for?" I asked, feeling that tension all up my back you only get when you're around a gun in the paws of somebody who don't know how to handle one.

He gesticulated again. Two people in the crowd ducked, so I knowed they was the sensible ones.

"I thought I might need it," he said, and stepped toward me.

I ducked this time, and Priya ducked, too. Miss Mosey swung to cover Oster with her own little rifle, and I wished I could tell him I didn't like his odds. But he took another step, like the damn fool he was, and I could see the red of his face and the white of his eyes.

Angel Maker's head went up and he snorted and sidled. I stayed with him, Priya ducking away from the other side, and then I heard her yell, "What on this earth is wrong with you?"

I looked up to see Oster steaming, leveling his six-shooter at Angel Maker. "That damn horse," he said. "Damn all of you. None of you respect me!"

Reader, I didn't think about it at all, I just stepped in front of the horse, and Priya stepped with me. Of course, Angel Maker was taller than both of us, and Oster was waving that gun around like it was a kid's doll.

When I heard a single shot, I wasn't sure at first if I had been shot, or Priya, or Angel Maker. I looked down at myself, then looked around wildly for blood on any of us.

Nothing. What I saw was Miss Mosey lowering her rifle, and Oster clutching his hand.

She had shot the six-shooter right out of his fingers.

He hopped up and down, a newspaper caricature of fury. "Destroy that animal!" he said. "This girl defied me! She ruined the stunt I planned!"

Somebody must have pried Black out of the armature and helped him to his feet. Or foot—there was a rag tied around his calf and he weren't weighting it. He leaned on Jonah Peace—I was pretty sure it was Jonah—and whatever rage had animated him previously was gone now. Resignation pinched his long face.

Black said, "You can't shoot that horse. He belongs to Miss Memery."

———

If Postlethwait had had a lick of sense, he would have run for the hills when he saw us all standing around Black and Black looking hangdog. Instead he bustled up like he owned the place, which I guess he thought he did, and said, "I'm here to take possession of this ranch."

Black looked at him with disgust. "No you ain't," he said. "This piece of shit is who I have been working for. He's got my daughter in that cult of his and doing his dirty work is the only way I get to see her."

Postlethwait looked around wildly. "That man is a murderer," he said. "Are you going to take his word over mine?"

Sheriff MacGregor looked from one man to the other a couple of times. He rubbed his mouth with the side of his finger and said, "Now we just got here, Father. How would you know that if you weren't involved somehow?"

Postlethwait spat like a wet cat. He rounded on Black. "I told you once that Hindu girl wrote the note to kill her!"

Black looked at him sadly. "These girls didn't do nothing deserving killing. Unlike you and me, Father."

Postlethwait said, "Well now we're both going to hang for your squeamishness."

Chapter Thirty-Three

Miz Kindness was back out of jail again before she even had time to send somebody for her knitting. Zenophon Charles kindly agreed to wait while she got fetched, and Priya and me put our heads together and agreed to loan Miz Kindness our first week's pay until she could pan up enough gold to pay us back. That, with what we had collected and what Otis had left, was enough to pay off the note on the ranch.

Miz Kindness asked Priya and me to be there when she signed the paperwork. We all gathered around her scrubbed table, and Priya set out a brand-new pen and a pot of ink.

She read Miz Kindness every word of those documents.

Miz Kindness looked down at the pen in her hand. She looked over at the deed, then pulled it over and made a little ceremony of squaring it off before herself. She sighed, and in a careful, unpracticed hand she wrote the date. Then she moved her hand an inch and let it hover.

"You make your mark here," said Mr. Charles, condescending.

She glanced up at him sidelong. "You think I don't know that? I'm thinkin'."

Charles frowned like he didn't know what there might be to think about, but he held his peace. Which was for the good, or I think Priya might have run out, got the Singer, and popped him one with her iron-clad fist.

Slowly, with great dignity, then, Miz Kindness lowered the pen. It scratched faintly as she wrote her name: MORNING KINDNESS.

The banker sniffed. "Are you sure that's spelled properly?"

"Do you think I don't know how to spell my own name, young man?"

Then she set the pen down on its little stand and sighed. "There," she said. "Done's done."

And held out her hand for the title.

Chapter Thirty-Four

There's some satisfaction to be had in knowing you behaved like the better person, it's true. Though even that satisfaction was feeling pretty skimmed and thin by the time I sat down at our slab table and picked up the block with the sandpaper wrapped around it.

I stroked it over the tabletop in gentle circles. It was going to be time to switch to finer grit soon, but the work was soothing.

I wanted to gloat, but I didn't have anything left in me to gloat with. Still, Angel Maker was outside in the stud corral and that was something to go forward on.

Priya came up behind me and put her hands on my shoulders. "You're brooding on that mare."

I started to protest, then sighed and said, "I am, in fact, brooding on that mare."

"If you spend *all* our money on horses, there won't be any left to feed them."

I said, "We need a horse for you. And you can just about ride Molly but you sure as hell can't ride Angel Maker. And what about if Molly decides she don't want to go?"

"Molly's a lot for me," Priya admitted. "I was thinking of building a fast mech."

I opened my mouth, but a mech weren't no more dangerous than a pony when it came down to it. I closed my mouth again, because the next thing I thought to say was, *And Copper would give us two mares and a stallion. We can breed some good stock off of these.*

I could hear Priya in my head as I thought it. *Ah. The truth will out.*

"All right," Priya said on a sigh, as if she'd had the same conversation in her head as I just had. "But I know you're plotting about colts."

That was when I put the telegram from our old friend Tomoatooah on the table and pushed it toward her with my fingertips.

MISS KAREN

SCOUT DROPPED FILLY FOAL BLUE ROAN NAMED FLINT STOP MEET NOVEMBER 5 TOMBSTONE ARIZONA TRADE HORSES END

TOMOATOOAH

"Well," said Priya, having read it five times over. "I knew what I was getting into."

"You'll be busy with your apprenticeship, anyway," I said.

She grinned. "That's right. I will."

Thank You

Thank you so much for reading! I have been working on sending Karen and Priya to the movies for almost ten years, and I am so pleased that you gave me the chance to share this story with you.

If you enjoyed their latest adventure, I hope you will tell someone about it or leave a review!

To stay up to date on what books I have coming next, you can also subscribe to my newsletter at https://buttondown.com/mat ociquala.

Recent Works by Elizabeth Bear

Karen Memory
Karen Memory
Stone Mad
Angel Maker

White Space
Ancestral Night
Machine
The Folded Sky

The Lotus Kingdoms
The Stone in the Skull
The Red-Stained Wings
The Origin of Storms

About the Author

Photo by Sharona Jacobs.

Elizabeth Bear was born on the same day as Frodo and Bilbo Baggins, but in a different year. She is the Hugo, Sturgeon, Locus, and Astounding Award winning author of over 30 novels and more than a hundred short stories.

Learn more and sign up for her newsletter at elizabethbear.com.